LAZARUS

LARS KEPLER

Translated from the Swedish by Neil Smith

HarperCollins*Publishers*

HarperCollins*Publishers*
1 London Bridge Street
London SE1 9GF

www.harpercollins.co.uk

HarperCollins*Publishers*
1st Floor, Watermarque Building, Ringsend Road
Dublin 4, Ireland

This paperback edition 2021
1
First published published in Great Britain by HarperCollins*Publishers* 2020

Originally published in 2018 by Albert Bonniers Förlag, Sweden, as *Lazarus*

Lars Kepler asserts the moral right to be identified as the author of this work

A catalogue record for this book
is available from the British Library

ISBN: 978-0-00-820598-0 (PB B-format)
ISBN: 978-0-00-824043-1 (PB A-format)

Typeset in Electra LT Std by Palimpsest Book Production Ltd, Falkirk, Stirlingshire

Printed and bound in Great Britain by
CPI Group (UK) Ltd, Croydon, CR0 4YY

MIX
Paper from
responsible sources
FSC **FSC™ C007454**

Prologue

The light of the white sky reveals the world in all its naked cruelty, the way it must have appeared to Lazarus outside the tomb.

The ribbed metal floor is vibrating beneath the priest's feet. He clings to the railing with one hand as he tries simultaneously to parry the rocking with his stick.

The grey sea is moving drowsily, like a billowing tent-canvas.

The ferry is being winched forward along the two steel cables stretched between the two islands. They rise dripping out of the water in front of the boat and sink back down behind it.

The ferryman brakes, foaming waves swell up and the gang-plank is extended to the concrete jetty with a clatter.

The priest stumbles slightly as the prow hits the fenders and the jolt echoes through the hull.

He's here to visit retired churchwarden Erland Lind, seeing as he isn't answering his phone and didn't show up for the Advent Service in Länna Church like he usually does.

Erland lives in the warden's cottage behind Högmarsö Chapel, it belongs to the parish. He suffers from dementia, but still gets paid to cut the grass and grit the paths when the weather turns icy.

The priest walks along the winding gravel track, his face turning numb in the cold air. There's no one in sight, but just before he reaches the chapel he hears the shriek of a lathe from the dry dock down in the boatyard.

He can no longer remember the Bible quote he tweeted that morning, he had been thinking of repeating it to Erland.

Against the backdrop of flat farmland and the strip of forest, the white chapel looks almost as if it's made of snow.

Because the place of worship is shut up in winter, the priest walks directly to the warden's cottage and knocks on the door with the crook of his stick, waits, then goes inside.

'Erland?'

There's no one home. He stamps his shoes and looks around. The kitchen is a mess. The priest gets out the bag of cinnamon buns and puts it down on the table next to a foil tray containing the cracked remains of some mashed potato, dried-up sauce, and two grey meatballs.

The lathe down by the shore falls silent.

The priest goes outside, tries the door to the chapel, then looks in the unlocked garage.

There's a muddy shovel on the floor, and a black plastic bucket full of rusting rat-traps.

He uses his stick to lift the plastic covering the snow-blower, but stops when he hears a distant moaning sound.

He goes back outside and walks over to the ruins of the old crematorium on the edge of the forest. The oven and the sooty stump of its chimney are sticking up from the tall weeds.

The priest walks round a stack of wooden pallets and can't help looking over his shoulder.

He's had an ominous feeling ever since he stepped on board the ferry.

There's nothing reassuring about the light today.

The odd sound rings out again, closer, like a calf trapped in a metal box.

He stops and stands still, not making a sound.

Everything is quiet as his breath steams from his mouth.

The ground is muddy and trampled down behind the compost heap. There's a bag of potting compost leaning against one tree.

The priest starts to walk towards the compost but stops when he reaches a metal pipe sticking out of the ground, some half a metre long. Perhaps it marks the boundary.

Leaning on his stick, he looks up at the forest and sees a path covered with pine-needles and cones.

The wind is whistling through the treetops, and a solitary crow cries in the distance.

The priest turns back, hears the strange moaning sound behind him and starts to walk faster. He passes the crematorium and cottage, glances over his shoulder and thinks that all he wants right now is to get back to his vicarage and sit down in front of the fire with a thriller and a glass of whisky.

A dirty police car is driving away from the centre of Oslo on the outer ring road. The weeds growing beneath the barriers shiver in the wind, and a plastic bag is blowing along the ditch.

Karen Stange and Mats Lystad have responded to the call even though it's late.

It's really time for them to knock off for the day, but instead they're on their way to Tveita.

A number of residents in an apartment block have been complaining about a terrible smell. The maintenance company sent someone to check the bins, but they were all clean. The smell turned out to be coming from a flat on the eleventh floor. The sound of quiet singing could be heard inside, but the occupant, a Vidar Hovland, was refusing to answer the door.

The police car drives past an industrial estate.

Behind the barbed wire fence sit skips, trucks, and depots full of salt, ready for winter.

The blocks of flats on Nåkkves vei look like a huge concrete staircase has fallen over and split into three parts.

A man in grey overalls is waving to them in front of a van with Morten's Lock Service Ltd emblazoned on the side. Their headlights sweep over him, and the shadow of his raised hand reaches several storeys up the building behind him.

Karen pulls over to the kerb and stops gently, pulls the handbrake on, switches the engine off and gets out of the car with Mats.

The sky is already closing up for the night. The air is cold, it feels like it might snow. The two police officers shake hands with the locksmith. He's clean-shaven, but his cheeks are grey, his chest seems shrunken and he moves in a twitchy, nervous way.

'Have you heard the one about the Swedish Police being called to a cemetery? They've already found almost three hundred buried bodies,' he jokes almost breathlessly, and looks down at the ground as he laughs.

The thickset man from the building maintenance company is sitting in his pickup smoking.

'The old guy's probably forgotten he's left a bag of rubbish containing fish in the hall,' he mutters, then shoves the car door open.

'Let's hope so,' Karen replies.

'I banged on the door and shouted through the letterbox that I was going to call the police,' he says, and flicks the cigarette butt away.

'You did the right thing calling us,' Mats replies.

Dead bodies have been found here twice in the past forty years, one in the car park and the other inside one of the flats.

The two officers and the locksmith follow the maintenance man in through the door and are hit at once by the nauseating smell.

They all try to avoid breathing through their noses as they get into the lift.

The doors close and they feel the pressure under their feet as they are carried upward.

'Floor eleven's a favourite,' the maintenance man says. 'We had a difficult eviction there last year, and in 2013 one of the flats was completely gutted by a fire.'

'On Swedish fire extinguishers it says they have to be tested three days before any fire,' the locksmith says quietly.

The smell when the lift door opens is so awful that they all get a slightly desperate look in their eyes.

The locksmith covers his nose and mouth with his hand.

Karen struggles to stop herself retching. It's as if her diaphragm is panicking and trying to push the contents of her stomach up through her throat.

The man from the maintenance company pulls his jumper over his nose and mouth and points out the flat with his other hand.

Karen walks over, puts her ear to the door and listens. There's no sound from within. She rings the doorbell.

A subdued melody rings out.

Suddenly she hears a weak voice from inside the flat. A man's voice, singing or reciting something.

Karen bangs on the door and the man falls silent, then starts again, very quietly.

'Let's go in,' Mats says.

The locksmith walks over to the door, puts his heavy bag down on the floor and unzips it.

'Can you hear that?' he asks.

'Yes,' Karen replies.

The door to one of the other flats opens and a small girl with tousled fair hair and dark rings under her eyes looks out.

'Go back inside,' Karen says.

'I want to watch,' the girl smiles.

'Aren't your mum and dad home?'

'I don't know,' she says, and quickly shuts the door.

Rather than use a lockpick, the locksmith drills the entire lock out. Shiny spirals of metal fly out and fall to the floor. He picks up the hot sections of the cylinder and puts them in his bag, pulls the bolt out and then backs away.

'Wait here,' Mats tells the maintenance man and locksmith.

Karen draws her pistol as Mats pulls the door open and calls into the flat.

'This is the police! We're coming in!'

Karen looks at the pistol in her pale hand. For a few moments the black metal object looks completely alien, its component parts, the barrel, bolt, and butt.

'Karen?'

She looks up and meets Mats's eye, then turns towards the flat, raises the pistol and goes inside with her other hand over her mouth.

She can't see any bags of rubbish in the hall.

The stench must be coming from the bathroom or kitchen.

The only sound is her boots on the plastic floor, and her own breathing.

She walks past a narrow hall mirror and into the living room, quickly securing the corners and glancing around at the chaos. The television has been tipped onto the floor, potted ferns are lying smashed on the floor, the sofa bed is standing askew and one of the cushions has been torn open, and the standard lamp is lying on the floor.

She turns her pistol towards the passageway leading to the bathroom and kitchen, lets Mats move past her and then follows him.

Their boots crunch on broken glass.

One wall lamp is lit, small dust-particles hovering in its light. She stops and listens.

Mats opens the bathroom door, then lowers his weapon. Karen tries to look in, but the door is blocking the light. All she can make out is a dirty shower curtain. She takes a step closer, leans forwards and nudges the door, and the light reaches across the tiles.

The handbasin is smeared with blood.

Karen shudders, then she suddenly hears a voice behind them. An old man, talking quietly. She's so startled that she lets out a whimper as she swings round and aims her pistol along the corridor.

There's no one there.

Full of adrenalin, she returns to the living room, hears a laugh and points her gun at the sofa.

There could easily be someone hiding behind it.

Karen hears Mats trying to say something to her, but doesn't catch what.

Her pulse is throbbing in her head.

She moves forward slowly, her finger resting on the trigger, then notices that she's shaking and supports it with her other hand.

The next moment she realises that the voice is coming from the stereo, as the old man starts to sing again.

Karen carries on round the sofa, then lowers her weapon and stares at the dusty cables and empty crisp packet.

'OK,' she whispers to herself.

On top of the stereo is a CD case from the Institute for Language and Folklore. The same track is playing on a loop, over and over again. An old man is saying something in heavy dialect, laughs, then starts to sing – *There's a wedding here at our farm, with empty plates and cracked dishes* – before falling silent.

Mats is standing in the doorway, gesturing to her to move on, keen to get to the kitchen.

It's almost dark outside now, the curtains are quivering gently in the heat from the radiators.

Karen follows her partner into the passageway, sways slightly and reaches out to the wall for support with the hand holding the pistol.

The air is thick with the smell of excrement and cadaver, strong enough to make their eyes water.

She can hear Mats taking short, shallow breaths, and focuses on not letting her nausea overwhelm her.

She follows him into the kitchen and stops.

On the linoleum floor lies a naked person with a bulging stomach and a head that's too big.

A pregnant woman with a swollen, grey-blue penis.

The floor lurches beneath her and her field of vision contracts.

Mats is leaning against the chest freezer, moaning gently to himself.

Karen tries to tell herself that it's just shock. She can see that the dead body is a man's, but the swollen stomach and spread thighs make her think of a woman giving birth.

She can feel her hands trembling as she puts her pistol back in its holster.

The body is in an advanced stage of decomposition, large parts of it look slack and wet.

Mats crosses the floor and throws up in the sink, so hard that it splashes the coffee machine.

The dead man's head looks like a blackened pumpkin that's been attached to his shoulders. His jaw has been broken off, and the gullet and Adam's apple have been pushed out through the deformed mouth by the gases that have built up inside.

There was a fight, Karen thinks. He got injured, broke his jaw, hit his head on the floor and died.

Mats vomits again, then spits out the slime.

Karen looks back to the stomach, parted legs, and the man's genitals.

Mats is sweating profusely and his face is white. She's about to go over and help him when someone grabs hold of her leg. Karen lets out a shriek and starts to fumble for her pistol, then realises that it's the girl from the neighbouring flat.

'You're not allowed to be in here,' she gasps.

'It's fun,' the girl says, looking at her with those dark eyes.

Karen's legs are shaking as she leads the child back through the flat and out into the stairwell.

'No one's allowed in,' she says to the man from the maintenance company.

'I turned away for a minute to open the window,' he replies.

Karen really doesn't want to go back into the flat, she knows she's going to end up having dreams about this, waking in the middle of the night with the man's spread legs etched on her retina.

When she enters the kitchen, Mats is turning off the tap in the sink. He turns to look at her with wet eyes.

'Are we done here?' she asks.

'Yes, I just want to look in the freezer,' he says, pointing to the bloody fingerprints around the handle.

He wipes his mouth, opens the lid and leans forward.

Karen looks on as his head jerks back and his mouth opens without a sound.

He staggers backwards and the lid slams shut with such force it makes a coffee-cup on the table jump.

'What is it?' she asks, walking closer to the freezer.

Mats is clutching the edge of the sink. He knocks over a plastic plant-spray and turns to look at her. His pupils have shrunk to the size of two drops of ink and his face is unnaturally white.

'Don't look,' he whispers.

'I need to know what's in the freezer,' she says, and can hear the fear in her own voice.

'For the love of God, don't look . . .'

2

Valeria's plant nursery in Nacka, outside Stockholm

Dusk is slowly falling, and the darkness only becomes apparent when the three greenhouses start to glow like rice-paper lanterns.

That's when you realise that evening has come.

Valeria de Castro has her curly hair pulled into a ponytail. Her boots are caked with mud and her padded red jacket is dirty, and tight across her shoulders.

Her breath is cloudy and the air has a crisp smell of frost.

She's done for the day, and pulls her gloves off as she heads up towards the house.

She goes upstairs and runs a bath, tossing her dirty clothes in the laundry basket.

When she turns towards the mirror she discovers a large smudge of dirt on her forehead, and a scratch on her cheek from the bramble patch.

Thinking that she needs to do something about her hair, she smiles wryly at herself because she looks so happy.

She pulls the shower curtain as far back as it will go, leans one hand on the tiled wall, and steps into the bathtub. The water is so hot that she waits a while before lowering herself in.

She leans her head against the edge of the bath, closes her eyes and listens to the drops falling from the tap.

Joona is coming this evening.

They had a row, it was so stupid, she felt hurt, but it was all a misunderstanding, and they sorted it out like adults.

She opens her eyes and sees the reflections of the water on the ceiling, as the rings from the drips spread out across the surface.

The shower curtain has slipped along the rail again, so she can no longer see the bathroom door and lock.

The water laps softly as she puts one foot up on the edge of the bath.

She shuts her eyes again and goes on thinking about Joona, then realises she's falling asleep and sits up.

Valeria is so hot now that she has to get out of the bath. She stands up and lets the water run off her body, then tries to look at the door in the mirror, but the glass is misted up.

She steps out of the bath onto the slippery floor, grabs a towel and starts to dry herself.

She nudges the bathroom door open, waits a moment, then looks out onto the landing.

The shadows on the wallpaper are still.

Everything's completely silent.

She isn't easily scared, but her time in prison has left her wary in certain situations.

She leaves the bathroom and walks across the cool landing and into the bedroom with her body steaming. It isn't completely dark yet, there are lines of translucent cloud visible against the sky.

She gets a clean pair of jeans from the chest of drawers and pulls them on, opens the wardrobe, takes out her yellow dress and lays it on the bed.

There's a noise downstairs.

Valeria stops moving instantly.

She holds her breath and stands there listening.

What could it have been?

Joona isn't due to arrive for another hour or so, but she's already made a spicy lamb stew with fresh coriander.

Valeria takes a step towards the window and starts to lower the blind when she catches sight of someone standing next to one of the greenhouses.

She jerks back and loses her grip on the cord, and the roll-blind flies up with a bang.

There's a rattling sound as the cord gets tangled up.

She quickly turns the bedside lamp out and goes back to the window.

There's no one there.

She's almost certain she saw a man standing motionless at the edge of the forest.

He was as thin as a skeleton, and was looking up at her.

The glass in the greenhouses is glinting with condensation. There's no one there. She can't let herself be afraid of the dark, that would make things impossible.

Valeria tells herself that it must have been a customer or supplier who disappeared when he saw her naked in the window.

She often gets visitors after the nursery has closed for the day.

She reaches for her mobile, but the battery has run out.

She quickly pulls on her long, red dressing-gown and starts to go downstairs. After a few steps she feels a cold breeze around her ankles. She carries on, and sees the front door standing wide open.

'Hello?' she calls quietly.

There are fallen leaves on the doormat, they've blown in across the wooden floor. Valeria slips her wet feet into her wellington boots, grabs the large torch from the coat rack and goes outside.

She follows the path down the greenhouses, checks the doors and shines the torch between the rows of plants.

The dark leaves light up in its beam as shadows and reflections play across the glass walls.

Valeria walks round the furthest greenhouse. The edge of the forest is black. The cold grass crunches beneath her feet as she walks.

'Can I help you with something?' she says loudly, shining the torch towards the trees.

The tree trunks look pale and grey in the light, but further in there's nothing but darkness. Valeria walks past her old wheel-barrow, and can smell the rust on it. Slowly she moves the beam of the torch from tree to tree.

The long grass looks untouched. She goes on aiming the torch at the trees. In amongst the trunks she catches sight of something on the ground. It looks like a grey blanket covering a log.

The light from the torch is getting weaker, and she shakes it. It grows stronger again, and she moves closer.

As she holds a branch out of the way she feels her heart start to beat faster, and the torch trembles in her hand.

It looks almost as if there could be a body under the blanket, someone hunched up, maybe missing one or both arms.

She has to pull the blanket off and look.

The forest is completely silent.

A dry branch snaps beneath her boot and suddenly the whole edge of the forest is bathed in white light. It's coming from behind her, and as it moves long, thin shadows merge with hers as they slip across the ground.

3

Joona Linna lets his car roll slowly towards the furthest green-house. The narrow, cracked tarmac track is edged with tall grass and tangled forest.

He has one hand resting on the steering wheel.

There's a thoughtful look on his face, a lonely look in his eyes, grey as sea-ice.

Joona keeps his hair cut short, because it starts sticking out in all directions if he lets it grow too long.

He's tall and muscular, the way you can only be from decades of hard exercise, when all your muscles, sinews and ligaments work together.

He's wearing a dark grey jacket, with an open-necked white shirt.

A wrapped bouquet of red roses is lying on the passenger seat beside him.

Before Joona Linna joined Police Academy he was in the military, part of the Special Operations Unit, where he qualified for a cutting-edge course in the Netherlands in unconventional close combat and urban guerrilla warfare.

Since Joona became a superintendent with the National Crime Division, he has solved more complex murder cases than anyone else in Scandinavia.

When he was sentenced to four years in prison, there were plenty of people who thought the entire trial in Stockholm Courthouse was unfair.

Joona didn't appeal against the judgement. He had known the risk he was taking when he tried to save a friend.

Last autumn Joona's sentence was reduced to community service as a neighbourhood officer in Norrmalm in Stockholm. He's been staying in a police service apartment on Rörstrandsgatan, opposite the Philadelphia Church. In a few weeks' time he's due to return to duty as a superintendent, and get back his office in Police Headquarters.

Joona turns the car round and stops, gets out and stands there in the cool air.

The lights are on in Valeria's little house, and the front door is wide open.

The light from the kitchen window is spreading out through the bare branches of the weeping birch and across the frost-covered grass.

He hears a snapping sound from the forest and turns. A weak light is moving amongst the trees, and leaves rustle as footsteps approach him.

Joona quickly unfastens his holster with one hand.

He steps aside when he sees Valeria emerge from the forest with a torch in her hand. She's wearing a red dressing-gown and wellington boots. Her cheeks are pale and her hair wet.

'What are you doing in the forest?' he asks.

She's looking at him oddly, as if her thoughts were a long way away.

'I was just checking the greenhouses,' she says.

'In your dressing-gown?'

'You're early,' she points out.

'I know, it's very impolite, I tried to drive slower,' he says, fetching the bunch of roses.

She thanks him, looks at him with her big brown eyes, and invites him up to the house.

The kitchen smells of cumin and bay, and Joona starts to say something about how hungry he is, then changes his mind and tries to explain that he knows he's early and that he's not in any rush to eat.

'It'll be ready in half an hour,' she smiles.

'Perfect.'

Valeria puts the flowers down on the table and goes over to the stove. She lifts the lid of the pan and stirs it, then puts her reading glasses on and checks the cookbook before adding the chopped parsley and coriander from the chopping board.

'You're staying the night, aren't you?' she asks.

'If that's OK.'

'I mean, so you can have some wine,' she explains with a blush.

'I guessed as much.'

'You guessed as much,' she says, imitating his Finnish accent with a wry smile.

'Yes.'

She takes two glasses from one of the top cupboards, opens a bottle of wine and pours it.

'I've made the bed in the spare room and left a towel and toothbrush.'

'Thanks,' Joona says, taking the glass.

They drink a silent toast, tasting the wine and looking at each other.

'I didn't get to do this in Kumla,' he says.

Valeria looks at the cut ends of the roses, puts them in a vase on the table, then turns serious.

'I'm going to say it straight out,' she begins, pulling at the belt of her old dressing-gown. 'I'm sorry I reacted the way I did.'

'You've already apologised,' Joona replies.

'I wanted to say it face to face . . . I behaved stupidly and immaturely when I found out you were still a police officer.'

'I know you thought I lied, but I—'

'It wasn't just that,' she interrupts, and blushes again.

'Everyone likes a police officer, don't they?'

'Yes,' she replies, trying so hard not to smile that the tip of her chin wrinkles.

She stirs the pot again, puts the lid back on and lowers the heat slightly.

'Let me know if there's anything I can do.'

'No, it's only . . . I was planning to sort out my hair and make-up before you came, so I'll nip off and do that now,' she says.

'OK.'

'Do you want to wait here or keep me company?'

'I'll keep you company,' Joona smiles.

They take their wine-glasses upstairs with them and go into the bedroom. The yellow dress is still lying on the neatly made bed.

'You can sit in the armchair,' Valeria mumbles.

'Thanks,' he says and sits down.

'You don't have to watch.'

He looks away as she takes the dressing-gown off, pulls on the yellow dress and starts to fasten the small buttons that run up from the waist.

'I don't often wear a dress, just the occasional day in the summer when I go into the city,' she says, looking at her reflection in the mirror.

'Really beautiful.'

'Stop looking,' she smiles as she fastens the last of the buttons over her breasts.

'I can't,' he replies.

She moves closer to the mirror and starts to put up her damp hair with hairclips.

Joona looks at her slender neck as she leans forwards to put lipstick on.

She sits down on the bed and picks up one of her earrings from the bedside table when she stops and meets his gaze.

'I think my reaction was because of that time in Mörby Centrum . . . I'm still ashamed of that,' she says quietly. 'I don't even want to think about what you must have thought of me.'

'That was one of my first operations with the Stockholm Rapid Response Unit,' he replies, looking down at the floor.

'I was an addict, a junkie.'

'People take different paths, that's just how it is,' he replies, looking her in the eye.

'But it upset you,' she says. 'I could tell . . . and I remember trying to counter that with a kind of hatred.'

'Do you know, I could only ever picture the way you were in high school . . . you never answered any of my letters, then I did my military service and ended up abroad.'

'And I ended up in Hinseberg Prison.'

'Valeria—'

'No, it was all so pointless, so fucking immature – I took every bad decision I possibly could . . . And then I came close to ruining things for us again.'

'You weren't expecting me to carry on in the police,' he says softly.

'Do you even know why I was in prison?'

'I've read the file, and it's no worse than what I've done.'

'OK, as long as you're aware that I'm no angel.'

'Of course you are,' he retorts.

Valeria goes on looking at him, as if there's more to see, as if there's something hidden that might soon become apparent.

'Joona,' she says seriously. 'I know you're convinced that it's dangerous to be together with you, that you expose the people you care about to danger.'

'No,' he whispers.

'You've been through some terrible things, for a very long time, but it isn't written in the stars that it always has to be like that.'

4

Joona is eating one last helping even though he's already full, as Valeria wipes the bottom of her plate with a piece of bread. They're sitting at the kitchen table, with the vase of roses moved to the worktop so they can see each other.

'Do you remember when we went on that canoeing course together?' Valeria asks, emptying the last of the bottle of wine in Joona's glass.

'I think about that summer a lot.'

It was high summer, and the two of them decided to spend the night on a small island they had spotted. It lay in an inlet, and was barely bigger than a double bed, with soft grass, a few bare rock outcrops, and five trees.

Valeria wipes the lipstick from the rim of her glass.

'Who knows how differently our lives might have turned out is that storm hadn't blown in,' she says without looking at him.

'I was so in love with you in high school,' he says, thinking that the same feelings are washing over him again.

'I don't think that ever really passed for me,' she says.

He puts his hand on hers and she looks at him with shimmering eyes before picking up another piece of bread.

Joona wipes his mouth on his napkin and leans back, making his chair creak.

'How's Lumi?' Valeria asks. 'Is she getting on OK in Paris?'

'I spoke to her on Saturday, she sounded happy, she was going to a party at Perottin, which apparently is a gallery I ought to know about . . . and I started asking if she was going to be out late and how she was going to get home.'

'The worried dad,' Valeria says with amusement.

'She said she'd probably get a taxi, and then I might have got a bit annoying, telling her to make sure she sits behind the driver and puts the seatbelt on.'

'OK,' Valeria smiles.

'I realised she wanted to end the call but I couldn't help telling her to take a photograph of the taxi-driver's licence and send it to me, and so on.'

'She didn't send the picture, did she?'

'No,' he laughs.

'Young people want us to care, but not too much . . . they want us to have faith in them.'

'I know, but it just comes out, I have trouble not thinking like a police officer.'

They remain seated at the table, drink the last of the wine, talk about the nursery and Valeria's two sons.

The darkness outside is thick now, as Joona thanks her for the meal and starts to clear the table.

'Would you like me to show you the guest bedroom?' she says shyly.

They stand up and Joona hits his head on the light, and it makes a metal clanging sound. They go up the creaking staircase together to a narrow room with a deep window alcove.

'Nice,' he says, stopping right behind her.

She turns and finds herself unexpectedly close to him, moves backwards and gestures slightly oddly towards the wardrobe.

'There are extra pillows in there . . . and blankets, if you're cold.'

'Thanks.'

'Or you could sleep in my bed, of course, if you like,' she whispers, taking his hand and leading him with her.

She stops in the doorway to her bedroom, stands on tiptoe and kisses him. He responds, puts his arms round her and almost picks her up.

'Shall we make the sheets into a tent?' he whispers.

'That's what we always used to do,' she smiles, and feels her heart beat faster.

She unbuttons his shirt and pushes it down over his shoulders, places her hands on his biceps and looks at him.

'It's funny . . . I remember your body, but you were only a tall boy back then, you didn't have all these muscles and scars.'

He unbuttons her dress, kisses her on the lips and the side of her neck, then looks at her again.

She's slim, with small breasts.

He remembers her dark nipples.

Now she has tattoos on her shoulders, and her arms are muscular and covered with scratches from thorny shrubs.

'Valeria . . . how can you be so beautiful?' he says.

She pulls down her pants and lets them fall to the floor, then steps out of them. Her pubic hair is black and tightly curled.

With trembling hands she starts to unbutton his trousers, but can't quite figure out how the catch on his belt works and only succeeds in pulling it tighter instead.

'Sorry,' Valeria giggles.

She blushes and forces herself not to stare too hard as he takes his trousers off.

They pull the large duvet over themselves, then sit beneath it on the bed, laughing and looking at each other in the soft light before starting to kiss again.

They roll to one side, push the duvet off, feeling like teen-agers, but simultaneously not. They're strangers, yet oddly familiar.

She sighs as he kisses her neck and lips, sinking back onto the bed and looking into his intense grey eyes, and feels a burst of giddy joy in her heart.

He kisses her breasts and sucks one of her nipples. She pulls his head towards her and he feels her heart racing.

'Come here,' she whispers, pulling him upwards and parting her legs as he lies on top of her.

Joona can't stop looking at her, those serious eyes, her half-open lips, her neck, the shadow of her collarbone.

Valeria pulls him closer and feels how hard he is as he slips inside her.

His weight presses her into the mattress, and the muscles in her thighs strain as her legs are pushed apart.

He feels her squeezing, moist warmth, then lets out a gasp as he changes rhythm.

She opens her eyes and sees the tenderness in his, the lust.

She responds to his movements and the soft light runs across her breasts, stomach, hips.

Her breathing speeds up and she raises her hips, leans her head back and closes her eyes.

The duvet slides to the floor.

The water in the glass on the bedside table is swaying, casting reflections that move in an elliptical pattern across the ceiling, over and over again.

5

It's Sunday, and the early winter's day is so dark that it feels as though the sun has already gone down. Joona has spent the past two nights at Valeria's, but is going back to work on Monday.

Valeria is sitting at the desk up in her bedroom, going through some quotes on her laptop when she hears a car.

She looks out of the window and sees Joona put his spade in the wheelbarrow and wave towards a white Jaguar that's approaching along the gravel track.

Joona tries to get Nils Åhlén to stop, but he drives straight over the row of potted hyacinths. There's a cracking sound as the pots break and damp compost sprays up around the tyres. The car comes to a stop with one wheel perched on the tall edging stone.

Valeria stands in the window and watches as a tall man in pilot's glasses gets out of the precariously balanced car. He's wearing a white lab coat under his unbuttoned duffel coat. His thin nose is crooked and his cropped hair grey.

Nils Åhlén is Professor of Forensic Medicine at the Karolinska Institute, and one of the leading forensic medical officers in Europe.

Joona shakes hands with his old friend and says he looks paler than usual.

'You should be wearing a scarf,' Joona says, and tries to fasten Åhlén's collar.

'Anja gave me the address here,' Nils says, without returning Joona's smile. 'I need to—'

He breaks off abruptly when he sees Valeria coming down the steps.

'What's happened?' Joona asks.

Nils Åhlén's thin lips are colourless, and he has a hunted look in his eyes.

'I need to talk to you in private.'

Valeria walks over to them and holds out her hand to the tall man.

'This is Valeria,' Joona says.

'Professor Nils Åhlén,' Åhlén replies formally.

'Nice to meet you,' Valeria smiles.

'I need to have a word with Nils,' Joona says. 'Is it OK if we go into the kitchen?'

'Of course,' she says, and leads them up to the house.

'I'm sorry to have to disturb you on a Sunday,' Nils Åhlén says.

'Don't worry, I was doing some work upstairs anyway,' Valeria says, and heads towards the stairs.

'Don't come down, I'll let you know when we're done,' Joona calls after her.

'OK.'

Joona shows Åhlén into the kitchen and invites him to sit down. The fire in the stove crackles.

'Would you like coffee?'

'No, thanks . . . I won't . . .'

He tails off and sinks onto a chair.

'So how are you doing really?'

'This isn't about me,' Nils replies, sounding troubled.

'So what's happened, then?'

Nils doesn't meet his gaze, just brushes the tabletop with one hand.

'I have a lot of dealings with my colleagues in Norway,' he begins tentatively. 'And I've had a call from the Norwegian Institute of Public Health . . . that's where their forensic medicine and pathology departments are based these days.'

'I know.'

Nils swallows hard, takes his glasses off, makes a half-hearted attempt to polish them and then puts them back on again.

'Joona, I'm sitting here, but I still don't know how on earth to tell . . . I mean, not without you . . .'

'Just tell me what's happened.'

Joona pours a glass of water and puts it down in front of Åhlén.

'As I understand it, the Norwegian Criminal Police have taken over from the Oslo police in the preliminary investigation of a suspected murder . . . They found a dead man in a flat. All the evidence suggested a run-of-the-mill drunken fight at first, but when they looked in the victim's freezer they found body parts belonging to a large number of different people, frozen at various stages of decomposition . . . They're working on the theory that the dead man was a previously unknown grave-robber . . . he may also have been involved in necrophilia and cannibalism . . . It seems he used to travel to antiques fairs and auctions as a dealer, taking the opportunity to raid local graves and help himself to souvenirs.'

Nils Åhlén takes a sip of water, then wipes his top lip with a trembling finger.

'What does this have to do with us?'

'I don't want you to get upset now,' Nils says, meeting Joona's gaze for the first time. 'He had Summa's skull in his freezer.'

'My Summa?'

Joona reaches out for the worktop and manages to knock over the empty wine bottle, but doesn't appear to notice as it clatters into the sink with the glasses and plates. His ears are roaring as memories of his wife flood his mind.

'Are you sure?' he whispers, looking out of the window at the greenhouses.

Nils Åhlén pushes his glasses further up his nose and explains that the Norwegian police have tried to find matches for DNA from the body parts found in the freezer in police databases held by Europol, Finland, and the Scandinavian countries.

'They found Summa's dental records . . . and seeing as I signed her death certificate, they called me.'

'I see,' Joona says, and sits down opposite his friend.

'They found all his travel documents in his flat . . . in the middle of November he was at a house clearance in Gällivare . . . that's not far from where Summa is buried.'

'Are you sure about this?' Joona repeats.

'Yes.'

'Can I see the pictures?'

'No,' Nils whispers.

'You don't have to worry,' Joona says, looking Nils in the eye. 'Don't do it.'

But Joona has already opened his case and taken out the file from the Norwegian Criminal Police. He lays one photograph after the other down on the kitchen table.

The first one shows the open chest freezer from above. A child's grey foot is sticking out of a frosted lump of white ice. A skeletal spine is nestled next to a bearded face and bloody tongue.

Joona leafs through photographs of the thawing body-parts on a stainless steel worktop. A human heart in an advanced state of decay, a leg cut off at the knee, an entire baby's body, three fleshless craniums, some teeth, and a torso complete with breasts and arms.

Suddenly Valeria walks into the kitchen and puts two used coffee-cups on the draining board.

'For God's sake!' Joona snaps, trying to cover the pictures even though he knows she's already seen them.

'Sorry,' she mumbles and hurries out.

He gets to his feet, leans one hand against the wall, stares out at the greenhouses, then back at the pictures again.

Summa's skull.

It's just a coincidence, he tells himself. The grave-robber didn't know who she was. There's no indication on the gravestone, and nothing in any public registers.

'What do we know about the perpetrator?' he asks, and hears Valeria go back upstairs.

'Nothing, they've got no leads at all.'

'And the victim?'

'All the evidence suggests a fight in the flat, he had a lot of alcohol in his blood when he died.'

'Isn't it a bit odd that the police don't have any leads on the other person?'

'What are you thinking? Joona, what exactly are you thinking now?' Nils Åhlén asks with apprehension in his voice.

6

Valeria is sitting at her computer upstairs when Joona comes up and knocks on the door.

She turns towards him and the pale light through the leaded window gives her hair a chestnut-red shimmer.

'Nils has gone,' Joona says in a subdued voice. 'Sorry I was angry, I just didn't want you to have to see that.'

'I'm not that fragile,' she replies. 'You know, I've seen dead bodies plenty of times.'

'But that was more than body-parts . . . this is personal,' Joona says, then falls silent.

There's a family grave in Stockholm with the names Summa Linna and Lumi Linna on the headstone, but the urns under the ground don't contain their ashes. The deaths of Joona's wife and daughter were fabricated, and they lived on for many years in a secret location with new names.

'Let's go down to the kitchen and heat that soup up,' Valeria says after a while.

'What?'

She gives him a hug, and he wraps his arms round her and rests his cheek against her head.

'Let's go and eat,' she repeats quietly.

They go down to the kitchen and she takes the soup they made earlier out of the fridge. She puts the pan on the stove and turns the hotplate on, but when she switches on the light in the extractor fan Joona walks over and turns it off.

'What's happened?' Valeria asks.

'Summa's grave has been vandalised and . . .'

Joona falls silent, turns his face away and she sees him wipe tears from his cheeks.

'You're allowed to cry, you know,' she says gently.

'I don't honestly know why this upsets me so much . . . someone has dug up her grave and taken her skull back to Oslo with him.'

'God,' she whispers.

He goes and stands by the window and looks out at the greenhouses and forest. Valeria can see that he's closed the curtains in the living room, and there's a knife lying on the old dresser.

'You know Jurek Walter's dead,' she says in a serious voice.

'Yes,' Joona whispers, closing the curtains in the kitchen window.

'Do you want to talk about him?'

'I don't think I can,' he says simply, and turns towards her.

'OK,' she replies in a composed voice. 'But you don't have to keep anything from me, I can cope with listening, I promise . . . I know what you did to save Summa and Lumi, so I understand that he's a monster.'

'He's worse than anything anyone could ever imagine . . . he digs his way inside of you . . . and leaves you hollowed out.'

'But it's over now,' Valeria whispers, and reaches out towards him. 'You're safe now, he's dead.'

Joona nods.

'This has dragged it all up again . . . it's like I could feel his breath on the back of my neck when I heard what had happened to Summa's grave.'

Joona returns to the window and peers out between the curtains. Valeria looks at his back in the gloom of the kitchen.

They sit down at the table and she asks him to tell her more about Jurek Walter. Joona puts his hands on the table to stop them shaking and says in a low voice:

'He was diagnosed with . . . non-specific schizophrenia, chaotic thinking, and acute psychosis characterised by bizarre and extremely violent behaviour, but that doesn't mean a thing . . .

he was never schizophrenic . . . the only thing that diagnosis shows is how terrified the psychiatrist who conducted the evaluation was.'

'Was he a grave-robber?'

'No,' Joona says.

'There you are, then,' she says, and tries to smile.

'Jurek Walter would never bother with trophies,' he says heavily. 'He wasn't a pervert . . . but he had a passion for ruining people's lives. Not killing them, not torturing them – not that he would have hesitated to do either in an instant, but to understand him you have to realise that he wanted to destroy his victims' souls, extinguish the spark inside them . . .'

Joona tries to explain that Jurek wanted to take everything away from his victims, then watch as they carried on living – going to work, eating, watching television – until the terrible moment when they realised that they were already dead.

They sit in near-darkness as Joona tells Valeria about Jurek Walter. Even though he was the worst ever serial killer in the Nordic countries, the general public know nothing because all information about him has been declared highly classified.

Joona explains how he and his partner Samuel Mendel began to close in on Jurek Walter.

They took turns to keep watch outside one particular woman's home. Her two children had gone missing in circumstances that were reminiscent of a number of other victims in the case.

It was as if the earth had opened up and swallowed them.

The pattern that had emerged showed that a disproportionate number of missing people in recent years came from families where someone else had already gone missing.

Joona falls silent and Valeria watches as he knits his hands together in an attempt to hold them still. She gets up, makes some tea and fills two mugs before sitting down again and waiting for him to go on.

'The weather had been mild for two weeks, it had started to thaw, but that day it started to snow again,' he says. 'So now there was fresh snow on top of what was already there . . .'

Joona has never spoken about those last hours, when Samuel arrived to relieve him.

A thin man had been standing at the edge of the forest, staring up at the window where the woman whose children had gone missing was lying asleep.

The man's face, so thin and wrinkled, was completely impassive.

Joona found himself thinking that the very sight of the building seemed to give the man a feeling of pleasurable calm, as if he were already dragging his victim off into the forest.

The thin figure did nothing but watch before turning away and vanishing.

'You're thinking of the first time you saw him,' Valeria says, putting her hand over his.

Joona looks up and realises that he's stopped talking, and nods before telling her that he and Samuel had got out of the car and followed the fresh trail of footprints.

'We ran along an old railway line, into Lill-Jans Forest . . .'

But in the darkness among the trees they suddenly lost the man's trail. With nothing else to go on, they turned to head back.

As they were retracing their steps along the railway track, they saw that the man had left the rails and had set off into the forest instead.

Because the ground beneath the fresh snow was wet, his shoes had left dark prints. Half an hour before they had been white, impossible to see in the weak light, but now they were as dark as granite, unmistakable.

As they headed through the forest they heard a whimpering, moaning sound.

It sounded like someone crying from the very depths of hell.

Between the tree trunks they spotted the man they had been pursuing. The ground was dark with freshly dug soil around a shallow grave. A filthy, emaciated woman was trying to get out of a coffin. She was sobbing as she struggled, but every time she almost got out, the man shoved her back down again.

They drew their pistols and rushed in, managed to get the man on the ground and cuffed his hands and ankles.

Samuel was sobbing as he called the emergency control centre.

Joona helped the woman out of the coffin and put his coat round her. As he held her and told her that help was on its way, he suddenly caught sight of movement between the trees. Some of the branches were moving, the snow on them falling softly to the ground.

'Someone had been standing there watching us,' he says quietly.

The fifty-year-old woman survived, despite having spent almost two years in the coffin. Jurek Walter had appeared from time to time, opening the coffin and giving her water and food. She had gone blind, was terribly emaciated, and had lost her teeth. Her muscles had withered away, and she was deformed by sores. Her hands and feet were both frostbitten.

At first the doctors thought she was merely traumatised, but it turned out she had suffered severe brain damage.

Large parts of the forest were cordoned off that same night. The following morning a police tracker-dog led them to a location two hundred metres from where the woman had been buried. Excavations uncovered the remains of a man and a boy, buried in a blue plastic barrel. It was later confirmed that they had been buried four years earlier, but hadn't survived for long despite the fact that the barrel was supplied with air through a tube.

Joona can see that Valeria is shaken; all the colour has drained from her face and she's got one hand clasped over her mouth.

She's thinking back to Joona's description of the first time he saw Jurek Walter, standing in the snow beneath the window of his next victim. It reminds her of the man she saw on Friday, at the edge of the forest next to the greenhouse. She should probably tell Joona about that, but doesn't want to give him any reason to think that Jurek is still alive after all.

7

A prosecutor took over responsibility for the preliminary investigation once Jurek had been arrested, but Joona and Samuel led the interviews with him, from the decision to remand him in custody until the main hearing.

'It's hard to understand, but somehow Jurck Walter got inside the head of anyone who came close enough,' Joona says, meeting Valeria's gaze. 'There's nothing supernatural about it, I'd put it down to a sort of cold awareness of human weakness . . . he would pick up on something fundamental that meant you completely lost any ability to defend yourself.'

Jurck Walter confessed to nothing during the whole of his time in custody. He didn't claim to be innocent either, just spent most of his time on a philosophical deconstruction of the concepts of crime and punishment.

'I only realised during the final hearing that Jurek's plan was to get me or Samuel to say that there was a possibility that he was innocent . . . that he had merely stumbled upon the grave and was trying to help the woman out when we arrested him.'

One evening when Joona and Samuel were running together, Samuel had raised the hypothetical question of what would have happened if anyone other than Jurek had been beside the grave when they arrived.

'I can't help thinking about it,' Samuel said. 'That anyone who had been standing by the grave at that moment would have been prosecuted.'

It was true that there was a lack of concrete evidence, and that it was mostly the circumstances of the arrest and lack of any adequate alternative explanation that had supported the prosecution.

Joona knew Jurek was dangerous, but had no idea at the time just what level of danger they were dealing with.

Samuel Mendel became more withdrawn, he couldn't handle it, couldn't bear to be in close proximity with Jurek, he said he felt dirty, that his soul was being poisoned.

'Almost against my will, I find myself saying things that suggest he could be innocent,' Samuel said.

'He's guilty . . . But I think he's got an accomplice,' Joona replied.

'It all points to a lone madman who—'

'He wasn't alone at the grave when we got there,' Joona interrupted.

'Yes, he was, that's just him manipulating us, because that could mean you saw the real perpetrator fleeing into the forest.'

Joona has thought about the last conversation he had with Jurek before the main hearing many times.

Jurek Walter was sitting on a chair in the heavily guarded interview room, his lined face staring down at the floor.

'It's completely irrelevant to me if I'm found guilty, even though I'm innocent,' he said. 'I'm not afraid of anything, not pain . . . not loneliness or boredom. The court's going to go along with the prosecutor . . . and my guilt is going to be regarded as proven beyond reasonable doubt.'

'You're refusing to defend yourself,' Joona says.

'I refuse to get bogged down in technicalities, seeing as digging a grave and filling it in are basically the same thing.'

Obviously Joona realised he was being manipulated, that Jurek Walter needed him on his side in order to be released. That was why he was trying to sow seeds of doubt. Joona knew what Jurek was up to, but at the same time couldn't ignore the fact that there was actually a crack in the case.

'He thought he'd won you over to his side,' Valeria says in a frightened voice.

'I think he took it as a promise.'

During the main hearing Joona was called as a witness to talk about the arrest.

'Is it possible that Jurek Walter was in fact trying to rescue the woman from the grave?' the defence lawyer asked.

An internal compulsion to agree with him was nudging Joona towards the edge. Such a possibility was obviously within the bounds of plausibility. Joona began to nod in response, but stopped and forced himself to go back to the exact memory of the appalling scene in the forest clearing, where Jurek Walter was unquestionably shoving the woman back into the grave every time she tried to crawl out.

'No . . . he was the person keeping her captive in the grave. He's the one who killed them all,' Joona replied.

After due consideration, the Chair of the Court declared that Jurek Walter was being sentenced to secure psychiatric treatment with specific restrictions applied to any eventual parole proceedings.

Before he was taken out of the court, Jurek Walter turned towards Joona. His face was covered with tiny wrinkles, and his pale eyes looked oddly empty.

'Now Samuel Mendel's sons are going to disappear,' Jurek said calmly. 'And Samuel's wife Rebecka will disappear. But . . . No, listen to me, Joona Linna. The police will look for them, and when the police give up, Samuel will go on looking. And when he eventually realises that he'll never see his family again, he'll kill himself . . .'

Light was playing through the leaves in the park outside, casting quivering, transparent shadows across his thin figure.

'And your little daughter,' Jurek Walter went on, looking down at his fingernails.

'Be careful,' Joona said.

'Lumi will disappear,' Jurek whispered. 'And Summa will disappear. And when you realise that you're never going to find them . . . you're going to hang yourself.'

He looked up and stared directly into Joona's eyes. His face was quite calm, as if things had already been settled the way he wanted.

'I'm going to crush you into the dirt,' he said quietly.

Joona goes over to the curtains and looks out at the darkness, where the branches of the birch trees are blowing in the wind.

'You've never told me much about your friend Samuel,' Valeria says.

'I've tried, but . . .'

'It wasn't your fault his family went missing.'

Joona sits down again and looks at her with moist eyes.

'I was sitting at home, at the kitchen table with Summa and Lumi . . . we'd just made spaghetti and meatballs when Samuel phoned . . . he was so upset that it took a while for me to realise that Rebecka and the boys weren't at the house on Dalarö that they'd set off for several hours earlier . . . he'd already been in touch with the hospitals and the police . . . he tried to pull himself together, tried to take deep breaths, but his voice broke when he asked me to check that Jurek Walter hadn't escaped.'

'Which he hadn't,' Valeria said breathlessly.

'No, he was locked in his cell.'

All traces of Rebecka and the boys stopped on the gravel track five metres in front of their abandoned car. Tracker dogs couldn't pick up any scent. For two months the police conducted a thorough search of the forests, roads, buildings, rivers and lakes. After the police and volunteers had given up, Samuel and Joona carried on looking on their own, without once discussing what they feared most.

'Jurek Walter had an accomplice, and he took them,' Valeria says.

'Yes.'

'And then it was your turn.'

Throughout this period Joona kept watch over his family, went with them everywhere, but obviously he realised that wasn't going to be enough, not long-term.

Samuel stopped looking and returned to work a year or so after his family went missing. He lasted three weeks before, having finally given up hope, he drove to his summerhouse, went down to the beach where his sons used to swim, and shot himself in the head with his service pistol.

Joona tried talking to Summa about moving, about starting a new life, but she couldn't appreciate just how dangerous Jurek Walter was.

To begin with he tried to find a way out for all of them together. Perhaps they could get new identities and live quietly in some distant country.

He called his old lieutenant on an encrypted line, but he was aware that wouldn't be enough. New, secret identities wouldn't be 100 per cent secure. They would merely buy them a period of grace.

'But why didn't you just take off together?' Valeria whispers.

'I would have given anything to be able to do that, but . . .'

When Joona realised what had to be done, it became an obsession. He started to work out a plan that could save all three of them.

There was one thing that was more important than him being together with Summa and Lumi.

Their lives were more important.

If he took off or disappeared with them, that would be a direct challenge to Jurek's accomplice to start looking for them.

And if you look for people who are trying to hide, sooner or later you always find them, Joona knew that.

So they mustn't be given any cause to look, he reasoned. That was the only sure way of not being found.

Which left him with one solution: Jurek Walter and his shadow needed to believe that Summa and Lumi were dead. Joona was going to arrange a car accident and make it look like they were both killed.

'But why not all three of you?' Valeria exclaimed. 'You could have pretended that you were in the car as well, that's what I'd have done.'

'Jurek would never have believed that . . . My loneliness was what tricked him, the fact that I lived alone for year after year . . . No one would be able to manage that, not without eventually being lulled into a false sense of security and giving in to the temptation to see their family.'

'So you thought you were being watched by the shadow the whole time.'

'I was,' Joona says in a hollow voice.

'We know that now, but had you ever seen anyone?'

'No.'

Now that it's all been over for a couple of years, Joona knows he did the right thing. They all paid a high price, but it saved Summa and Lumi's lives.

'Jurek's twin brother Igor was helping him all along,' Joona says. 'It was appalling . . . he had no life of his own, he was so mentally traumatised that his only purpose in life was to obey Jurek.'

Joona falls silent and thinks of the scars on Igor's back, evidence of a lifetime of abuse from a razor strap.

When Jurek escaped after fourteen years in isolation, he carried on with his plan as if nothing had happened.

A lot of people lost their lives during those terrible days when Jurek Walter was free.

'But both Jurek and his brother are dead now,' Valeria points out.

'Yes.'

Joona remembers the moment he shot the brother three times in the heart from close range. The bullets went right through his body, and Igor was thrown backwards into a gravel pit. Even though Joona knew Jurek's twin brother had to be dead, he still shuffled down the steep slope to make absolutely sure.

Saga Bauer shot Jurek Walter and saw his body get carried away down a river and washed out to sea.

By the time Joona was finally reunited with his wife Summa, she was dying of cancer. He took her and their daughter Lumi to a house in Nattavaara, in the far north of Sweden. The little family had six months together. When Summa died, they buried her where her grandmother grew up, in Purnu in Finland.

It wasn't until a year later that Joona finally dared to believe it was really over, when Saga found the remains of Jurek's body, and the fingerprints and DNA analysis confirmed that it was definitely him.

It was as if Joona could finally breathe again.

For all those involved, the grief and wounds from those years will always be there. Saga Bauer hasn't been the same since she went undercover to investigate Jurek Walter. She's become darker, and sometimes Joona can't help thinking that Saga's trying to run away from her fate.

8

Saga Bauer is running fast across the old Skansbron through the damp shadows of the newer bridges up above.

Heavy traffic is thundering past her.

She lengthens her stride as she approaches the end of the bridge.

Her sports top is dark with sweat across her chest.

Almost every day she runs all the way to Gamla Enskede after work and collects her half-sister Pellerina from school.

Saga has reconnected with her father after a rift that started when she was a teenager. Though the worst of the misunderstandings have been sorted out now, Saga is finding it hard to slip back into being someone's daughter again. Maybe they'll never be able to patch things up completely.

Saga speeds up as she passes beneath the echoing viaduct carrying Nynäsvägen and the railway lines.

She's muscular, like a ballet dancer, and beautiful in a way that catches people's attention. Her long blond hair is plaited with colourful ribbons, and her eyes are strikingly blue.

Saga Bauer is an Operational Superintendent with the Swedish Security Police, but this autumn her boss has made her write reports and take part in turgid meetings about cooperation between the police in Sweden and the USA. In order to avoid open disagreement and internal criticism, it has been decided to declare the collaboration a great success. Amongst other things, both Saga Bauer and Special Agent López have been forced to become friends on Facebook.

Saga passes the dismal-looking sports hall and carries on into the old garden suburb, then sprints the last stretch before she gets to Enskede School.

Dust is flying up from the football pitch, drifting through the tall chain-link fence.

Pellerina is twelve now, but isn't allowed to go home on her own after school. She has to stay behind and participate in after-school activities until she's picked up.

Pellerina has Down Syndrome, and was born with Fallot's Tetralogy, a combination of four different heart defects that prevent blood getting to her lungs. She had a shunt installed when she was four weeks old, and had to undergo serious heart surgery before her first birthday.

She has learning difficulties, but is able to attend a regular school with the help of specially trained assistants.

Saga's pulse-rate and breathing calm down as she walks round the main school building and approaches the Mellis out-of-school club. She can see her little sister through the ground-floor window. Pellerina looks happy, she's jumping about and laughing with two other girls.

Saga opens the front door, walks through the cloakroom and takes her shoes off beside the line of tape on the floor, then goes into the club. She can hear music from the dance and yoga room, and stops in the doorway.

A pink shawl has been draped over a lamp. The bass of the music is making one of the windows rattle, and the paper snow-flakes stuck to it seem to dance.

Saga recognises Anna and Fredrika from her sister's class, they're both a head taller than Pellerina.

They're all barefoot. Their sausagy socks are lying in the dust beneath one of the chairs. They're standing in a row in the middle of the floor, counting themselves in, then wiggling their hips, taking a step forward, clapping their hands and spinning round.

Pellerina is smiling broadly as she dances, unaware of the string of snot hanging from her nose. Saga can see she's doing it well, she's learned all the moves, but she's a bit too enthusiastic, jutting her hips out more than the other two girls.

Anna turns the music off. Out of breath, she tucks a lock of hair behind her ear and claps her hands.

From her vantage point over by the door, Saga sees the two girls exchange a look above Pellerina's head, and Fredrika pulls a moronic face, which makes Anna laugh.

'Why are you laughing?' Pellerina asks, still panting for breath as she puts her thick glasses back on.

'We're laughing because you're so clever and pretty,' Fredrika says, stifling a giggle.

'You're both clever and pretty too,' Pellerina says with a smile.

'But not as pretty as you,' Anna says.

'Yes, you are,' Pellerina laughs.

'You should think about going solo,' Fredrika says

'What does that mean?' Pellerina asks, pushing her glasses further up her nose.

'That it might be better if we filmed you dancing on your own —'

Fredrika stops abruptly when Saga walks into the room. Pellerina runs over and hugs her.

'Are you having fun?' Saga asks calmly.

'We're practising our dance,' Pellerina replies.

'Is it going well?'

'Really well!'

'Anna?' Saga says, looking at the girl. 'Is it going well?'

'Yes,' she says, and glances at Fredrika.

'Fredrika?'

'Yes.'

'I can tell you're both nice girls,' she says. 'Keep it that way.'

Saga waits in the cloakroom as Pellerina hugs her special-needs helper several times before pulling on her winter overalls and putting her drawings in a bag.

'They're the coolest girls in the class,' Pellerina explains as they walk across the schoolyard hand in hand.

'But if they tell you to do funny things, you must say no,' Saga says as they walk home.

'I'm a big girl.'

'You know I'm a worrier,' Saga explains, and feels a lump in her throat.

She takes hold of Pellerina's hand and thinks about the girls pulling faces over her head. It sounded like they were thinking of filming Pellerina to mock her, and spread the clip.

Afterwards everyone always claims it was just an innocent game that got out of hand, when there was never any doubt that it was simply cruel. Dark energy fills the room and you choose to carry on regardless.

9

Pellerina lives with her dad in a bright-red plastered house with a red-tiled roof on Björkvägen in Gamla Enskede.

The old apple trees and lawn are sparkling with tiny ice crystals.

As Saga closes the gate Pellerina runs to the door and rings the bell.

Lars-Erik Bauer is wearing cords and a white, crumpled open-neck shirt. He could have done with getting his hair cut a month ago, but his unkempt, greying hair makes him look appealingly eccentric. Every time Saga sees her father she's struck by how old he is now.

'Come in,' he says, and helps Pellerina out of her overalls. 'You're welcome to stay for dinner, Saga.'

'I haven't got time,' Saga replies automatically.

Pellerina's thick glasses have steamed up. She takes them off and clambers up the stairs to her room.

'I'm making macaroni cheese, I know that's one of your favourites.'

'It was when I was little.'

'Just say what you'd like then – I can go to the shop,' her dad says.

'Stop it,' she says with a smile. 'It doesn't matter, I'll eat anything. Macaroni cheese will do fine.'

Lars-Erik looks genuinely delighted that she wants to stay for a while. He takes her coat, hangs it up and tells her to make herself at home.

'I'm worried that a couple of the girls at Mellis aren't being very nice,' Saga says.

'In what way?' her dad asks.

'I don't know, just a feeling, they were pulling faces.'

'Pellerina usually handles most things pretty well on her own, but I'll have a word with her,' he says before they head upstairs to her sister's room.

Lars-Erik is a cardiologist, and has bought a professional ECG-machine so he can monitor Pellerina's heart, seeing as she could suffer a recurrence of her earlier problems.

Saga looks at her sister's latest drawings while their dad connects the electrodes to her chest. The pale scar from her operations runs vertically down her breastbone.

'I'm going to start dinner,' Lars-Erik says, and leaves them.

'I've got a silly heart,' Pellerina sighs, putting her glasses back on.

'You've got the best heart in the world,' Saga says.

'Daddy says I'm all heart,' she smiles.

'He's right – and you're the best little sister in the whole world.'

'You're best, you look just like Elsa,' Pellerina whispers, reaching out for Saga's long hair.

Usually it annoys Saga whenever anyone compares her to a Disney princess, but she likes the fact that Pellerina sees herself and Saga as the two sisters in *Frozen*.

'Saga?' Lars-Erik calls from the bottom of the stairs. 'Can you come down here for a moment?'

'I'll be back soon, Anna,' she says, patting her sister's cheek.

'OK, Elsa.'

Lars-Erik is chopping leeks when Saga walks in. There's a parcel on the kitchen table. It's wrapped in aluminium foil and has a paper heart stuck on top, with the words *To my darling daughter, Saga*.

'I ran out of wrapping paper,' he says apologetically.

'I don't want presents, Dad.'

'It's nothing, just a little token.'

Saga tears the foil off and crumples it into a shiny ball, and puts it down next to the flowery cardboard box.

'Open it,' Lars-Erik says with a wide smile.

The box contains an old-fashioned porcelain Christmas elf, packed in shredded paper. He's wearing a tree-green outfit, has rather piercing eyes, pink cheeks and a cheerful little mouth.

There's a large porridge bowl in his arms.

Her Christmas elf.

It used to get brought out every Christmas, and the pot filled with pink and yellow toffees.

'I've been looking for one . . . well, for ages, really,' Lars-Erik says. 'And today I happened to wander into an antiques shop in Solna and there he was.'

Saga remembers that her mum threw the elf on the floor once when she was angry with her dad, smashing it to pieces.

'Thanks, Dad,' she says, and puts the box down on the table.

When she goes back up to see Pellerina, she notices that her heart rate has increased, as if her sister had been running. Pellerina is staring at her phone open-mouthed, with a look of horror on her face.

'What's happened?' Saga asks in a concerned voice.

'No one can see, no one can see,' her sister says, pressing the phone to her chest.

'Dad!' Saga calls.

'It's not allowed!'

'Don't worry, sweetheart,' Saga says. 'Just tell me what you were looking at.'

'No.'

Lars-Erik hurries up the stairs and comes into the bedroom.

'Tell Daddy,' Saga says.

'No!' Pellerina cries.

'What is it, Pellerina? I'm in the middle of cooking,' he says, to encourage her to speak.

'It's something on her phone,' Saga explains.

'Show me,' Lars-Erik says, and holds out his hand.

'It's not allowed,' Pellerina sobs.

'Who says so?' he asks.

'It says in the email.'

'I'm your dad, so I'm allowed to see.'

She hands him the phone and he opens and reads it with a frown.

'Oh, sweetheart,' he says with a smile, putting the phone down. 'That isn't real, you know that, don't you?'

'I have to send it on, otherwise—'

'No, you don't have to. We don't send silly emails in this family,' Lars-Erik says firmly.

'One of those chain emails?' Saga asks.

'Yes, a really silly one,' he replies, then turns back towards Pellerina. 'I'll get rid of it.'

'No, please!' she pleads, but Lars-Erik has already deleted it.

'It's all gone now,' he says, and hands the phone back to her. 'We can forget all about it.'

'I get chain emails too,' Saga says.

'But do they come to see you too?'

'Who?'

'The clown girls,' Pellerina whispers, pushing her glasses further up her nose.

'That isn't real, it's all made up,' her dad says. 'It's just some little kid who's made it all up to scare people.'

After Lars-Erik removes the electrodes and switches the ECG-monitor off, Saga carries her little sister downstairs and lays her down on the sofa in front of the television. She tucks her up in a blanket, and puts *Frozen* on, as usual.

It's dark outside now. Saga goes into the kitchen to help her dad with the cooking. As soon as he's finished pouring the cream, eggs and grated cheese onto the macaroni, she picks up a pair of silicone oven-gloves and puts the dish in the oven.

'What did the email say?' she asks quietly.

'That you have to send the email to three other people to escape the curse,' he sighs. 'Otherwise the clown girls will come when you're asleep and poke your eyes out – that sort of thing.'

'I can see why she'd be frightened,' Saga says.

She goes and checks on Pellerina, who's fallen asleep. Saga takes her glasses off and puts them down on the coffee table.

'She's sleeping,' Saga says when she comes back into the kitchen.

'I'll wake her when it's time to eat – this always happens, school wears her out.'

'I have to go,' she says.

'Haven't you got time to eat first?' he asks.

'No.'

He goes into the hall with her and passes her her coat.

'Don't forget your elf,' he reminds her.

'He can stay here,' Saga says as she opens the door.

Lars-Erik stands in the doorway. The light plays on his lined face and unkempt hair.

'I thought you'd like it,' he says quietly.

'It doesn't work like that,' she says, and walks away.

10

It's three o'clock and the white sky is already starting to grow darker.

Joona has never had any objection to being on patrol, but after Nils Åhlén's visit it feels like the world has become a more dangerous place.

He's walking past the wrought-iron railings outside Adolf Fredrik Church, and sees a black-clad group standing around an open grave. The surrounding gravestones have been vandalised and are covered with swastikas.

As Joona passes Olof Palmes gata he notices someone waving behind the window of a Thai restaurant.

An intoxicated woman has stood up from her table and is staring at him.

As he moves closer she spits on the window right in front of him.

He carries on towards Hötorget, where the market traders are busy selling fruit and vegetables. His mind keeps wandering to the grave-robber in Oslo. As soon as he gets Summa's cranium back from Norway, he's planning to rebury it with the rest of her remains. He hasn't yet decided whether to tell Lumi about what's happened. It would upset her terribly.

Joona has just passed the Concert Hall when he hears a man yelling in an aggressive, drunken voice. There's the sound of a glass bottle breaking, and Joona spins round and sees shards of green glass on the road.

People are keeping their distance from a man who's clearly under the influence of narcotics. He's unshaven, and his blond hair is gathered in a messy tangle at the back of his head. He's wearing a battered leather jacket and jeans that are dark with urine around the crotch and down one leg.

The man isn't wearing shoes or socks, and Joona can see he's injured one foot and is bleeding on the pavement.

The man is swearing at a woman who's hurrying away, then he stands still with an imperious expression and points one finger at the people around him as if he were about to say something incredibly important.

'One, two, three, four . . . five, six, seven . . .'

Joona walks closer and sees that there's a young girl standing behind the confused man. Her dirty face is upset, and she looks like she's about to burst into tears. A pink tracksuit top is her only protection from the cold.

'Can we go home now?' she asks, tugging tentatively at the man's jacket.

'One . . . two . . . three . . .'

He loses his thread and reaches out for the lamppost to stop himself falling. His eyes look drugged, his pupils have shrunk to pinpricks and there's snot streaming from his thin nose.

'Do you need any help?' Joona asks.

'Yes, please,' the man mutters.

'What can I do?'

'Shoot the ones I point at.'

'Are you armed?'

'I'm pointing at all the ones who—'

'Stop that,' Joona interrupts calmly.

'OK, OK,' the man mutters.

'Are you armed?'

The man points at a man who's stopped to look, then at a woman walking past with a pushchair.

'Daddy,' the girl pleads.

'Don't be frightened,' Joona says to her, 'but I need to find out if your dad's got a weapon of any sort on him.'

'He needs to get some rest, that's all,' she whispers.

Joona tells the man to put his hands behind his head, and he does as Joona says. But when he lets go of the lamppost he loses his balance and stumbles backwards, into the shadow of the blue wall of the Concert Hall.

'What drugs have you taken?'

'Just a bit of ketamine, and some speed.'

Joona crouches down next to the girl. Her father has started to point his finger discreetly at different people again.

'How old are you?'

'Six and a half.'

'Do you think you could look after a teddy bear?'

'What?'

Joona opens his bag and pulls out the stuffed toy. In the run-up to Christmas the police have been given teddy bears that they can give to any child in trouble or who's witnessed anything violent. Often that's the only present they're going to get in families with drug problems.

The girl stares at the little bear, which has a stripy top and a big red heart on its chest.

'Would you like to look after it?' Joona smiles.

'No,' she whispers, and glances up at him shyly.

'You can have it if you want,' Joona explains.

'Really?'

'But it needs a name,' Joona says, handing the stuffed toy over to her.

'Sonja,' the girl says, pressing the bear to her neck.

'That's a lovely name.'

'It was my mum's name,' she tells him.

'We need to take your dad to hospital – is there anyone you can stay with in the meantime?'

The child nods and whispers something in the teddy bear's ear.

'Grandma.'

Joona calls an ambulance, then contacts an acquaintance at Social Services and asks her to collect the girl and take her to the address they've looked up.

As he finishes explaining everything to the girl, a police car arrives at the scene. Its blue lights flash across the tarmac.

Two uniformed colleagues get out of the car and nod to Joona.

'Joona Linna? Your boss has contacted me over the radio,' one of them says.

'Carlos?'

'He wants you to answer your phone.'

Joona takes his phone out and sees that Carlos Eliasson – head of the National Operational Unit – is calling him, though there's no ringtone.

'Joona,' he says as he answers.

'Sorry to disturb you while you're working, but this is top priority,' Carlos says. 'A superintendent with the German police, Clara Fischer at the BKA, is trying to get in touch with you as soon as possible.'

'What for?'

'I've said you can help them with a preliminary investigation . . . The police in Rostock are looking into a death at a camping site, probably murder . . . Victim's name is Fabian Dissinger . . . a serial rapist who was recently released from a secure psychiatric unit in Cologne.'

'I'm still on probation, I'm on patrol duties until—'

'She asked for you specifically,' Carlos interrupts.

11

Joona is driving past pale green fields and large stone houses with tarmac drives full of cars and bicycles.

The plane from Stockholm landed at Rostock-Laage Airport an hour ago. Joona hired a BMW and set off north on Autobahn 19.

He doesn't know why Superintendent Clara Fischer has requested assistance from him specifically. They've never been in contact before, and the man who was found dead at the campsite has never cropped up in any of Joona's cases.

Clara Fischer didn't specify precisely what she thought Joona would be able to contribute, but because the German and Swedish police forces have a long history of cooperation, Carlos gave the go-ahead.

During the flight Joona had time to read three of the case files relating to the murder victim that he had been sent by the Bundeskriminalamt.

Fabian Dissinger was convicted of twenty-three violent rapes of both men and women in Germany, Poland and Italy. According to one psychiatric report, he had an antisocial personality disorder with sadistic tendencies and elements of psychopathy.

Joona turns sharp left and drives through a patch of woodland. He catches sight of a muddy motocross course in a clearing on his right, then there's nothing but trees until he reaches the camping site, Ostseecamp Rostocker Heide.

Joona parks just outside the police cordon and walks over to the group of German police officers waiting for him.

The winter sun is glinting off the cables and satellite dishes on the roofs of the caravans.

Superintendent Clara Fischer is a tall woman with dark brown eyes; something about her proud bearing suggests that she would be quick to take offence. Her penetrating gaze seems to grow sharper as she watches Joona approach. Her short curly hair is greying at the temples. She's wearing a black leather jacket that reaches below her hips, and black leather boots with low heels that are now completely grey with mud from the wet ground.

Clara studies Joona as if the slightest shift in his expression is of great significance.

'Thanks for coming at such short notice,' she says, not breaking eye contact as she shakes his hand.

'I like campsites . . .'

'Great.'

'But I'm wondering why I'm here,' he concludes.

'Certainly not because Fabian Dissinger's death is a great loss to Germany,' Clara Fischer replies, setting off towards one of the plots.

Joona follows her along one of the tarmac paths that crisscross the campsite. The winter air is cold as the white rays of sunlight shine through the bare treetops.

'I'm not saying he got what he deserved, but if I had my way he'd have spent the rest of his life in prison,' she says calmly.

'Not an unreasonable opinion.'

They pass the shower block and a small kiosk. A few campers are standing outside the cordon taking pictures of the crime scene on their phones. The red-and-white plastic tape is rippling in the wind.

'Not an unreasonable opinion,' Clara repeats, and glances at him. 'I know that some of our colleagues in Berlin refused to work on a case last week . . . A known paedophile was found drowned in a ditch near a school . . . I can understand that, when at the same time they're having to drop the investigation into the mugging and murder of a young woman in Spandau.'

An empty beer can rolls across a patch of sand surrounding a cluster of recycling bins. Broken glass sparkles in the sunshine, and there's a bundle of bubble-wrap wedged between two of the containers.

Joona and Clara walk on in silence through a group of older caravans that have been shut up for the winter.

Two uniformed officers are guarding the inner cordon. They greet Clara with respectful salutes.

'A Cabby 58 from 2005,' she says, nodding towards the caravan. 'Dissinger had been renting it for the past two months and four days.'

Joona looks at the boxy caravan, perched on breezeblocks. Trickles of red-brown rust have run down the side from a crooked aerial on the roof.

Two forensics officers in white overalls are examining the ground around a camping table on the gravel outside the caravan, and numbered sticks mark the site of any finds. There's a sooty aluminium saucepan full of rainwater and dead flies.

'I presume you haven't had time to look at the reports we sent through.'

'Not all of them, no.'

She smiles bleakly.

'Not all of them,' she repeats. 'We've found a huge quantity of violent porn on his computer . . . so I think we can surmise that eleven years of psychiatric treatment didn't sort out all his problems. He was locked up, medicated, just ticking over . . . and all the while waiting for a chance to pick up where he left off.'

'Some people are like that,' Joona replies simply.

A tall forensics officer in protective white overalls leaves the caravan to make space for them, and says something to Clara that Joona doesn't hear.

They step up onto the step-shaped stool in front of the open door.

Clara watches his every move without embarrassment. It's as if she's on the verge of asking a question but keeps stopping herself.

Translucent plastic mats have been laid out on the cork floor to protect it. The floor of the caravan creaks under their weight.

There's a brown jacket with threadbare lapels and blood-stained sleeves lying on the sun-bleached, pale blue fitted benches.

'Someone ought to have heard the fight,' Clara says quietly.

The glass top covering the small sink and gas-hob is laden with test-tubes of biological samples and plastic bags containing seized items – coffee-cups, beer glasses, cutlery, toothbrushes, and cigarette butts.

'Dissinger received a visitor, he was probably planning on the usual, but time had got the better of him, he was weaker, older . . . and the tables turned and he was assaulted and killed by the person he was planning to rape.'

Sunlight is streaming in through the grimy windows and stained cream curtains. The remains of broken spiders' webs are trembling in the draught from the open door.

'He was found by two youngsters . . . It seems he told one of them a few days ago that he'd be happy to offer them a drink.'

'I'd like to talk to them,' Joona says, looking at the blood on the rounded corner of one of the cupboards.

'They're pretty shaken, but if they hadn't arrived too late for that drink they'd probably be in a considerably worse state than that.'

The double bed is stained with blood and one of the reading lights set into the headboard has been pulled out and is hanging by its wires. Someone was dragged off the bare mattress, then shoved back and dragged along the side of the caravan when they tried to escape.

'His relatives aren't exactly queuing up to organise his funeral, so I left him hanging in there until you got here,' Clara concludes, and gestures towards the closed door to the bathroom.

'Thanks.'

12

Joona opens the sliding door to the bathroom. A large man, bare-chested, is hanging from an overhead locker between the cassette toilet and washbasin. His feet reach the floor, but both his legs have been broken at the knee, rendering them incapable of supporting his weight.

He has a length of steel wire round his neck. It has cut into his skin below his Adam's apple, to a depth of at least five centimetres.

Blood has run down his hairy chest and bulging stomach to his jeans.

'You're certain about the ID?'

'Hundred per cent,' Clara says, looking intently at Joona again.

The man's face has been smashed in, there isn't much left of his features.

The hands hanging by his sides are black with hypostasis.

'He must have had plenty of enemies after the trial,' Joona says thoughtfully. 'Have you—'

'Statistically, revenge is an unusual motive,' Clara says, cutting him off.

Joona looks at the wall behind the body. The dead man evidently struggled for a long time before he was asphyxiated. In his efforts to loosen the wire by swinging back and forth, he managed to break the basin. Even though it can't be counted as an out-and-out hanging, seeing as the dead man's feet are touching the ground, Joona is certain they're going find fractures to the hyoid bone and at the top of the thyroid cartilage.

'I'm working on the hypothesis that he managed to lure a young man whose life had gone off the rails – care-homes, petty crime, prostitution, steroids, Rohypnol,' Clara continues, pulling on a pair of white latex gloves.

'There wasn't a fight,' Joona says.

'No?'

'He should have been able to put up a decent fight, but his knuckles aren't damaged at all.'

'We'll get the body to the lab now that you've seen it,' she mutters.

'He's got no other defensive injuries either,' Joona goes on.

'He must have,' she says, turning the dead man's arms round to look.

'He didn't defend himself,' Joona says calmly.

Clara Fischer sighs, lets go of the arms and stares intently at Joona.

'How can you know so much?'

'What am I doing here?' Joona asks.

'That's what I was thinking of asking you,' Clara says, taking a plastic sleeve from her bag and showing him an old-fashioned mobile phone.

'A phone,' he says.

'A phone that we found between the cushions on the sofa . . . It belonged to Fabian Dissinger,' she says, switching it on inside the plastic. 'Two days ago he called this number – do you recognise it?'

'That's my number,' Joona says.

'One of the last calls he made in his life was to your personal phone.'

Joona takes out his mobile and sees that he missed the call.

'Tell me what you know,' Clara says.

'Well, now I know why you wanted me here.'

'You need to tell me why he called you,' she says impatiently.

Joona shakes his head.

'Fabian Dissinger hasn't featured in any of my investigations.'

'Tell me the truth,' Clara says irritably.

'I have no idea.'

She blows a strand of hair away from her mouth.

'You have no idea. There must be a connection, though,' she persists.

'Yes,' Joona nods, taking a step closer to the hanged man and looking at his eyes.

One of them is hidden by blue-grey swelling and pulpy red flesh, but the other is open, and the mucous membrane is punctuated by small dots of blood.

He realises that Clara Fischer held back from telling him about the phone to see if his reaction to the crime scene might reveal a connection that he would otherwise have denied.

'Give me something,' she says, staring at him.

In spite of the cold air in the caravan, she has tiny beads of sweat on her top lip.

'I'd like to be present for the post-mortem,' Joona replies.

'You said there wasn't a fight.'

'The violence was one-sided . . . an almost uncontrolled explosion of aggression, but employing certain military techniques.'

'You were in the military – the Special Operations Unit – before you joined the police.'

They move away from the bathroom so that two forensics officers can go in. They lay a body-bag on the floor, then fasten plastic bags round the victim's hands, cut the wire and lift the big, rigid body down.

The dead man's weight makes the officers groan, and they keep giving each other instructions as they carry him feet-first out through the narrow doorway. Joona gets a glimpse of Fabian Dissinger's broad back and hairy shoulders as they set him down on the bag.

'Hang on, turn him over,' Joona says, moving closer.

'*Könnten Sie bitte die Leiche auf den Bauch wenden*,' Clara says in a neutral voice.

The forensics officers stare at them, but open the bag again, turn the body over, then make room for Joona and Clara.

Joona feels his heartbeat increase as he looks at the lower part of the victim's back: the skin from the bottom of his shoulder blades down to his buttocks is unnaturally striped, as if he'd been lying on a reed mat.

'What's happened to his back?' Clara whispers.

Without bothering about protective gloves, Joona crouches down and gently runs his fingertips over the damaged skin; hundreds of parallel scars made by wounds that have bled and healed over and over again.

'I know you've got a legendary reputation as a detective,' Clara says slowly. 'But you've also got a criminal conviction, you're on probation, and I'm going to arrest you and take you in for questioning unless you can explain how—'

Joona stands up, pushes past her and accidentally knocks over some of the evidence bags containing glasses and ashtrays when he reaches out to the stove for support before going on through the door and out into the sunshine.

'I've got you, Joona – haven't I?' Clara says, hurrying after him.

He doesn't reply, just walks across the gravel towards the gate, pushing aside a forensics officer who's standing poking at his phone.

Behind him he hears Clara say, 'Stop him,' but there's no sense of urgency in her voice.

Ready to put down anyone who tries to stop him, Joona passes two uniformed officers.

Obviously recognising the intent in his face, they back away cautiously.

The dead man in the caravan shows signs of having been beaten.

Jurek Walter's twin brother had similar scars on his back. He had been whipped for years with a shaving strop, a length of coarse leather used to sharpen razor blades.

Joona doesn't yet know what these similarities mean, but there's no doubt that they're a message for him.

He starts to run towards the car park, jumps into his car and spins it round, sending mud flying up over the sides.

As he drives away from the campsite he calls the Norwegian Criminal Police. He needs to know if there were any injuries on the back of the grave-robber who was found dead in Oslo, the man who had Summa's skull in his freezer.

13

Joona has taken a taxi straight from the airport to the Karolinska Institute's Department of Forensic Medicine on the outskirts of Stockholm.

There are electric Advent lights in the windows of the red brick building and black rosehips covered in frost on the bare bushes outside.

Joona hasn't taken his medication today because it makes him feel as if he's not as sharp as he could be.

As a result of an accident many years ago, Joona suffers from cluster migraines. Sometimes an attack will knock him out completely for several minutes, and sometimes it sweeps past like a threatening storm. So far, the only thing that helps is an anti-epilepsy drug called Topiramate.

Joona walks through the glass doors and turns left into the corridor, where he bumps into the elderly cleaner with his cart.

'How's Cindy getting on?' Joona asks.

'She's much better now, thanks,' the man says with a smile.

Joona can't count the number of times he's stood in this corridor during his years in the police, waiting to hear what Nils Åhlén has found out.

Things are different today, seeing as the bodies they're going to analyse are only present in photographic form.

Fabian Dissinger, the sex-offender found dead in Rostock, had been abused over a long period of time. The scars were consistent with his having lain still on his front while someone beat him from the side. The wounds healed, were opened up again by fresh blows, then healed once more.

The Oslo grave-robber had no scars on his back. But shortly before his death five severe blows had been delivered with either a belt or a strop.

The lights are on in the main post-mortem lab.

Saga is crouching down with her back against the tiled wall, and Nils is standing in his medical coat, rubbing his thin hands.

'The Norwegian Criminal Police have sent the pictures, I received them in the car on the way here. I've forwarded them to you,' Joona explains.

'Thanks,' Nils says.

'Don't I get a hug?' Saga says, getting to her feet.

Her blond hair is in plaits, and as usual she's wearing faded jeans and a jacket from her boxing club.

'You look happy,' he says, walking over and giving her a hug.

'I suppose I am,' she replies.

He takes a step back and looks her in the eye. She keeps hold of his arm with one hand for a few moments.

'Even though you're dating a police officer.'

'Randy,' she smiles.

Nils Åhlén opens his computer, finds the emails and clicks on the attachments. The three of them gather in front of the screen as Nils brings up the images from the two crime scenes.

'What's this all about?' Saga eventually says. 'Both men were assaulted and killed, with extreme force, excessive brutality . . . neither of them made much effort to defend themselves . . . and both have been whipped across the back.'

'In the same way as Jurek's brother,' Joona says.

'That's debatable,' she says.

'Fabian Dissinger has exactly the same sort of scars as Jurek Walter's twin brother . . . although the brother's were much worse, of course, a lot older, and—'

'In which case they're not the same,' she points out.

'Both victims had direct connections to me,' Joona says.

'Yes,' she replies.

'We know everyone says Jurek Walter is dead,' Joona says after a pause. 'But I've been thinking that . . . well, perhaps that isn't the case.'

'Stop that,' Saga says in a tense voice.

'Joona,' Nils Åhlén says, nudging at his glasses nervously. 'We've got a body, we've got a one hundred per cent DNA match—'

'I want to go through the evidence again,' Joona says, cutting him off. 'I need to know if there's even a theoretical possibility that he could still be alive, and—'

'There isn't,' Nils interrupts.

Saga shakes her head and starts walking towards the door.

'Wait, this affects you too,' Joona says to her back.

'I'll get the file,' Nils Åhlén says. 'We'll do it your way.'

'You're both mad,' Saga mutters as she turns and walks towards them.

Nils unlocks his filing cabinet and pulls out the folder containing the reports and photographs relating to Jurek Walter. From the cold store he fetches a sealed jar containing a finger preserved in formalin. The glass enlarges the finger slightly. Small white particles are swirling around the swollen finger, as pale as ice.

'The only evidence we have that Jurek is dead is one finger,' Joona says.

'It was an entire damn torso,' Saga says, raising her voice. 'Heart, lungs, liver, kidneys, intestines—'

'Saga, listen,' Joona says. 'I just want us to do this, I want us to go through what we know together. Because that will either help us relax, or—'

'I shot him, I killed him,' Saga says. 'He could have killed me, I don't know why he hesitated, but I shot him in the neck, the arm, the chest—'

'Calm down,' Nils says, and pulls over an office chair for her.

Saga sits down, puts her face in her hands for a few moments, then lowers her hands and takes a deep breath.

'Jurek Walter died that night,' she goes on, her voice breaking. 'I don't know how many times I've been through it all in my head . . . how hard it was, running through the deep snow, the way the flare reflected off the tiny crystals . . . I had a clear view of him, and I shot him with my Glock 17. The first shot hit him in the neck, the second in his arm . . . I walked towards him and shot him again, with three shots to the chest. Every single damn shot hit him, and I saw the blood spray from the exit wounds onto the snow behind him.'

'I know, but—'

'It's hardly my bloody fault that he fell into the rapids, but I fired into the water and saw a cloud of blood billow out around him, and I followed him downstream, firing and firing until the body was swept away by the current.'

'Everyone did what they had to – and more,' Nils Åhlén says slowly. 'The police sent divers down that same night, and the following morning they searched the banks with sniffer dogs for more than ten kilometres downstream.'

'They should have found the body,' Joona says in a subdued voice.

He knows that Saga carried on looking on her own. The search probably formed part of her long road back to life, a way for her to work through what had happened privately. She's told him about how she followed the river all the way to the sea near Hysingsvik, then marked out an area on the map and systematically searched the archipelago by dividing it into squares. She studied tidal currents and went out to every single island and skerry along a hundred-kilometre length of coast, spoke to residents and summer visitors, fishermen, people who worked the ferries, oceanographers . . .

'I found him,' Saga whispers, looking at Joona with bloodshot eyes. 'Damn it, Joona, I found him.'

He's heard her explanation of how, after more than a year of looking, she bumped into a man on the rugged north coast of Högmarsö. He was a retired churchwarden, collecting driftwood from the beach. She spoke to him and discovered that he had found the dead body of a man at the water's edge five months earlier.

Saga had gone with him to the inhabited part of the island. The churchwarden's cottage and the old crematorium were tucked behind a sugar-white chapel.

'Jurek's body had been carried on the current and washed

ashore during the storms we had at the end of that winter,' Saga says, without taking her eyes off Joona.

'That all checks out,' Nils says. 'Do you get that, Joona? It all makes sense. He's dead.'

'The only parts of Jurek Walter that were left were his torso and one arm,' Saga goes on. 'The churchwarden told me he carried the swollen body through the forest in his wheelbarrow, and left it on the floor of the toolshed behind the chapel. But the smell drove his dog mad, so he ended up having to move it to the old crematorium.'

'Why didn't he call the police?' Joona asks.

'I don't know. He made his own hooch and was fiddling his benefits,' she says. 'Maybe he'd already started to go senile . . . But he took pictures of the body on his phone in case the police did show up asking questions . . . and he kept one of the fingers at the back of his freezer.'

Nils Åhlén pulls a printed picture from the file and passes it to Joona.

He takes the photograph and angles it so the reflection of the fluorescent lights in the ceiling of the post-mortem lab don't get in the way.

On a cement floor beside a red lawnmower lies a bloated body with no head. A pool of water has spread out around it. The loose covering of white skin has slid off the chest, and the three jagged entry wounds gape like craters.

Saga has come and stood next to him so she can see the picture.

'That's Jurek, that's where I hit him.'

14

Nils Åhlén very calmly lays out copies of the scanned fingerprints, Jurek Walter's DNA profile taken at the time of his arrest, and the laboratory's response.

'The match is exact because we've got both DNA and fingerprints . . . not even identical twins share the same fingerprints,' he explains.

'I don't doubt that that's Jurek Walter's finger,' Joona says quietly.

'It was cut off an already dead body,' Nils Åhlén says emphatically.

'Joona, he's dead, aren't you listening?' Saga asks, wiping tears from her cheeks.

'One dead body part is enough,' Joona replies. 'The finger could have been cut from an amputated hand that had been lying in brackish water for the same length of time as the body.'

'Oh, for God's sake,' she groans.

'Purely theoretically,' Joona persists.

'Nils, tell him that's not possible.'

Nils Åhlén pushes his glasses up his nose again and looks at Joona.

'You're suggesting he could have cut his own hand off in order to . . .'

He trails off and meets Joona's gaze.

'Let's say Jurek was incredibly lucky and somehow survived

being shot, swam with the current, made it to land and survived,' Joona says seriously.

'Those shots were fatal,' Saga protests.

'Jurek started out as a child soldier,' Joona says. 'Pain is irrelevant to him, he would have cauterised the wounds himself and amputated his own arm if that's what it took.'

'Joona, you do realise that this is impossible,' Nils says wearily.

'It's only impossible if it genuinely can't be done.'

'OK, we're listening,' Saga says, sinking back onto her chair.

Joona's face is pale and impassive.

'Jurek finds a man with roughly the same build as him, the same age,' he says. 'He shoots his victim the same way you shot him . . . then he removes the dead man's head and leaves the rest of the body to soak somewhere along the coast . . . in some sort of cage or crate.'

'Along with his own hand,' Nils says quietly.

'It wouldn't even be that bizarre for him – he used to keep people buried alive in coffins, only checking on them from time to time.'

'To do that, he'd have had to have the cooperation of the churchwarden Saga met.'

'Jurek has ways of making people obey him.'

Drips from a tap glint in the drainage gulley in the floor.

Joona looks at Nils and Saga. His pale grey eyes look almost black now, and his face is beaded with sweat.

'Am I right: there's a theoretical possibility that Jurek is still alive?' he asks in a whisper.

'Joona,' Nils pleads, then he nods in response.

'That's nonsense, it isn't enough, this is nothing, for God's sake!' Saga exclaims, sweeping the reports and photographs onto the floor.

'I'm not saying I believe that he's alive,' Joona says tentatively.

'Good, Joona, because that would have felt kind of weird,' she blurts. 'Seeing as I shot him and then found his body.'

'It was actually only a finger.'

'In theory, Joona's right,' Nils says.

'OK, what the hell,' Saga says, sitting back down on her chair. 'So you're right in theory, but no matter how you look at it, there's no logic to the entire premise. Why the fuck would Jurek want to whip and kill two perverted ex-cons in Norway and Germany?'

'That doesn't sound like Jurek Walter,' Nils Åhlén concedes.

Joona closes his eyes and his eyelids tremble as he tries to compose himself enough to pursue his line of reasoning.

'Jurek had three types of victim,' he begins, opening his eyes. 'The true victims, his primary targets, were the ones he didn't kill himself, like Samuel Mendel.'

'Which is why it was so hard to establish a pattern,' Nils says.

'The second category were the people he took from his prime targets, the people who made their lives worth living.'

'Children, wives, siblings, parents, friends.'

'Jurek didn't actively want to kill them either. As individuals, they had no significance to him.'

'Which is why he kept them locked up or buried in coffins and drums,' Nils says, nodding in agreement.

'The third category were people who happened to get in his way . . . he didn't want to kill them either, but he did so for practical reasons, to remove them as obstacles.'

'So he never really set out to kill anyone?' Saga says.

'He didn't get anything out of the act of killing itself, there was no sexual motive, it wasn't even about domination, just his own personal sense of justice . . . he wanted the first category, the primary victims, to be broken down to the point they would choose death over life.'

He looks down at the floor and the photographs of the decayed torso, whipped backs and lab reports.

'Now we have two victims with no apparent connection to each other, with injuries inflicted in a way that is reminiscent of what happened to Jurek's brother. One victim had Summa's skull in his freezer, and the other had tried to contact me.'

'That can't be coincidence,' Saga says quietly. 'But these murders don't fit Jurek Walter's persona.'

'I agree, I completely agree, I don't think it's Jurek either, but maybe someone's trying to tell me something, and maybe that person has some sort of connection to him,' Joona says.

'What if there are other victims?' Saga says, and looks him in the eye.

15

Stellan Ragnarson is a lanky man with kind eyes and a somewhat uncertain, beseeching smile. He's started cutting his hair very short after it got too thin to look boyish.

This evening he's wearing his shiny black jogging bottoms and a washed-out grey hoodie with the New York Rangers logo on it.

He takes half a kilo of steak from the fridge, tears off the plastic and tips the meat into a large stainless steel bowl.

Marika is sitting at the drop-leaf table with her phone and a bar of chocolate.

She's five years younger than him, and works at the petrol station in the E65, opposite the ICA Kvantum supermarket.

'You spoil him' she says, breaking off three chunks of chocolate.

'I can afford it,' he replies, and puts the bowl down on the floor below the kitchen window.

'Today, maybe.'

Stellan smiles as the big dog devours the meat with a snap of its neck. Rollof is an impressive-looking Rottweiler, self-assured and calm. His tail was docked when he was a puppy because it was coiled up over his back.

Stellan is unemployed, but he won some money on the horses yesterday and surprised Marika by buying her a rose.

They go and sit on the sofa and eat ham-and-mustard toasted sandwiches, and watch the television show *Stranger Things*.

Marika's phone rings just as they're finishing. She looks at the screen and says it's her sister again.

'Take it,' he says, standing up. 'I'll go up and play for a bit before I take Rollof out.'

'Hi, Sis,' Marika answers with a smile, and plumps up the cushion behind her back.

Stellan gets a can of beer from the fridge and goes upstairs to his computer.

Six months ago he began to explore the Dark Web, the invisible part of the World Wide Web that's said to be five thousand times the size of the ordinary Internet.

Even if you haven't studied software programming and Internet protocols, most people are aware that every computer and phone has its own individual IP address, a combination of letters and numbers that can be used to identify the user and locate them geographically.

Stellan was attracted to Darknet, part of the Dark Web which employs servers without IP addresses. That's where most of the really dangerous deals and developments are happening: guns, drugs, rape, contract killings, slave trade and organ theft.

But after what happened eleven days ago, he stopped looking at the Dark Web altogether. He cut off all contact and tried to get rid of the software, without success.

It doesn't matter, he tells himself.

He's not using the Dark Web any more, from now on he'll make do with a bit of online gaming.

He's started to get caught up in the game Battlefield.

It's intense, but only a game nonetheless.

You have to put together a team to carry out a military operation; players spend most of the time talking about the mission, but it's still fun getting to know new people from all corners of the world.

Stellan puts his beer down on the desk and sticks a plaster over the camera lens on the computer before putting on his headphones and microphone and getting going.

His team's task in the game is to liquidate a terrorist leader in a run-down building in Damascus.

They've been given satellite pictures of the building, and have been flown in from their base by helicopter.

Stellan takes one hand off the handset to open the can, but doesn't have time before he has to get back to the game.

They force entry through a back door and enter the building in two pairs. Stellan and his backup, who goes by the name Straw, run through a pillared walkway along the side of a courtyard, with cracked marble tiles and rusting military equipment among desiccated palm trees.

'Take it nice and slow now,' Stellan says over the voice-chat.

'I can take the lead if you're getting cold feet,' Straw says, then lets out a belch.

'You haven't even seen the guards, have you?' Stellan says quietly.

The guards' cigarettes are barely visible in a dark corner. When they inhale, the light of the burning tobacco glints off their automatic rifles.

Straw sighs in Stellan's headphones, then walks straight out and shoots the terrorist leader's guards. The heavy fire echoes through the walkway and off the walls.

'Fuck, you can't do that before we've checked the courtyard,' Stellan says, reaching for the can of beer again.

He tries to open the ring-pull as Straw's avatar saunters into the courtyard with his gun hanging by his hip.

'Do you need help with that can?' he asks.

Stellan pulls off his headphones and stands up so fast that his chair topples over behind him. He stares at the screen, looks at the plaster covering the lens, then hears a voice from the headphones, now lying on the desk next to the handset.

'Sit back down,' Straw calls.

Stellan walks closer and pulls out the headphones, forces the computer to shut down, unplugs it and tries to figure out how anyone could see him as he carries the laptop to the wardrobe, stuffs it inside and shuts the door.

He goes over to the window and looks out at the dark street. There's a parked car with misted-up windows outside. Stellan lets the blinds fall with a clatter, picks up the chair from the floor and sits down, his heart racing.

'What's going on?' he whispers to himself.

He tucks the handset and headphones away in one of the desk drawers with trembling hands.

He thinks it must have something to do with what happened eleven days ago.

'Fuck, fuck, fuck . . .'

Even if he did spend two years in prison studying IT, he now realises how stupid it was to dabble in Darknet. There's no real anonymity, there's always someone who can outsmart the system.

But until eleven days ago he had been obsessed with it, unable to resist the temptation.

He went way too far before realising he was in very deep water, that he was in a league way beyond anything he could have imagined. Some of the people on Darknet were lethal, they knew no boundaries at all. In real time he had watched two men shoot a boy sitting in front of his computer. Blood sprayed across the Star Wars posters and saggy mask of Trump's face that was lying on the floor.

Stellan read up about the risks, and found out that anyone who hooked up using the Vidalia browser became accomplices in all activity on the Dark Web.

But Tor software is supposed to protect users, making them impossible to trace.

It's all a matter of mix cascades, a relay system that means that your signals are sent through a random sequence of proxy servers around the world.

Stellan doesn't understand it completely, but his reading of it was that the software would give him access to the darkest parts of the Internet without anyone being able to identify or trace him.

16

Stellan gets up on shaky legs, nudges the blinds aside and looks out at the street again. The car has gone. He goes downstairs and pulls the cable out of the router in the living room. Marika is sitting on the sofa in front of the television, and pats the seat beside her when she sees him.

'I have to take Rollof out,' he says in a toneless voice.

She pulls an exaggeratedly upset face.

'You always put the dog first.'

'He needs the exercise, he's a big dog.'

'What's the matter? You don't look great,' she says.

'It's just . . . we can't use the Internet any more.'

'Why not?'

'We need to switch network, we've got a virus that will ruin everything if we try to get online.'

'But I need to go online.'

'Now?'

'Yes, I've got to pay the bills, and—'

'Go round to your sister's and use her computer,' he says, cutting her off.

Marika shakes her head.

'This feels pretty messed up.'

'I'll call the support number after I've been out with Rollof.'

'This shouldn't be allowed to happen,' Marika mutters.

Stellan goes out into the hall, and the moment he takes the

leash down and the silvery links rattle, Rollof comes rushing over.

It's a quiet, rainy winter's evening in the south of Sweden. The fields are brown and bare. Stellan and Rollof set off along the side of the E65 as usual. Heavy trucks thunder past occasionally. Stellan can't help looking over his shoulder at regular intervals, but they're alone.

Thin mist is hanging over the allotments on the other side of the wide road. Rollof sticks close to him, breathing calmly.

It's a raw night, dark and cold. They turn right onto Aulinvägen and walk along the yellowed grass, with the big industrial estate to their left. The huge car parks are deserted at this time of night.

Stellan is aware that he isn't thinking very clearly, that he might be behaving irrationally, but he's decided to burn down the workshop. If he burns it down, he'll be able to get an insurance payout, move away from Ystad, change his Internet supplier and get new electronic equipment.

There's a light in one of the old greenhouses up ahead. Rollof stops, then barks and growls at the dense bushes in the deserted plot.

'What is it?' Stellan asks in a low voice.

The leash is taut around the dog's thick neck, making his breathing sound strained. Rollof is dependable, but he can be a real handful when he encounters other male dogs.

'No fighting, now,' Stellan warns, pulling him away.

The other dog doesn't bark back, but some of the branches in front of the greenhouse start to sway.

Stellan feels a shiver run down his spine. For a moment he thought there was someone standing over there.

He heads into the big industrial estate. The streets are empty, and between the streetlamps everything is pitch-black. His shadow grows longer, then has time to disappear altogether before he reaches the next circle of light. His footsteps echo off the brick and corrugated metal façades.

It isn't easy for anyone with a criminal record to succeed in the job market in Sweden. Stellan was convicted of a double murder when he was twenty years old.

Since his release he's had a number of temporary jobs, has

been on loads of courses, trying to get better qualifications, but mostly he's lived off social security benefits.

His restless search of the Darknet, his voyeuristic observation of what other people were getting up to, all had its roots in an old fantasy. Even in prison he had talked about getting hold of some girls and letting them earn money for him. He had read about it, thought about it, considered the risks and decided to figure out the best way to succeed.

That was what was in his mind when he ventured into the Dark Web. He'd advertised in a couple of forums that he wanted to buy three girls, but hadn't got any responses.

When he made the adverts more specific and explained that he wanted to keep the girls in cages and exploit them sexually, he suddenly started to get responses. Many of them were provocative, and some tried to frighten him off. Others seemed serious, but when he made further enquiries they appeared to be connected to organised crime.

Stellan doesn't know why he can't stop thinking about keeping them in cages. Maybe it's the idea that it might actually be achievable.

Ten years ago he inherited an old industrial unit that he had tried to rent out. While he was waiting for more responses on the Dark Web marketplaces, he built a sturdy inner wall towards the back of the long, narrow building. Without measuring the walls inside and out, it was impossible to tell that there was a hidden room containing five cages equipped with beds, a shower, toilet, and a small kitchen area with a fridge.

Stellan had almost finished work on it when he was contacted by Andersson.

He didn't appreciate how dangerous he was – if only he had.

Andersson showed an interest in his plans, and was prepared to deliver five young girls from Romania.

The offer was perfect in every detail. It all sounded great – like getting an inside tip on the horses.

But at the same time, Andersson radiated a compromising seriousness that made Stellan shiver with fear.

He did more research into the Tor network.

Provided he was careful, he couldn't be traced, because his

information was relayed via countless nodes and was encrypted until it reached its recipient.

The deal was a bit too big for him.

But if he managed to build up a client base, he could earn a fortune.

Stellan couldn't stop thinking about the imprisoned girls. Despite that, he didn't actually know what he was going to do with them.

He didn't want to rape them, he didn't want to beat them. He fantasised about them becoming so demoralised that they would consent to anything without resistance.

Andersson got him to divulge details of his background, and asked complicated questions about loyalty.

He felt annoyed by that, and created a sort of Trojan horse in the form of a PDF document as a way of gaining the upper hand.

When the attachment was opened, Andersson revealed his exact location.

So now Andersson knew that he knew.

Stellan had his address.

Don't fuck with me, that had been the thought in his mind.

Andersson's response had been as rapid as it was unexpected.

'You shouldn't have done that,' he wrote. 'The only way you can regain my trust is by filming yourself slicing through your Achilles tendons.'

That was eleven days ago.

Stellan pretended to believe it was all a joke, but deep down he knew Andersson was mad.

Without making a big deal of it, he tried to pull out of the arrangement, explaining that he'd run into difficulties and was going to have to put the whole thing on ice.

It's too late for that, Andersson replied.

What do you mean?

I'll be paying you a visit soon.

Andersson, I'm very sorry, Stellan wrote. *I didn't mean to—*

He stopped when the fan on his computer started to run at top speed.

I own you, Andersson replied.

The next moment Stellan's screen went black. The room went dark. The computer restarted, the hard-drive rattled, the screen flickered, then the connection came back up and suddenly Stellan saw himself on the screen.

Andersson was controlling his laptop remotely, and had activated the camera and seen him sitting at his desk without a top on, a coffee mug next to the keyboard.

With his heart pounding, Stellan left the Dark Web, went into his system settings, closed off the Internet connection and tried to remove the Tor browser from his computer.

Since then Stellan hasn't ventured onto Darknet. The suffocating feelings of being watched and observed have grown worse with each passing day.

The gates of Herrestadsgatan 18 are open. Rollof raises his leg and pisses on the post, as usual. They pass Jeppsson Engineering and the blue canvas covering an old trolleybus.

Stellan and the dog leave the gravel drive and carry on across the wet grass, past a big, silver-coloured building, towards a long, narrow industrial yellow-brick unit with a flight of metal steps in front of it.

The sign announcing *Ystad Tyre and Mechanical Workshop* is still there, though the business is long gone.

Stellan ties the leash to a concrete block meant to support roadworks signs, kneels down, ruffles the loose skin on the back of Rollof's neck and tells him that he'll be back soon.

He switches the lights on and the fluorescent strip-lights flicker and buzz into life, spreading their harsh glare across dirty benches and heavy mountings. The cement floor is covered with oil stains and drill-holes where machinery once stood. There's evidence of the defunct workshop everywhere. Anything that could be sold at the auction that followed the bankruptcy had been removed and taken away.

As he approaches the false wall, he hears Rollof start to growl outside. Stellan unlocks the door of the cleaning cupboard, pulls out the industrial vacuum cleaner, takes down the topless calendar, inserts the long key into the lock and pushes the hidden door open.

Inside the secret room he has constructed three cages out of heavy-duty wire mesh, firmly fixed to the concrete floor.

All that they contain at the moment is three plain, unmade beds from Ikea and three plastic bedpans.

The ceiling lamp is casting chequered shadows across the mattresses.

The little kitchen consists of an all-in-one unit containing a sink, hotplate, a hand-held shower to fit on the tap, a microwave oven and a small fridge.

He's aware that the sensible thing to do would be to dismantle the cages before he sets light to the workshop. Stellan walks over to the furthest cage and inserts the crowbar between the brick wall and the mesh frame and pushes.

He's planning on siphoning off the diesel from the bus outside Jeppsson's once he's destroyed the cages, drenching everything, then starting the fire in here using one of the radiators.

The workshop isn't insured for its full value, but he can hardly call and ask to change the terms now.

Stellan wrenches one side of the frame out, pushing it away from him as it falls. His phone buzzes and he hooks the crowbar on the mesh as he takes it out and looks at the screen. He's received a text message from a number he doesn't recognise: *Pour petrol over yourself and . . .*

Stellan doesn't finish reading the text, just throws his phone at the wall, unable to figure out how Andersson could have got hold of his phone number.

'What's going on?' he whispers, stamping on the phone until it shatters.

He decides not to bother dismantling the cages. They'll probably burn along with everything else, so he won't be found out.

Suddenly the lights go out. The fuse must have blown. Stellan feels his way out, stumbling over the paper bag containing screws, angle irons and a random assortment of other spares. The heavy security door is closed and he pulls it open, goes into the cleaning cupboard, then the workshop. All the lights have gone out. Weak grey light is coming in through the windows that haven't been covered with plywood. Stellan can see that the door to the fuse box with its old enamel fuses is already open.

Outside, Rollof starts barking. The dog is clearly agitated, he's pulling at his leash, then starts growling and barking again.

A shadow passes one of the windows. Someone's creeping round the building.

Stellan's heart is beating so hard that his throat hurts.

He looks at the door in front of him, unsure what to do.

The chain from the broken winch is swinging behind him.

Stellan spins round but can't see anyone.

He starts walking towards the door, hears quick footsteps behind him and then feels a flare of pain in his head.

He staggers sideways, aware of an excruciating pain in his temple.

His legs buckle and he collapses on the floor, and hears himself making guttural moaning sounds.

His back arches in cramp, his body tenses, then starts to jerk uncontrollably. Someone grabs him by one leg and starts to drag him across the floor.

'I'm sorry,' he gasps, blinking the blood from his eyes.

The man shrieks something, then stamps on his mouth. Stellan feels him carry on stamping until he loses consciousness altogether.

When he comes round, his face feels wet and warm.

He's lying on his side, and tries to raise his head as he sees the man overturn the old desk, then come back with a rusty saw in one hand and kick him in the stomach.

Stellan's breathing rattles off the concrete floor.

He's thinking that he has to crawl out and release Rollof.

The man stamps on the base of his spine several times, then walks round him.

Stellan feels the man take hold of the back of his head, put the jagged blade to his neck, then start to saw.

He hears the sound change, and just has time to think that the pain is utterly unbearable before everything fades away.

17

Joona and Nils Åhlén are standing in the lift in silence, not looking at each other. The floor is wet with melted snow. The only sound is the swishing of the cables in the lift-shaft as they head up to the conference room on the eighth floor.

Nathan Pollock from the National Murder Commission has already called the first meeting. Within the National Operations Unit, he's responsible for the search for victims who might fit the pattern of the two known cases.

The look on Joona's face is one of intense concentration, focus. The collar of his coat is uneven, half up, half down.

Seeing as they agree that there's a theoretical possibility that Jurek Walter survived Saga's gunshots, Joona has to follow this to the end of the road.

The reason he can't fend off a feeling of impending disaster is that the choice of victim doesn't fit with Jurek's sense of balance.

Neither the choice of victim nor the method makes sense.

Jurek isn't interested in excessive violence, he simply does whatever is necessary to achieve the result he's after.

The dead men in Germany and Norway both have a link to Joona, but there's nothing to indicate any clear connection to Jurek Walter.

The fact that the victim at the campsite in Rostock had been whipped doesn't necessarily mean anything. He could have been a masochist, he could have self-harmed, or been assaulted by the other patients in the secure psychiatric unit.

It hasn't even been established beyond reasonable doubt that he was beaten using a shaving strop. Maybe Joona is getting carried away by his imagination.

And the man in Oslo only had a few scars on his back. They could have been caused during the assault that caused his death.

Joona forces himself to pay attention as Nils tells him that his assistant Frippe has started playing golf with his wife.

Joona tries to smile, and thinks once more that he's probably overreacting.

Jurek is dead.

The man in Oslo and the man at the campsite must have been killed by the same person, and there was a definite connection to him in both cases.

Joona has been trying to figure out how the murdered sex-offender could have got hold of his private telephone number.

Fabian Dissinger hasn't cropped up in any Swedish investigation, at least not since Joona started working in the police.

Same thing with the grave-robber in Oslo.

The lift slows down, stops, and the doors slide open.

Anja is waiting for them. Without saying a word she hugs Joona tightly, then takes a step back.

She shows them into the conference room with a satisfied smile. Three smaller tables have been pushed together. On one of them there's a closed laptop and two bundles of papers and folders. There's an Advent candelabra with a dusty cable poking out of the bin.

The inner courtyard is visible through the low windows, the flat roofs covered with masts and satellite dishes, the exercise yard of the custody unit and the spire of the old police head-quarters.

'You were quick,' Nathan says behind them.

As usual, his grey hair is tied in a ponytail and he's wearing a black jacket, narrow trousers and shoes with Cuban heels.

'How's things?' Joona asks, shaking his old friend's hand.

'Shit but OK, thanks,' Nathan replies, as usual.

He walks over to the wall and pulls down a Christmas picture and a poster telling police officers to keep an eye on their teenage children.

'Nathan thinks Christmas is bad for the room's feng shui,' Anja says.

'What have you got?' Joona says, sitting down on one of the chairs.

Nathan jerks his head slightly to get his ponytail in the right place, then opens the laptop and starts to tell them about his dealings with Europol.

'We asked about victims in the past six months who were serious criminals or mentally ill . . . violent assaults, sexual offences.'

'With particular emphasis on signs of beatings and whipping,' Anja adds.

'We asked them to discount terrorism, organised crime, the drug trade, and financial crimes,' Nathan goes on.

'Their response was that there aren't any murders that fulfil those criteria,' Anja says, filling four glasses from the carafe of water.

'But there must be some, purely statistically,' Nathan continues. 'So we contacted the national police authorities, then moved on to separate districts and departments.'

'I don't want to say it's been tough, but there are forty five different nation states in Europe, so that means an awful lot of heads of department,' Anja explains. 'Some of them are suspicious and don't want to reveal details, but the biggest problem is probably . . .'

She tails off and sighs.

'This all gets a bit grubby,' she goes on. 'But in general the police don't put a huge amount of effort into cases of one crim-inal killing another. And if any of their worst offenders dies, the usual reaction is relief. That isn't the official attitude, of course, but it's inevitable . . . no one becomes personally motivated when a paedophile dies, you don't spend a lot of time calling other districts, other countries.'

'I spoke to a Hungarian officer who said he didn't want to sound like Duterte . . . but he explained that even if they wouldn't go so far as to encourage murders of any sort, they really don't have any objection to society being cleaned up,' Nathan says.

'And I spoke to an English superintendent who said he'd put our murderer on the payroll if he moved to Tottenham.'

Joona raises his glass, looks at the surface of the water and the round, translucent shadow on the table, and feels a degree of relief for the first time.

Jurek isn't trying to make the world a better place, he would never feel any obligation to punish offenders – that isn't how he works.

'But I want to stress that we're far from finished with our inquiries,' Nathan says, taking an apple from the bowl in the middle of the table. 'We just thought you'd want to see the three responses we've received so far that match the criteria.'

A roaring sound fills Joona's head.

'Match?' he repeats, putting his fingertips to his left temple.

'Let's see,' Nathan says, opening a file on the laptop. 'This one took a lot of persuasion . . . at first they said they didn't have any murders at all, then I was eventually put through to a superintendent in Gdansk . . . And without any hesitation he told me that they'd found a middle-aged man in the abandoned branch of the River Vistula known as "the Dead Vistula" . . . The man hadn't drowned, he'd been beaten to death. His face had been bitten and his head was almost severed from his body.'

'He'd been in prison for three murders and the desecration of a corpse,' Anja says.

'What else?' Joona asks, his mouth suddenly dry.

'I spoke to Salvatore Giani this morning – he sends his regards,' Nathan says, and takes a bite of the apple.

'Thanks,' Joona whispers.

'Salvatore had a murder in Segrate, on the outskirts of Milan . . . Last Thursday a woman by the name of Patrizia Tuttino was found with her neck broken in the boot of her own car, outside the Department of Reconstructive Surgery at the San Raffaele Hospital . . . During the search of her house they discovered that she had carried out at least five contract-killings before she embarked upon her gender realignment.'

Nathan frowns as he taps at the laptop, then turns it towards Joona to show him a picture.

The shadow of the hospital building's cupola reaches across

the pavement to a red Fiat Panda with a damaged front bumper. There's a dead body lying in the open boot. The plastic bag over her head is smeared with lipstick on the inside. Her dress and fur coat are black with mud. She's a tall woman, with full breasts, broad thighs, and thick knees.

'And the third victim?' Joona asks.

Nathan rubs his forehead.

'There's a popular national park outside Brest-Litovsk in Belarus, the Białowieża Forest. Last week a man's body was found in the undergrowth behind some rubbish bins at the new tourist attraction based around Ded Moroz, who's a sort of eastern Slavic Father Christmas . . . The victim was a man who worked as a warden in the park. He's been brutally assaulted, both his arms were broken and he'd been shot in the back of the neck. His name was Maksim Rios.'

'I see,' Joona says.

'Our Belarusian colleague said the man had been whipped in the past year, "like some poor kid in an orphanage", as he put it.'

'I need to think,' Joona says.

'We're still waiting for pictures, as well as responses from plenty more countries . . . As Anja says, the problem is that most of them don't have any objection to some of their offenders disappearing.'

Joona sits with his hands over his face as he listens while Nathan relates the sarcastic response of the police in Marseille.

Serial killers like this don't exist, Joona is thinking.

Occasionally a serial killer will try to excuse his urge to kill with the idea that society needs to be cleansed, but on those occasions the victims are usually homosexuals, prostitutes or specific ethnic or religious groups.

It can't be Jurek.

He would never kill anyone for demonstrating a lack of morality.

That is of no interest whatsoever to him.

Unless there's some advantage to it, Joona suddenly thinks, and gets up from his chair.

The murders are nothing to do with cleansing society.

It's a competition, a contest, they're dealing with a knockout challenge.

'He's alive,' Joona whispers, pushing his chair under the table.

Jurek Walter is alive, and he has been recruiting and testing to see who would be most suitable as an accomplice.

He's restricted his search to people with no moral boundaries.

Jurek needs someone to take his brother's place, someone who's utterly loyal, who's prepared to accept punishment for the slightest mistake.

Jurek didn't plan for the man in Oslo to take Summa's skull, he didn't want the man at the campsite to call me – those acts were merely by-products of his indoctrination.

The accumulation of dead bodies means that the selection is complete.

The victims that have been found so far are the ones who didn't get through to the next round.

That's the motive.

The motive they hadn't been able to identify.

Joona is aware that Nathan is saying something to him, but he can't hear him, he can't take anything in.

'Joona? What is it?'

Joona turns away and walks unsteadily towards the door and opens it. He checks he's got his pistol in the holster under his arm, and starts to walk towards the lifts as he pulls out his phone and looks up Lumi's number.

Anja catches up with him in the corridor.

'What's going on?' she asks anxiously.

'I have to go,' he says, reaching out for the wall with one hand.

'We've just received an email from Ystad that you should see: the police there have found a man's body in an industrial estate . . . his head, face, and chest have been completely smashed in . . .'

Joona accidentally pulls down a poster for a women's indoor hockey tournament as he makes his way to the lifts.

'It fits the pattern,' Anja calls after him. 'The victim's name is Stellan Ragnarson, he served time for cutting the throats of his girlfriend and her mother.'

Joona quickens his pace and puts the phone to his ear as the call goes through. He presses the button for the lift, but when it doesn't come he starts to run down the stairs.

'Lumi,' she answers in a subdued voice.

'It's Dad,' he says, and stops moving.

'Hi, Dad . . . I'm in a lecture, I can't—'

'Lumi,' he interrupts, trying to suppress the panic that's building up inside him. 'Listen to me . . . I was wondering, do you remember the solar eclipse in Helsinki?'

For a few moments she says nothing. Anxious beads of sweat have broken out on Joona's forehead and neck.

'Yes,' she eventually replies, and swallows hard.

'I was just thinking about that day, but we can talk about it later . . . I love you.'

'I love you, Dad.'

18

Lumi drops her iPhone in her rucksack and closes her notebook with trembling hands. If Professor Jean-Baptiste Blom hadn't had to interrupt his lecture because of a problem with his laptop, she'd never have taken the call.

She can't believe this is happening for real, that her dad has called to ask her about the solar eclipse.

It was never supposed to happen, not really.

Winter light is flooding into the lecture theatre through the large windows. The walls are patchy, the floor shabby.

The art-history students are still sitting in their places, talking quietly or checking their phones while the professor tries to get his laptop to work.

'I have to go,' Lumi whispers to Laurent, who's moved to sit closer to her.

'Who was that?' he asks as his warm hand slides down her back.

Lumi puts her notebook and pens in her rucksack, stands up, removes her boyfriend's hand from her backside and starts to make her way along the row.

'Lumi?'

She doesn't answer, pretends not to hear, but realises that he's gathering his things and is coming after her.

Lumi reaches the aisle and sees the professor smile through distinctly uneven teeth when the first picture appears on the large screen. It's Robert Doisneau's photograph of a man swimming with a floating cello.

She walks quietly towards the door as the professor resumes his argument about the dramaturgy of the moment.

She emerges into the corridor and puts her jacket on. She glances towards the toilets, feeling like she's about to throw up, but carries on towards the exit.

'Lumi?'

Laurent catches up with her and takes hold of her arm. She spins round, adrenalin pumping through her body.

'What's going on?' he asks.

She looks at his concerned face, his stubble and long, boyish hair, messy and charming, like he's just got out of bed.

'There's something I need to sort out,' she says quickly.

'Who was that who called you?'

'A friend,' she says, backing away.

'From Sweden?'

'I've got to go.'

'Is he here in Paris? Does he want to see you?'

'Laurent . . .' she pleads.

'You're really weird, you know that, right?'

'It's something private, nothing to do with—'

'You do know I've moved in with you?' he interrupts with a smile. 'And you remember what we did last night, and again this morning . . . and are going to do again tonight?'

'Stop it,' she says, feeling that she's liable to burst into tears any second.

He sees the look on her face and turns serious.

'OK,' he says.

The second-hand on the big wall-clock is slowly ticking round. A police car drives past somewhere nearby. She lets him hold her hand in both of his, but can't bring herself to look him in the eye.

'But you're still coming to the party later, aren't you?' he asks.

'I don't know.'

'You don't know,' he repeats quietly.

Lumi pulls away and hurries for the exit, passes through the glass doors, turns left along the pavement and crosses the Rue Fénelon.

She stops in front of the broad flight of steps leading up to the church, removes a peace badge from her jacket and uses the needle to remove the SIM card from her mobile.

She drops it on the ground, stamps on it to destroy it, then hurries on.

On the other side of the Boulevard de Magenta she tosses her mobile phone in a bin, then walks to the Gare du Nord, where she takes the metro to the huge railway terminus of Gare de Lyon.

Her neck is throbbing with anxiety, and she's having trouble breathing as she pushes her way through a group of tourists.

The concourse is full of the noise of excited travellers, freight wagons, braking trains and echoing public announcements.

The throng of people is reflected in the great glass roof, like some huge single organism.

Lumi hurries past the flower stalls, newsagents and fast-food joints, takes the escalator beneath the main station passageway and passes the security control to reach the left-luggage lockers.

She's breathing hard as she stops in front of the small lockers, taps in a code and removes the bag from the locker, then goes into the women's bathroom, locks herself in the last cubicle, takes her jacket off and hangs it up on the hook. She opens the bag, takes out a small penknife, selects the screwdriver tool, then crouches down under the washbasin and runs her hand over the wall. Just above the overflow pipe, a few centimetres off the floor, she finds the painted-over screws. She fits the screwdriver into their slots and removes the panel concealing the valves in the pipes. She reaches in and pulls out the package, screws the hatch back in place, stands up and looks at herself in the mirror.

Her lips are white with stress and her eyes look oddly shiny.

Lumi tries to concentrate on what she's about to do, though she still can't quite believe it's happening.

She loosens the string and is about to remove the paper from the parcel when she hears someone come into the bathroom.

She hears a woman talking, complaining in a slurred voice about high-class prostitutes. She walks along the cubicles, hitting each door with the palm of her hand as she goes.

Without making a sound, Lumi removes the paper from the pistol, a small Glock 26 with a night sight.

She inserts one of the magazines and tugs the gun away in her bag.

The woman outside is still ranting to herself.

With very deliberate movements, Lumi takes the envelope of cash out of the bag, divides the bundle of notes in two, puts one in her purse and replaces the other in the bag. She picks out one of the passports, checks the name, mouths it to herself, then takes one of the mobile phones out of the bag.

The woman is quiet now, but Lumi can hear her heavy breathing.

Something falls to the floor with a clatter.

Lumi switches the phone on and taps in the PIN-code.

She's worried something bad has happened to her dad, that's her main concern. Lumi didn't ask any questions, but she can't help hoping that he's wrong. Part of her is wondering if he's been expecting disaster to strike for so long that he couldn't bear it any longer, and has seen it coming even though it doesn't really exist.

But now he's called her and asked if she remembers the solar eclipse in Helsinki.

That means just one thing: their disaster plan has been activated.

She said yes.

Meaning that she thinks she can carry out her part of it.

Lumi wipes the tears from her cheeks, tries to breathe calmly, puts on her new jacket, tucks the old one in her bag, pulls the hood up over her head, then flushes the toilet and leaves the cubicle.

A large woman is standing in front of the mirror at one of the basins. The floor below her is soaking wet.

Lumi hurries out and goes to one of the counters in the departure hall, takes a numbered ticket, then when it's her turn buys a return ticket on the next train to Marseille. She pays cash, then makes her way to the platform.

The heavy smell of the train brakes hangs in the air.

Lumi waits with her head lowered, her bag between her feet.

The sign on the platform says the train won't be there for another twenty minutes or so.

She thinks back to those months in Nattavaara. The last time she spent with her mum was also the first she spent with her dad. She didn't really know him before then, all she'd had to go on was a few random memories and stories.

But she loved being close to him, those evenings at the dinner table, the early mornings.

She loved the fact that he had trained her, patiently and tirelessly.

They grew close to each other through their preparations for worst-case scenarios.

Lumi lifts her chin and listens. The tannoy is announcing delays.

There's the sound of train whistles in the distance.

A thin man in a lead-coloured coat is walking along the opposite platform, making his way through the waiting passengers before suddenly running for the stairs.

Lumi lowers her gaze and thinks back to when Saga Bauer came to see them, to tell them that Jurek Walter's body had been found.

It had felt like throwing open the doors to the garden on a summer's morning. She could walk out into a new world, she could move to Paris.

A train is approaching, rattling as it passes a set of points before pulling up at platform 18 with a hiss. Lumi picks up her bag, climbs on board and finds her seat. She sits with her bag in her lap, looking out of the window, when she suddenly sees the man in the grey coat outside the train.

She quickly sinks down onto the floor, making out that she's looking for something in her bag, and checks the time.

They should have set off by now.

She doesn't answer when the woman next to her asks if she can help with anything.

A whistle blows on the platform and the train starts to move. She waits for a long while before sitting back up in her seat and apologising to the woman.

Lumi closes her eyes tightly to stop herself from crying.

For some reason she finds herself thinking back to the end of her first term, when she accidentally insulted another student by suggesting that his photographs might be sexist. At the exhibition later that month he had scrawled 'five sexist pictures by a sexist' across the photographs.

They ended up going out with each other after that, and this summer he moved in with her, to see if they could make it work.

She opens her eyes, but can still picture him in front of her. Laurent, with his untidy hair and pilled sweaters. Those intense brown eyes. Laurent, with his beautiful smile, Southern French accent and pouting lips.

Paris and its sprawling suburbs are already long gone.

Lumi thinks of how she pulled away from Laurent and ran from him like Cinderella.

When the train pulls into Lyon two hours later, she gets to her feet, pulls the hood of her top over her head and steps out onto the platform.

The wind is warmer here.

Lumi never had any intention of travelling all the way to Marseille.

She joins the stream of people moving through the huge station, takes the escalator to the lower floor and walks along a tiled passageway to the Hertz Car Hire desk. She takes out her fake passport, fills in all the forms, pays cash and is given the key to a red Toyota.

If she takes the A42 autoroute she can be in Switzerland in two hours.

19

Joona Linna is driving as fast as he can along Järlasjön. The heavy snowfall vanishes without a trace the instant it hits the dark surface of the lake. He tries calling Valeria again but there's no answer.

Panic flashes through his mind. It's as if Jurek Walter were sitting in the darkness on the back seat of the car, leaning forward to whisper to him:

'I'm going to crush you into the dirt.'

Joona is cursing himself for being so slow, for not spotting what Jurek was doing earlier.

Valeria isn't answering her phone.

If he meets a vehicle coming the other way he's going to have to assume that it's Jurek or one of his accomplices. He'll have to block the road with the car and throw himself into the ditch, ready to jump to his feet and shoot the driver through the windscreen.

He's able to drive even faster when he reaches the narrow road past Hästhagen. The swirling snow behind the car glows red in the glare of the rear lights.

The forest opens up, and the dark soil of the fields has recently been covered by a layer of snow.

The falling snowflakes are smaller now; they fly up into the air as he turns into the drive that leads to Valeria's nursery.

There are fresh tyre tracks from a heavy vehicle on the drive and turning circle. They weren't made by Valeria's car, which is parked in its usual place with a thin layer of snow covering its roof, windscreen and bonnet.

The lights are on in the greenhouses, but he can't see anyone inside.

Joona turns the wheel sharply to the left, heading towards the deep ditch, then reverses and stops, so the car is blocking the road for any other vehicles.

He takes the bag from the passenger seat and gets out of the car, then puts his hand under his jacket and draws his Colt Combat.

The windows of Valeria's house are dark. There's no sound. The snow is slowly drifting down, white against the white sky.

As he approaches the first greenhouse he sees signs of recent movement on the ground.

A bucket full of Leca balls has been overturned.

Joona walks along the glass walls, peering in. There are green leaves pressed up against the glass, which is foggy with condensation.

He hears the sound of a dog barking in the distance.

When he reaches the furthest greenhouse, he sees Valeria's red padded jacket lying on the floor next to one of the benches.

He cautiously nudges the door open, walks into the humid air, stops to listen, then carries on between the benches with his pistol aimed at the floor.

He moves between the steaming vegetation, a striking contrast to the world outside, which has gone into hibernation for winter.

He hears a clatter, possibly a pair of scissors landing on a cement floor.

Joona moves his finger to the trigger and crouches beneath the branches of a row of Japanese flowering cherries. There's someone moving about further inside the greenhouse, rapid movements through the damp foliage.

Valeria.

She's got her back to him, and is holding a knife in her hand.

Walking slowly, Joona puts his pistol back in its holster and holds a protruding branch aside.

'Valeria?'

She turns round with a surprised smile. She's dressed in a dirty Greenpeace T-shirt, and her curly hair is pulled up in a thick ponytail. There's a streak of compost across her left cheek.

She puts the knife down on a stool and pulls off her gloves.

He sees that she's been grafting new branches onto apple tree rootstock, binding the grafts with twine to hold them in place, then painting them with wax to seal them.

'Careful, I'm a bit dirty,' she says, stifling a smile in a way that makes the tip of her chin wrinkle.

She leans forward and kisses him on the lips without touching him.

'I've been trying to call you,' Joona says.

Valeria feels the back pockets of her jeans.

'Must have left my phone in my jacket.'

Joona glances out at a dark branch when a gust of wind passes through the trees.

'I thought we were going to meet at Farang?'

'We need to talk, things are happening which . . .'

He falls silent and takes a deep breath. Valeria swallows hard and her face tenses.

'You think he's alive,' she whispers. 'But they found the body, it was his body, wasn't it?'

'I've been through it all with Nils, but it isn't enough . . . Jurek Walter's alive. I didn't think he was, but he's alive.'

'No,' she says, quietly but firmly.

Joona looks over his shoulder, but he can't see the door of the greenhouse, there are too many plants in the way.

'You need to trust me,' he says. 'I'm going to get Lumi to a safe place abroad and try to protect her, and – well, I'm asking you to come with me.'

Valeria's face has turned grey, it does that when she's worried. The wrinkles around her mouth become more defined, and her face becomes less expressive.

'You know I can't do that,' she says quietly.

'This is a difficult decision.'

'Is it? Because I'm almost starting to wonder what this is all about . . . I don't want to exaggerate my own significance, but this has come right at the start of us having a serious relationship . . . I've wanted you to know you weren't under any sort of pressure, I'm not trying to compete with Summa, because I can't, I know that.'

Joona takes one step to the side so he can get a better view of the greenhouse behind her.

'I hear what you're saying, but—'

'Sorry, I didn't mean . . . that was a silly thing to say.'

'I do understand,' he says. 'We can discuss everything, but Jurek's alive . . . and he's killed at least five people in the past month.'

Valeria rubs her forehead with her dirty fingers, leaving two black streaks above her right eyebrow.

'Why haven't I read anything about that in the papers?' she counters.

'Because the victims are spread across Europe, and because the victims are criminals as well, murderers and sex offenders . . . Jurek's looking for someone he can work with, he's been testing various candidates and killing the ones who don't make the grade.'

He looks at his watch, then glances up towards the dark house.

'Do you genuinely think it's dangerous for the two of us to stay here?'

'Yes,' he says, looking her in the eye. 'There's a good chance you're already being watched. He'll have been watching you, getting to know you, your routines.'

'It sounds so over the top.'

'You have to come with me,' Joona pleads.

'When are you thinking of leaving?' she says after a pause.

'Now.'

She looks at him in astonishment and moistens her lips.

'Can I join you later?'

'No.'

'You're saying I just have to pack a bag and leave?'

'There's no time to pack.'

'How long are we going to be in hiding?'

'Two weeks, two years . . . as long as it takes.'

'All this would be ruined, everything I've worked so hard to achieve,' she says in a toneless voice.

'Valeria, you can always start again, I'll help you.'

She stands there silently, her eyes lowered.

'Joona,' she says, and looks up. 'You've done what you could, I appreciate that this could be serious, but I don't have a choice.

'I can't leave, I've got my greenhouses, my client-base . . . This is my home . . . and I'm going to celebrate Christmas with my boys for the first time . . . you know how much that means to me.'

'You could be back in time for Christmas,' Joona says, feeling desperation rising. 'Listen, Valeria – when Jurek escaped I was living with a woman, Disa . . . I never thought I'd ever dare to do that again.'

'Disa? Why haven't you ever mentioned her?'

'I didn't want to frighten you,' he says heavily.

She shuts her eyes when she realises what he means.

'He killed her.'

'Yes.'

She wipes her mouth with the back of her hand.

'That doesn't mean he's going to kill me,' she says in a shaky voice.

'Valeria,' Joona begs, feeling more helpless than at any point in his life.

'I can't, I just can't,' she says. 'How am I supposed to leave the boys again?'

'Please, you—'

'I can't,' she interrupts.

'I'll organise police protection.'

'Never,' she says, then lets out a surprised laugh.

'You wouldn't have to see them.'

'Joona, listen to me, no cops, not on my property . . . except you.'

He stands with his head bowed for several seconds, then opens his bag, takes out a pistol in a shoulder holster, removes it and hands it to her.

'This is a Sig Sauer. It's loaded, eleven shots in the magazine . . . Carry it with you at all times, keep it with you even when you're in bed . . . See here, all you have to do is release this catch, hold it with both hands, aim and fire. Don't hesitate if you get the opportunity, shoot immediately, several times.'

She shakes her head.

'I'm not going to do that, Joona.'

He puts the gun down on the stool next to her knife and takes a deep breath.

'The other thing I need to do is give you a warning. From now on you have to regard anything that isn't absolutely familiar to you as a trap. Unexpected visitors, a new customer, someone who's changed their car or has turned up at the wrong time . . . No matter what it is, you call this number.'

Joona shows her a number on his mobile, then sends her the contact details.

'Keep that number, and make sure it's always the first option when you open your phone . . . It won't be enough to save you immediately, Jurek's too quick for that, but this number belongs to a friend of mine, Nathan Pollock . . . he'll be able to see where you are, and that increases the chances of them tracking and rescuing you.'

'This all sounds crazy,' she says simply, fixing her eyes on him.

'I'd stay with you if it wasn't for Lumi, I have to look after her,' he says.

'It's OK, I understand, Joona.'

'I've got to go now,' he whispers. 'If you want to come with me, you'll have to come as you are, in boots and dirty trousers . . . I'll go back to the car and wait twenty seconds.'

She doesn't answer, just looks at him and tries to hold back the tears and swallow the lump in her throat.

Joona walks out of the greenhouse and gets in his car, reverses to the turning circle and stops.

He looks at his watch.

Snowflakes are falling through the glow from the big green-houses.

The seconds tick past, he should have left by now.

He leans against the cold seat and puts his right hand on the gearstick.

Everything is quiet and still.

He starts the engine again and the headlights form a swirling tunnel down towards the edge of the forest.

The fans whirr as the car heats up.

Joona stares ahead of him, then glances at his watch again, changes gear and drives slowly round the turning circle. He looks at the greenhouses in the rear-view mirror and he drives slowly away from Valeria's nursery.

20

Erica Liljestrand is sitting on her own at the counter in the Pilgrim Bar, waiting for a friend from her biotechnology course.

Sleet is running down the window facing the street.

She puts her phone down beside the glass of wine and looks at the fingerprints on the screen before it goes dark.

She and Liv agreed to meet here at ten o'clock to discuss the New Year's Eve party, but Liv is over an hour late now, and she's not answering her phone.

There are hardly any customers in the Pilgrim Bar this evening, probably because the building's being renovated and the façade on Regeringsgatan is covered up. The entrance is hidden by scaffolding and dirty white nylon netting.

The three guys at the table at the back have started glancing in her direction, so she sticks with the bartender, chatting to him and checking her phone.

Weird that a woman sitting alone in a bar has to think of herself as fair game, she thinks.

Erica knows she isn't exactly pretty, and she's a long way from being a flirt. Even so, the simple fact that she's there on her own is enough for them.

The bartender, who says his name is Nick, seems to assume that he's irresistible. He's a suntanned, wrinkled man in early middle-age, with blue eyes and a fashionable haircut. His short-sleeved shirt is tight across his bulging biceps, and only half covers the fuzzy tattoo on his neck.

So far Nick has told her about mountain-climbing in Thailand, skiing in the French Alps, and the jittery stock market.

Erica glances surreptitiously at the older, pink-cheeked couple chatting over at one of the corner tables. They look happy with their bottle of wine and nachos with salsa and guacamole.

She calls Liv again, and lets it ring for a ridiculous amount of time.

Dirty water is dripping from the scaffolding outside.

She puts her phone down and traces a scratch in the polished wood of the bar counter with her fingernail, then stops when she reaches the foot of her glass and takes a sip.

The bell jangles as the door opens.

Erica turns to look.

It isn't Liv, but a man the size of a bear. He brings cold air from the street in with him, then takes off his black raincoat and squeezes it into a plastic bag.

The man is wearing a dark blue knitted sweater with leather patches on the elbows, cargo trousers and military-style boots.

He says hello to the bartender and sits down a metre or so away from Erica, with one chair between them, and hangs the plastic bag from a hook under the bar.

'It's a blowy night,' he says in a deep, soft voice.

'Looks that way,' the bartender replies.

The large man rubs his hands together.

'What vodkas have you got?'

'Dworek, Stolichnaya, Smirnoff, Absolut, Koskenkorva, Nemiroff,' Nick says.

'Black Smirnoff?'

'Yes.'

'I'll have five doubles of Smirnoff, then.'

Nick raises his eyebrows.

'You want five glasses of vodka?'

'Room temperature, if that's OK,' the man smiles.

Erica looks at the time on her phone and decides to wait another ten minutes.

The bartender places five shot glasses in front of the large man, then fetches a bottle from the shelf.

'And refill her glass, seeing as we're celebrating,' he says, nodding in Erica's direction.

Erica has no idea what he's talking about. Maybe it was just a joke that didn't quite work. She looks at him, but he doesn't look back. His face looks sad, and his thick neck has settled into folds, his hair is cropped and he has beautiful pearl earrings in each earlobe.

'Do you want another glass of wine?' the bartender asks Erica.

'Why not?' she replies, stifling a yawn.

'Seeing as we're celebrating,' Nick says, then fills a fresh glass.

The large man has taken out a book of matches and is now chewing on one of them.

'I used to have a bar in Gothenburg,' he says, then gets to his feet.

He stands still, as if he can no longer understand where he is. Slowly he turns to look at the bartender, then Erica. His pupils are dilated, and the match falls from his lips. He keeps turning, looks at the older man at the corner table, then one of the young men, before licking his lips and sitting back down again.

He clears his throat and empties the first glass of vodka, then puts it down on the bar.

Erica looks at the flat matchbook lying next to the line of glasses. The black cover is decorated with what looks like a small white skeleton.

'Are you spending Christmas in Stockholm?' Nick asks, putting a bowl of large green olives in front of Erica.

'I'll be going to my parents' in Växjö,' she replies.

'Nice, Växjö's a good town.'

'You?' she asks politely.

'Thailand, as usual.'

'I don't think so,' the large man says.

'Sorry?' Nick says in surprise.

'Not that I can see into the future, but—'

'Can't you?' the bartender interrupts. 'That's a relief, you almost had me worried there for a moment.'

The large man has lowered his gaze and is looking at his stubby fingertips. The young men get up noisily and leave.

'It's complicated,' the large man says after a while.

'Isn't it just,' Nick says tartly.

The man doesn't answer, carries on picking at his matchbook. The bartender stands and looks at him for a while, waiting for him to look up, then he starts wiping the counter with a grey cloth.

'Nice earrings,' Erica says, and hears the bartender let out a laugh.

'Thanks,' the man says in a serious voice. 'I wear them for my sister, my twin sister, she died when I was thirteen.'

'That's terrible,' she whispers.

'Yes,' he says simply, and raises his shot glass towards her. 'Cheers . . . cheers, whatever your name is . . .'

'Erica,' she says.

'Cheers, Erica . . .'

'Cheers.'

He drinks, puts the empty glass down, and licks his lips.

'They call me the Beaver.'

The bartender turns away to hide his smile.

'It's a shame your friend's late,' the Beaver says after a pause.

'How did you know that?'

'I could say it's deduction, a logical conclusion,' he says. 'I watch people, I saw the way you've been looking at your phone, the way you turned towards the door . . . And I've also got a sixth sense.'

'A sixth sense, like telepathy?' she asks, forcing herself not to smile.

Nick removes her first wine-glass and wipes the counter.

'It's hard to explain,' the Beaver goes on. 'But in layman's terms I should probably call it precognition . . . Along with claircognizance, intrinsic knowledge.'

'That sounds pretty advanced,' Erica says. 'So you're some sort of medium?'

She can't help feeling sorry for him. He seems completely unaware of how weird he comes across.

'My abilities aren't paranormal . . . there's a logical explanation.'

'OK,' the bartender says sceptically.

They wait for him to go on, but instead he empties the third shot glass with very precise movements, then sets it down beside the others.

'Almost every time I'm with other people, I know the order in which they're going to die,' he says. 'I don't know when it's going to happen – in ten minutes or fifty years . . . but I can see the order.'

Erica nods. She regrets having encouraged him to talk. She only felt obliged to be a bit friendlier because Nick was starting to act like a bully. She's wondering how soon she can leave without it looking like she's trying to get away from him when her mobile buzzes.

21

Erica turns her phone round, hoping it will give her an excuse to leave the bar at once. It's a text from Liv, apologising for not showing up, and saying she had to help a friend who'd drunk too much get home.

Erica's thumbs feel oddly numb when she replies that she understands and that they can meet up tomorrow instead.

'I have to go,' she says, pushing her almost untouched glass of wine away.

'I didn't mean to scare you,' the large man says, looking at her intently.

'No, it's . . . I believe everyone has abilities that they don't use,' she replies rather vaguely.

'I'm aware it sounded overdramatic, what I said, but I never seem to be able to find the right words to describe it.'

'I understand,' she says, looking at the screen.

'Sometimes I only have time to count everyone, but sometimes I can do everyone in a room . . . It's like I see a big clock-face with Roman numerals, and when the hand points to the number one, I find myself looking at the first person in the room who's going to die, I don't know how, but it's just what happens. Tick tock, the hand moves to the number two, and I'm looking at another person . . . often I catch sight of my own face in a mirror before I lose contact.'

'Can I settle up?' Erica says to the bartender.

'I scared you,' the Beaver says, still trying to catch her eye.

'Can you leave her alone, now?' Nick says.

'Erica, I just want to say that your number wasn't the first to come up in this room.'

'Stop it,' the bartender says, leaning across the bar.

'I'm stopping,' the Beaver says calmly, and tucks the flat little matchbook in the chest pocket of his sweater. 'Unless you'd like to know who number one was?'

'Excuse me,' Erica says, and heads off towards the toilets.

The bartender watches her go, and sees her wobble and hold one hand out to the wall to steady herself.

The Beaver empties his fourth glass of vodka, then puts it down silently next to the last one.

'OK, who's going to die first?' the bartender asks.

'You . . . which isn't really surprising,' the Beaver replies.

'Why isn't it surprising?'

'Because I'm here to cut your throat,' the Beaver replies calmly.

'Am I going to have to call the police?'

'You've already dosed her glass with Xyrem, haven't you?' the Beaver asks.

'What the hell do you want?' Nick hisses.

'Did you know that one of your girls died in the ambulance?' the Beaver says, turning the last glass on the bar.

'You're mentally ill,' Nick tells him. 'You may not be aware of it yourself, but . . .'

He falls silent when Erica returns to her stool. Her cheeks are pale and she sits quietly for a while with her eyes half-closed.

'I'm fairly sure I'm going to succeed, seeing as you're number one, and I'm number five,' the Beaver says quietly.

The older couple call out their thanks, put their coats on and leave the bar. Now there are just the three of them left in the room.

'I should probably go,' Erica says, slurring her words. 'I'm not feeling too good . . .'

'Would you like me to call a taxi?' Nick asks amiably.

'Thanks,' she manages to say.

'He's only pretending to call,' the Beaver says. 'That's his way of getting you to stay here until the bar's empty.'

'Drink up and leave,' the bartender says.

'When my sister died, I—'

'Shut up,' the bartender says, getting his phone out.

'I want to hear,' Erica says, and feels a fresh wave of tiredness wash over her.

'I had a permanent stomach ache when I was a child,' the Beaver says. 'It felt swollen and heavy . . . and when I was thirteen it had got so big that I couldn't hide it any more. They took me to see a doctor who concluded that it was a tumour . . . not an ordinary tumour, though, but my twin sister, a so-called "foetus in foetu".'

He pulls up his knitted sweater and white vest to reveal a long, pale scar across the side of his fat, hairless stomach.

'Bloody hell,' Erica murmurs.

'Behind my peritoneum was a sort of capsule of tissue, twenty-five centimetres long . . . that was where she was,' he says. 'I saw the pictures afterwards, when she was dead: thin arms and big hands, stomach, small, stick-like legs, her spine and a bit of her face . . . but no brain. My blood was the only thing keeping her alive.'

Erica feels nausea rising in her gullet, and stands up and tries to put her coat on, but one of the sleeves is inside out and she stumbles, and only just manages to grab the bar in time.

'They also found parts of her in my brain,' the Beaver goes on. 'But they were too difficult to remove . . . so they'll have to stay where they are as long as they don't metastasise . . . I can feel her most of the time. You can't exactly see it on an MRI, but I think I've got her tiny brain inside mine . . . that's why I've got an extra sense.'

Erica drops her handbag on the floor, and her glasses case and eyeliner roll out and disappear under the barstool. She feels like she's about to be sick, and wonders if she's eaten something that's disagreed with her.

'God,' she whispers, and feels that her back is wet with sweat.

She sinks to the floor to put her things back in her bag, but she's so tired she has to lie on her side and rest for a moment before she can get back up again.

The floor feels cool against her cheek. She closes her eyes but starts at a sudden noise. It's the bartender, shouting at the Beaver.

'Get out!' he roars.

Erica knows she has to get up, she has to go home. She forces her eyes open and sees the bartender backing away with a base-ball bat in his hands.

'Just fuck off!' he shouts.

The large man who said he was known as the Beaver sweeps several bottles off the bar, then moves quickly towards Nick.

Erica hears thuds and deep sighs.

The bartender hits the floor hard and rolls over, sending two chairs flying before he crashes into the wall.

The Beaver follows him with long strides. He grabs the base-ball bat from Nick and hits him over the legs three times, yelling something in a ragged voice before he smashes a table. He tosses the broken bat at Nick, then stamps on the remains of the table, kicking the pieces away.

Erica tries to sit up, and looks on as the Beaver drags Nick to his feet again before shoving him hard in the chest and screaming into his face.

'OK, just calm down,' Nick pants.

He can't put any weight on his right leg, and there's blood running down his face from a cut above one eyebrow. The Beaver grabs him by the neck with one hand and punches him in the face with the other. He pushes Nick down onto a table, knocking glasses and a candleholder to the floor, then shoves the table into the wall, knocking it over and sending Nick sprawling across the floor.

Erica has to lie down again, and watches as the Beaver stands astride the bartender, hitting him in the face.

Nick is trying to get away from the big man. Blood sprays from his mouth as he coughs and begs him to stop. The Beaver grabs him by one hand and breaks his arm at the elbow.

Nick lets out a shriek of desperation as the Beaver yanks at the arm and tries to break it again.

The Beaver is panting heavily as he takes hold of Nick's neck with both hands, then squeezes so tightly that his face turns white, and he roars and thuds the bartender's head against the floor, before suddenly letting go and stepping away from Nick, who splutters and tries to catch his breath.

The Beaver staggers backwards.

When he pulls something from his pocket, the little matchbook falls out and lands on the floor.

He flicks open a broad-bladed knife with a click, then walks forward again, yelling so hard that his uneven teeth glint in the glow of one of the wall lights.

'I'm sorry I was rude to you, I didn't mean it,' Nick groans. 'You don't have to kill me, I promise . . .'

Erica feels heavy steps across the floor against her cheek.

The Beaver reaches Nick, holds his raised hand aside and stabs him with the knife.

The blade penetrates deep into his chest.

Blood sprays up into the Beaver's face as he pulls the knife out.

He lets out a roar of rage and stabs again.

Nick has almost lost consciousness, and is merely whimpering weakly now.

The Beaver spins him round, grabs hold of his hair and sets about trying to scalp him. He cuts off a large chunk of skin and tosses it aside.

It's as if he's taken some sort of terrible drug.

The Beaver drops the knife, lets out a roar, then drags the lifeless body over towards the door by one leg.

Nick must surely be dead by now, but the Beaver goes on beating him and stamping on his stomach. He pulls a framed photograph of John Lennon off the wall, smashes it, sending pieces of glass flying in all directions, then tosses the remnants of the frame onto the bloody body.

He tips a table on top of Nick, then backs away gasping before turning round and looking at her.

'I'm not involved in this,' she says weakly.

He walks towards her and picks the flick knife up from the floor. A string of congealed blood is hanging from the blade.

'Please . . .'

Erica doesn't even have the energy to lift her head from the floor as he walks over to her and grabs her by the hair.

The pain really isn't that overwhelming as the blade cuts through tissue, sinews and blood vessels. Far worse is the ice-cold storm wind in her face, combined with the feeling of being asphyxiated from within.

22

When Saga wakes up she can hear Randy moving about in the kitchen. He often spends the night at hers, and sometimes sleeps in the old photographic studio he rents. Randy comes in with a cup of coffee and a croissant with jam for her.

He's five years younger than Saga, and has a shaved head, calm eyes and a sceptical smile. He's a police inspector, and is part of a team investigating online hate crimes.

'Whenever I go home to Örgryte, Mum brings me breakfast in bed,' he says.

'You're spoiled,' Saga smiles, and sips the coffee.

'I know your mum was—'

'I don't want to talk about her,' she interrupts.

'OK, sorry,' he says, lowering his eyes.

'It doesn't do me any good, which is why I've got this rule. It's better to avoid the subject altogether, I've already said that.'

'I know, but—'

'This isn't about you.'

'But I'm here,' he says quietly.

'Thanks,' she replies curtly.

When he's gone she wonders if she might have sounded too dismissive. There's no way Randy could know what she's been through. She texts him to say sorry and thank him for breakfast.

After work Saga collects her half-sister from school and takes her to see her hearing consultant. On the way home she asks her about the clown girls.

'Dad says they're not real,' Pellerina says.

'That's right, they're not,' Saga tells her.

'I still don't want them to find me.'

Their dad isn't in when they get home. Saga hopes he'll be back soon, she wants to talk to him about the present she couldn't accept because it reminded her too much of her mum's illness.

Now Pellerina is standing at the kitchen worktop wearing a polka-dot apron and whisking cake mixture while Saga greases the tin.

The doorbell rings and Pellerina squeals that it's their dad.

Saga wipes her hands on some kitchen roll, then goes into the hall to answer the door.

It's Joona Linna.

His face is serious, his grey eyes icy cold.

'Come in,' she says.

He looks over his shoulder, then walks into the hall and closes the door behind him.

'Who else is in the house?'

'Just me and Pellerina,' she replies. 'What's happened?'

He looks over at the wooden staircase, then the door to the kitchen.

'Joona, I realise that you really believe Jurek's still alive,' she says.

'At first it was only a theoretical possibility . . . but now I've identified the pattern,' he says, peering through the spyhole in the front door.

'Wouldn't you like to come in and have coffee?' she asks.

'I haven't got time,' he replies, looking back at her again.

'I know recent events have stirred up loads of old memories,' she says. 'But I honestly don't think Jurek's behind this. Look at the level of violence; it's aggressive in a way that Jurek never was . . . and yes, I know you're going to say it was his accomplice. I hear what you're saying, I know that so far as you're concerned there's a clear pattern, but I just can't see it.'

'Saga, I'm only here to say you need to go into hiding, you

need to find a safe place for yourself and your family . . . but I'm starting to realise that you won't be doing that.'

'I'd never manage to get Dad and Pellerina to come with me . . . I'm not even going to try, I don't want to frighten them.'

'But—'

A door slams in the kitchen, and Joona's hand reaches instinctively for the pistol under his jacket before he hears Pellerina laughing.

'If Jurek's alive, it's my fault,' Saga says in a low voice. 'You know that, I was the one who let him out . . . so it's my responsibility to stop him.'

'It isn't worth it,' he says. 'You're like a sister to me, I don't even want you to try to stop Jurek, I just want you to hide.'

'Joona, you're doing the right thing from your point of view, you're convinced about all this and you need to protect Lumi,' she says. 'But for me, the right thing is staying and trying to find the person who's behind these murders . . . and I'm not ruling anything out, not even Jurek Walter.'

'Then work with Nathan . . . I've sent everything I've got to him.'

'OK, I'll talk to him.'

'Saga!' Pellerina calls from the kitchen.

'I need to get back to her,' she says.

'Don't think Jurek's like everyone else,' Joona goes on. 'He didn't treat you differently because you're so beautiful . . .'

'And there was I thinking you'd never even noticed,' she smiles.

'I've noticed, Saga,' he says. 'But Jurek doesn't care about how you look, he's interested in your mind, your soul . . . your darkness, what he likes to call your catacombs.'

'You do know I've spoken to Jurek Walter, don't you? More than you have, actually,' she reminds him.

'But back then you were merely a tool for him, a Trojan horse—'

'OK, fine,' she says, raising her hands to get him to stop.

'Saga, listen to me . . . if you stay, you're going to see him again.'

'That's just an idea you've got into your head,' she says.

'You don't have to listen to me, but I can't go without giving you three pieces of advice first.'

'I'm listening.'

She leans against the doorframe and folds her arms over her chest.

'One . . . don't try to talk to him, don't try to arrest him, don't worry about any ethical considerations if there aren't any witnesses – you need to kill him at once, and make sure he's dead this time.'

'He's already dead.'

'Two . . . remember that he isn't on his own, and that—'

'If your theory's correct,' she interrupts.

'Jurek's used to having a brother who would obey him like a dog . . . these murders mean he's recruited an accomplice – and that means he can be in more than one place at the same time.'

'Joona, that's enough now,' Saga says.

'Three,' Joona goes on. 'If what can't happen happens anyway, you need to remember that you can't make any agreements with him, because they'll never work in your favour . . . He won't let go, and with each agreement you make with him, you'll end up deeper in his trap . . . Jurek will take everything from you, but it's you he wants to get at.'

'I want you to leave now,' she says, and looks him in the eye. 'Maybe that would be just as well.'

23

As Joona pulls out onto the roundabout he can't help thinking he stayed too long at Saga's. He realised almost immediately that she wasn't going to heed his advice, but perhaps she'll remember some of what he said if she does encounter Jurek.

A dusty cement-lorry is parked in a cloud of exhaust fumes at the petrol station, and there's a group of schoolchildren approaching over the footbridge.

As Joona turns onto Nynäsvägen he spots the white van for a second time.

It was parked outside the church down the street as he hurried along the pavement after his meeting with Saga.

The branches of the trees were reflected in the windscreen, but they weren't just moving in time with the wind – sometimes they shuddered and lurched.

There was someone inside the van.

That doesn't necessarily mean he was being watched, but under the current circumstances it's a sensible assumption.

He can't afford to dismiss anything odd as mere coincidence.

Joona changes lane and pulls out onto the Johanneshov Bridge, keeping pace with the fast traffic as the dark water sparkles far below.

Two police cars rush past in the opposite direction, sirens blaring.

There's a shredded tyre lying in the middle of the road.

In the rear-view mirror he sees the van pull out onto the bridge. It's several hundred metres behind him, but it hasn't lost touch.

Joona would never take it for granted, but he imagines he'd win in close combat if he met Jurek face to face. The reason he's running is that Jurek would never get into close combat with anyone he couldn't beat.

It's impossible to defeat Jurek, because he exploits the fact that human beings love each other.

Joona overtakes a battered delivery van on the inside, then pulls in front of it and increases his speed.

The windows let out a little sigh and all sound is muffled as the car heads into the entrance to the Söderleden Tunnel.

He has precisely 1,520 metres to come up with a solution.

The dirty grey walls and green emergency exits flash past, and the glare of the strip-lights pulses evenly through the car.

He speeds up and unfastens his seat belt as he passes the junction for Medborgarplatsen. The vehicles around him are making a monotonous roar.

Joona pulls into the right-hand lane and sees the signs for the exit to Nacka. He looks in the rear-view mirror and veers even further to the right, until he's driving on top of the dotted line separating the two lanes.

The turning is approaching fast, and the vehicles around him are sounding their horns and keeping their distance.

The dotted line becomes a solid line as it disappears beneath the front of the car. If he doesn't make a decision now he'll drive straight into the wall dividing the two roads.

Joona glances quickly in the rear-view mirror and brakes so hard that the tyres skid across the tarmac and into the hard shoulder. The ridged lines on the road make the entire chassis rumble before the car comes to a stop centimetres from the low crash barrier that's designed to cushion any impact with the wall separating the two tunnels.

Heavy vehicles thunder past on both sides.

Joona slips out of the car and runs several metres at a crouch down the tunnel leading to Nacka.

No sooner has he tucked himself away in the darkness behind

the row of columns than he hears a vehicle brake and stop behind his.

It stops on the hatched area between the lanes.

A taxi heading for Nacka sounds its horn irritably.

Dust and rubbish swirl through the air.

Joona draws his Colt Combat from the holster under his right arm, feeds a bullet into the chamber, then stops and listens.

All he can hear is the rumble of the traffic in the tunnel, and the sound of the fans in the roof.

Lead-coloured dust covers the floor and the rubbish that's collected in the space behind the pillars.

There's a rustling sound from some old plastic bags behind him.

He's put his pursuer in an impossible position by stopping right where the tunnel divides, like a snake's tongue.

Whichever road they take could turn out to be the wrong one.

His pursuer has been forced either to give up or surrender any attempt at stealth.

Now he's sitting there with the engine in neutral, unsure what to do.

It probably feels like a trap.

The pursuer doesn't know if Joona's hiding in the car, or if he's continued on foot and possibly even left the tunnel through the emergency exit up ahead.

Joona creeps forward slowly between the pillars. As long as he stays out of reach of the lights in the roof, he's invisible.

Every time a vehicle passes he pulls back slightly to stop himself being lit up by the headlamps.

Black dust swirls in the backdraught from each car.

With his pistol pointed at the floor, Joona hurries forward the moment a motorbike has passed him.

He has to know if the person who's stopped behind his car is Jurek.

Very slowly, he moves towards the light, and sees the filthy emergency telephone on the wall, the striped shadows across the rough concrete.

It's still impossible to see the other vehicle clearly.

He moves cautiously to one side to get a better angle, and can now see part of the back of the van.

There's no doubt that it's the same white van he saw parked in Saga's street.

The cloud of exhaust fumes swirls about each time a vehicle passes.

Joona moves as far as he can, and sees that the driver is sitting at the wheel, but it's impossible to make out a face because of reflections in the glass.

A truck passes by, heading towards the city centre. Its weight makes the ground shake, and the headlamps light up the van long enough for Joona to see a large man with sloping shoulders.

An air-freshener dangling from the rear-view mirror is obscuring most of his face.

But Joona is certain that it isn't Jurek Walter. Maybe he's just had his first glimpse of Jurek's new recruit.

It's impossible to know.

Joona lowers his pistol.

If it had been, he could have shot him the next time a large vehicle drove past, but because he can't be certain that the man in the van is Jurek's accomplice he can't do that – as long as the man remains passive.

The van shakes slightly as the man inside moves.

Joona stands motionless with his pistol aimed at the ground. He can hear rats rustling amongst the plastic bags behind him.

The van rocks again.

A large, noisy bus is approaching.

Joona moves back slightly.

The glare of the headlamps fills the tunnel, and the light hits the cab of the van from the side.

The large man is no longer sitting behind the wheel.

He's gone.

As the bus passes the ground trembles.

The air fills with dust and rubbish.

The only sound is the distant rumble of the large fans in the roof.

Joona crouches down and tries to see under the van, but it's too dark, he can't tell if his pursuer is hiding there or not.

He waits for the next vehicle and aims his pistol towards the gloom between the front and rear wheels.

Joona can see the lights from another vehicle approaching in the distance, and as it approaches the beam bounces across the carriageway until it reaches the van.

For a moment the muddy chassis, driveshaft, and tyres are lit up.

There's no one there.

Joona lowers his pistol again and is just getting to his feet when the van starts to reverse, then it stops before turning left and disappearing into the tunnel leading to the city centre.

Joona listens as the sound of the engine fades away.

He waits several minutes, then approaches his own car at a crouch with his pistol aimed in front of him, checks beneath the car, looks around and then gets back in the driver's seat.

He reverses, then drives to the central station, pulls up in front of the main entrance and stops in a no-parking zone.

He walks round the car, pulls out his mobile and sees that Valeria has called. He removes the SIM card and destroys it, then opens the boot of the car.

There are two black shoulder-bags in the space where the spare wheel should be, one large, one small. He takes them both out, then gets back in the driver's seat. One of the bags contains a short knife designed for close combat. He fastens it to his lower left arm with tape, puts the pistol in the glove compartment, locks the car and walks away.

The car will soon be removed by the Transport Police and stored in a compound outside the city until he collects it.

Joona walks in through the main entrance and glances up at the departure board. He moves through the slow-moving crowd with his head lowered.

He walks straight to the plate-glass window of the bookshop and stares intently at the reflections of the people moving behind him.

No one seems to be following him.

He walks over to the counter and buys a ticket to Copenhagen, paying for it with cash.

The train leaves in eleven minutes, and is already waiting at Platform 12.

He walks over to the platform, past the information boards

and ticket machines. A cold wind is blowing along the tracks. Crows are circling the dark, canopied roofs. There's a beggar sleeping beside one of the bins, wrapped in a padded green quilt. Joona drops his mobile phone in her cup, then climbs onto the train.

24

Joona has an aisle seat and is reading Keith Richards' autobiography. From time to time he looks up to observe his fellow passengers. The woman on the seat next to him has her face turned towards the window and is talking on her phone in a monotone. On the other side of the aisle is an older man with dirt-marks on the trousers of his pale brown suit. He's leafing through the free magazine from the pocket on the back of the seat in front, before leaning his head against the head-rest and closing his eyes.

The train crosses the long viaduct and stops at Södertälje Syd station. A large man sits down in one of the seats a few rows behind Joona.

A heavy smell of aftershave drifts along the carriage.

The conductor passes through, asking for new passengers, and clings onto the parcel shelf when the train jolts before he moves on to the next carriage.

The landscape is frosty and grey.

The large man must have joined the train in Stockholm seeing as the conductor didn't want to check his ticket, but waited until they had passed Södertälje before taking his seat.

The thin thread of a migraine flares behind one of Joona's eyes. His vision loses its clarity and he has to shut his eyes for a while before he can go on reading.

Keith Richards is describing with great enthusiasm a recipe involving sausages.

After a while Joona stands up and glances back down the carriage.

He can't see the tall passenger's face, he's looking out of the window and is wearing a black woollen hat.

Joona takes the smaller bag with him but leaves his jacket hanging on a hook by his seat and the larger bag up on the rack.

He walks to the buffet car and buys a cheese sandwich and a mug of coffee. When he turns back he sees someone watching him from the noisy space between the carriages. He can't tell who it is through the glass door, but as soon as he starts to move in that direction the figure disappears.

Joona returns to his carriage and notes that the tall man is sitting in his seat as if he hasn't moved.

They pass a set of points, and the rumble from the wheels travels down the train.

Joona sits back down in his seat and carries on reading.

The train is approaching Norrköping.

There are many hours to go before they reach Copenhagen.

The landscape flattens out.

The woman next to him is looking through a report from the Central Bank on her laptop.

Putting his book down on the seat, and leaving the coffee-cup and half-eaten sandwich on the table, Joona takes the small bag and goes and stands outside the toilet, waiting for it to become free.

The train slows down and shudders as it changes track and approaches the platform. Just as the train pulls to a halt at the station, Joona moves into the next carriage.

A group of passengers is lined up in the aisle, waiting with their bags and pushchairs to get off. The doors open with a wheeze and Joona leaves the train under cover of the group. He stops behind a large vending machine on the platform, kneeling down so he won't be seen, pulls out the dagger and conceals it against his body, then waits.

The larger of his two bags is still on the rack above his seat, his jacket is hanging from the hook, and his coffee-cup is on the table.

The air is full of the smell of the train's brakes. There are cigarette butts and portions of chewing tobacco on the ground.

The conductor blows his whistle and the doors close with a hiss. Slowly the train sets off from the platform as the electric cables hum.

Joona tucks the dagger away in his bag, then gets to his feet and runs towards the station building. A bus is pulling away as he turns the corner. There are two cars waiting at the taxi-rank, and Joona opens the door of the first one, gets in and explains quickly to the driver that he needs to get to Skavsta Airport in a hurry.

As the taxi pulls away from the station Joona watches as the train accelerates.

The taxi slows down to let an old woman with a rollator use a pedestrian crossing. Some magpies are picking through the rubbish in front of a hotdog kiosk.

The taxi is cruising along Norra Promenaden when the train stops in the distance, close to the imposing bulk of the police station.

Someone's pulled the emergency brake.

The taxi passes some large buildings, blocking Joona's view of the train. The driver tries to engage him in conversation about taking a trip to the sun, but Joona keeps his replies short as he looks behind them.

Just before they head down into the tunnel under the goods yard Joona catches sight of the train again. A man is running along the track towards the station.

Thirty-six minutes later the taxi stops outside the grey terminal building at Skavsta Airport. Tossing his bag over his shoulder, Joona goes in through the main entrance, passes beneath the plane hanging from the roof and makes his way to the customer service desk. He takes a numbered ticket and waits with his back to the wall, his hand clasping the dagger inside the bag.

People come and go through the doors. The pale sky glints in the glass every time the doors swing open.

A tired-looking man is trying to check in a full set of golf equipment for a flight to the Canary Islands, and a very old woman needs help phoning her sister.

When it's Joona's turn he walks up to the woman at the desk.

She stares into his eyes as he asks for a ticket to Béziers in the South of France.

'France? You don't fancy staying in Nyköping instead?' she says with a smile, then blushes.

'In another life,' he replies.

'You know where I am.'

After getting his boarding card he goes into the bathroom, carefully wipes all traces of his fingerprints from the knife, wraps it in toilet paper and drops it in the bin.

Only once the last call for boarding has been announced does he pass through security, making sure he's the last passenger on board. The door swings shut behind him, the plane starts to taxi and the purser steps into the aisle to begin the safety demonstration.

Joona turns to look through the window. He feels the plane's engines start to roar, then the whirr as the flaps extend. He's sent detailed instructions to Nathan Pollock. The first thing Nathan needs to do is make sure Valeria gets police protection, at the very highest level.

When Joona lands in France he'll change his identity. He has a different passport in his bag, a new driving licence, cash in various currencies, everything he needs.

If Jurek figures out that Joona has gone to France, he'll assume that Joona's going to meet Lumi in Marseille, but Joona will be driving his rental car in the opposite direction, to pick up a bag in Bouloc, north of Toulouse.

To the right of the Rue Jean Jourès, before you enter the town, is a small farm on the edge of a field.

Joona has buried an aluminium case there, next to the slurry pit.

It contains two pistols, ammunition, explosives and detonators.

Once he's collected the case he'll make his way to Geneva on minor roads to meet up with Lumi.

25

Saga's knees are resting on the matt-black petrol tank, and she can feel the vibrations from the engine against the insides of her thighs. She's heading along the motorway in sixth gear, parallel to the railway line, then leans gently to the left and takes the exit for Sollentuna, eases up on the throttle, changes down through the gears and turns so sharply that one of the silencers scrapes the tarmac.

She hasn't quite got used to how little lean this motorbike tolerates.

When her old Triumph reached the end of its life, her dad let her borrow his Indian Chief Dark Horse, seeing as he only uses it in perfect summer weather.

Her dad's sentimental about the brand, and the fact that it was a guy from Småland who founded Indian and built the first motorbike. When Lars-Erik was young he lived in San Francisco for a while, and rode a clapped out 1950 Indian.

Now that he's middle-aged and can afford it, he's indulged himself by buying a new one, but he's grown too accustomed to creature comforts to use it.

She brakes on the steep hill leading to Nathan Pollock's driveway and pulls up behind his SUV.

They're due to have a meeting with their respective bosses at the headquarters of the Security Police in Solna, but wanted to look through the material Joona has had couriered to Nathan before that.

The black villa is situated on a slope, and looks out across the dark, choppy waters of Edsviken.

Saga hangs her helmet on the handlebars and walks round Nathan's car.

Dead plants are rustling on a flaking trellis surrounding a bench.

Saga carries on towards the house and sees a bag of groceries on the path some ten metres from the veranda. Bread, a bag of frozen peas and three packs of free-range bacon have spilled out onto the yellow grass.

She stops and listens. She can hear thudding sounds from inside the house. It sounds like a door being slammed five times, then the noise suddenly stops.

Saga sets off towards the veranda but comes to an abrupt halt when she hears a woman's voice shouting inside the house.

Saga crouches down and pulls her Glock from its holster, feeds a bullet into the chamber, then walks around the house with the barrel aimed at the ground.

She can see into the living room through the first window. A high-backed chair is lying on the floor.

Saga squeezes the trigger until it reaches the first notch, and walks past an apple tree to get a view through the second window. In the gap between the curtains she can see Nathan's wife. She's standing in the door to the living room wiping tears from her eyes.

Slowly Saga moves sideways, and sees Nathan enter the room and empty a drawer of colourful underwear on the floor.

His wife yells something at him, but he doesn't answer, just goes out again with the empty drawer.

They're obviously in the middle of a big row.

Saga puts her pistol back in the holster and walks round to the front of the house, and is about to get back on the motorbike and ride home when the front door opens and Veronica comes out with a packet of cigarettes in her hand, and catches sight of her.

'Hello,' she says quickly, and lights a cigarette.

'Is this a bad time?'

'Quite the contrary,' Veronica says, without looking at Saga.

Nathan is standing in the porch behind her.

'She wants a divorce,' he says.

'Shall I come back later?'

'No, it's no big deal, she'll probably change her mind.'

'I won't,' Veronica says bitterly, and takes a deep drag on the cigarette.

'Maybe not, I'm sure you're right, why would you stay with me?' he says, holding the door open for Saga.

Veronica lowers her cigarette and looks at Saga with an exhausted expression.

'Sorry about the mess,' she says. 'I'll let Nathan explain the pile of underwear in—'

'Nicky, I just think—'

'Don't call me that,' she interrupts sharply. 'I hate it, I've always hated it, I only pretended to think it was cute back at the start.'

'OK,' he smiles, and goes into the hall with Saga. He helps her out of the leather jacket she's wearing over her hooded top.

'You don't need a reason to get a divorce in Sweden, but—'

'I've got a thousand reasons!' Veronica calls from outside.

'But if one person objects, then there's a delay, the court will give the couple six months' thinking time,' he says.

Saga isn't sure how many times he's been married, but she remembers his previous wife, a blonde woman the same age as him, and before her he was married to a forensics expert called Kristina.

They carry on through the glazed veranda, with its cane furniture and potted ivy plants. The leaded windows rattle when the front door opens and shuts again.

'Veronica isn't keen on the six months' thinking time, and I can understand that. Things are very fraught right now,' he says in a carefree voice.

'Are you upset about the divorce?'

'You know,' he says, 'I'm fairly used to getting divorced by now.'

'Well I'm not, and I'm upset,' Veronica says behind them.

'You weren't supposed to hear that,' Nathan says over his shoulder.

'Of course I was,' she says wearily.

'All I'm saying is, you should think about it – that's why the law's been designed this way,' he replies with irritating calmness.

'I've already thought about it, you know that perfectly well, this is just you throwing your weight about.'

'She wants to sell the house and divide the contents before the divorce goes through,' Nathan says to Saga.

'What difference would that make to you?' Veronica says, wiping the tears that have started to fall again. 'It's going to happen, whether you like it or not.'

'In which case I'm sure you can wait another six months, Nicky.'

'Am I going to have to hit you?' she asks provocatively.

'I've got a witness,' he smiles, tossing his long, silver-grey ponytail over his shoulder.

Veronica sighs, whispers something to herself, retrieves an item of clothing from the floor and puts it on one of the cane chairs, then picks up a mug of tea from the table.

'Don't get married to him,' she says to Saga, then leaves the veranda.

Saga and Nathan walk through the living room, lined with bookcases and with a brown tiled fireplace.

'Her underwear,' he says, gesturing towards the floor. 'I thought she could make a start by selling that, then we could divide the profits.'

'Don't be mean, Nathan.'

'I'm not,' he replies.

The deep lines on his face and wrinkles around his eyes make him look tired, but his eyes are as impenetrable as stone.

'Shall we take a look at what Joona sent?' she asks.

'It'll take a while.'

He shows her into the kitchen, where there are ten removal boxes on the floor. He's started to unpack one of them, and the table is already covered with maps of the sites where the bodies were found, as well as railway maps and photographs.

'Joona's written down a few notes,' Nathan says, showing her a full page of writing in a notepad.

'OK,' she says, looking at a photograph of the graves in Lill-Jans Forest.

'The first thing he wants us to do is get protection for Valeria.'

'I can understand that, looking at it from his point of view,' Saga says.

'It isn't that straightforward, though,' Nathan goes on. 'He says it has to be done in secret, because she doesn't want protection.'

He shows Saga a sketch Joona has made of Valeria's nursery, and the best locations to post ten police officers.

'That looks good,' Saga nods.

'Obviously he says it's impossible to protect yourself against Jurek . . . but that you can destroy a spider's web with a stick.'

'Jurek's dead,' Saga mutters.

'The second thing he wants us to do is interview the church-warden who was keeping Jurek's finger in a glass jar.'

'He's senile, it's impossible to get any sense out of him.'

'Joona's aware of that, but he still thinks we could get something if we give the old boy some time . . . because Jurek's plan would never have worked without the churchwarden's involvement.'

'I saw the body, the decayed torso, the bullet holes exactly where I shot him.'

'I know,' Nathan says, digging out the letter from the papers on the table. 'This is what Joona says: "The chapel on the island is the only way into Jurek's world that we've found so far . . . that's the crack he crawled out of, that's where you . . ."'

There's a loud thud from upstairs, followed by the sound of something shattering on the floor.

'I collect art glass,' he says laconically.

'Shall we get going?'

26

In the north-eastern part of Huvudsta is an area known as Ingenting, 'Nothing'. The name can be traced back to an eighteenth-century estate. And this where the new headquarters of the Swedish Security Police is located.

Because information-gathering is at the core of the Security Police's activities, the institution is characterised by paranoia. The fear of bugging is so widespread that they have more or less built a prison for themselves, with extreme security measures.

The same firm that built the high-security prisons at Kumla and Hall constructed the secure seven-storey building with its balustrades and glazed entrance.

Saga and Nathan get out of the lift and head past the large windows along the open walkway. Saga still has the hood of her tracksuit top pulled up after her bike ride. Nathan's silver ponytail bounces against his back with each step.

Both of their bosses are already in the room when they arrive. It looks as if they've had a brief preliminary meeting.

Verner Sandén is sitting at the table in his suit and tie, his long legs crossed. One trouser leg has ridden up, revealing a stripy black sock.

Carlos Eliasson is wearing a burgundy sweater and white shirt. He's sitting slouched in one of the armchairs, holding a clementine in his hand.

The large windows of Verner's office look out onto a building site, with some industrial units and Ingenting Forest beyond. The world outside looks oddly soft around the edges through the reinforced security glass.

'What's for lunch today?' Saga asks as she sits down at the oval table.

'That's a secret,' Verner says, without smiling.

'One of the murders in question took place in the south of Sweden,' Carlos begins as he peels the clementine. 'And five took place outside our borders, two of them in—'

'Joona thinks Valeria de Castro needs police protection,' Saga interrupts.

'So he told me in the message he left on my phone . . . and obviously she'll get it, like anyone else in the country, if there's a clear threat against her,' Carlos replies calmly.

'Joona thinks there is.'

'But the person responsible for the threat is dead,' Carlos says, and pops three segments in his mouth.

'In theory there's an infinitesimal possibility that Jurek Walter is still alive,' Saga says.

'Naturally, we don't believe that,' Nathan interjects.

'But Joona's convinced that Jurek is alive, and is behind the murders of these criminals around Europe,' Carlos goes on.

'And if he's right, the threat against Valeria is pretty damn extreme,' Saga says, placing the sketch-map of Valeria's nursery and possible police positions on the table in front of Verner.

'It's clear that what unbalanced Joona was the fact that two of the victims had connections to him,' Verner says, without looking at the map. 'That's understandable, it's deeply upsetting that his wife's grave was vandalised, truly awful, but the man in Oslo had collected body parts from thirty-six different people.'

Carlos stands up and throws the clementine peel in the bin.

'As for the second victim . . . it's undeniably difficult to explain why a German sex offender would try to call Joona shortly before he died,' Carlos says.

'Why a Swedish police officer?'

'We have no idea. But the victim had been locked away in a secure psychiatric unit for years, and – according to files I've received – he was in a ward containing at least three inmates who were active in Sweden.'

'And you can find Joona's phone number on the Internet if you know where to look,' Verner says.

'We're not going to drop this, absolutely not,' Carlos says, taking a seat at the table. 'But we can't devote a lot of resources to it either.'

'OK,' Pollock says quietly.

'It would have been good if Joona could have been here for this meeting,' Carlos says, holding his mobile up for no apparent reason.

'He's probably left the country by now,' Saga says.

'Because of this?' Carlos asks.

'I think he's doing the right thing,' Saga says, looking him in the eye.

'You think—'

'Hold on,' she says, cutting him off. 'I'm sure I killed Jurek Walter, but I still think Joona's doing the right thing seeing as he personally isn't convinced Jurek is dead . . . So I'm glad he's gone off to protect his daughter and has left the investigating to us.'

Carlos shakes his head doubtfully.

'I'm going to make sure he sees a psychologist when he gets back,' he sighs.

'The killer is someone – or possibly more than one person – who's taken upon themselves the task of cleaning things up around Europe,' Verner says.

'But that's not Jurek's style – why would he want to clean up society?' Carlos says.

'Joona believes that Jurek Walter has recruited an accomplice,' Saga says. 'That he's spent several years testing candidates . . . and now he's killing the ones that didn't make the grade.'

Verner gets up and fetches a laptop from his desk.

'Joona left Carlos a message saying that Jurek Walter had whipped the man at the campsite the same way he used to whip his twin brother,' he says, connecting the laptop to the socket on the table.

'Yes, I know,' Saga nods.

'And when Joona found out about a murder in Belarus where the victim had similar wounds on his back, he took that as proof that Jurek is responsible for the murders of criminals all over Europe,' Carlos says.

'We've now received a recording from the Belarusian police. Some surveillance footage that caught the killer on camera,' Verner says, tapping the laptop. A large screen on one wall comes to life.

'You can see the murderer?' Nathan asks.

'The national park is closed at night. It's not quite ten o'clock, and the security guard is doing his rounds,' Verner replies cryptically as he turns the lights off and clicks to play the soundless footage on the screen.

Three words in white Cyrillic lettering appear at the bottom of the screen, next to a counter.

The security camera is pointing at an ornate house built of dark wood, with a wealth of carving and exuberant detailing. The walls, veranda, railings, and pillars are covered with fairylights, all of them switched off.

'A gingerbread house,' Nathan murmurs.

'Their version of Santa Claus is called Ded Moroz, and apparently this is where he lives,' Verner rumbles.

The wintry park is dark. The only light is coming from what look like electric torches with pointed glass domes which line the paths. A uniformed guard in a fur hat checks that the door to the house is locked, then walks back down the steps. His breath clouds around his mouth in the cold air. He carries on along the ploughed path lined by an ornate wooden fence.

'The Belarusian authorities haven't confirmed this,' Verner says, 'but we know that the victim was previously employed by the secret service to deal with critics of the government.'

The guard stops and lights a cigarette before carrying on towards the left of the screen.

A large shape emerges from the darkness between the trees and follows the guard.

'Bloody hell,' Saga whispers.

The black-and-white recording is low resolution, and the pursuer's movements seem to be subject to some sort of lag, as if part of his dark persona lingers like an elastic shimmer.

'Watch this,' Carlos says quietly.

The thickset figure has pulled a silenced pistol from his bag, and is obviously moving silently across the snow seeing as the guard doesn't react.

'That's not Jurek,' Saga says, staring at the recording.

The man catches up with the guard beside a plastic snowman and shoots him in the back of the head without any preamble. The end of the silenced barrel flares for an instant. Blood and fragments of bone burst from the guard's mouth like some terrible attack of projectile vomiting. His teeth and tongue follow, spraying across the snow.

The cigarette is still clasped between his fingers as his legs give way. The large man hits him in the head with the butt of the pistol.

The dead body subsides onto the snow, but the attacker doesn't stop. He slips, takes a step to the side, puts the pistol away, then goes back and starts kicking wildly at the body.

'What's he doing? The man's dead,' Nathan whispers.

The man grabs one of the guard's arms and drags him off behind the fence, leaving a dark trail of blood across the snow. His mouth is opening as if he's shrieking as he smashes the guard's head against a rock.

'Christ,' Carlos groans.

The man straightens up, evidently out of breath, then stamps on the guard's face and chest over and over again, then drags the body out of shot by one leg.

'The body was found twenty metres away behind some bins,' Verner says.

The large man returns, but it's still too dark for his face to be seen clearly. He wipes his mouth, then turns and walks back a short way, kicks and smashes one of the glass lanterns lining the path, yells something, then disappears.

The recording flickers and comes to an end.

'This disproves Joona's theory one hundred per cent,' Carlos concludes.

'It could be the accomplice,' Saga says.

'The secret accomplice who kills other secret accomplices in Belarus,' Verner mutters.

'We do realise how this sounds,' Saga sighs.

'There's no logic to it,' Carlos says, not unpleasantly. 'If Jurek's alive and has an accomplice, then surely the accomplice ought to do what Jurek wants, and bury people alive – not clean up society.'

'We'd still like to conduct a preliminary investigation,' Saga persists.

'Into the murder in Sweden, then,' Carlos replies.

'This is a serial killer,' she says.

'We can't go outside the country if no one's requested our help . . . people are only too relieved to get shot of some of their worst criminals.'

'Give us a month,' Nathan asks.

'You can have a week, just the two of you, and that's being generous,' Carlos says, glancing at Verner.

27

Valeria has gathered her curly hair into a thick ponytail and changed into a clean pair of jeans and white vest. There's a cup of tea on the kitchen table, next to a paperback edition of *My Brilliant Friend* and her cheap reading glasses.

She's standing at the window talking on the phone to her younger son Linus as she gazes out at the dark greenhouses.

Linus lives in Farsta, only twenty minutes away from her if he drives through Älta. She's promised to let him have an old bureau that's been standing in the attic for years.

'I'll pick it up next week,' Linus is saying.

'Have a word with Amanda and see if you'd like to stay for dinner,' she says.

'Will Joona be there?'

'He's away at the moment.'

'How are things going with him?' Linus asks. 'You've sounded happier recently.'

'I have been,' she says.

They end the call and Valeria puts her phone down on the table and looks at her reading glasses. One of the screws fell out some time ago, so one arm is held on with a paperclip.

She's used to being on her own. Her years in prison have made loneliness a part of her, but when Joona comes back home she's planning to ask if he'd like to try living together, to see how it goes. He can hold onto his flat, there's no hurry to do anything, but she'd love to spend more time with him, doing ordinary, everyday things.

She gets a glass out of one of the top cupboards and half fills it from the wine-box on the counter, then walks into the living room and glances at the dark television and black windows before switching on the record player and playing the album already on the turntable. The speakers crackle, then Barbra Streisand's 1980s album *Guilty* starts to play.

Valeria sits down on the arm of the sofa and thinks about how odd it is that she's met up with Joona again after so many years.

She thinks of her car journeys to Kumla Prison, and the anxiety she felt when the steel gates clanged shut behind her. She felt the same panic every time she passed the guards, walked in through Door 3, handed over her ID, was given a visitor's badge and told to hang her coat and leave any loose items in one of the lockers. She would nod and smile at the immaculately made-up women who were always there with restless children milling around their legs. The waiting room contained a bathroom, several sofas, information for visitors, and a rocking-horse with worn rockers.

You weren't allowed to wear a bra with a catch on it, nor tampons or pads. You had to put your shoes on a conveyor-belt before you walked through the security gate and were searched.

But she still loved the dull visiting room. She loved Joona's attempts to make it nice with napkins, coffee and biscuits.

And now he was free.

He's spent the night with her, they've made love and worked in the garden together.

Valeria drinks some more wine and starts to sing along to 'Woman in Love' before she realises and stops, embarrassed.

She goes out into the hall and stops in front of the mirror, where she blows a lock of hair away from her face, raises her chin and concludes that she does in fact look happy.

The tattoos on her shoulders have become blurred over the years, and her arms are muscular from hard work, and scratched by brambles.

She carries on into the kitchen, puts the wine-glass down on the counter and turns out the light that Joona always hits his head on.

The music in the living room is muffled by the walls, as if a neighbour was having a party in the flat next door.

She thinks of the fear she saw in Joona's eyes when he asked her to leave everything and go away with him.

It frightened her that he genuinely seemed to believe that Jurek wasn't dead.

She understands why he might think that. A trauma never really leaves you, it just hides in the shadows, ready to leap out on you at a moment's notice.

It's good that he's gone to see Lumi.

Valeria hopes it will help calm him down, spending a few days with her in Paris, seeing that she's doing well there.

The wind has got up, and is whistling in the chimney.

Valeria is about to pick up her book and reading glasses when the light from a car's headlamps shines through the kitchen window. They flicker between the trees like the images in a kinetoscope.

Her pulse-rate speeds up as she sees the unfamiliar vehicle stop in the turning circle. Its headlamps are shining right into the first greenhouse, lighting up the plants and casting multiple shadows.

Valeria goes out into the hall and pulls on her raincoat, then puts her boots on, reaches for the torch on the shelf and opens the door to the cold evening air.

The strange car is parked motionless outside. A cloud of exhaust fumes is billowing gently in the red glow of the rear-lights.

She thinks momentarily of the pistol in the drawer of her bedside table.

The gravel crunches under her boots.

The driver's door is open, the seat empty.

There's someone in the nearest greenhouse, a dark shape moving between the racks and plants.

Valeria turns the torch on as she gets closer, but the beam fades almost instantly, so she shakes it and points the weak light towards the greenhouse.

It's Gustav Eriksson, from Hasselfors Garden Supplies. One of his colleagues is standing a little further in among the benches.

Valeria waves to them, then walks closer and pulls the door open.

Gustav is a thickset man in his sixties who always starts to rattle the coins in his pocket whenever he talks business. He has glasses and a salt-and-pepper moustache, and always wears baggy jeans and pink or yellow shirts and jackets.

Valeria's been buying compost and manure from Hasselfors for over ten years.

She assumes he must have been passing and wanted to check if she was likely to place another order before spring.

'Gustav?'

'Spring'll be with us before you know it,' he says, rattling the coins in his pocket.

His heavily built colleague picks up a potted tomato plant and some of the soil runs out through the hole at the bottom.

'I'm still working it out,' she says. 'But I'm going to need quite a lot this year.'

He lets out a low, embarrassed chuckle.

'You'll have to excuse me calling in so late, I very nearly turned back, but when I saw that you already had a customer in here, I assumed it was OK to—'

There's a heavy thud and Gustav stops mid-sentence. Then there's a second, wetter thud and Gustav slumps onto the cupboard in front of her.

She doesn't understand.

His legs are jerking spasmodically, but his face is slack even though his eyes are wide open.

Valeria sees the other man beside him, and is about to tell him to call an ambulance when she sees the hammer in his hand.

A dark pool of blood is spreading out beneath Gustav.

The man with the hammer is almost two metres tall, with a thick neck and round shoulders. His nostrils are flaring and he looks tense. His breathing is rapid and his pearly earrings are swaying in an agitated manner.

It's like a dream.

She tries to move backwards, away from him, but her legs feel oddly numb, as if she were wading through water.

The man tosses the hammer aside, as if he no longer understands what he's holding, and turns towards her with a quizzical expression.

'Don't go,' he mumbles.

'I'll come back,' she whispers, and turns slowly towards the door.

'Don't go!' the man bellows, and sets off towards her.

Valeria breaks into a run, and overturns the bench holding the blackberry bushes behind her, and hears him trip over it and roar like an animal. She rushes between the shelving, jumping over bags of compost.

She realises that he's right behind her, and bumps into one of the shelves as she passes through the beam from the car's headlamps, knocking two terracotta pots to the floor.

Valeria reaches the door and just manages to grab hold of the handle when the man catches up with her.

She spins round and lashes out with the torch, hitting him hard in the cheek. He staggers sideways and she kicks him between his legs. She sees him bend double and sink to his knees.

She turns back to the door again.

The old lock has caught, and she hits the rusty latch with her knuckles and tugs at the door.

Reflected in the shaking glass she sees the man creeping towards her.

Valeria turns the handle and hears herself whimper as he grabs hold of one of her legs. With a single tug he pulls her to the floor. She collapses onto her front and puts her hands out to brace her fall, then rolls onto her side and tries to kick him.

He yanks her backwards hard.

Her raincoat slides up and she scrapes her stomach and chin.

Before she has time to get to her feet he's on top of her, hitting her in the back. She loses her breath, coughs and is struggling to breathe when he hits her again.

He backs away from her, growling, breaking the pieces of the fallen pots.

Gasping, she gets up on all fours and sees the man pull plants onto the floor as he makes his way back to Gustav. He starts kicking the lifeless body and roaring with rage.

She gets to her feet and reaches out to the glass to steady herself as he returns to her.

'Leave me the fuck alone!' she manages to blurt out, and tries to fend him off with one hand.

He catches hold of her arm and hits her hard across her left cheek, and she stumbles to the right, hitting her head against the glass and falling to the ground in a shower of broken glass.

He stamps on her chest, yelling that she's about to die, that he's going to slaughter her, and is coughing and bellowing as he sits astride her, grabs hold of her throat with both hands and starts to squeeze her neck.

She can't breathe, and struggles to get him off her, but he's too strong. She twists sideways and tries to reach his face.

He starts to hit her against the floor. The third time the back of her head flares, she loses consciousness.

She dreams that she's in a lift, heading down to the ground fast, and wakes up because of an excruciating pain in one leg. The man is biting her thigh through her jeans, then he gets up with a roar and kicks at her feet.

Warm blood is oozing from the bite.

Only half-conscious, she watches as he tears plants down from the benches, then picks up a pruning knife from the floor.

The large man goes back to Gustav and slits his throat with a deep cut, then slices him open from his navel to his neck. He heaves Gustav up onto his shoulder and walks to the door. Little spasms run through his body, and blood pours down his back.

He passes Valeria and kicks the greenhouse door open. The hinges break and the glass shatters as it hits the ground.

Valeria gets to her feet, and almost throws up from the pain. Blood is running down under her raincoat from the back of her head. She staggers forward, fumbling for support, and slips out through the door.

There's a muffled explosion from the turning circle as the car starts to burn. Dirty petrol flames are tossed sideways by the wind. The large man smashes the windows with a spade, then takes a step back as the flames flare up and fixes his gaze on Valeria.

She turns and starts to run into the forest, gasping with pain from her thigh. Whimpering, she forces her way through the undergrowth, almost falling but somehow managing to stay on her feet.

His heavy breathing is right behind her. She treads in a water-filled hole and is trying to shield her face from low-hanging branches when he hits her on the back of the head with the shovel.

Knocked out, she falls headfirst through the dry branches onto the frosty lingonberry twigs. With a roar he lashes out again but misses her head and loses his grip on the shovel.

She comes round and realises that the man is dragging her through the forest by one leg. Valeria has lost her boots and her raincoat is dragging behind her. She tries to grab hold of a slender birch tree, but isn't strong enough.

28

Joona Linna is now a Finnish landscape architect called Paavo Niskanen, according to his passport and bank card. Apart from his actual body, there's no longer anything that can be linked to his true identity and life in Stockholm.

No paperwork, no electronics, not even any items of clothing.

He's cut open the spare tyre, stuffed it with explosives and detonators, then welded the rubber wall closed again.

Distances in western Europe are short compared to Sweden.

It's only five hundred kilometres from Béziers in the South of France to Geneva in Switzerland on the A9 autoroute, but because he chooses to drive on smaller roads the trip takes seven hours.

Joona keeps telling himself that everything's going to be all right. He knows that Nathan will have made sure Valeria has got protection. It would have been better if she'd come with him, but she'll be safe until Joona manages to find Jurek.

He crosses the narrow extension of the La Laire Rau river and the unmanned Swiss border, drives along the Chemin du Moulin-de-la-Grave and approaches Geneva beneath a sky heavy with rain.

Joona parks in Rue de Lausanne and slings his bag over his shoulder. He walks through the extravagant entrance of the railway station, into the café, and fetches the envelope from the counter containing the key card from Lumi.

That means she's here.

She managed to escape from Paris.

Before Joona walks into the marble-clad reception of the Warwick Geneva Hotel he covers his head with the hoodie.

As he's heading up to the second floor he keeps his head lowered so the security cameras in the lift don't pick him up.

The carpet in the corridor silences his steps. He stops outside room 208 and knocks.

The peephole in the door goes dark.

He knows Lumi is standing to one side, covering the lens with something – a sofa cushion, maybe – in case the person outside is ready to shoot through the door the moment she looks through it.

The corridor is still empty, but he can hear faint music from somewhere.

The peephole gets lighter, then darker again.

Joona nods and Lumi opens the door. He goes inside quickly, locks the door behind him and puts his bag down on the floor.

They hug, he kisses her on the head, breathing in the scent of her hair, and holds her tight.

'Dad,' she whispers to his chest.

He smiles as he looks down at her, she's got her light brown hair pulled back into a neat ponytail, and she seems to have grown slightly slimmer, her cheekbones are more pronounced and her grey eyes darker.

'You look great,' he says.

'Thanks,' she says, lowering her gaze.

He walks further into the double room, turns the light out, closes the curtains and turns back towards her again.

'Are you absolutely sure?' she asks seriously.

'Yes.'

He can see that she's trying not to say anything. She just nods and goes and sits down on one of the armchairs.

'Have you got rid of everything?' he asks as he fetches his bag from the hall.

'I've done what we agreed,' she replies in a heavy voice.

'Did it go OK?'

She shrugs and looks down.

'I'm so sorry you're caught up in this,' Joona says, pulling out a plastic bag. 'Put these clothes on . . . they're probably a bit too big, but we can buy more on the way.'

'OK,' she murmurs and gets to her feet.

'Change everything, underwear, hairclips—'

'I know,' she interrupts, then goes into the bathroom with the bag swinging from her hand.

Joona takes the pistols out of his bag. He slips one into the shoulder holster beneath his left arm, then tapes the other to his right shin.

Lumi emerges as he's adjusting his clothes. Her new sweater is baggy and the trousers hang loosely from her slender hips.

'Where's your gun?' he asks.

'Under the pillow on the bed.'

'You've checked the hammer and spring?'

'You did that before I got it,' she says, folding her arms over her chest.

'You don't know that.'

'Yes, I do,' she insists.

'Do it yourself, that's the only way to be sure.'

Without saying anything she goes over to the bed, pulls out her Glock 26, removes the magazine, takes the bullet out of the chamber and disassembles the gun, putting the pieces on the bed and then examining the recoil spring.

'I'm starting to get used to disappearing,' Joona says, trying to smile. 'And I know all this can feel a bit over the top.'

Lumi doesn't respond. She puts the gun back together again, tests the mechanism a couple of times, then reinserts the magazine.

Joona goes into the bathroom and finds her discarded clothes in the bathtub. He puts them all in a bin-bag, gathers up the rest of her things, grabs her shoes from the floor next to the door and leaves the hotel again.

The air is chill and the sky a steel grey. Dark streaks of cloud are hanging above the huge railway station. The streets have been decorated for Christmas, with sparkling Christmas trees and garlands on the lampposts. The pavements are full of people and there's still a lot of traffic. Joona walks with his head down, turns left down Place de Cornavin, past a basic hamburger joint and a brasserie. By the large pedestrian tunnel leading to the station he sets about discarding Lumi's things in different bins.

On the way back he goes into a Chinese restaurant and orders a takeaway. While he's waiting in the dimly lit bar area he thinks about the time he spent with Lumi up in Nattavaara, and how they got to know each other again, talking about all the things they'd been through in all the years that had passed while they were apart.

Lumi looks like she's been crying when she lets him back into the room. He follows her to the sitting area and puts the food down on the table by the sofa.

'Do you drink wine?' he asks.

'I live in France,' she says quietly.

He takes out the cartons of food, then gets out glasses, napkins, and chopsticks.

'What's been happening at college? How's it all going?' he asks, taking a bottle of red out of the minibar.

'I'm happy there . . . there's a lot going on at the moment.'

'That's the way it should be, though, isn't it?'

'How about you? How have you been getting on, Dad?' Lumi asks, opening the cartons.

While they eat he talks about what's happened since he was released from prison, about his work as a neighbourhood police officer, and about Valeria and her nursery.

'Are you going to move in with her?'

'I don't know, I'd like to, but she's got a life of her own, so . . . well, we'll have to see.'

She puts her chopsticks down and turns away.

'What is it, Lumi?'

'It's just that . . . you don't really know anything about me,' she says.

'I haven't wanted to bother you, you've got a whole new life . . . which I'd love to be part of, but I understand that having a dad who's a police officer isn't much to boast about among all those artists and authors.'

'Do you think I'm ashamed of you?'

'No, but . . . I only meant that I don't exactly fit in.'

Her voice reminds him of Summa's. He feels like saying that, but holds back. They finish eating in silence, then drink the last of the wine.

'We'll be leaving early,' he says, starting to clear the table.

'Where to?'

'I can't say.'

'No,' she whispers, and turns her face away.

'Lumi,' he says, 'I understand that you don't want to go into hiding, that it doesn't fit in with the way your life looks now.'

'Have I complained?' she asks in a thick voice.

'You don't need to.'

She sighs and runs the palm of her hand quickly over her eyes.

'Have you seen Jurek Walter?'

'No, but his accomplice was following me, and—'

'What accomplice?' she interrupts.

'Jurek's been watching you,' Joona goes on. 'He's been mapping your life, he knows your routines, and he knows who you spend time with.'

'But why would Jurek get an accomplice?'

'If he's going to get his revenge the way he wants, he needs an accomplice who's as loyal as his brother was,' Joona explains. 'He knew I'd drop everything and try to protect you the moment I realised he was still alive . . . and his strategy was to grab you before I could get to Paris, while his accomplice would seize Valeria in Stockholm. That had to happen simultaneously, he thinks like a twin.'

'So why was the accomplice following you, then?'

Joona puts the empty cartons in the bin, feels a sting of pain behind his eye and grabs hold of the writing desk with one hand to keep his balance.

'Because I realised Jurek wasn't dead just moments before he launched his plan,' he replies, turning back towards her. 'I called you, you did exactly what you had to do, and you managed to get away from Paris . . . Sending the accomplice after me was an emergency solution, an attempt not to lose the only way he could find you . . . We were quick and managed to get a small head start, but that's all.'

'There's no logic to any of this, Dad . . . besides the fact that there's no evidence that Jurek's alive, no one's seen him, not even you . . . I mean, why would the person who was following you have any connection to Jurek?'

'I know Jurek's alive.'

'OK, let's assume that – after all, that's why we're sitting here.'

'I killed his twin brother, but not him,' Joona goes on.

'And who am I in all this?' she asks.

'My daughter.'

'I'm starting to feel like some sort of hostage,' she says, then holds her hands up in a gesture of resignation. 'Sorry, that was an exaggeration . . . but this is affecting my whole life, so I have a right to know what we're doing.'

'What do you want to know?' Joona says, sitting down on the sofa.

'Where are we going tomorrow, what's the plan?'

'The plan is to stay alive until the police catch Jurek . . . I've given them loads of material, so it's not impossible that they'll be able to find Jurek if they get a move on.'

'How are we going to stay alive?' Lumi asks in a gentler voice.

'We're going to drive up through Germany and Belgium to Holland . . . there are some derelict buildings surrounded by fields in the province of Limburg, not far from Weert.'

'And that's where we're going to hide?'

'Yes.'

'For how long?'

He doesn't answer. There is no answer.

'Will you feel calmer there?' Lumi asks, sitting down on the armchair.

'Have I ever told you about my friend Rinus?'

'You mentioned him when we were practising close combat in Nattavaara,' she nods.

After his time as a paratrooper, Joona was recruited for a top-secret training course in the Netherlands, where he was trained by Lieutenant Rinus Advocaat.

'Rinus has always been a bit paranoid, and has created the closest thing you can get to a completely safe house . . . It looks like a group of derelict buildings from the outside, but . . .'

'So what?' she sighs.

Joona is about to say something, but a second, worse stab of the migraine hits him. A sharp pain behind his left eye, followed by a debilitating feeling of his ears being filled with water.

'Dad? What's happening?'

He presses his hand to his left eye as the storm sweeps past and the pain eases.

'It's been a long day,' he explains, then stands up and goes to brush his teeth.

When he returns to the bedroom Lumi is sitting on the edge of the bed with a watch in her hand.

'What's that?' she asks.

'A present,' she replies.

'You'll have to leave it behind.'

'There's nothing funny about it,' she replies firmly, pulling it over her wrist.

'Probably not, but the only rule that works is making a complete break.'

'Fine, but I'm not leaving my watch – you can check it, it's only a watch,' she says, handing it to him.

He takes it, turns the bedside lamp on to see better, turns it in the light, checks every link of the chain, and looks to see if any of the tiny screws on the back are scratched.

'No secret microphones or transmitters?' she asks, unable to hide the sarcasm in her voice.

He hands the watch back to her without answering, and she puts it on her left wrist in silence. They pack their bags without speaking, get dressed as if they were about to leave, with their shoes on and pistols in their holsters, before lying down on either side of the bed.

29

Saga Bauer and Nathan Pollock have been sitting in the National Operational Unit with their phones and computers for fourteen hours now.

The three windows look out onto the covered inner courtyard, the enclosed rest area of the prison, and roofs covered with ventilation units and satellite dishes.

The walls of the room are covered with maps, satellite images, photographs and lists of names and telephone numbers for various contacts around Europe.

On the table are pads full of notes and highlighted ideas. A crumpled napkin in a mug has turned dark and the only thing left on what was a plate of buns is some icing sugar and a few pieces of old chewing gum.

'It isn't Jurek, it's a serial killer . . . and we've got one week to find him,' Saga says, closing her stinging eyes for a few seconds. 'What's the next step? The pictures from Belarus are too poor – you can't even see if he's got a face.'

'Six victims in six different countries, and the same thing everywhere. It's crazy,' she says. 'No witnesses, no pictures, no matches in the DNA database.'

'I'll call Ystad again – there must be some sort of security cameras in an industrial estate, for God's sake.'

Exhaustion has made the lines in Nathan's thin face deeper than ever, and his sharp eyes are bloodshot.

'Go ahead,' she sighs. 'They'll only say that their forensic examination is ongoing, and that they don't need any help from Stockholm.'

'We should go down there anyway.'

'There's no point.'

'If we had just one reasonably sharp picture, a single witness, a name, anything at all, then we'd be able to find him.'

Saga looks at the map of the industrial estate in Ystad again.

A convicted double murderer was beaten to death in a workshop that he himself owned.

His head was smashed to a pulp with a hammer, then severed from his body, which was then dangled from a hoist.

His dog was killed and impaled on a railing outside.

Several windows in the building opposite were smashed, and a motorbike in a neighbouring property was vandalised.

Saga wonders if the perpetrator has abnormal levels of serotonin in his prefrontal cortex, and increased activity in his amygdala.

'He's extremely violent . . . But there's another side to him as well,' she says. 'Seeing as the victims are so specific, he must have done a lot of research, hacking or somehow gaining access to a whole range of databases . . . He's mapped the victims and probably established some form of contact with them well before the attacks.'

Nathan's phone rings on the desk and Saga has time to see a picture of his wife on the screen before he rejects the call and goes over to stand in front of the long list of countries, districts and names of detectives and other police officers.

They've already crossed out four hundred names and eight countries.

Saga opens a PDF of a Europol report and thinks about all the sacrifices Joona has made over the years. He let go of his family, missed years of his daughter's life and based his entire life around trying to escape Jurek's vengeance.

It's clearly become something of an obsession.

The fact that the grave-robber in Oslo had Summa's skull in his freezer was simply too much for him.

Joona's paranoia created a scenario in which the murders

around Europe were committed by Jurek Walter, as he dispensed with candidates who hadn't made the grade.

But Jurek Walter is dead, and this killer has nothing to do with him.

Nathan looks up from his computer and starts saying once again that the common denominator between all the victims is that they had all been found guilty of serious sexual or violent offences.

'Without getting caught up on that . . . one plausible theory is that the perpetrator has some sort of warped moral motivation,' Nathan says. 'He thinks he's on a mission to clean up society, maybe even make the world a better, safer place.'

'A superhero . . . or the hand of God.'

She and Nathan start searching the Internet for people advocating harsher punishment and purification of society, but the number of results is way too large to be any use.

Predictable, perhaps.

Hundreds of thousands of people declaring that the streets need to be cleaned up.

There are plenty of police officers among them, complaining about the rules, about the courts, and politically correct colleagues, about excessive respect for the rights of criminals.

The phone rings and Saga picks it up, sees that it's a foreign number and takes the call. Superintendent Salvatore Giani in Milan. He tells her apologetically that the murder of Patrizia Tuttino outside the San Raffaele Hospital has gone cold.

'We've examined the recordings from all the security cameras, we've talked to all the staff in the hospital . . . there are no leads, no witnesses, nothing,' he says.

'What about forensics?'

'I'm sorry, but we're no longer prioritising this investigation,' Salvatore explains.

'I see,' Saga says. 'Thanks for letting me know.'

She puts her phone down, sighs and meets Nathan's weary gaze.

'I'll have another go with Volgograd,' he says, and is reaching for his phone when Veronica calls again.

'Take it,' Saga says.

'She only wants to tell me I'm an idiot for ignoring her calls.'

'So stop ignoring them, then.'

He takes a sip of cold coffee, tosses the plastic cup in the bin, and picks the phone up.

'Hello, darling.'

Saga can hear from Veronica's voice that she's upset.

'I'm not ignoring you,' Nathan says. 'But I've got a job that . . . OK, Nicky, we don't agree on that . . . Fine . . . but apart from that, was there anything in particular you wanted to talk about . . . ?'

He falls silent and puts his phone down.

'Well, at least we're friends again now,' he says sardonically.

Saga stands up and goes over to the wall with the blurred pictures from security cameras, and the photographs of the brutal-ised bodies.

'This isn't just going to blow over . . . because this superhero isn't going to stop until he's caught,' she says.

'Agreed,' Nathan says.

'If the quality of the Belarusian footage hadn't been so poor, we might already have been able to issue a description,' she says. 'I mean . . . he's going to make a mistake sooner or later, if he hasn't already.'

Saga picks up her phone and weighs it in her hand. It's warm, and the dark screen reflects the lights in the ceiling. She looks at the notes on the pad in front of her and decides to call their contact at the national police centre in Poland.

Nathan has already had twenty-three conversations with various Russian authorities, the FSB, SVR, and regional police chiefs in all the federal districts.

'I feel like I'm in telesales,' Nathan mutters and he calls the Russian narcotics unit, Gosnarkokontrol.

After several misunderstandings he is put through to an elderly superintendent named Jakov Kramnik, and quickly explains why he's calling.

'Yes, we received your request via Interpol,' the Russian super-intendent replies. 'I'm sorry I haven't got back to you, but we still have some of our old bureaucracy left in certain areas.'

'Don't worry,' Nathan says, rubbing his forehead.

'Thanks for understanding, that's good of you,' he says. 'It warms my heart . . . Because we do actually have one suspected murder that matches several of your criteria. On Monday an Igor Sokolov was found with his throat cut in a warehouse on the outskirts of St Petersburg. He'd previously served nineteen years in Kresty for narcotics offences, but was also suspected of four murders . . . It was an execution . . . one of his knees was broken, and the internal carotid artery severed. It looks like our special forces had done it . . . but they'd never attempt to remove his spine.'

'His spine?'

'Sokolov was subjected to extreme violence long after he was dead – I can send our report if you like.'

'Do you have any idea who the perpetrator might be?' Nathan asks, as Saga's phone starts to ring.

'Igor Sokolov fought for our country in Afghanistan, then got caught up on heroin addiction and serious crime . . . but he served his sentence and was rebuilding his life, and I respect that . . . We've got no leads on the perpetrator, but it looks like an old enemy from the underworld caught up with him.'

Reflected in the window, Nathan sees Saga stand up so abruptly that her office chair rolls backwards and thuds into the wall.

'You've checked the security cameras in the area around the warehouse?' he asks.

'Nothing,' the Russian superintendent replies.

Nathan ends the call with mutual expressions of thanks and hopes of continuing cooperation in the future.

He puts his phone down on the table, watches as it spins round once, then turns to Saga.

She's standing with her phone pressed to her ear, and is leaning forward and scribbling something on the pad in front of her.

'We're on our way, we'll be there as soon as possible,' she says.

30

Two police cars are blocking one side of Regeringsgatan, and the entire pavement in front of the scaffolding and the workmen's portacabin with its barred windows is cordoned off with blue-and-white tape that flutters in the wind.

'I don't know . . . it just sounded a lot like our perpetrator,' Saga says.

'We spend hours making calls to every corner of Europe, but we don't even know what's going on in our own fucking backyard,' Nathan says as he pulls over to the kerb.

'Because they're convinced it's to do with a protection racket,' Saga says. 'Apparently this bar has been the target of extortion attempts before.'

'Everyone guards their own little patch like a bunch of squabbling kids.'

'Look, we're both tired, but we're here now, so let's try to be calm. I mean, this could be what we've been looking for,' Saga says, opening the car door. 'And as far as I'm concerned, they're welcome to think Black Cobra are behind this, as long as they let us in.'

An older man is waiting on the pavement under an umbrella. Senior Prosecutor Arne Rosander from the Central Stockholm office.

He has thinning hair and a neat beard, and is wearing silvery glasses and a wax-cloth raincoat over a check blazer.

'I've heard about you, Saga Bauer, but I thought they were exaggerating,' he says, holding the umbrella over her head.

'Have the victims been identified?' she asks.

'Erica Liljestrand . . . twenty-eight years old, single . . . studying biotechnology at the Royal Institute of Technology . . . Niklas Dahlberg, also single, a bartender here at the Pilgrim Bar.'

The dirty white nylon mesh covering the scaffolding is billowing like a sail.

'We haven't found any connection between the victims,' the prosecutor goes on, shepherding them towards the crime scene. 'All the evidence suggests that she was the last customer in the bar.'

'Alone?' Nathan asks.

'She didn't have a date, but she was supposed to be meeting a friend,' Arne Rosander explains. 'She probably got caught up in it by accident.'

They walk into the passageway beneath the scaffolding. Rain is seeping through the makeshift plywood roof. Forensics have set up an airlock outside the entrance to the bar for people to put protective clothing on and write their names on a list before entering the crime scene.

Well used to the procedure, Arne quickly slips into the protective outfit and waits patiently as Saga and Nathan sign the list.

'What do you think happened here, Arne?' Nathan asks, tucking his ponytail in before pulling the blue plastic hood over his head.

The prosecutor's warm eyes take on a despairing look.

'It's Black Cobra, you'll see the excessive brutality used . . . but obviously it'll be hard to put a prosecution together. We have to link the perpetrator to the organisation, then show that he was given explicit orders to do this.'

They step into the blinding light of the floodlamps. Around a dozen forensics officers are working inside the bar in silence.

'The bodies have been moved to the Institute of Forensic Medicine,' Arne says quietly, 'but apart from that I've kept the crime scene as intact as possible.'

Saga inspects the locations where the bodies were found. All the evidence suggests an extremely violent incident. Blood has been trodden across the floor, the bodies were evidently dragged between the furniture, and in two places it looks like the bodies were at least partially dismembered.

There is a strong smell of alcohol and sour wine in the air from the smashed bottles behind the bar. There's broken glass everywhere, strewn amongst the shattered furniture and splintered wood. If it wasn't for all the blood, you might have thought a tornado had blown through the room.

They go further in and stop next to the bent metal frame of a table that's lying beside a bloody wooden baseball bat.

Saga looks out across the room and tries to reconstruct the course of events. The bartender seems to have been the primary victim, or at least the focus of the perpetrator's aggression. The woman had her throat cut, and was then dragged several metres through the room before her body was dumped.

'Is it our killer?' Nathan asks in a low voice.

Saga turns round slowly and looks at the smashed-up bar. It seems to her that it started with a fight, lots of punching and kicking, before it turned into an out-and-out assault with the baseball bat.

She looks at a large pool of blood by the opposite wall, and notes that the blood sprayed out at considerable pressure, reaching the pink lampshades of the wall lights.

That was where the most extreme violence started.

Forensics have probably already found the knife.

Several stabs to the heart and lungs.

Then the body was dragged towards the door. She follows the trail of blood and heavy footprints with her eyes.

The victims were still alive – one bloody hand tried to cling onto a pillar.

'It's him,' she says.

'Looks like it,' Nathan nods.

'Is there any indication of sexual violence?' Saga asks.

'No,' the prosecutor replies.

'You've checked all the security cameras in the area?' Nathan asks.

'Unfortunately the only relevant ones are covered by scaffolding . . . but they probably wouldn't have given us much, given that it was dark and the weather was so bad.'

'I see.'

'But we've got three witnesses who saw a thickset man in the street outside . . . shouting and acting aggressively.'

'I'd like to read their statements,' Saga says.

'One of them was able to give a pretty good description,' Arne says, searching for an audio file on his iPad.

They move closer to him, he presses play, and they listen as an elderly woman starts to speak, in an attractive, slightly fragile voice.

'At first I only heard shouting, a man screaming . . . which was obviously very unpleasant . . . but then I caught sight of him beneath the scaffolding. He was a big man, in his fifties, maybe two metres tall, broad shoulders . . . he was wearing a black raincoat, plastic, not nylon . . . and he was moving jerkily . . . When he reached Nalen the light hit him and I saw that he had blood on his face . . . he was acting extremely aggressively, shouting and kicking out at parked cars, then he picked up a stone and threw it at a group of youngsters on the other side of the street before he disappeared.'

'Can you describe his face?' the interviewer asked.

'I don't know, what struck me most was the blood, I thought he'd hurt himself . . . but he had a big head and a thick neck . . . I don't know, it's very difficult . . . I thought he looked like a Russian hooligan, but I'm not entirely sure what I mean by that.'

The Institute of Forensic Medicine at the Karolinska Institute is housed in an unassuming red-brick building on the northern outskirts of Stockholm. Advent stars and electric candelabra shine weakly from the windows behind the blinds.

Rubbish from the overflowing bins has blown in amongst the bare rose bushes.

Saga and Nathan pull into the car park and get out of the car.

A white Jaguar is parked crookedly on one side of the entrance, and as they push their way past it Saga sees that there's a black briefcase lying on the roof of the car.

She grabs the briefcase and follows Nathan into the building.

The floor of the empty corridor is worn from heavy use. The doorframes and skirting boards are badly scratched and dented.

The door to the professor's room is open.

Nils Åhlén is sitting at his computer in his medical coat. His thin face is clean-shaven and sad, his grey hair cropped short.

Someone has sprayed *Twisted Christmas* on his window in fake snow.

Saga knocks and steps into the room.

'I've got one just like that,' Nils says when he sees the briefcase.

'Found it on the roof of your car,' Saga says, putting the briefcase down on his desk.

'Well, it's not supposed to be there,' he replies, and logs out of his computer.

'We've come straight from the Pilgrim Bar, where we spoke to Arne Rosander, who said you were looking at the bodies.'

'Have you given up this idea about Jurek Walter?' Nils asks.

'It isn't him, we've got witnesses and some blurred security camera footage,' Nathan replies.

'When we find the real perpetrator, these murders will stop . . . and as soon as Joona hears that, he can come home,' Saga says.

Nils nods and his thin lips form themselves into a gloomy smile. He puts both hands on his desk and heaves himself to his feet.

'Then let's get going,' he says, and leaves the room.

Saga and Nathan follow him to the post-mortem lab closest to his office. The automatic doors swing open. The white tiles on the walls reflect the glare of the fluorescent lights.

Saga walks over to the dead woman, who's lying with her eyes open, her lips shrunken. Her naked body is grey and pale, and the deep wound in her neck is gaping dark red. The plastic surface of the post-mortem table, with its gullies and troughs, is dark with blood.

'Who confirmed the ID?' she asks.

'Erica Liljestrand's sister, even if she had trouble recognising her, she kept saying there must be some misunderstanding before I realised she was talking about the eyes.'

'What about them?' Nathan says, leaning forward.

'Everyone gets brown eyes because of the haemolysin . . .

regardless of what colour they used to be . . . and that can confuse relatives.'

'What can you tell us about her?' Saga asks impatiently.

Nils lifts up one of the dead woman's arms.

'Well, you can see here that the livor mortis is fairly faint . . . it's really only visible where the body was pressing directly against the floor.'

'So she lost a lot of blood.'

'I'm a long way from finished with my examination, but the cause of death is somewhere between loss of blood and inhalation of blood . . . her neck was cut and her spine broken.'

'The prosecutor's convinced it's a criminal gang making a show of strength.'

'That could be right,' Nils said, nudging his pilot's glasses further up his nose.

'If it wasn't wrong,' Saga says quickly.

'You sound like Joona,' he says.

'No, but I know the prosecutor's wrong, because this is the same killer as the one down in Ystad . . . I've asked them to send you their post-mortem report.'

'It hasn't arrived.'

'Well, it's the same perpetrator,' she says, 'and we need his DNA. The victims put up resistance, it must be possible to find something.'

'Yes, but that sort of analysis takes time,' he says.

Saga's face is pale and tense, her eyes blank from lack of sleep.

'We're aware that you're not finished yet,' Nathan says. 'But we know you think the man is the prime target.'

Nils pulls his mask down under his chin and looks at them both.

'Seeing as the man and woman were basically killed at the same time, it's impossible to tell – from body temperature and decay – which of them died first, but of course that isn't what you're asking.'

Saga lets out a loud groan.

'We want to know if the perpetrator really only wanted to kill one of them,' Nathan says.

'The man, as you know, is in a far worse state, but that doesn't necessarily mean he was the primary target.'

'How do you mean?' Nathan asks, noting that Saga has turned to face the tiled wall.

'For instance, if the man was driven by jealousy and was planning to harm the woman, when he sees a man in her company, he could be seized by a sudden, terrible fury against the man.'

'In which case she'd be the primary target even though he was subjected to a more violent attack,' Nathan says.

'But if we're looking at a show of strength from a criminal organisation . . . Then it's far more likely that the man is the target and the woman merely a witness who needed to be silenced,' Nils goes on.

'Yes,' Saga says, still facing the wall.

'On the other hand, she had been drugged, which puts the spotlight back on her again . . . I've just received the toxicology report, which shows that she had gamma-hydroxybutyrate in her blood.'

Saga turns and looks at Nils.

'GBH . . . ? Was she even conscious when she was murdered?'

'She must have been incredibly tired, but I'm sure she was awake because she was holding on to something so tightly . . . otherwise she would have dropped it.'

'What was she holding?'

Nils goes over to a cabinet and returns to Saga with a plastic bag containing a small matchbook, the sort where you open the lid and pull out a match to light it.

Saga holds the bag up to the light and angles it to avoid reflections.

The little matchbook is a promotional product. The black front is decorated with a headless skeleton holding a skull in each hand.

As if he can't work out which one is his, Saga thinks. Like Hamlet confronted with a new problem.

There are three matches missing.

On the back is nothing but the word Head in white lettering. Perhaps this is the mistake they've been waiting for.

31

Following their meeting with Nils Åhlén it doesn't take Saga and Nathan long to track down the unlicensed club, Head, in basement premises at Ringvägen 151, next to Lilla Blecktornsparken. The borderline-illegal hard rock club is open on Fridays and Saturdays, from midnight until six in the morning.

They've got no way of knowing if the matchbook belonged to the perpetrator, but the victim's friends are pretty adamant that she didn't go to hard rock clubs.

Nathan has gone home to talk to Veronica. He's going to deal with the meeting with the prosecutor tomorrow morning, and has offered Saga a lie-in if she's willing to go to the club.

The plan is for her to go there tonight and talk to the bouncers, find out if there are any membership lists or security cameras.

Saga has been home and had three hours' sleep to prepare for her visit to the club.

She's showered and changed her clothes, and she's due to meet Randy in an hour.

She picks up her phone and calls Pellerina. After a long pause her dad answers instead and says her sister's hands are covered in chocolate cake mix.

'Is everything OK with her?'

'Same as usual,' he replies.

'You sound a bit low.'

She hears him walk out of the kitchen.

'Oh, it's just that I've been trying Internet dating . . . there are apps you can put on your phone,' he tells her.

'What does Pellerina think about that?'

'I haven't mentioned it to her, it all feels a bit embarrassing, actually.'

'Everyone does it these days.'

'I'm wondering what you do when you meet up for real.'

'I don't know,' she replies, and goes over to drink from the glass of water on her bedside table.

'Because I've been emailing a researcher at the Uppsala University Hospital, and I was wondering about asking her out for dinner.'

'Do it,' she replies.

'Would you be able to keep Pellerina company on Monday?' he asks with a smile in his voice.

'This coming Monday?'

'In the evening.'

'I can't, I'm working late,' she replies, and hears her sister shout out in the background that she's washed her hands now.

'It's not that I'm desperate or anything. I thought it might be fun, that's all,' her dad says.

'Can I talk to Pellerina?'

'But it's OK with you if I start dating?'

'Stop it – what do you think?' Saga says impatiently.

'Pellerina Bauer,' her sister says, taking the phone.

'Hi, this is Saga.'

'I've washed my hands now.'

'Are you baking?'

'Sticky chocolate cake.'

'Yummy.'

'Yes,' Pellerina says quietly.

'What's on your mind?'

'Dad's allowed to cry too.'

'Of course, but why do you say that? Has Dad been sad?'

'Yes.'

'Do you know why?'

'He doesn't want to talk about it.'

'I'm sure the cake will make him feel happier.'

'Yes.'

After a break-up, Randy has been renting premises from an old friend who's put his advertising business on hold. A lot of the equipment is still there, or piled up in boxes lining one wall. The studio is in a dirty yellow-brick industrial building in Västberga, filled with a mixture of studios, body-shops, dentists, and gynaecologists, investment companies and tyre specialists.

Saga takes the big industrial lift up to the top floor and walks along the corridor to the old photographic studio.

'Did you see the pizza delivery guy?' Randy asks, giving her a hug.

'No.'

Randy works as a police officer but he's a passionate photographer. He takes pictures of her every time they meet.

Twelve pictures, half frame.

The only furniture Randy brought with him is a double bed. It's standing in the middle of the studio surrounded by camera tripods, professional flashlights, reflectors, and backdrops.

The sky outside the big windows is dark.

They sit down on the bed and eat pizza and drink wine from coffee-cups in the light of a standard lamp.

Randy reaches for a wine-box that's perched on a black box of lighting gear and fills their mugs.

'I can stay till twelve,' she says, feeding him some pizza.

Randy was adopted from China, and is still in contact with his biological mother in Yuxi, in Yunnan province. He grew up on Lidingö and graduated from Police Academy five years ago.

On the walls there are already several large photographs of Saga, so intimate that the small hairs on her body are visible.

Beside the bed are several pencil sketches for his latest idea, which would have her lying inside a large heptagram of cherries, photographed from directly above.

Saga picks up one of the sheets and looks at the sketch.

The lamp shines through the paper. Randy has drawn her face as an oval and the cherries as small dots forming a seven-pointed star.

'It's an old symbol of the creation, the seven days,' he says. 'God created man and woman on the sixth day . . . and He made them both to rule over all the creatures on earth.'

'Equal from the start,' she says.

'We don't have to do this particular picture . . . You can give the whole creation story the finger instead, as a little greeting to Ai Weiwei.'

'No,' she smiles.

'Or we could just eat all the cherries.'

'Stop it, let's do it now, it's a fun idea.'

Randy lays the cherries out on the floor and then starts to rig up the camera, reflectors, and lights.

Saga gets up from the bed, takes off her jeans and hangs them over a spare tripod. She unzips her old Adidas jacket and walks over to a full-length mirror leaning against the wall.

Without realising that Randy has stopped working, she lets her jacket fall to the floor, then pulls off her worn old T-shirt. He can't help staring as she stands there in her underpants applying cherry-red lipstick to her lips and nipples.

There's a bang and she looks up. Randy has dropped the heavy lead of one of the stands on the floor, and mumbles an apology as he picks it up.

'Are you cold?' he asks in a hoarse voice.

'Not yet.'

'The lamps will soon warm things up.'

She screws the lipstick back down, takes off her underpants and follows his instructions as she lies down in the middle of the star so that her nipples are in line with the cherries on the floor.

Last weekend she took his picture as he sat naked with angel's wings on his back and a bottle of calvados in one hand.

Randy has already mounted the camera on a pantograph that he moves along a rail in the ceiling to be able to photograph her from above. He climbs up a stepladder, looks at her, climbs back down and moves the ladder.

'Ready for the first picture?'

'You want me to just lie here?'

'You're so incredibly beautiful, it's insane,' he says, and squeezes the black rubber bulb at the end of the long shutter-release cable.

He climbs up and winds the film on, climbs back down, moves the ladder out of the way and adjusts one of the studio lights and a silver-coloured screen.

'Great,' he mutters. 'This is going to be really great . . .'

Saga raises one knee a little more.

'Good, that's great, stay like that.'

'Are you coming with me to see Dad and Pellerina for the Lucia celebrations?'

'I told you, I'd love to,' Randy replies, still taking pictures.

His gaze is introverted now, he's already seeing the developed pictures, her white skin and luminous beauty inside the pointed star of cherries. Her ribs stand out beneath her skin like rippled sand, and her blonde pubic hair shifts from bronze to glass.

After the final picture Saga gets up and eats some of the left-over cherries from a bowl. She has red marks on her back from lying on the hard surface.

'Are we nearly done with the foreplay?' she asks.

'Maybe,' he replies.

Saga angles the floor lamp away from her and lies down on the side of the bed and waits while he disconnects the last of the cables. She has a couple of hours before it's time to go to the hard rock club. Randy sits down on the bed and pulls his T-shirt off. She rolls onto her back and he kisses her neck and breasts.

She parts her legs slightly and closes her eyes, but she can still feel his eyes burning her skin. Randy kisses her stomach and the inside of her thighs, and she can feel his breathing as he starts to lick her, gently and rhythmically.

She disappears into the soft heat of his mouth.

The hot metal of the lamps clicks around them.

She puts one hand on his stubbled head and hears his breathing get quicker. The pulsating heat spreads through her whole body.

'Slower,' she whispers.

He carries on, light as a feather, and shifts sideways slightly, not noticing that he knocks the floor lamp over with his foot. She sees it fall, and feels him tremble between her legs as it hits the floor and goes out.

'God, that gave me a fright,' he smiles.

'I noticed,' she laughs.

'OK?'

She smiles and nods, helps him take his trousers off, then pushes him down onto his back. She looks at his naked body, his muscles, narrow hips, straight black pubic hair and semi-erect penis.

Saga takes a condom out of the packet on top of his iPad next to the bed, opens the wrapper and meets his eye. She takes him gently in her mouth until he gets hard, then holds his erection with one hand and rolls the condom on.

She leans over him, opens her mouth and feels the taut, plasticky rubber against her lips and tongue.

'Come here,' he whispers.

She sits astride him and lets him slide all the way into her, squeezes him tight and starts to move her hips.

She leans forward, resting her hands on his chest, and slides back repeatedly, sighing. He starts to breathe faster, holding her backside with both hands, then throws his head back and ejaculates.

Saga didn't have time to reach an orgasm, wasn't even close, it all happened too fast, but she's learned that that's how he works, they'll carry on again shortly, and she'll have longer the second and third times.

Randy pulls the condom off and ties a knot in it. They lie beside each other without speaking. His breathing is still fast. After a short while he leans over her and starts to suck gently at one of her nipples.

Saga is stroking his damp neck when her phone rings from the pile of clothes on the floor. She gets to her feet, finds her jacket and pulls out her phone.

'Bauer,' she answers.

'I know it's late, but in my defence I'm only remembering what you said about getting in touch if we had the smallest detail that could help piece together a picture of the perpetrator,' Senior Prosecutor Arne Rosander says.

'Absolutely,' Saga says very professionally.

She takes a few more steps away from the bed. Her whole

body is still tingling. Through the window she sees that part of the building on the other side of the street is being redecorated, they've left the lights on and there's a stepladder in the middle of the floor.

'It might be nothing,' Arne Rosander goes on. 'But I've spoken to our eyewitness specialist . . . and today she interviewed another woman who saw the perpetrator in the street outside the bar . . . This woman wasn't able to give any sort of description earlier – that's the way it is sometimes – but last night she had a dream about him.'

'I'm listening.'

Saga turns back to look at the studio again. Randy is lying naked on the bed, looking over at her with shining eyes.

'A large man with a thick neck, cropped hair and a bloody face . . . and listen to this, this is pretty interesting – he was wearing pearl earrings.'

'Did she remember him wearing them in real life?'

'No, that was in the dream, but the hair and blood match what the other witnesses said.'

Saga thanks him for calling, then goes back to Randy. She settles down on his arm and feels his other hand make its way between her legs.

Saga stops a short distance away from the entrance to the club. It's got colder again. Crisp, tiny snowflakes are drifting in the glow of the bare light-bulb that illuminates the unassuming door to the club.

A tall bouncer in a protective vest and with his blond hair pulled back in a ponytail is watching some black-clad young men who are smoking behind the rubbish bins. The bouncer's bare neck is blue-grey with tattoos.

Large nylon sacks of builders' rubble have been piled up along the edge of the pavement.

It's half past four in the morning, but music is still thudding out onto the street from the basement.

Saga fell asleep after having sex with Randy a second time, and didn't wake up until quarter to four. Before she set out she locked her pistol and police ID in his gun-cabinet. She knows she'd never get permission from her boss to visit an illegal club in her capacity as a Security Police agent. There was more than enough fuss about her trip to Chicago in pursuit of the Rabbit Hunter.

Saga approaches the entrance as an unlicensed cab pulls up in front of her. Three youths in long black coats get out and exchange a few words with the bouncer on the door before going inside and vanishing down some steps.

The bouncer steps aside so he's not blocking the light as Saga walks up to him.

'Are you sure you haven't come to the wrong place, princess?' he asks, his face breaking into a network of wrinkles as he smiles.

'Yes.'

'Your decision,' he says, and opens the door. The music instantly gets louder.

'Do you have security cameras?' she asks.

'No, why do you . . . ?'

'Nowhere inside?'

'We don't have a licence for that.'

Saga can't help smiling at the fact that an illegal club is worried about licences. She goes down a steep flight of concrete steps as the bouncer closes the door behind her.

She can hear some sort of roaring over the thud of the bass.

At the foot of the stairs is a security check before you get inside the actual club. Ahead of Saga, the three youths sign their names on a membership list, then pay a fee and walk through a metal detector.

The music is making the walls shake, and the framed pictures of famous visitors rattle against the concrete.

The security guard is a large woman with a double chin, a shaved head, round glasses and black leather trousers.

The boys laugh as she pats them down.

As she signs herself in and pays, Saga looks at the list, which consists solely of first names and email addresses. She walks through the detector, wondering if the list only exists in case there's a raid – so that they can use the loophole in the law about alcohol and private gatherings – then gets thrown away after the club closes.

A T-shirt with the text Tribe 8 is stretched across the security guard's chest. Her thick, pale arms are covered with beautiful garland tattoos.

The three boys in the long coats are yelling at each other over the music, and one of them pushes his way towards the toilets.

Saga walks over and stands with her arms outstretched, and is quickly patted down by the guard.

'I signed the list, but . . .'

'What?' the guard says.

'I signed the list,' Saga says, louder. 'But I don't know if I'm on the membership database.'

The guard shrugs her shoulder and gestures to her to move. More people are on their way down the stairs.

'Keep moving.'

'Is there a membership database that . . . ?'

The guard's face is shiny with sweat, her eyes beady behind her round glasses.

'What the fuck are you talking about?' she asks.

Saga looks away and moves on into the cloakroom. She looks around. The door to the women's toilet opens and a young woman with dark lipstick emerges.

Saga catches a glimpse of the crowd in front of the mirrors before the door closes again. She steps over the legs of a man who's sitting on the floor with a phone pressed to his ear, and makes her way into the main part of the club.

She passes through two heavy doors with thick rubber fringes along the bottom, and has to stop for a moment in the sudden darkness.

The level of noise is extraordinary.

A band is playing on stage, and the rapid thud of the bass vibrates through her body. The crowd is pressing forward, jumping and holding their hands in the air.

The room is packed.

It's all but impossible to move in any direction.

A wave passing through the throng forces her sideways and she's pushed up against the wall, then another wave leaves her stumbling back into the sudden void.

The audience is pushing and shoving, dancing, singing along.

There are banks of speakers and other equipment mounted on the ceiling. Smoke streams through rotating beams of light.

There's no way any sort of conversation is possible here. Until she manages to find one of the organisers, there's nothing for her to do except look for a thickset man in his fifties.

If he is here, it shouldn't be hard to spot him, because most of the clientele are young men with long hair and black clothes.

Saga apologises and tries to make her way along the inner wall, as far away from the chaos on stage as possible.

The bass and double-pedal bass-drum are keeping up a frenetic pace, and the guitar is playing rapid, repetitive power chords.

The singer is wearing black jeans and a T-shirt with the name Entombed emblazoned on it in ornate lettering.

A roar is coming from the speakers, followed by guttural growling, a sort of deep, moaning throat-song.

The audience moves backwards, pressing Saga against the wall again. She struggles to hold them off, pushing the bodies away with both arms.

As the wave changes direction she feels a hand between her legs. She turns, but can't work out who grabbed her, it's too dark and everyone is already tumbling forward again.

A man with a beard and a shiny head is dancing and kicking the air. He loses his balance, falls to the floor, and rolls several metres.

Saga tries to make her way to the bar. She shoves forward along the wall.

The audience is jumping about and pressing against the edge of the stage, yelling with cracked voices and waving their hands in the air.

The music is hammering against Saga's chest and neck.

A woman in a short back vinyl skirt spills beer as she tries to drink from a plastic cup. A man with greasy hair is standing behind her, squeezing her breasts. She makes a feeble attempt to resist, but goes on drinking.

Saga pushes forward, shoving someone who's blocking her path out of the way, and ignores the shove in the shoulder she gets in return as she pushes through the men.

She reaches a raised mixing desk with scratched plexiglass screens and cables taped to the floor.

The air is hot, laden with the smell of sweat, beer, and dry-ice.

The lights from the stage sweep across the crowd.

Over by the bar Saga catches a glimpse of the silhouette of a man who's almost thirty centimetres taller than everyone around him.

She's almost certain his head is shaved.

Saga tries to weave round the mixing desk but gets pushed back by the crowd.

The music slows down and seems to hang in the air. The bass drum has fallen silent and the cymbals tinkle gently.

The singer pulls his T-shirt down over his stomach, stands

right on the edge of the stage, raises his right arm, and then makes a slow chopping motion in front of him.

The audience parts on either side of the line, moving out of the way to free up a path down the middle.

There's some rubbish, empty plastic cups, and a denim jacket on the floor.

The two halves of the audience stand facing each other, panting, expectant.

Suddenly the music gets ridiculously fast again and the men on both sides of the empty space rush towards each other, screaming as they collide and fall. One blond boy crashes to the floor and several other men stumble over him. Another staggers away with his hand over his mouth and blood streaming between his fingers.

The music is thudding in her ears as stroboscopic light sweeps the stage.

Saga pushes past the booth and gets elbowed in the cheek by a man trying to climb onto his friend's shoulders.

Sweat is running down her back when she finally reaches the throng around the bar. She scans the crowd for the thickset man. People are leaning over the bar, passing large plastic cups of beer behind them.

One young man with long, wavy hair hanging down his cheeks looks Saga in the eye and says something inaudible with a crooked smile.

The singer divides the crowd again.

Saga makes her way towards a man with a tattooed head who's standing between the bar and the sea of people. She forces her way through to him and asks if he's seen an older man with a shaved head. She has to shout into his ear for him to hear her. He looks at her drunkenly, says something, then staggers away.

Only then does she realise that he asked her if he looked like the sort of person who likes the police.

The music is rumbling slowly as a crash of thunder approaches.

Hazy lights sweep across the crowd and Saga catches sight of the tall man with the shaved head. He's standing in an alcove next to the door to the staff area. The light flickers past and then everything goes dark again.

The music explodes and the screams from the stage drown out everything else as the two halves of the audience rush towards each other again.

They collide and fall.

One girl is dragged across the floor.

Two boys start kicking and fighting until they're pulled apart.

Saga manages to push her way along the bar to the alcove. The tall man can't be any older than twenty. He's leaning against the wall with his thin, tattooed arms hanging by his sides.

She keeps going and checks the next alcove, looking at all the faces in the dim light.

The crowd is jumping about and shoving.

The guitars are playing rapid chromatic chord sequences. The singer is clutching the microphone with both hands and growling.

On a silver-painted podium to one side of the stage a young woman is dancing in her underwear beside a vertical metal pole, circling it, hooking one leg around it and spinning round as she slides down it.

Saga sees the man with the tattooed head pushing his way through the crowd towards the entrance.

She sets off after him, but someone shoves her in the back and she stumbles into a man who helps her regain her balance.

33

Saga tries not to let the man with the tattooed head out of her sight.

The crowd pushes backwards and she's swept up in the movement, and almost falls as beer splashes her face. She collides with the mixing booth, hitting her head against the plexiglass.

She presses on along the back wall, treading on a stray trainer and fending off a man who's flailing wildly about him before she finally reaches the door and emerges into the cloakroom.

Cooler air is streaming in from the entrance, and although the music is thudding through the walls, it's still much quieter there.

People are coming back down the stairs after going outside to smoke. They show their stamps to the guard.

There's a pile of matchbooks with skeletons in a cigarette machine.

The man with the tattooed head disappears into the men's toilet with his phone pressed to his ear.

Saga follows him, and is hit by an intense stench of urine and toilet-cleaner. The entire floor is awash, and covered with wet paper towels, plastic cups and discarded chewing tobacco.

She sees drunken young men lined up at the urinals. One of them is leaning against the wall with one hand as he aims his penis with the other. His urine swirls around the small portions of chewing tobacco in the urinal, hits the edge and splashes onto the wall and floor.

The man with the tattooed head emerges from one of the cubicles. The toilet seat is lying on the wet floor beside the toilet.

'I didn't hear what you said in answer to my question,' Saga says, standing in front of him.

'What?' he mutters, looking her in the eye.

'I'm looking for a man in his fifties who—'

'She just wants a fuck,' another man says.

'I don't know what you're talking about,' the man with the tattooed head says.

'I think you do.'

'Leave me the fuck alone,' he says, and shoves her in the chest.

She follows him out into the cloakroom, to the sound of applause and wolf-whistles behind her.

This is hopeless, she thinks, standing still. The matchbook didn't necessarily belong to the murderer, and even if it did, that doesn't have to mean he comes here regularly.

But at the same time, it's all they've got to go on for the time being.

A possible connection between the murderer and a hard rock club.

Hoping to catch a glimpse of him in the crowd is pointless.

But the club is about to close, so it will be easier to figure out who works here.

Someone must know something.

Saga returns to the main room. The audience is leaping about, fists raised in front of the stage where the guitarist is playing fast with both hands on the neck of his instrument.

The music switches to a fanfare-like rhythm, the chord changes become heavier, slower.

The performance climaxes with a single howl.

It's six in the morning.

The band leave the stage and roadies immediately move in to dismantle their kit.

The lights go up as the music is still ringing in everyone's ears.

Saga tries to see everyone's faces as they stream out. Security staff go round waking men who have fallen asleep by the walls, helping the drunkest of them to walk.

The floor empties, revealing a few discarded items of clothing among the plastic cups and other rubbish.

The stage, its black paint peeling off, is already deserted.

A few drunken youths are laughing and jeering as they make their way up the steps towards the street.

A red cabinet containing fire-extinguishers has come away from the wall and is standing on the floor.

Saga moves through the thinning stream of people and approaches the staff who are still standing behind the bar. The pole-dancer is now wearing a dressing-gown, and the sound engineer with grey stubble is talking to the female security guard with round glasses.

The bartender is pouring them beer and Coke.

Saga goes up to them and sits down on one of the fixed barstools, then turns to the man behind the bar.

'I'd like to be put on the mailing list,' she says.

'We haven't got one,' he says abruptly as he wipes the bar.

'How do you get information to your members . . . through Facebook, or—'

'No, not like that,' he interrupts, looking at her.

'Why do you ask so many fucking questions?' the security guard asks.

'I'm trying to find someone who comes here,' Saga says, loudly enough for them all to hear.

'And who are you?' the bartender says, scratching his ear.

'A friend.'

'Whose friend?' he asks, tapping the bar.

'We're closing now,' the security guard says.

'I'm looking for a man in his fifties, he's been here,' Saga goes on. 'He's thickset, has a thick neck, cropped hair.'

'A hell of a lot of different people come here,' the bartender replies.

'People who aren't young guys in black clothes?' Saga asks.

'He was trying to help,' the security guard said sharply.

'I mean that the person I'm trying to find ought to stand out,' Saga explains.

'Fifty years old, shaved head, thick neck,' the bartender says, and points to a photograph behind him.

It's a picture of the singer, Udo Dirkschneider, when he was visiting the club. A plump man with cropped blond hair, a leather jacket and a plastic glass of beer in one hand.

'The man I'm looking for sometimes gets extremely angry and breaks things,' Saga says.

The bartender shrugs his shoulders and the security guard looks at the time on her phone. A roadie who's been gathering cables from the stage comes over to the bar to get a glass of water.

'What's going on?' he asks, looking at Saga.

'How often is there trouble here?' she asks.

'You mean the audience . . . that's not trouble, that's just the mosh-pit. I swear, it's one hell of a buzz,' he says, empties his glass and starts walking towards the door.

'We never have trouble here,' the security guard says.

'There's a possibility that he wears pearl earrings,' Saga says, and from the corner of her eye sees the dancer turn away.

'You'll have to look for Daddy somewhere else,' the bartender says, dragging a beer-barrel out of the way.

The guard laughs and repeats what he said about Daddy. Saga watches as the dancer sets off towards the staffroom.

There was something about her face as she turned away.

As if she'd been caught out.

Saga starts to follow her, and notices that the woman speeds up before she reaches the door and presses the handle.

'Wait a moment,' Saga says sternly.

The dancer disappears into the staffroom. Saga runs the last steps and catches the door before it closes.

'You can't go in there,' the guard calls after her.

'I know,' Saga says almost silently as she goes in.

The staffroom is a windowless space with a row of metal lockers, a battered sofa and armchairs around a badly scratched table, and a small kitchen corner.

The dancer hurries into the toilet and locks the door. The security guard comes into the staffroom as Saga knocks on the toilet door.

'Come out here, I need to talk to you,' Saga says, banging on the door.

'You can't be in here,' the guard says behind her.

'I know,' Saga replies. 'But I think she knows something about the man I'm looking for.'

'Come with me and we can talk about it.'

'In a moment,' Saga says, and knocks on the door again.

'You're starting to cause trouble for me now,' the guard goes on. 'I need to do my job, the club's closed and I can't let you be in here.'

'I hear what you're saying, but I need to speak to —'

'Are you slow on the uptake, or what?' the guard interrupts.

Saga brushes the hair from her face and glances at her.

'This is important,' she says. 'You've probably noticed that, and I'd be really grateful if you could give me ten minutes.'

She turns back towards the toilet door, and when the guard puts one hand on her arm she pulls loose and looks her in the eye.

'Don't touch me,' Saga says coolly.

'I've tried to be nice and tell you that you have to leave – but what the hell am I supposed to do if you won't listen?'

'Open up!' Saga says, banging on the door.

The guard grabs hold of her upper arm again. Saga turns and shoves her in the chest, making her take a step back to keep her balance.

The guard pulls a telescopic baton from her belt and opens it up to its full length.

'I can see I'm going to have to deal with you and —'

'Shut up,' Saga interrupts. 'It's late and I'm starting to get really fucking tired, but if you don't stay out of the way —'

Saga sees the baton coming from the side and moves nimbly out of the way.

She hasn't fought competitively for several years, but she still trains at the boxing club four days a week.

The guard moves after Saga and tries to hit her on the shoulder. The baton swings down at her with full force.

Saga slides out of the way and puts her elbow in the way of the guard's lower arm. The woman groans and the baton spins through the air and hits one of the metal lockers.

The guard moves like a kick-boxer and throws a left hook.

Instead of rolling past the punch, Saga tilts her head back, beyond the guard's reach, to lure her into trying even harder next time.

A sort of Ali-shuffle.

The guard takes a step forward and swings again.

Saga jabs with her left hand to gauge the precise distance and moves simultaneously to one side, out of her opponent's central line.

'A little boxer,' the guard laughs, trying to catch her.

Saga lands a perfect right hook to her face. The woman's glasses go flying in a spray of sweat.

The guard looks confused, one leg is wobbling and she staggers sideways from the blow.

Saga meets her unbalanced movements with a low left hook to her ribs.

The guard whimpers, sinks down onto one knee and reaches out for a box of toilet cleaner with one hand, gasping as blood seeps from her lip.

Saga is already on her again, with a right cross from above, aimed right at the bridge of her nose.

It's an extremely hard punch.

The guard's head flies back as if her neck muscles had stopped working. Her body follows and she tumbles backwards helplessly, dragging a mop and bucket down with her.

Without giving the guard another look, Saga goes back to the toilet door, knocks on it and shouts at the dancer to open up.

'Fuck, fuck, fuck,' the guard groans, trying to sit up as blood streams from her nose.

'Stay there,' Saga says, then kicks at the toilet door.

There's a crash as the lock shatters and its metal components clatter to the floor.

'Don't hit me,' the dancer pleads, sinking down beside the sink.

'I only want to talk,' Saga says, pulling her out from the toilet.

34

It's starting to get light as Saga puts two cups of coffee down on the table. McDonald's on Götgatan has just opened for the day. Before they left the club, Saga took the dancer's ID out of her purse, photographed it and confirmed her address and phone number.

Her name is Anna Sjölin, she's twenty-two years old and lives in Vårby.

Now she's wearing jeans and a red padded jacket. Her gloves and knitted hat are on the table in front of her, and her long brown hair is gathered into a knot.

'Drink some coffee,' Saga says, sitting down opposite her.

Anna nods and puts both hands round the cup, as if she were trying to warm them up. Her thin face is pale as she hesitantly answers Saga's questions.

'How long have you worked at the club?'

'About a year,' Anna says, tasting the coffee.

Saga massages the sore knuckles of her right hand as she observes the young woman's impassive face and slow movements.

'Pole-dancing is a sport,' Anna says without looking up.

'I know,' Saga says.

'Not like this, though. I just do simple things so I don't get too tired, because I have to dance all night.'

'What do you do between shifts?'

Anna rubs her nose and looks at Saga. She has dark rings

under her eyes from lack of sleep, and there are fine lines running across her forehead.

'Can you tell me why we're sitting here?' she asks, pushing the mug away.

'I work for the Security Police.'

'The Security Police,' she smiles. 'Can I see some ID?'

'No,' Saga says.

'How am I supposed to—'

'Tell me about the man with the pearl earrings,' Saga interrupts.

Anna lowers her gaze and her eyelashes flutter.

'What's he done?' she asks.

'I can't talk about that.'

Anna looks out of the window just as the streetlights go out along the pavement. A homeless woman with an overloaded shopping trolley stops outside the window and stares at them.

'You've seen a thickset man with pearl earrings at the club,' Saga says once more, to get Anna to go on.

'Yes.'

'Is he there a lot?'

'I've seen him maybe five times.'

'What does he do?'

'He keeps to himself, he doesn't join in, doesn't dance . . . he stays a few hours, drinking vodka shots and eating chilli nuts.'

She pulls the coffee towards her again, then reaches for the sugar before changing her mind.

'Have you ever talked to him?' Saga asks.

'Once, when some guys tipped beer over him . . . He looks a bit . . . special, like a big kid . . . with those earrings and, oh . . . I don't know . . .'

She falls silent again with a deep furrow between her eyebrows. Saga tries to think of a way to get Anna to tell her more, give her something that will help the investigation along.

'Did he get angry when they tipped beer on him?'

'No, he just tried to explain the pearls. They weren't listening . . . but I heard what he said . . . They're a tribute to his sister who died when she was thirteen, they were her earrings, and he said he didn't care if people laughed . . . he's happy to take whatever abuse he gets for them.'

179

'What's his name?'

'He calls himself the Beaver,' Anna says with a tired smile. 'He doesn't exactly make things easy for himself.'

She drinks some coffee and wipes her lips with her hand.

'So you've talked to him?' Saga prompts.

Anna shrugs her shoulders.

'A bit.'

'About what?'

'All sorts,' she says, and seems to drift off in thought for a few seconds. 'I'm not saying I believe it, but he told me he had a sixth sense, that he always knows who's going to die first when he enters a room.'

'How do you mean?' Saga asks.

'He said it like it was obvious, and pointed at Jamal, a guy who . . . well, he wasn't to know that I knew him . . . three days later I heard that Jamal was dead, a blood vessel burst in his brain, he was born with it, apparently . . . No one knew about it, not even Jamal.'

Anna puts the mug down, picks up her hat and gloves and gets to her feet.

'We're almost done,' Saga says.

Anna sits down again.

'Do you know what the Beaver's real name is?'

'No.'

'Have you got his contact details, anything concrete?'

'No.'

'Have you ever seen him with anyone else?'

'No.'

'Did he hit on you?'

'He spoke about starting a club of his own, and asked if I'd be interested in changing jobs.'

'What did you say?'

'That I'd think about it.'

'Where does he live?'

Anna sighed and leaned back.

'He seemed a bit rootless, didn't have a fixed address, kept moving round all the time, at least that's how I understood it.'

'Did he mention any address at all? Did he say where he

was living at the moment? Did he mention any friends, anything?'

'No.'

Anna stifles a yawn with her knuckles.

'OK, let's go through the whole conversation again, bit by bit,' Saga says. 'He must have said something . . . something that would help me find him.'

'Look, I need to get some sleep, I work at Filippa Krister during the week. He never said where he lived.'

'How were you going to let him know about the job?'

'I don't know, it was too soon for that, he hasn't even got a club,' she replies.

'So it was all talk?'

'I honestly don't know, he said he was an entrepreneur, a renaissance man . . . he said loads of weird stuff, I didn't understand all of it, he talked about buying a deserted research centre in Bulgaria, some state-run laboratory that was abandoned after the fall of communism, but I don't really remember.'

'Is he from Bulgaria?'

'I don't think so, he hasn't got an accent . . . Sorry, I'm too tired to think straight,' she whispers.

'A psychologist who specialises in interviewing eyewitnesses will be getting in touch with you tomorrow, she'll help you to remember better,' Saga says, getting to her feet.

35

It's quarter past eight on Sunday evening and Saga and Nathan Pollock are reluctantly calling an end to the day's work.

On one wall of the room is a map of Europe, along with larger-scale maps of the locations where the victims were found. On the other are a series of printouts from the Belarusian security-camera footage. The recording was made in darkness and the picture quality is poor, but the man who calls himself the Beaver is still visible. His height, build, those big, sloping shoulders are all clearly evident. When seen from certain angles, a little of his thick neck, jawline, and the shape of his head stand out against the background.

The glare of the desk lamp catches on the scratched lenses of Nathan's reading glasses next to his computer, and the reflection quivers on the ceiling as he knocks the edge of the table when he stands up.

He jerks his head to get his grey ponytail to hang down his back.

The witnesses outside the Pilgrim Bar described an aggressive man who resembles the man in the security-camera footage from Belarus.

The Swedish police have searched the home of the murdered bartender and found videos of drugged women being raped. He had twice been cleared of charges of rape in court in Stockholm.

The dancer, Anna Sjölin, has told them about her conversation with a man who fits the description of the perpetrator.

The Beaver wears pearl earrings, sees himself as an entrepreneur, and wants to buy an old laboratory complex in Bulgaria.

For some reason he seems to think he has special powers. It sounds like he has a fairly inflated view of himself, a sense of superiority, which would fit with a murderer who sees himself as a superhero charged with cleansing society from criminals the justice system has failed to punish sufficiently.

Two hours ago, when Saga spoke to specialist interviewer Jeanette Fleming, the psychologist was sitting at Anna's kitchen table out in Vårby. It was too early to discuss the conversation with the Beaver, but Jeanette said that they were weaving Anna's memories into an increasingly fine-meshed net.

Nathan starts to pack his briefcase and explains that he has to get home to Veronica to explain how the courts deal with cases of divorce. A few strands of grey hair from his ponytail have caught on his jacket.

'You ought to sign the papers,' Saga says.

'I'm not in any hurry.'

Saga has also decided to go home; she's thinking of going for a ten-kilometre run and then calling Randy. She ought to talk to her dad as well, but she doesn't feel up to that. The last time they spoke he tried to ask for advice on how to behave with an internet date, as if she'd ever tried online dating. The whole conversation left her feeling impatient, it was as if her dad was pretending everything was fine, that they had a relaxed, adult relationship.

Saga goes over to the best picture they have of the Beaver's face. Grease from the Blu Tack has stained the corners of the printout.

The camera caught him seconds before he kicked and smashed an outdoor lamp in the shape of a flame.

The glow from it lights up his backwards-tilted face from below.

In spite of the poor resolution, it's possible to make out his round cheeks, his forehead, and the sparkle of what could be a pearl earring.

'Now we know that the Beaver is capable of sitting down and

holding a conversation,' she says. 'He can even be provoked without getting angry . . . but at the same time we've seen the sort of rage he's capable of.'

'What else do we know?' Nathan asks quietly.

Saga meets his weary gaze.

'He calls himself the Beaver, he's a thickset man in his fifties, has cropped hair, wears earrings, two pearls that belonged to his dead sister,' Saga says.

'He claims to have a sixth sense, and is cleansing Europe,' Nathan says.

'He speaks Swedish without an accent, probably has no fixed address, says he's going to start a club and buy an old research centre in Bulgaria . . . He makes out he's an entrepreneur, but that could be all talk . . . I haven't been able to find any old laboratories that are for sale.'

Silence fills the room again. The whole building is quiet, there aren't many people in the headquarters of the National Operational Unit at this time on a Sunday evening.

The windows of Nathan's office are streaked with dirt. The telecommunications mast and the spire of the old police head-quarters stand out against the dark sky. In the centre of one of the windows is the imprint of a forehead. Fragments of small, pale brown leaves lie strewn on the windowsill around a potted plant.

'How long has Jeanette been talking to the dancer now?' Nathan asks, folding a napkin and tossing it in the bin.

'I don't want to interrupt them, Jeanette will call when she's finished.'

They leave the room and walk down the corridor, leave their mugs in the kitchen and switch the lights out behind them. On the way to the lift they pass Joona Linna's empty room.

'We need to find some way to let Joona know it isn't Jurek who's trying to clean up society,' Nathan says.

36

The streets are almost deserted when Saga goes home. A few snowflakes are swirling around the streetlamps and illuminated advertisements. At first the cold wind in her face bothers her, but it becomes slightly numbing and leaves her feeling an odd inner warmth. She's already started to get used to her dad's motorbike, and has come to appreciate its low centre of gravity in the urban traffic.

It occurs to Saga that Joona is bound to get in touch at some point to ask about the investigation. Otherwise he'd end up in hiding forever, and would never know that they've identified a completely new serial killer.

She turns into Tavastgatan, stops, and covers the bike with its tarpaulin.

The thin, silvery-grey material rustles in the evening wind.

Up in her apartment Saga locks her pistol in the gun-cabinet, leafs through the post, drinks some orange juice straight from the carton and changes into her running clothes.

Just as she's putting on her trainers in the hall her mobile rings. She hunts through her bag on the floor, finds her phone, sees that it's Pellerina and answers.

'What are you doing?' her half-sister asks, almost too quietly to hear.

'I'm going to get some exercise, you know, go out for a run.'

'OK,' Pellerina says, and her breathing echoes down the line.

'Why aren't you asleep? It's quite late,' Saga says tentatively.

'It's really dark,' she whispers.

'Turn on your heart light.'

'You mustn't forget to turn it off,' her sister replies.

'I promise, you're allowed to turn it on,' Saga says. 'Can you go and see Dad and give him the phone?'

'No.'

'Why don't you want to go and see Dad?' she asks.

'I can't.'

'Is he downstairs in the kitchen?'

'He's not home.'

'Are you on your own?'

'Maybe.'

'Tell me what's happened . . . Your painting class finished at eight o'clock and then you went home with Miriam's mum as usual, and Dad usually has your tea ready.'

'He wasn't home,' her sister replies. 'I think he's cross with me.'

'Maybe Dad had to go to the hospital – you know, because he helps people who have problems with their hearts.'

Saga can hear her sister's breathing.

'I heard giggling outside,' Pellerina whispers, almost inaudibly. 'I thought it was the clown girls.'

'They're not real – you know that, don't you?'

Saga can't help thinking that it might have been the girls from school who sent the chain email.

'Have you turned the lights on?' she asks.

'No.'

Suddenly Saga is worried that the girls might get inside the house and harm Pellerina for real, hold her down and pick out her eyes with a screwdriver. She knows it's just her imagination running riot, but at the same time all children need to test their boundaries, and it's easy for that to get out of hand, it happens everywhere.

'Put the lights on now.'

'OK.'

'I'll be with you as soon as I can – how does that sound?' Saga says.

They hang up and Saga calls her dad as she pulls her white leathers over her running clothes. There's no answer, so she tries again as she hurries downstairs. She leaves a voicemail telling him to call her as soon as he can.

She looks up the number of the Thoracic Intensive Care Unit at the Karolinska Hospital, but Lars-Erik Bauer isn't working tonight.

Saga removes the tarpaulin, puts her helmet on and starts the motorbike.

While she's riding to Gamla Enskede she thinks through the last conversation she had with her dad. She can't imagine how he could have misunderstood her. He wanted to invite the researcher he'd met on line out to dinner, and asked if she could babysit.

Maybe she misunderstood which day he meant. Perhaps she was distracted and said yes without being aware of it.

There are white-windowed cars parked in front of all the houses, and the lawns are sparkling with frost.

Saga stops and opens the wrought-iron gate, rides the heavy motorbike into the drive, switches off the engine, props it up, then goes and closes the gate behind her.

She takes her helmet off and looks up at the house.

All the windows are dark.

The light from a streetlamp further down the road reaches into the garden. The bare branches of the apple tree cast a network of shadows over the brickwork.

Pellerina's pink bicycle, with tassels on its handlebars, is lying on the grass with flat tyres.

Saga walks towards the house with the faint light behind her. She sees her shadow get paler and longer.

She looks along the curved driveway down to the garage in the basement. There's a plastic football lying in front of the door.

She stops at the front door and listens. She can hear a faint thudding sound, like someone running on a treadmill.

She pushes the door handle down and pulls.

The front door is unlocked.

The thudding sound stops the moment she opens the door.

She looks into the dark hall.

Complete silence.

The rug is lying slightly crooked.

Saga puts her helmet on the stool, takes off her boots and walks in. The worn parquet floor is ice-cold under her feet. She turns the main light on and a yellow glow spreads across the walls.

'Hello? Pellerina?' Saga calls.

The house is so cold that her breath clouds in front of her mouth. She passes the passageway and door leading to the basement and sees her dad's coat hanging over the back of a chair in the kitchen.

'Dad?'

Saga switches the kitchen light on and sees that the door to the back garden is wide open.

She walks over to it and calls to Pellerina.

There are some dull noises from the boiler down in the basement, then silence again.

Saga looks at the damp glass of the greenhouse, which is reflecting the light from the kitchen. She sees herself standing in the doorway in the form of a black silhouette.

The bare bushes against the neighbour's fence are moving in the wind. The swing is creaking gently on its frame.

Saga gazes out into the garden, at the darkness between the trees, then closes the door.

The chain email said that the clown girls come at night, grab hold of you, then paint a laughing mouth on your face to make you look happy when they prick out your eyes.

She goes back to the passageway and stops at the door to the basement. Pellerina never goes down there. All that's there is the boiler, the washing machine and mangle, and a garage full of garden tools and furniture.

But Pellerina is scared of the boiler, because on really cold nights the banging noise it makes can be heard throughout the house.

Saga walks over to the staircase and sees that someone has gone up it with dirty shoes.

'Pellerina?' she calls upstairs.

Saga creeps up the stairs, and when her head reaches the level of the landing she stops and looks along the thick floorboards.

She sees the grain of the wood, the frayed edges of the rugs, the crack under the door to the bathroom.

She can hear a very faint voice, but can't tell where it's coming from. It sounds like monotonous singing.

Saga turns back quickly and looks downstairs, puts a hand on one of the steps, kneels down and checks that the door to the basement is closed.

She carries on up the stairs, walks through the darkness to Pellerina's room, listens, then carefully opens the door.

In the gloom she can make out the grey plastic case of the ECG-machine, a pair of pink ballet shoes and the closed wardrobe door.

Saga goes in and sees that the bed has been used but is now empty. She hears a creaking sound from the attic. The loose cable of the satellite dish is swaying outside the window.

'Pellerina,' Saga says quietly.

She switches on the lamp with the heart-shaped shade and the pink glow spreads across the wall behind the chest of drawers, up to the ceiling.

Saga looks under the bed, and sees some sweet wrappers, a dusty extension lead and a plastic skeleton with red eyes.

She gets to her feet and goes over to the wardrobe, and puts her hand on the bronze-coloured handle.

'Pellerina, it's only me,' she says, opens the door.

The hinges creak and Saga catches a glimpse of the clothes hanging inside as a large shape sweeps towards her. She throws her head back and her hand reaches automatically for her pistol as the huge teddy bear lands on the floor and sits there on its backside in front of her.

'I very nearly did you a lot of damage,' Saga says.

She closes the wardrobe and hears the singing again. The voice is very weak, almost impossible to hear. She turns round slowly, listens and thinks that it seems to be coming from the guest bedroom.

Saga walks out of the room, past the dark staircase, then nudges open the door of the room where she usually sleeps. Someone's pulled the bedclothes onto the floor and is sitting under them on the other side of the bed.

'Not here, not here, not here,' Pellerina is chanting in a high voice.

'Pellerina?'

'Not here, not here . . .'

When Saga pulls the covers back her sister lets out a shriek of fear. Her hands are clamped over her ears and she looks terrified.

'It's me,' Saga says, taking her into her arms.

Her sister's heart is beating fast and her small body is sweaty.

'It's only me, don't worry, it's only me.'

Pellerina hugs her tightly and whispers her name over and over again.

'Saga, Saga, Saga, Saga . . .'

37

They sit on the bed with their arms wrapped tightly round each other until Pellerina has calmed down, before going downstairs to the kitchen. Her sister stays close to Saga the whole time as she switches on every lamp they pass.

Saga opens the fridge and finds some leftovers from the previous day's meal, beef stew and boiled potatoes.

'You'll have to go to bed as soon as we've finished eating,' Saga says, taking out a carton of cream.

'Daddy was cross and didn't make any tea,' Pellerina whispers.

'Why do you keep saying he was cross?'

'I sent a picture of my first painting.'

'From painting class?'

'Yes, and he phoned and said it was a really lovely dog, and that he'd pin it up in the kitchen, but when I told him it was a horse he got cross and hung up.'

'What? What did he say?' she asks.

Pellerina nudges her glasses further up her nose.

'He just hung up,' she says.

'There must have been a problem, sometimes the battery runs out, I promise, he wasn't cross,' Saga smiles as she starts to heat the food up on the stove.

'Why doesn't he want to come home, then?'

'That might be my fault, I'd forgotten that Dad was going to meet a girl.'

'Has Daddy got a date?' Pellerina smiles.

'You know I'm seeing Randy, don't you?'

'He's really cute.'

'Yes, he is.'

As the food warms through Saga makes a sauce. She dissolves a stock cube in cream, then adds some pepper and a teaspoon of soy sauce.

'So what's Daddy's girlfriend called?' Pellerina asks.

'I don't remember – Annabella, maybe?' Saga says, picking a name at random.

'Annabella,' her sister laughs.

'With big brown eyes, dark hair and bright red lipstick.'

'And a sparkly gold dress!'

'Exactly.'

Saga gets out two plates and glasses, takes out the lingonberry jam, some sheets of kitchen roll and a jug of water.

'He's probably put his phone on silent so he can kiss Annabella,' she goes on.

Pellerina laughs out loud. The colour's come back to her face now. They sit down and Saga makes sure Pellerina takes her heart medication before they start to eat.

'Didn't Dad tell you about his date?' she asks after a while.

'No,' Pellerina says, and takes a sip of water.

'But he told you I'd be coming tonight?'

'I don't know,' Pellerina says, eating some of the stew. 'I don't think so.'

When they've finished, Saga brushes Pellerina's teeth, then goes into her bedroom with her.

'I went and hid when I got scared,' Pellerina says as she puts her nightdress on.

'I'll give you a little piece of advice,' Saga says, brushing the hair from her sister's face. 'If you really want to hide, you have to stay completely quiet. You can't say "not here, not here", because then they'll know that you're there.'

'OK,' her sister nods, and lies back in bed.

'And don't hide under the blankets,' Saga goes on. 'Hide behind the curtains or behind an open door and stand there nice and still until I find you.'

'Because you're the police.'

'Shall I leave the light on?'

'Yes.'

'But there's nothing to be scared of – you know that, don't you?' Saga says, sitting down beside her.

'Aren't you ever scared?' Pellerina asks.

'No, I'm not,' Saga replies, taking her sister's glasses off and putting them on the bedside table.

'Goodnight, Saga.'

'Goodnight, little sister,' she says, just as her phone starts to ring in her pocket.

'Maybe Dad's had enough of kissing,' Pellerina smiles.

Saga takes her phone out and sees that the call is from Jeanette Fleming.

'It isn't him,' she says. 'It's my work, I need to get this, but I'll come and see you again in a little while.'

Leaving the door ajar, Saga takes the call as she walks downstairs.

'Sorry to call so late, but you said you wanted a report after each session,' Jeanette says.

'How did it go?' Saga asks.

'I probably need another couple of evenings.'

'Can't we just tell her to take some time off work?'

'You get better results if you fit in with them, and I'm OK with the late evenings.'

'As long as you don't wear yourself out,' Saga says.

'The baby likes it when I work, stays nice and quiet.'

Jeanette's divorced, but is finally pregnant after wanting children for years. Saga thinks she went to Denmark to be artificially inseminated like she talked about, but she's been oddly secretive about how it all happened.

'What's she said?'

'It might be better if you heard it for yourself, I'll send the audio, there's only a few minutes where she's remembering new things, the rest is all preamble and structure.'

'Great, thanks.'

Saga hangs up and retrieves the file, opens it, sits down at the kitchen table and looks out at the old apple trees in the light of the window as the recording begins in the middle of a sentence:

'. . . and that too. No, it isn't mine, it's—'

Anna knocks something over and swears.

'Fuck.'

Chair legs scrape the floor, then footsteps and the sound of a tap running. Jeanette is a long way from the microphone, her voice is barely audible.

'Shall we go back to what you said before, about him saying he was going to buy a research centre in Bulgaria?'

'He said all sorts of things,' Anna replies, breathing heavily.

'But you remember the bit about the old laboratory in Bulgaria? Did you understand what he wanted it for?'

'No idea, he seemed interested in the chemical industry – how the hell could anyone be interested in that? He talked about a company in Norrtälje as well, one that makes . . . what's it called, the stuff that makes cars shiny?'

'Polish?' Jeanette suggests, sitting back down at the table.

'No, wax.'

'Car wax?'

'Yes, they make something that's in car wax . . . He was talking about buying a majority of shares in the company.'

'Did he work there?'

'No, but he was hanging about down there at the time.'

'In Norrtälje?'

'He took the ferry from Solö,' she replies.

'Where to?'

'I don't know.'

'But he took the ferry to get home?'

'That's how I understood it, but he . . .'

Anna falls silent when the doorbell rings, mutters that it's Fredrika, and leaves the kitchen.

Saga sits in silence for a while before she gets up and starts to clear the table. She rinses the plates and cutlery, sets the dishwasher going, then heads back upstairs to check on her sister.

Saga walks round the house, turning out the lights and making sure the doors are locked and the windows closed before she goes to the guest bedroom.

She picks up the bedclothes from the floor, makes the bed, then tries to call her dad again.

It's strange that he hasn't been in touch, even if he is on a date, she thinks.

His phone must be broken, unless he's lost it.

If he'd had an accident, she'd have heard by now.

Saga turns the bedside lamp off and closes her eyes, but opens them again when she imagines she sees movement through her eyelids. She looks up at the ceiling in the darkness, and the lamp swaying almost imperceptibly.

The vine growing up the wall has grown around the window of the guest bedroom, and its dry branches scrape against the windowsill.

She thinks through that day's work, her conversations with Nathan, the short audio file from Jeanette, the Beaver's interest in the chemical industry, and a ferry outside Norrtälje.

The boiler starts to clank down in the basement. It sounds like someone with cramp in an empty bathtub.

She should be asleep by now, but now that the thought's in her head she can't help switching the light back on, grabbing her mobile and looking up ferries from Solö on the Internet.

Almost at once she manages to find a timetable, and reads the names of the various stops, and sees that the ferry passes Högmarsö.

It's just one of many islands that the ferry calls at.

Even so, Saga's heart has started to beat faster.

Högmarsö was where Jurek Walter's body drifted ashore, and that was where she met the churchwarden and was given the severed finger. That was where Joona thought she and Nathan should start their search.

He wanted them to go there because he thought that would give them an opening into Jurek's world.

Saga realises that her hands are shaking as she looks up Anna Sjölin's phone number and calls her.

'Fuck,' a hoarse voice says. 'I was asleep . . . . What's going on? This is—'

'Did the Beaver say he lived on Högmarsö?' Saga interrupts. 'What?'

'Did he live on an island in the archipelago called Högmarsö?'

'I don't know,' she says. 'I don't think so.'

'But he took the ferry from Solö?'

'That's what I thought he said . . . look, I need to get some sleep . . .'

'One more thing,' Saga says.

'What?'

'Are you listening?'

'Yeees.'

'Did the Beaver mention a churchwarden?'

'I don't know . . . Actually – yes, he said he was sleeping in a church.'

38

Joona and Lumi are approaching the small border town of Waldfeucht along a narrow road, Brabanter Strasse.

The agricultural landscape is flat and wide, like a moss-green sea. White wind turbines stand out against the low winter sky.

A flock of jackdaws takes off from a dark tree as they drive past.

They left their hotel yesterday morning and drove north, through Switzerland and into Germany.

They kept to minor roads close to Autobahn 5 up to Karlsruhe, driving for hours through smaller towns such as Trier and Düren in grey rain.

Joona keeps one hand on the wheel as he talks through various points of strategy with Lumi, the various escape routes and meeting places.

He tells her how to get her bearings in the landscape when it's dark, with the help of simple trigonometry using visible phone masts.

After the run-through they sit in silence, side by side, deep in thought. It's impossible to tell where the sun is behind the white sky.

Lumi's face is turned away. The landscape runs quickly over her grey eyes.

'Dad,' she says eventually, taking a deep breath. 'I'm doing this because I promised I would . . . but I don't want to.'

'I understand that.'

'No, I don't honestly think you do,' she says, looking at him from the side. 'You've been waiting for this to happen, it's almost as if you've been looking forward to it . . . I mean, all the preparations, all the sacrifices you've been forced to make suddenly mean something.'

They drive straight through the German border town. It only takes a matter of minutes. Brown-brick buildings and an attractive church disappear behind them.

In the distance a yellow tractor is rolling across a field. The sky reflects off a grain silo.

There's no border check between the countries. The narrow road simply carries on past a sign, into the Netherlands.

'One thing I don't understand, Dad . . . the way you just left everything, I mean, you're the expert on Jurek, you know everything about him, but now that you think he's back, you suddenly vanish and leave your colleagues to look for him.'

'Even if I was still there, I wouldn't be allowed to take part in the investigation,' Joona explains. 'But I've given Nathan Pollock my notes and background information, and he'll be able to put together a large team along with Saga Bauer.'

'While you're hiding,' she says quietly.

'I'll do whatever it takes not to lose you,' he says honestly.

'And Valeria?'

'It would have been better if she'd come with me, but she'll have protection and that's the important thing, ten police officers, heavily armed,' he says.

'How can you live with that fear all the time?'

'Lumi, I know practically every time you've seen me I've been frightened, like up in Nattavaara,' Joona says, glancing at her quickly with a smile. 'But the truth is that I'm very rarely frightened.'

They're driving through a straight avenue of bare trees, past the occasional dark-brick house, with more farms visible in the distance.

'Mum told me you were the bravest man in the world,' Lumi says after a while.

'I'm not that, but I'm pretty good at what I do,' Joona replies.

As they drive up through the southern Dutch province of Limburg it starts to rain again.

The mechanical sound of the windscreen-wipers fills the car.

Rows of plastic-covered bales of silage lie on the black fields like shiny white fruit.

'Have you and Saga Bauer ever got it together?' Lumi asks.

'No, never,' he smiles. 'She's always been more like a sister.'

Lumi looks at herself in the small mirror in the sunshade.

'I've only met her once, when she came to say she'd found Jurek's body . . . I don't know, I haven't been able to stop thinking about her, she's so ridiculously beautiful, perfect.'

'You're perfect,' Joona says.

Lumi looks out of the side window and sees a large crucifix by the side of the road surrounded by iron railings.

'I don't get why she joined the police when she could have been a supermodel, or anything else, really.'

'Just like me,' he jokes.

'There's nothing wrong with wanting to be in the police, you know that's not what I mean, but it doesn't suit everyone.'

'As I understand it, Saga had a difficult childhood – her mum suffered from mental illness. She never talks about it, but I think her mum committed suicide . . . Whenever I've tried raising the subject, she tells me she doesn't want to talk about it – that it's one of her rules, seeing as thinking about her mum makes her unhappy. She's very particular about that.'

They drive past a petrol station with a red neon strip around the flat canopy above the pumps.

'What was it like when your dad died?' Lumi asks.

'Dad,' Joona says quietly.

'I mean, I know you were only eleven,' she says. 'Do you remember him? Properly, I mean?'

'I've been worried about forgetting . . . when I was younger I used to panic when I thought I couldn't remember his face or his voice . . . but the memory works in other ways, I've realised . . . I still dream about him a lot, and then I can see him perfectly clearly.'

The wiper blades are moving quickly across the windscreen, sweeping the rain away.

'Do you dream about your mum?' Joona asks after a while.

'A lot,' Lumi replies. 'I miss her so much, every day.'

'I miss her too,' Joona says.

Lumi lowers her face and quickly brushes her tears away with the back of her hand.

Joona slows down at a junction on the outskirts of Weert. The red traffic light reflects off the wet tarmac. A crow lands heavily in the crown of a bare tree.

'I remember once when Mum and I . . . We'd been watching a large fire,' Lumi said. 'A warehouse at the station was burning. I think it was the same day we sat and had ice-cream on the steps of the cathedral, and she told me about my wonderful dad who was no longer around.'

The light turns green and they start moving again.

'Do you remember anything about life in Sweden?' Joona asks.

'Mum told me I used to have a little toy cooker,' Lumi says. 'And that you used to play with me when you got home.'

'I used to have to be your child, or a yappy dog, or I had to lie on the floor while you fed me . . . you were always very patient . . . I used to fall asleep after a while, and then you'd cover me with plates and cutlery.'

'What for?' she smiles.

'I don't know, maybe I was a table?'

They overtake a truck close to a grubby-looking chapel. Water cascades over the windscreen and the slipstream makes the car judder.

'This might be something I've dreamed,' Lumi says slowly, 'but I think it's a real memory: us saying goodnight to a grey cat.'

'We did,' he says. 'I read you stories every night I was home . . . and before you fell asleep we used to wave to the neighbour's cat.'

39

It stops raining as they slow to a halt on Rijksweg, which runs almost parallel to the E25. They're not far from the industrial zone on the outskirts of Maarheeze.

There are about thirty sheep standing in a field, all facing the same way in the wind. On the other side of the motorway is the grey surface of a large dam.

They turn off onto a narrow tarmac road, where badly dented signs indicate that it's a dead end, and that the area is private property.

Tall grass brushes against the sides of the car.

Joona pulls up in front of a rusty boom, goes out into the cold air and removes a spike that's been stuck in the chain in place of a padlock.

At the end of the road is a cluster of derelict buildings, with a wide view stretching out in all directions.

The place is perfect, carefully chosen.

No one can approach without being seen from a distance, and it's only seventy kilometres to the Belgian border.

They drive into the yard and Joona parks behind the main building. The windows are covered with plywood and the door is nailed shut.

A gravel track, dotted with water-filled potholes, loops round a meadow to the old workshop. It's a large building with white tin walls. Part of one end seems to be hanging off, swaying slowly in the wind.

They take a shortcut across the meadow and step over an abandoned electric fence. The wires are missing and several of the posts are lying in puddles with their porcelain insulators.

'It isn't mined?' Lumi asks.

'No.'

'Because that would give the hiding place away,' she says to herself.

They follow a heavily rutted tractor track through patches of ground elder and reach the gravel drive. The remains of a threshing machine are lying in the weeds beside the workshop.

Joona draws his pistol and holds it close to his body as they walk round the workshop. The windows upstairs are shuttered. Red-brown rust has run from the studs in the dirty white tin façade. The end of the building consists of two doors that are big enough to drive a heavy loader through. One of the doors is hanging loose and is moving back and forth in the wind.

The whole workshop looks like it's been abandoned for years.

An empty plastic oil-bottle is rolling in the wind at the bottom of the cracked concrete ramp.

Joona stops and looks back quickly across the meadow, the narrow track, and the car parked outside the main house.

He opens the door, looks inside the gloomy workshop and sees a concrete floor covered with old oil-stains, a box of tin nails, and some rolls of industrial plastic.

The paint has been scraped off the pillar closest to the door, the result of years of mechanical wear and tear.

'I think he's got a surprise for us,' Joona says, and steps inside.

Lumi follows him with nagging anxiety in the pit of her stomach. Dry autumn leaves have blown in across the floor.

Instinctively she sticks close to her dad.

The large workshop is almost completely empty.

The wind lifts the door behind them for a moment, then it swings shut with a creak, leaving them in almost total darkness.

The sound of their steps echoes off the walls.

'This doesn't feel good,' she whispers.

White light from the sky reaches in as the wind pulls the door open again. The pale light moves across the floor like a scorch-mark, stops at an internal wall, then retreats again.

The room is spacious, but not quite large enough to fill the entire building.

Lumi tries to pull Joona towards the entrance. There's a strange sucking sound, and a moment later a hydraulic steel door crashes down behind them.

It hits the floor and locks into place. The exit is completely blocked now, from floor to ceiling.

'Dad,' Lumi says, with fear in her voice.

'Don't worry,' he replies.

The lights go on and they see that the smooth walls are made of rough steel, welded at the corners.

Four metres up there are surveillance cameras and firing slots. There's nothing to hide behind, nothing to climb up.

They see themselves reflected like two grey shadows in the reinforced wall in front of them.

Lumi is breathing fast, and Joona puts a hand on her arm to stop her reaching for her pistol.

A steel door opens in the wall and a shortish man in black jogging bottoms and a knitted black top comes limping into the room. His face is badly scarred, he has close-cropped white hair, and is holding a pistol in his hand.

'I'm very unhappy with you,' he says in deadpan English, gesturing towards Joona with the pistol.

'Sorry to hear—'

'Did you hear what I said?' the man interrupts, raising his voice.

'Yes, Lieutenant.'

The man walks round Joona, inspecting him and shoving him in the back, forcing him to take a step forward to keep his balance.

'How does it feel to lie on the floor in your own blood?'

'I'm not.'

'But I could have shot you – couldn't I?'

'No one's going to come in here unless you repaint the pillar.'

'The pillar?'

'The paint's been worn off it the whole way up, and if you look up to the roof you can see the whole mechanism,' Joona says.

The man holds back a contented smile and turns towards Lumi for the first time.

'My name is Rinus,' he says, shaking her hand.

'Thanks for letting us come,' she says.

'I tried to knock some sense into your dad once upon a time,' he explains.

'So he's said,' Lumi says.

'What's he told you?'

'That it was like being on holiday,' she replies with a smile.

'I knew I was too easy on him,' Rinus laughs.

Rinus tells them how he bought the property thirty years ago with the aim of running the farm himself, but that never happened. When he left the military he was instead recruited by the AIVD, the Dutch national intelligence service.

Although the AIVD were directly subordinate to the Interior Ministry, Rinus became aware that a situation could arise that would require him to go into hiding for a long period of time.

'The intelligence service's own safe-houses aren't safe enough, and you can't always trust your own team completely,' he says, as if that was obvious. 'I was leading an extremely sensitive secret investigation that appeared to point at parts of our own organisation, and that was when I felt it was time to make sure I was prepared.'

The property consists of four hectares of land, and is close to Belgium, Germany, Luxembourg and France, in case he ever has to leave the country in a hurry and seek asylum elsewhere.

The main building is merely a front in case anyone gets curious; an abandoned, boarded-up house that he never uses.

The real living quarters are hidden inside the old workshop.

Rinus shows them past the kitchen on the upper storey into a passageway with doors leading to four bedrooms, each one containing two bunk-beds.

At the end of the corridor is a sealed emergency exit. Rinus has scrawled 'Stairway to Heaven' on the door, seeing as he's removed the escape ladder and taken it to the tip.

The only way in is through the workshop, but there's a hidden underground escape tunnel that runs two hundred metres to a patch of woodland in the field behind the building.

Joona lays the table for three as he heats up frozen lasagne in the microwave. He fills three glasses with water and tells Lumi about his training under Rinus. Once he was dropped into the sea five kilometres from the coast with his legs tied together and his hands cuffed behind his back.

'A beach holiday,' Rinus smiles as he comes into the kitchen after moving their car to the hidden garage.

He sits down and tells Lumi that he's lived in Amsterdam for years, though his family comes from Sint Geertruid in the south of the Netherlands, not far from Maastricht.

'People down here tend to be Catholic, far more religious than on the other side of the rivers,' he explains as he starts to serve the food.

'What does Patrik say about you disappearing like this?' Joona asks.

'I hope he'll have time to miss me, but I suspect he's actually relieved to be shot of me for a while.'

'I thought you made him breakfast in bed every morning,' Joona smiles.

'Well, if I'm already up anyway,' Rinus says with a shrug.

He looks at Lumi, who's blowing on a forkful of steaming hot lasagne.

'So, Police Academy after art school?'

'No way,' she replies with a short laugh.

'Your dad's artistic too,' he says, glancing at Joona.

'I'm not,' he protests.

'You drew a —'

'Let's forget all about that, shall we?' Joona interrupts.

Rinus chuckles silently to himself as he looks down at his plate. The deep scars across his cheeks and one corner of his mouth are as pale as lines drawn in chalk.

After the meal Rinus leads them downstairs, through a curtain and into a dimly lit room with shutters over the windows.

One wall is lined with wooden boxes of weapons – pistols, semi-automatics and sniper rifles.

Rinus goes through the tactical plan and order of command in case of attack, and shows them the monitor and alarm system.

Taking the location of the shutters upstairs as the starting point, they divide the surroundings into different surveillance areas and draw up a rota of duties.

Joona stands with a pair of binoculars and watches the approach road and the barrier across the track while Rinus shows Lumi how the Russian detonators work, in case they have to mine the workshop.

'Electric detonators are better, but these mechanical ones are more reliable . . . even if they've been lying in their boxes for thirty years,' he says, putting one down on the table in front of her.

The detonator looks a lot like a ballpoint pen, with a small fuse and a pin at one end.

'I assume that's where you attach the line,' she says, pointing at the large ring.

'Yes, but first you stick the point about five centimetres into the explosive charge, then prime it with a line to the pin, like you say . . . then release the catch.'

'And if someone walks into the line, the pin is pulled out.'

'And the hammer hits the cap, which triggers the detonator,' Rinus says. 'The cap's no worse than the cap in a toy gun, but if the detonator explodes you lose your hand, and obviously if the explosives get set off, you're dead.'

40

Saga and Nathan Pollock don't take the ferry from Solö like the Beaver did, but drive as far as they can across the bridges linking the islands to catch the regular cable ferry from Svartnö.

Her dad still hadn't got home when she dropped Pellerina off at school. The school was closed for teacher training, but the out-of-school club is open all day and Pellerina's special needs assistant is on duty.

Saga's been trying not to worry, telling herself that her dad's phone might be broken, or that he's gone straight to work the morning after his date.

But when she called the Karolinska he wasn't there.

She's now called all the hospitals in Stockholm, and spoken to the police.

She feels like the parent of a teenager.

All she can do is hope that he's fallen so head over heels in love that he's forgotten about everything else.

That wouldn't be like him, but she'd be simultaneously relieved and extremely angry.

Nathan brakes and turns off highway 278, onto a gravel track that leads off through a pine forest to the right of the road.

They're heading out to Högmarsö to try to talk to the church-warden, to find out if the Beaver really did stay in the chapel for a while.

If they're lucky, they'll soon know the Beaver's real name. The

207

churchwarden may even be forwarding his post to a new address if he's left his contact details.

But Saga knows it isn't going to be easy.

Erland Lind has been suffering from dementia for several years, and any communication with him up to now has been hopeless.

They stop in front of the boom blocking the way to the quay. This is where you have to queue until it's time to board the ferry.

The road is empty.

No one else is waiting to go across.

Saga looks at the dark island on the other side of the water and the approaching cable ferry.

Her and Nathan's search for the large man calling himself the Beaver has disconcerting connections with the final chapter in Jurek Walter's story, and the precise location where his remains were found.

There's a scraping sound as the ferry pulls in.

The water beyond is completely still.

When the barrier rises they drive onto the quay, and a man in waterproofs waves them on board. The ramp clanks against the quay as the car's weight presses it down.

The deck is black and wet, and the railings and ferryman's cab are painted mustard yellow.

Nathan and Saga stay seated in the car, which starts to shake as the ferry gets under way. The trembling moves through their legs, pelvises, and stomachs.

Beneath the surface of the water two sturdy steel cables run in parallel between the two islands. They get pulled out of the water and passed through the ferry's powerful winch before being dropped down again.

Saga looks back and watches as the swell makes the frozen yellow reeds on either side of the quay sway.

Joona is convinced that Jurek Walter is alive, and that he's devoted the last few years to finding a replacement for his brother.

Saga has always been convinced she killed Jurek.

The reason she spent a year searching for his body was so she could calm Joona down.

It was her fault that Jurek escaped, so she felt it was her duty to prove to Joona that Jurek was dead, if that was at all possible.

She vividly remembers meeting the churchwarden on Högmarsö. He was gathering driftwood from the rocks, and told her he'd found a man's body five months earlier.

He'd kept the body in the toolshed, but when the stench got too bad he burned it in the old crematorium.

He cut off one of the fingers and kept it in his fridge in a jar of vodka.

Saga and Nils Åhlén studied the photograph he had taken of the swollen torso and bullet holes.

It was Jurek, every detail fitted.

And when the DNA and fingerprint turned out to be a one hundred per cent match, they were convinced.

Saga wishes Joona had waited a bit longer before disappearing, that he'd had time to see the security-camera footage from Belarus.

She'll never forget the look on his face when he came to warn her.

She almost didn't recognise him; the theft of his wife's skull had made him paranoid.

Suddenly he was convinced that Jurek was alive – that he'd found a man the same age and build as him, shot him in the same places Saga had shot him, then amputated his own hand or part of it, and left the amputated body part to soak in seawater for six months.

Joona's conclusion was that the churchwarden must have helped him, that Jurek either forced or persuaded Erland Lind to photograph the dead man's torso and then cremate it, cut off and save the finger from Jurek's rotted hand, and burn the rest.

Saga thinks back to Erland Lind's drink-ravaged gaze, his taciturnity, his shabby clothes. She tried to interview him on several occasions after that first meeting, but he'd descended so far into dementia that it was pretty pointless.

The water is almost black this morning, there's no wind and the surface is still. Thin mist is hanging between the islands in the distance.

The ferry slowly approaches Högmarsö.

Bare trees stand motionless beyond the empty quay.

The ferry slides up the underwater rails with a dull rumble, and the ramp scrapes across the concrete quayside before the ferry comes to a halt.

The swell laps against the rocky shore.

Nathan gives Saga a look, starts the car and rolls ashore. They drive up the hill, past summerhouses boarded up for the winter.

It only takes them a couple of minutes to reach the boatyard. The glare of a welding torch bounces between the buildings. The dusty yard is full of clutter and covered boats.

Nathan turns left, past some small fields and a patch of woodland. The chapel glints between the black tree trunks, as white as sugar.

They slow down, drive up a hill and stop. A large anchor is propped up in the yellow grass.

The cold air carries the smell of the sea. The cries of gulls can be heard from the harbour.

Saga walks up the gravel path and tries the door of the chapel. It's locked, but the key is hanging from a nail under the railing beside the steps.

She unlocks the door, pushes the handle down, and Nathan follows her inside, onto the creaking wooden floor. The pews have been painted green, and there are votives on the walls. The cream-coloured dado rail reflects the winter light from the arched windows. They walk up to the simple altar, turn back, and stop in front of a muddy blanket lying on the floor.

There are some cans of beans and meat stew by the wall, next to the hymn books.

Nathan and Saga go outside again, lock the chapel and carry on towards the churchwarden's cottage. The bell tower looms like a hunting platform between the trees.

As they knock on the door the sun breaks through the mist. They wait a few seconds then go in.

The tiny house consists of a kitchen with a bed in an alcove, and a small bathroom.

On the table, the remains of a meal have curled up and dried out. Beside the coffee-maker is a plastic bag full of mouldy cinnamon buns. The narrow bed in the alcove has no sheets. He's been sleeping on the bare mattress with only a blanket to cover him. A watch with a scratched glass face is lying on a stool next to the bed.

The cottage has been abandoned.

Saga remembers the smell of cooking and damp the first time she was here. Erland Lind had been drunk, but at least his mind was relatively clear back then.

The next time she came he had been introverted and confused. The process seemed to have been very rapid.

Saga thinks he must have ended up in care, and none of his relatives has managed to deal with his effects yet.

'This is where he kept the finger in an old jam-jar,' she says, opening the fridge.

The dirty shelves are strewn with bottles with no labels and packs of rancid and rotten food. She looks at the best-before dates of a carton of cream and a pack of bacon.

'He hasn't been here for four months,' she tells Nathan, and shuts the fridge.

They leave the house and go to the garage.

A dirty spade with a rusty blade is lying on the floor surrounded by dry soil. They can see part of Erland's illegal still behind the covered snow-blower.

'This was where Jurek was lying, liquid was leaking from his body down into the drain,' she says, pointing.

They walk outside again and look back towards the car and chapel.

'Shall we go and ask the neighbours if they know where he's gone?' Nathan asks in a low voice.

'I'll call the parish office,' Saga says, turning back the other way.

The remains of the crematorium's foundations are hidden in the tall weeds, but the brick chimney sticks up four metres from the ground.

'That was where he burned Jurek's body,' Nathan says.

'Right.'

They walk through the grass and stop in front of the sooty oven. Saga carries on cautiously to the edge of the forest, looks

211

at the pitchfork sticking out of the compost heap, then moves on towards the soil between the trees.

It feels as if all the air vanishes when she sees a metal tube sticking out of the ground.

She has to grab one of the trees to stop herself falling.

With her heart pounding she walks over and feels her heels sink into the loose soil. Thoughts are swirling through her head. She kneels down, leans forward and smells the tube, then stands up, coughing, backs away and spits on the ground.

Rotten meat.

The edge of the forest slides away as she turns, searching for something to focus on. She takes a few steps, looking at the crematorium and churchwarden's house.

'What is it?' Nathan asks anxiously.

She can't answer, just runs to the garage, grabs the spade, runs back and starts digging in the softly packed soil, shovelling it into the tall weeds.

Sweat trickles down her back.

Her throat makes a whimpering sound as she presses the blade into the earth with her foot and heaves the soil away.

Panting hard, she makes the hole bigger, then climbs into it and keeps digging.

Seventy centimetres down the spade hits a coffin. She sweeps the loose soil aside with her hand. The pipe leads through the lid, and the hole has been sealed with silver duct tape.

'What is this?' Nathan asks.

She clears the whole top of the coffin, forces the blade of the spade beneath the lid and breaks it open. She tosses the spade aside and grabs hold of it with both hands, jerks the lid sideways and pulls the last of the nails out.

Nathan takes the lid from her and puts it beside the shallow grave.

They both stare down at the remains of the churchwarden.

Erland Lind's body is swollen and oozing, some parts have almost dissolved, while others, including his hands and feet, seem to be intact. His face is emaciated, his eyes black, his fingertips torn to shreds.

'Jurek did this,' Saga whispers.

She clambers out of the grave, hurries back towards the chapel and stumbles over part of the crematorium's foundations.

'Wait!' Nathan calls, hurrying after her.

'He's got my dad!' she screams, and starts running towards the car.

41

Police officers Karin Hagman and Andrej Ekberg are sitting in patrol car 30-901 on Palmfeltsvägen close to the Globe Arena.

It's a quiet morning. The rush-hour traffic heading into Stockholm has thinned out, the queues on Nynäsvägen have gone and, apart from one minor collision in which no one was hurt, things have been very calm.

Karin and Andrej have driven around the slaughterhouse district, and pulled up behind a parked van with a pornographic image painted across its door. Karin checked the registration number in the criminal database in the hope that they could have intervened on stronger grounds than bad taste alone.

Now they're driving slowly along the shaded road that runs beside the underground line, beneath deserted footbridges and dark, empty brick buildings. The area is still a mess after a concert the previous evening.

'Life's too long to have the energy to have fun all the time,' Karin sighs.

'You said you were going to tell Joakim how you're feeling,' Andrej says.

'It won't make any difference . . . he doesn't seem to want anything any more, he just doesn't care.'

'You need to split up.'

'I know,' Karin whispers, then drums the steering wheel with her hand.

They pass someone collecting discarded cans to get the deposit back on them. He's dressed in a filthy military coat and fur hat as he walks along the ditch dragging a bin-bag behind him.

Karin opens her mouth to say that Joakim will do anything to avoid having sex when they get a call from Central Command.

She answers the call and notes that the operator's voice sounds unusually stressed when he says they have a Priority 1 alarm from a colleague.

The pale glow from the POLMAN radio makes her hand look as white as snow as she reaches for the gear-stick.

The alarm concerns an ongoing kidnapping at Enskede School, at the Mellis out-of-school club on Mittelvägen.

The operator does his best to answer their questions calmly and efficiently, but there's clearly something about the situation that's got to him.

As Karin understands it, they're dealing with the violent kidnapping of a twelve-year-old girl with Down Syndrome. The suspected perpetrator is believed to be extremely dangerous, possibly armed.

The address appears on their screen.

They're close.

Karin switches the flashing lights on and turns the car round, sending the blue light pulsing across a brown brick wall with shredded awnings.

The operator tells them that they're coordinating their response with Södermalm Hospital and the National Operational Unit.

'But we're closest, we're going to be first on the scene,' he says.

Karin switches on the hi-lo siren, puts her foot down, and feels the car's acceleration push her into her seat. There's a cyclist up ahead to their right, and a truck approaching from the opposite direction.

In the rear-view mirror the man collecting cans in the ditch stands and watches them go.

She slows down at the large junction to make sure that everyone has stopped to let them across before accelerating again.

Andrej asks the operator if he knows how many children are in the club, and is told that there are probably fewer than normal because the school is closed for the day.

Karin thinks it sounds like a custody battle that's got out of hand, some aggrieved ex-husband who feels hard done by.

They pass the yellow façade of the Catholic school, turn sharp right at the roundabout and speed up past the large sports field.

Silvery fencing in front of the row of football pitches flickers past.

As Karin drives, Andrej keeps talking to the operator. They've received a number of calls from the public about a disturbance, as well as gunshots.

She's driving a little too fast when they reach the next roundabout and the tyres lose their grip as she turns left.

They slide across the loose grit on the tarmac and end up on the pavement, scraping a sign pointing to Enskede Church.

'Take it easy,' Andrej mutters.

Karin doesn't answer, just puts her foot down again as they drive along the edge of Margareta Park.

Several birds take off from a rubbish bin.

The winter grass in the park is brown and the bare trees shade the network of paths.

They spot the tiled roof of the school above the surrounding buildings and Karin turns the siren off. She turns sharp right onto Mittelvägen, slows down and stops right in front of the entrance.

They get out of the car and check their weapons and protective vests. Karin tries to control her breathing.

The brown leaves that have gathered at the base of a spiral fire-escape are rustling in the wind.

Andrej confirms that they're on the scene. Karin looks on as he listens and nods before ending the call.

'The operator told us to be careful,' he says, looking her in the eye.

'Careful? I've never heard that before,' she says, without quite managing to summon up a smile.

'That was from the colleague who raised the alarm.'

'Careful,' she repeats in a low voice.

She looks at the single-storey building that houses the out-of-school club, which has been squeezed into a gap between the far taller school buildings on either side. Its brick walls have been painted yellow, and there's moss growing on the red-tiled roof.

There are lights on behind the curtains but there's no one in sight.

Everything is quiet.

'Let's go in and take a look,' Andrej says.

With their pistols drawn, they run across the wide pavement, then creep along the wall to the dark-red door.

Andrej pulls it open and Karin takes a couple of steps into the cloakroom.

There's a large plastic box of discarded clothing in the middle of the floor. Boots and trainers are lined up next to a drying-cupboard.

Andrej moves past Karin and gestures towards the next door, and she follows him into a large room with tables laid out for chess and backgammon.

The curtains in front of all the windows are closed.

The only sound is the rustle of their uniforms and the noise of their boots on the plastic floor as they move between the low tables.

The door to one of the toilets at the far end of the room is closed.

They stop.

They can hear a clicking, bubbling sound.

Karin exchanges a glance with Andrej, and he immediately moves to one side. She walks closer to the toilet door, thinking about the unusual exhortation to be careful, and realises that she's shaking as she reaches her hand out and pushes the door handle.

42

Karin yanks the door open, backs away and aims her pistol into the darkness, but the door swings shut before she has time to see anything.

She reaches forward and opens the door again.

There's no one there.

The tap is on and an even trickle of water is running down the plughole with a gentle tinkling sound.

'Where the hell is everyone?' Andrej whispers behind her.

They carry on into the dining room. Three circular tables are spread out across the floor. On one of the tables is a glass of chocolate milkshake and a plate with half a sandwich on it.

Karin spots a shoe on the floor between the tables and chairs, close to the half-closed door to the kitchen.

Andrej goes over to the window, nudges the curtain aside and looks out. There's no sign of the rapid-response unit, but a white van has stopped at the end of the block.

'There's a van further down the street,' he says quietly.

Karin looks at the pistol in her hand, moves a chair out of the way and walks over to him.

She stops and looks back towards the kitchen again.

She can see a bare foot among the tables.

'Andrej,' she says in a tense voice.

She turns and hurries across the dining room, her pulse racing. In the doorway to the kitchen a large woman is lying on her stomach, completely motionless. The sliding door is half-closed, so that only the bottom half of her body is visible.

Both her shoes are missing.

Her heels are pink, the wrinkled soles of her feet almost white.

Karin looks at the faded jeans and tasselled back pockets across the woman's large backside.

A horizontal-striped Marimekko T-shirt is stretched across the woman's back.

Aiming her pistol towards the kitchen, Karin reaches out her other hand and slowly slides the door open.

She gasps when, instead of hair and the back of her head, she finds herself looking at the woman's face.

It's been pulled back hard.

Her neck has been broken so brutally that the ligaments have torn and the soft tissue between the first and second vertebrae has been crushed.

'What the hell's happened here?' Andrej whispers.

'Check the next room,' she says, unnecessarily loudly.

The woman's face is white, her lips closed, eyes wide open, and blood is running from her nose.

Karin keeps her pistol pointing into the kitchen as she crouches down to feel the woman's neck.

She feels cool, must have been dead for several hours.

Thoughts are swirling through Karin's head. The alarm was raised far too late, there's no point setting up roadblocks, and they don't need the support of the rapid-response unit.

She stands up and is walking in to look at the trashed kitchen when Andrej calls to her. Karin turns, steps past the dead woman and accidentally walks into a chair, knocking it against the table with a bang.

Andrej is standing in the gloom of the dance and yoga room. The curtains are half drawn, and the pink glow of a mood-enhancing lamp is shining off a guitar hanging on the wall.

A glitterball is rotating up in the ceiling, its tiny reflections sliding across the walls.

Karin follows Andrej's gaze and looks at the far corner.

A man with a black beard and thick eyebrows is sitting on a yoga mat, leaning against a rib-backed chair. His head has been smashed in. His forehead has been pushed in by at least five centimetres, and his face and chest are covered with dark blood.

Andrej mutters that they've got here too late and leaves the room.

Karin doesn't move, just listens to her pulse racing in her ears.

Even though she can see the man is dead, she still goes over and feels his neck.

She wipes her hand on her trousers, then starts to walk back towards the cloakroom.

When she emerges into the cool air outside the building, Andrej is sitting on a bench next to a dark wooden table.

They can hear sirens in the distance. A tattooed man is pulling a heavy hose from the van down the street.

'He killed the staff and took the girl,' Andrej says without looking at her.

'Looks like it,' she replies. 'Have you reported back?'

'I'm doing it now.'

While Andrej talks to their immediate superior Karin goes to the car and fetches the roll of cordon tape. She ties one end to the spiral fire-escape, runs it around the shed and trees, then round the entire building, before she starts to make some notes about what's happened.

The yellow glare of the streetlamps lights up the leaves on the tarmac. At this time of year the lamps are on almost all day long.

The first ambulance turns into Mittelvägen, drives up onto the pavement to get past their police car, and stops outside the cordon.

Karin goes over and explains the situation to the paramedics. They follow her into the out-of-school club and check the first body.

They move on into the dimly lit dance and yoga room together.

Karin stops in the middle of the room and watches as the paramedics crouch down next to the dead man. The reflections from the glitterball are playing across the dead face and beard.

'We'll get the stretcher,' one of the paramedics says in a heavy voice.

Karin goes over to the window and pulls one of the curtains back to let in the light of the streetlamp outside.

When she pulls the curtain back she gets such a shock that her head instantly fills with adrenalin.

Her pulse is thudding in her ears.

A little girl is standing completely still with her hands clamped over her mouth, with her eyes screwed shut behind thick glasses.

'Oh, sweetheart,' Karin manages to say.

The girl must have been hiding behind the curtain for several hours. When Karin touches her gently on the shoulder, she opens her eyes and wobbles.

'There's no need to be scared now, he's gone,' Karin says.

The girl's lips are white and she looks exhausted. Suddenly her legs give way and she sinks to the floor. Karin kneels down and holds the child, feeling the tense, trembling body.

'Can I carry you?'

Very carefully she picks the girl up and walks out of the dance room. She holds her in such a way that she can't see the dead man or the woman in the entrance to the kitchen.

'Who's been here?' she asks as they move between the tables.

The girl doesn't answer. Karin can feel her warm, damp breath against her shoulder, and whispers to her that she doesn't have to be scared now.

They agree that Andrej should wait for the forensics team and detectives while Karin goes with the child in the ambulance. She sits down next to her, holds the girl's hand, and asks again who she was hiding from, but the girl doesn't answer, just holds her hand tight. Her eyelids are half-closed, as if she's about to fall asleep.

43

Lars-Erik Bauer wakes up with a feeling of catastrophe in his body. Something's very wrong, but his sluggish brain can't process the information from his senses.

It's cold, he's lying down, and the ground seems to be shaking beneath him.

The moment before he opens his eyes he thinks about the peculiar phone call from Kristina.

She sounded different.

Something had happened.

He's never heard such a lonely voice before. She must have apologised at least ten times, saying that the battery in her car was flat.

She'd given her son a lift to Barkarby Flying Club, south of Järvafältet. On the way back, in the middle of the forest, her car conked out.

There was no answer when she tried calling different break-down services, and in the end she just locked herself inside the car, too afraid to walk through the forest.

If he set off at once with his jump-leads he'd have time to get back and make Pellerina's tea on time.

They were actually supposed to be meeting for the first time next week, he'd already booked a table at Wedholm's fish restaurant.

Lars-Erik groans when his back is hit hard.

He opens his eyes, blinks, and sees the full moon glinting above treetops flashing past.

It's like a dream.

His jaw snaps shut when his head hits something hard.

He can't make sense of what's happening. He's being dragged on a tarpaulin along a path in a pine forest. Time and again his head and back hit rocks and roots.

He can't move his hands or legs, and realises that he's been drugged. His mouth is dry and he has no idea how long he was out.

His eyes close once more, he can't keep them open.

He thinks about the effects of the anaesthetic gases that used to be widely used, such as Halothane, in combination with opioids and overdoses of muscle relaxants injected into the spinal column.

Immediate anaesthesia and lingering paralysis.

It must have been a trap.

Kristina tricked him, got him interested, lured him into the forest.

The last thing he remembers is parking his car on the dark forest road.

The headlights were pointing at Kristina's car on the gravel road. The surrounding trees and the undergrowth in the ditch looked like a grey theatre set.

Then Pellerina sent him a picture of a painting she'd done at school, and he called her and said it was a lovely dog.

It looked like a brown lump with four legs.

He saw in the wing-mirror that someone was approaching the car from behind as Pellerina explained that it was a horse, not a dog, and that his name was Silver.

Someone in a black rain poncho was approaching very quickly from behind the car, turning red in the glare of the rear lights.

Lars-Erik opened the door, but doesn't remember what happened after that.

He remembers the tall grass lining the verge bending under the car door as it opened.

A car park ticket blew off the dashboard in the draught.

Then the faint sound of glass against glass.

He loses consciousness again and doesn't come round until

the person dragging him through the forest stops and lets go of the tarpaulin.

Lars-Erik's head sinks heavily to the ground.

He looks up at the moon and the black treetops surrounding the clearing.

Everything is cold and silent.

He opens his mouth and tries to say something, but he has no voice, all he can do is lie there on his back, breathing in the smell of the moss and damp earth.

His toes are itching and tingling.

He makes an attempt to move but his body won't obey him. All he manages to do is turn his head slightly to one side.

Footsteps are approaching on the soft ground.

He looks around at the trees.

A branch breaks, then he sees a thin man walking along the path.

Lars-Erik tries to call for help, but no sound comes out.

The figure passes a fallen tree, then becomes visible in the moonlight.

His thin face is covered by a network of wrinkles.

The man walks past Lars-Erik, very close, without so much as glancing at him, then stops somewhere outside his field of vision before returning.

He's rolling a large plastic barrel.

Lars-Erik tries to tell him to get help. But the sound that emerges from his mouth is no louder than a whisper.

The man carefully lifts his feet into the opening of the barrel, then pulls it up over his legs, all the way to his hips.

Lars-Erik still can't move, all he can do is toss his sluggish head from side to side, towards the mute, dark trees.

The old man says nothing, and doesn't look him in the eye, it's clear that he's just doing a job. With brusque movements he stuffs Lars-Erik's lower half into the barrel.

He handles Lars-Erik as though he were a slaughtered animal, a carcass.

With a hard jerk he stands the barrel up and Lars-Erik's legs give way beneath him. He slumps into the barrel, up to his armpits. His shirt slides up and he cuts his stomach on the sharp edge of the plastic.

He still can't understand what's going on.

The old man tries to push him down into the barrel.

He's unexpectedly strong, but it's impossible, his arms are dangling over the sides and half his upper body is still above the rim.

The man takes several steps to the side and returns with a spade.

Now Lars-Erik notices a deep hole in the ground next to the barrel. On the grass beside the hole is a roll of plastic and a bucket containing a white liquid.

The thin man walks over to him again, raises the blade of the spade and brings it down hard on his shoulder.

Lars-Erik groans with pain as his left collarbone breaks. He's breathing hard through his nose and tears are running down his cheeks.

The man tosses the spade on the ground and leans over him.

The pain is so bad that Lars-Erik's vision fades as the man squeezes his shoulder to get it past the edge of the barrel. His right arm is sticking straight up, but the man folds it down over his neck, then pushes his head down and puts a lid on the barrel.

The old man rocks the barrel a few times until it tips over, then rolls it into the large hole.

The impact makes Lars-Erik pass out. When he comes round he can hear a clattering sound, like a heavy shower of rain.

After a few moments he realises that the man has stood the barrel up in the bottom of the hole and has started to fill it in. The clattering sound becomes more and more distant, then stops altogether.

The moist air inside the barrel smells of plastic, and there isn't enough oxygen.

His body is still paralysed, and he tries to twist his head in panic, and sees a small point of light on the side of the barrel.

Lars-Erik stares at the light, and realises that it's moonlight shining through an air-tube in the lid of the barrel.

His contorted shoulder and broken collarbone are throbbing with pain. His fingers are ice-cold, his circulation isn't reaching them.

Lars-Erik realises that he's been buried alive.

44

Saga drives past the open ambulance entrance at Södermalm Hospital, pulls up onto the pavement and gets out of Nathan's car without closing the door. She runs past stretchers and discarded prams and carries on into the children's emergency room, past a metre-high green plastic frog.

The waiting room is full of people, crying babies, and pale youths. There are information leaflets scattered across the floor. One man is engaged in a heated conversation on his phone.

Jurek made his move early that morning, thirty minutes after Saga dropped Pellerina off at the out-of-school club and set off for the ferry to Högmarsö.

He had plenty of time.

He killed the staff inside the club, the manager, and special needs assistant.

The police officers who were first on the scene found Pellerina hiding behind a curtain.

If Saga hadn't told her how to hide and stay completely silent, Jurek Walter would have snatched her that morning.

She would never have seen her sister again.

Ignoring the queuing system, Saga walks straight up to the desk, shows her ID, and asks to see Pellerina Bauer.

Her sister is in one of the emergency rooms.

Saga starts to run along the corridor, pushing a cleaning trolley out of her way.

The mop topples over and she hears the handle hit the floor.

Wheelchairs, drip-stands, and blue-mattressed trolleys are lined up along one wall.

A nurse is moving a crash cart.

Saga slows down as she approaches the uniformed police officer standing outside the last door before Lift B.

'Are you alone?' she asks, showing her police ID.

'Yes,' the man replies, without taking his eyes off her.

'What the . . . ?' she sighs, then goes in.

The lighting in the cramped, windowless treatment room is subdued. Pellerina is sitting in the bed with a yellow blanket round her shoulders.

On the bedside table beside her there's a glass of juice and a cheese sandwich on a paper plate.

Saga hurries over and puts her arms round her. As she holds her sister she allows the relief to wash over her for the first time. She presses her face into Pellerina's tangled hair. 'I came as quickly as I could,' she says.

They hug for a long time, then Saga looks at Pellerina, forces herself to smile and strokes her cheek.

'How are you feeling?'

'Fine,' the girl replies seriously.

'Really?' Saga whispers, fighting to hold back the tears.

'Can we go home to Dad now?'

Saga swallows hard. She keeps having to stop her own thoughts, force herself not to imagine what might have happened to her dad.

'Were you scared?'

Pellerina nods and lowers her gaze, takes off her glasses and picks at the corner of one eye. Her pale eyelashes cast small shadows across her round cheeks.

'I can understand that,' Saga says, brushing some hair from Pellerina's forehead.

'I hid behind the curtain and I was as quiet as a mouse,' she smiles, and puts her glasses back on again.

'That was really clever,' Saga says. 'Did you see him?'

'A bit, before I closed my eyes . . . It was a man, but he was really quick.'

Saga feels her heart speed up and glances over at the door.

'We have to go now,' she says. 'Has the doctor looked at you?'

'She's coming soon.'

'How long have you been waiting?'

'I don't know.'

Saga presses the alarm button and after a while a carer comes in, a middle-aged man with a round stomach and glasses.

'I want a doctor to look at her before we leave,' Saga says.

'Doctor Sami will be here as soon as she can,' the man replies, with already strained patience.

'Pellerina is only twelve years old, and I don't know how long you've made her wait so far.'

'I appreciate that it's annoying, but we have to prioritise the most acute cases, I'm sure you can—'

'Listen to me,' Saga interrupts sharply. 'You're in no position to evaluate the urgency of this case.'

She shows the man her ID, he studies it carefully, then hands it back.

'This child is a priority,' Saga says.

'I can ask the triage doctor to come and make a new assessment—'

'There's no time for that,' she cuts in. 'Just get any damn doctor who's qualified.'

The man doesn't answer, just leaves the room looking agitated.

'Why are you so angry?' Pellerina asks.

'I'm not angry, I'm really not, you know I sometimes sound angry when I get stressed.'

'You swore.'

'I know, I shouldn't have done that, that was very silly of me.'

After a while they hear voices outside the door, then the doctor comes in, a short woman with light brown eyes.

'I heard you wanted to talk to me,' she says warily.

'Just examine her,' Saga says impatiently.

'I don't understand,' the doctor smiles.

'We can't stay here, we're in a hurry but first I want to make sure she's OK.'

'I won't stop you as long as you can prove you're her guardian.'

'Just do as I say!'

The police officer comes in with his hand on his holster.

'What's going on?'

'Guard the door!' Saga snaps. 'You don't leave that door, and for God's sake fasten your protective vest!'

The police officer doesn't move.

'What kind of threat are we expecting?'

'I haven't got time to explain . . . and it really doesn't matter, you wouldn't stand a chance anyway,' she says, and tries to calm down.

She looks the doctor in the eye and takes a couple of steps towards her, trying to talk quietly so Pellerina won't hear.

'Listen, I work for the Security Police as an operational superintendent, and I need to interview this girl in a place of safety . . . It's possible that she witnessed a double murder, and it's highly likely that the murderer will come after her . . . Trust me, you don't want us in this hospital any longer than necessary. We'll leave as soon as you're done. She's had an operation for a heart defect, Fallot's Tetralogy . . . I know you've done an ECG, but I need to know if she's showing any signs of serious trauma.'

'I understand,' the doctor says. Her eyes are dark with stress.

While the doctor is talking to Pellerina, Saga leaves the room, checks the corridor and looks over towards the entrance, scrutinising the people waiting beyond the glass screen in the reception area.

Her immediate evaluation was that the churchwarden had been dead for two weeks, but the dates on the food in the fridge suggest that he was buried in the grave more than four months ago.

The Beaver is the accomplice Jurek picked. She may have toyed with the idea before, but she always considered it impossible.

Now she knows Joona was right all along.

The Beaver stayed in the chapel, keeping an eye on the grave, keeping the churchwarden alive.

Four months in a grave, she thinks.

And now Jurek has taken her dad.

She tries calling him again, but Lars-Erik's phone is still switched off.

Saga puts out an alert for her dad's car, then calls the Security Police and asks one of the technical experts to track his mobile.

While she's talking she sees a thin man walk through the door. She breaks off the call and cautiously draws her pistol. When she's sure it isn't Jurek she slips it back in its holster.

She glances the other way along the corridor, then takes out her phone again and calls Carlos Eliasson's direct line at the National Operational Unit.

'Jurek Walter's back,' she says bluntly.

'I've heard what happened at your sister's school.'

'She needs a secure apartment at once,' Saga says, looking over towards the entrance again.

'We can't provide that, that's not how it works, the personal security unit need to conduct an evaluation. Being worried isn't enough, you know that, the same rules apply for everyone.'

'Then I'm taking a leave of absence, I need to find somewhere to hide.'

'Saga, you're starting to sound like a certain superintendent with a Finnish—'

'Valeria,' she interrupts, raising her voice. 'Has she got protection? Tell me she's got protection!'

'There's no tangible threat,' Carlos says patiently.

'She has to have protection! This is your damn responsibility . . . You know what? Just shut up, Jurek's back, that's what's happening.'

'Saga, he's dead. You killed him, then you found his—'

'Just make sure Valeria gets protection,' Saga interrupts, then ends the call.

She looks around the corridor again as thoughts whirl through her head. Joona was right all along, and she and Nathan Pollock have wasted valuable time on a distraction. Joona took the threat seriously, he had his escape route prepared, and managed to save both himself and his daughter.

The police officer guarding the door looks at her with bemusement as she walks back into the treatment room.

The doctor shakes Pellerina's hand, then comes over to Saga.

'She's a lovely girl, really smart.'

'She is, isn't she?' Saga says with a terrible weight in her chest.

'There are no problems with her heart,' the doctor goes on. 'But Pellerina has had a terrible fright. I don't think she saw the violence, she seems to have had her eyes shut the whole time . . . It's a bit hard to tell, but she's not showing any signs of dissoci-ation or disorientation, and she has no psychomotor problems.'

'Thanks.'

'I'd prefer her to see a psychologist, because she's going to need to talk about what's happened.'

'Of course.'

'If she starts to get anxious or has trouble sleeping, you'll have to come back. Sometimes it—'

'Good,' Saga interrupts, and goes over to Pellerina.

She quickly wraps the yellow blanket round her sister and picks her up, walks past the doctor into the corridor, and orders the police officer to walk with them to the car.

She puts Pellerina in the back seat, fastens her seat belt, then thanks the policeman.

Saga drives away from the hospital, thinking that they should head north, to some place that has no connections to her. She'll find some isolated summer cottage, break in and hide out there with her sister. They can stay there while the police do their job. But first she needs to get a new phone so she can't be traced. Saga pulls over to the kerb at Skanstull and is searching online for shops that sell used mobiles when Carlos calls.

'Saga,' he says in an unsteady voice. 'I sent one of our cars that was in the area to check on Valeria and . . . I don't know how to say this, but she's gone, she's been taken . . . We found a man's remains in a burned-out car, there's blood everywhere, the greenhouses are wrecked . . .'

'Have you set up roadblocks?' she asks, almost in a whisper.

'It's too late for that, this all happened several days ago . . . we should have handled this differently.'

'Yes.'

'I've organised a safe apartment for your half-sister,' Carlos says in conclusion.

45

Valeria twists sideways a little to relieve the pressure on the sores on her heels and injured shoulders.

As before, the low lid of the box stops her moving too much. She has to sink down onto her back again.

It's totally dark, and she's long since lost all perception of time.

The pain in her thigh from where she was bitten was horribly intense at first.

She's wet herself twice, but that's almost dried now.

She doesn't think about hunger, but she's extremely thirsty, her mouth is completely dry.

Occasionally she sleeps, an hour or so, maybe less. There's no way of knowing. Once she heard a thudding sound and a woman screaming in the distance.

It's as cold as a fridge, maybe colder. She can keep her fingers warm, but her toes have gone numb.

Behind the sweet smell of the wooden box, she can detect the stale odour of soil.

She stopped calling for help fairly early on, when she realised it was Jurek Walter who had done this, just as Joona had predicted.

She's been buried alive.

This is Jurek's doing, and the stocky man who came to her greenhouse is his new accomplice.

He was horrifically strong and aggressive.

She had already lost her wellington boots when he grabbed

232

her by one ankle and pulled her into the forest. Her raincoat slid up and dragged behind her like a cape. When it got caught on a branch he stopped and tore it off her.

He threw her in the boot of a car and drove off along a bumpy track.

Valeria tried to open the boot with her wounded hands, but lost her balance when the car lurched badly.

She was bleeding from the bite on her thigh.

She tried again, but it was impossible.

Suddenly she remembered what Joona said about situations like this. Sometimes he would tell her about the training he'd given his daughter up in Nattavaara.

The jack, she thinks.

There's almost always a jack in the boot of a car.

Valeria felt across the floor of the boot in the darkness, found the catches for the hatch, loosened them, then managed to move sideways and open the panel. She felt around the edge of the spare tyre, fumbling across a wrench and a warning triangle before she found a nylon bag containing the jack.

She positioned it as close to the lock as she could, then turned the screw with her fingers until it reached the lid of the boot, then fixed the handle in place.

The car lurched and she slumped onto one shoulder, but managed to hold the jack in place and started to turn it.

The boot was so cramped that she scraped her knuckles with each turn.

The metal started to squeak as the lid was forced upward, but then the car came to an abrupt halt.

She went on turning the handle as fast as she could, but gave up when the engine was switched off and the driver's door opened.

She fumbled for a weapon, got hold of the wrench just as the boot-lid opened, and lashed out. But he was prepared, grabbed the wrench, threw it away, yanked her hair back and pressed an ice-cold rag to her mouth and nose.

When she came round she was in this darkness. She's called for help, tapped out SOS, searched for anything she could use to open the box, she's pushed her hands and knees up and to the sides with all her strength, but the most she's heard is a faint creak in the wood.

She warms her fingers under her thighs and dozes off, but the pain from the sores in her heels wakes her up and she tries to move her feet.

Suddenly she hears a thudding sound above her, then the heavy dragging. Her heart starts to beat faster when she hears voices. She can't make out the words, but it's a man and woman arguing.

Valeria thinks she's been found and starts calling for help when there's a sudden bang as someone stamps on the box.

'For fuck's sake, she needs water, otherwise she'll die today, maybe tomorrow,' the man says.

'It's dangerous, though,' the woman says in an agitated voice. 'It's far too—'

'We can do it,' the man interrupts.

'I'll hit her if she tries to get out,' the woman says. 'I'll split her head open!'

The sudden light burns Valeria's eyes when the box opens. She squints and sees a man and a woman standing above her.

Valeria is lying beneath the floor of a room with bullfighting posters on the walls.

A hole has been sawn through the tiles, insulation and floorboards.

The man is pointing a hunting rifle at Valeria and the woman is holding an axe. They look perfectly ordinary, like neighbours, or the sort of people you'd see in the supermarket. The man has a blond moustache and anxious eyes, the woman's hair is pulled up into a ponytail and she's wearing pink-framed glasses.

'Please, help me,' Valeria gasps, putting one hand on the edge of the box.

'Stay there!' the man commands.

The coffin is lying on the ground in the sealed crawl-space beneath the house. Valeria is weak, but tries to sit up. The man hits her in the face with the butt of the rifle. Her head lurches back, but she keeps hold of the edge of the box.

'Stay where you are, you bitch!' the man roars. 'I'll shoot you, OK! I'll shoot!'

'Why are you doing this?' she sobs.

'Lie down!'

Warm blood is trickling down her cheek. Valeria reaches up with one hand and grabs hold of the floor. The woman brings the axe down, but Valeria has already lost her grip when the blade cuts deep into the floorboard.

The man shoves her in the chest with the barrel of the rifle and she falls back into the coffin, hitting her head on the bottom.

She had time to see the thick straps in the ground next to the coffin. They're the same sort as the ones she uses in her nursery, and she knows the winches have a tensile strength of ten tons.

'Give her the water,' the woman says in a tight voice.

Valeria is gasping for breath, she knows she needs to establish contact with them, she mustn't get hysterical.

'Please, I don't understand—'

'Shut up!'

A teenage girl with a length of wood in one hand approaches the coffin with a look of terror in her eyes. She tosses a plastic bottle of water into the coffin, then pushes the lid shut again with her foot.

46

Pellerina was immediately placed in the police protection programme, with the highest level of security the state could offer.

Saga bought two used phones with pay-as-you-go accounts, and added the other number to each phone so that she and Pellerina could talk to each other.

She made sure she wasn't being followed, and drove around Stora Essingen before heading to Kungsholmen and driving into the car park beneath Rådhusparken, where she parked next to a black van with blacked-out windows.

The lenses of all the security cameras had already been covered over.

Saga got out of the car, walked round and shook hands with the tall, blonde bodyguard.

'I'm Sabrina,' she said.

'The threat level is extremely high,' Saga said. 'Don't trust anyone, and don't reveal the address to anyone, no matter who they are.'

Saga fetched Pellerina, said a quick goodbye and promised to come and see her as soon as she possibly could, then opened the door of the van and strapped her sister in.

'I want my own phone,' Pellerina said when Saga gave her the used one.

'You'll get it when I come and see you, it's broken and I need to get it mended,' Saga lied.

Pellerina looked at her helplessly through her thick glasses and started to cry.

'I was really careful with it.'

'It's not your fault,' Saga says, wiping the tears from her sister's cheeks.

Because Saga has been involved in personal security operations before, she knows that the apartment allocated to Pellerina is on P O Hallmans gata 17, and has an advanced security system, with reinforced doors and bulletproof windows.

Saga gets back in Nathan's car and watches as the van backs out and disappears through the folding doors and up the ramp.

As she was driving from Högmarsö to Södermalm Hospital she made three calls to the IT and telecoms department of the Security Police. They're trying to trace her dad's mobile, but it can't be activated remotely and it isn't giving off any kind of signal. The last time he used it was when he spoke to Pellerina in her painting class, and at that point his signal was picked up by a base station in Kista.

She knows they're trying to get information from other masts to try and triangulate the signal and identify his location at the time of the call more precisely.

Saga knows there's no point, but she keeps trying to call her dad. The endless ringing without any answer is like a dark memory of the night her mum died.

The voicemail clicks in and she ends the calls before she hears her dad's formal message and calls Nathan Pollock instead.

He's still out on Högmarsö with the forensics team. The sharp wind distorts his voice.

'How's Pellerina?' he asks.

'She's going to be OK, she's in a secure location now,' Saga replies, swallowing the lump in her throat.

'Good.'

'She was lucky.'

'I know, it's incredible,' Nathan says.

'But Jurek's got my dad,' she whispers.

'Let's hope that isn't the case,' Nathan says.

'I know he's taken Dad and Valeria.'

She takes a deep breath, clears her throat, and presses one hand against her eyes. Tears are burning behind her eyelids.

'Sorry,' she says quietly. 'This is all so hard to accept, even though I was warned.'

'We're going to solve this,' Nathan says. 'We need to focus on—'

'I have to look for my dad,' she interrupts. 'That's my duty, it's all I can think about, he's probably still alive, and I have to find him.'

'We will, I promise,' Nathan says. 'We've got plenty of people out here, we've already searched every inch of the churchwarden's home and the garage, but there's nothing that can be linked to Jurek or the Beaver . . . Erland Lind didn't have a computer, but we found his phone under the bed.'

'Maybe that can give us something,' Saga whispers.

'The dogs have been right through the forest, but there don't seem to be any more graves out here.'

There's a lot of disruption on the line and she hears shouting in the background.

Saga leans back against the headrest and runs her fingers over the rough leather of the steering wheel.

'I'd be happy to come back out, if that would be useful?' she asks. 'We need to talk to Carlos about whether to issue a nation-wide alert or—'

'Hang on a moment,' Nathan interrupts.

Saga sits with the phone to her ear and hears him talking to someone. The wind keeps catching the microphone and the voices vanish.

A woman gets into her car, starts the engine and drives to the ramp, and waits while the doors open.

'Are you still there?' Nathan asks.

'Of course.'

'You need to hear this: forensics have found something on the inside of the coffin lid,' he says. 'They've taken photographs of it using raked light, and have discovered two words . . . the churchwarden must have scratched the letters with his nails before he died, they're almost illegible.'

'What does it say?' she asks.

'It says "Save Cornelia".'

'Save Cornelia?'

'We have no idea who—'

'The churchwarden's sister is called Cornelia,' Saga interrupts, starting the car. 'She didn't have any contact with her brother. She lives fairly close to Norrtälje – that's less than twenty kilometres from the river where I shot Jurek.'

47

Saga drives to Svartnö, turns the car round and pulls over to the side of the road. She watches the quayside and dark grey water in the rear-view mirror.

When she sees the ferry approaching land she gets out of the car and walks down the slope.

Nathan is standing alone on deck with both hands on the railing.

The cables cut through the water with a hiss.

The ramp lowers and scrapes the quayside.

Nathan waves to the ferryman in his cab, then walks ashore. Saga hands him his car keys and gets in the passenger seat.

Nathan gets in, adjusts the seat and starts the engine.

Cornelia lives on the outskirts of Paris, a small residential area just east of Norrtälje.

'There was nothing else on the coffin lid,' Nathan says.

'Jurek probably threatened to kill Cornelia to make the church-warden cooperate,' Saga says, checking that the ringtone of her phone isn't switched off.

'So what was he thinking in the coffin?' Pollock goes on. 'He must have realised he was going to die, that was why he wrote the message, he hoped someone would find the grave and rescue his sister.'

'Jurek must have terrified him to make sure he wouldn't tell the police the truth . . . perhaps he'd already been given a taster of the grave, or had seen his sister in one . . . his dementia developed pretty rapidly after I first met him.'

They're driving past meadows edged with pine forest, and pass beneath the E18.

Nathan's left hand is holding the bottom of the wheel. Despite his impending divorce, he's still wearing his slim wedding ring.

Saga forces herself not to tell him to call and put pressure on the dog handler.

According to the car's satnav, they've got less than five kilometres to go.

As they drive they receive a few brief updates over the comms terminal in the car: Cornelia isn't answering her phone, and in the past month a number of bills have been passed to the bailiffs due to non-payment.

Before she retired, she worked as a nurse at Norrtälje Hospital.

Cornelia is seventy-two years old, and single.

The screen shows a broad-shouldered woman with short white hair and reading glasses hanging on her chest.

'Who interviewed her?' Nathan asked.

'No one,' Saga replies. 'I shot Jurek six months before the churchwarden found the body. There was no reason to think there was any connection between him and the sister.'

'But she lives less than twenty kilometres from where he disappeared.'

'I know, but we knew that Jurek was dying – how far could he get? We spoke to everyone who lived within ten kilometres of the river . . . that alone meant seven hundred interviews.'

She remembers that they discussed expanding the search area to twenty kilometres, but that would have included the built-up area of Norrtälje and would have increased the number of interviews by more than twentyfold.

'I mean later, though, when the body was found and the churchwarden developed dementia,' Nathan says, glancing quickly at her.

'I phoned and spoke to her,' Saga says. 'She hadn't been in touch with her brother for ten years, and had nothing of interest to say.'

They turn off onto a narrow gravel road with a strip of frosted yellow grass in the middle that leads directly into the thick forest.

Saga stares at the dark tree trunks slipping past.

Maybe Jurek is keeping Valeria and her dad on Cornelia's land.

Her mouth goes dry and she reaches for the plastic bottle of mineral water.

That's not impossible, it wouldn't be unlike him to gather the graves in groups.

She's always wondered how he managed to remember all those unmarked graves.

'What are you thinking?' Nathan asks, giving her a sideways glance.

'Nothing – what do you mean?'

'You're shaking.'

She looks at the bottle in her hand, drinks some more, then puts it down in the cup-holder in the central console and squeezes her hands between her thighs.

'I'm worried about my dad,' she says.

'I can understand that,' Nathan replies.

Saga turns to look at the green-black fir trees and the scrappy heather and blueberry twigs.

She can't bear the thought that she exposed her dad to this. It's all her fault, it's her responsibility and she has to save him.

They're several kilometres from the other houses when the dark forest opens out into a clearing. Nathan slows down as a red house with white eaves and windows comes into view.

'The dog handler knew it was urgent, right?' she says.

'She set off immediately,' Nathan says.

'There ought to be dogs closer, though. Maybe in Norrtälje?'

'Amanda's the best,' he replies patiently.

They roll slowly towards the little house. A muddy Jeep Wrangler from the 1980s is parked in a carport with a canvas roof, beside a wall of stacked birchwood.

Saga draws her Glock from her shoulder holster and feeds a bullet into the chamber.

They stop on a weed-ridden gravel drive leading up to the house. Saga gets out of the car without a word, holding her pistol close to her body, pointed at the ground, as she strides forward.

She hears Nathan shut the car door behind her.

She's fairly confident that Jurek isn't here; that wouldn't fit his way of operating, far too easy to trace.

She moves off to one side, looking for bare soil, signs of recent digging. Her eyes roam anxiously towards the edge of the clearing, in behind the carport, to the bare bushes beside the house.

Without waiting for Nathan, she hurries round to the shaded rear of the house. The ground is drier there, covered with pine-cones.

In the lawn between the house and the dark edge of the forest are two huge fir trees, with heavy, contorted branches.

There's a stepladder lying in the grass behind the larger of the trees.

Saga walks past a water-filled wheelbarrow and looks inside a small greenhouse full of dead plants. She can't see any obvious sign of graves, no vegetable patch, or bare corner of the garden.

'Saga? Talk to me,' Nathan says as he comes round the corner.

'They could be buried in the forest,' Saga says.

'I know how it feels, but we need to do this in the right order, we start by talking to Cornelia.'

Nathan returns to the front of the house, leaving Saga to gaze out at the trees for a while.

She's about to turn round and follow him when there's a crunching sound at the edge of the forest. Saga spins on her heel and raises the pistol, squeezing the trigger until she feels it catch; she focuses her gaze, scanning for movement.

All she can see are tree trunks.

She moves slowly sideways and hears the crunching sound again. She thinks it must be an animal foraging in the under-growth, and moves cautiously towards the edge of the forest.

She stops and stands completely still for a moment, scanning the trees.

Seeing nothing, she turns and starts to walk back to the front of the house, but stops and looks towards the trees again where she heard the noise before carrying on round the house.

Nathan rings the doorbell and takes a step back.

Saga stands next to him and notices a sign indicating that a duty nurse lives here.

Cornelia's been running a private nursing clinic from her home, she thinks.

Nathan rings the bell again. The sound is clearly audible through the walls. He waits a moment, then tries the door.

It's not locked, and swings silently open on its three hinges.

'Put your pistol away,' he says.

Saga wipes the sweat from her hand on her jeans, but keeps her pistol in her hand as she follows him into a waiting room containing a television, two hard sofas, and a magazine rack.

They cross the pale grey linoleum floor, check the visitors' toilet, then carry on through the door to the treatment room.

There are two large paper fans blocking the views from the windows facing the carport. The sun is only just reaching above the treetops. The windowpanes are dirty and there are dead flies on the sills.

Along one wall is a bunk covered with coarse protective paper, and on the other a desk with a computer, phone, and printer.

Beyond the desk is a door with a frosted-glass window at face height.

The room behind the door is dark.

Saga sees her own hazy reflection in the clouded glass as she approaches and opens the door. The only thing visible in the darkness is the metallic glint of a strip of evening sunlight.

She reaches in with one hand, feeling across the wall, and the thought that someone could be standing in there watching her flits through her head. Her fingertips find the light-switch, she presses it, and raises her pistol.

She walks slowly inside and shivers as she looks round.

Cornelia's living room with its open fireplace has been turned into an operating theatre. The curtains are closed and held shut with clothes pegs.

Motes of dust sparkle in the air in the glare of the ceiling light.

Nathan stops next to Saga and looks at the well-used equipment.

The operating table may only be around ten years old, but the ECG machine isn't even digital, and prints out its readings on graph paper.

There's a round operating lamp next to a drip-stand, and a

stainless steel trolley. On top of the trolley are a capnograph and cylinders of oxygen, medicinal air and carbon dioxide.

'This is too advanced for a nurse's clinic,' Nathan says beside her.

'I'm starting to realise where we are,' Saga replies.

48

Saga walks through the operating room with her pistol raised and pushes open a door that leads to a small bedroom. The bed is neatly made, with a crocheted bedspread. There's a pill box on the bedside table, next to a Bible.

They go into the kitchen, which contains a pine table and four rib-backed chairs with red cushions tied to them. Above the sink is an old-fashioned storage unit, with glass-handled scoops for flour, sugar and oats tucked into wooden cubbyholes. A stained coffee-cup and a plate with crumbs on it are standing in the sink.

'He's taken her,' she says.

'Amanda will be here with the dogs in an hour,' Nathan says.

Saga lowers her pistol, pauses for a few seconds, then puts it back in her holster. She walks slowly over to the window and looks out at the huge pine tree and the stepladder lying in the grass.

The forest isn't particularly large, possibly no more than a thousand hectares, but it's started to get dark and the search will take time.

They return to the living room and stop in front of the protective plastic that's been spread out on top of the fitted carpet beneath the operating table.

'Should we call forensics?' Nathan asks.

'Yes,' she sighs.

Saga looks at the closed curtains. The strip of light has almost vanished now. Someone could already be standing outside watching them without them knowing.

'So this was where Jurek ended up after you shot him,' Nathan says.

Saga nods and goes over to a tall glass-fronted cabinet. She studies the array of saws, scalpels, hooked suture needles, and haemostats. On the top shelf is an old-fashioned, bound journal.

The acrid smell of disinfectant hits her as she opens the cabinet and takes the book out.

In the 'admission date' column, Cornelia has entered the date Saga thought she had killed Jurek Walter, and in the column for 'name and place of abode' she has written 'Andersson'.

The most common surname in Sweden.

That's followed by a fifteen-page handwritten account of the first four months, followed by three pages of sporadic notes of treatment leading up to this summer.

As Saga and Nathan stand side by side reading about everything that happened in this room, they grow more and more astonished at the accuracy of Joona's guesses.

Cornelia had been standing smoking in the car park of the Bergasjön nature reserve when her dog picked up a scent. A body had been swept along on the current and had got stranded in the shallows just before a wide curve in the river.

She thought he was dead when she backed her Jeep down the gentle slope and out into the water. It wasn't until she lifted the man onto the back of the Jeep that she realised he was conscious.

In spite of the cold and the severity of his injuries, he had somehow managed to persuade her not to take him to hospital.

She must have realised from the gunshot wounds that he was probably wanted by the police, but still saw it as her duty to try to save his life.

She told him she was a nurse, and that she could patch him up enough for him to be able to get to a doctor he trusted, but once they got to her house he asked her to conduct the necessary operations herself.

The journal doesn't say how she got hold of the equipment – maybe she had a set of keys to the store at her former hospital.

In the journal she gives a scrupulous account of the patient's condition and care.

He had three life-threatening injuries, and a number of less serious wounds.

The shots fired by Saga are all accounted for.

Two or three high-velocity projectiles had ruptured the front lobe of his left lung, and fractured his left shoulder blade.

Cornelia wrote that she wasn't qualified to administer strong sedatives, but that the patient had refused even basic painkillers.

He lost consciousness several times during the operations that followed.

She describes the patient's condition as critical until she saved his lung and stopped the bleeding from his upper arm.

'She gave him her own blood . . . because she's blood group O, she knew she could give blood to anyone no matter what group their blood was,' Saga says.

'Unbelievable,' Nathan whispers.

Later that night she began to operate on his injured hand. Large parts of it had been destroyed by the shot, literally torn away.

Traumatic injury to the artery, a complete rupture. There was no way of saving it.

'She amputated his hand,' Saga whispers.

Moment by moment, Cornelia describes how she removed the hand without specialist equipment, using a Gigli saw, filed the exposed bones, isolated the blood vessels and nerves, inserted a double catheter for drainage, then shaped the stump using a flap of tissue and skin.

'Why didn't Jurek destroy the journal, burn the house down, something like that?' Nathan wonders when they finish reading.

'Because he knows that none of this could lead back to him until he'd carried out his plan,' Saga replies. 'Jurek isn't afraid of prison or secure psychiatric care, that wasn't why he escaped.'

She walks out of the house and looks off along the road through the forest.

A crow is crying in the distance.

She looks in the Jeep in the carport, then circles the house. She stops in front of the curtained window of the operating room and imagines how things unfolded.

Fairly soon after the operation Jurek must have started to look for a man the same age and build as himself.

He probably drove around in Cornelia's Jeep long before he had recovered, searching among beggars and the homeless.

When he found the right person, he shot him in the same places he had been shot, then let him die.

Perhaps he had the whole thing planned from the start, perhaps it occurred to him when his own hand had to be amputated.

Despite the large quantities of antibiotics, Jurek suffered a secondary infection in the afflicted arm which led to gangrene.

Cornelia fought the infection as long as she could, but eventually decided to perform a second amputation, above the elbow. By this point Jurek must already have left his hand and the stranger's torso to rot in the sea.

In the spring following the second amputation, Jurek took the decayed body parts to Cornelia's brother, the churchwarden. Jurek forced him to photograph the torso, cut the finger from the hand, put it in alcohol, and cremate the rest of the remains.

The idea was probably that the churchwarden would contact the police to inform them of the body he'd discovered, but before he had time to do that he met Saga on the shore.

The wind blows through the trees, knocking more pine cones to the ground.

Saga stands still in the garden.

The water in the wheelbarrow is as black as pitch.

The Earth has continued to turn, and the last of the evening sun lights up the large pine tree from a different angle – and now Saga sees a new shadow on the grass.

It reveals what's been hidden at the back of the tree.

A body is hanging from a high branch.

That's why the stepladder is lying where it is.

Saga walks round the tree and looks up at the dead woman with the rope around her neck.

Cornelia has hanged herself.

Her wellingtons have fallen to the ground beneath her.

She has ingrained blood on her fingertips and on her chest.

She must have done it around three weeks ago, kicking the stepladder away, then fighting instinctively to get free.

She was probably already dead by the time the churchwarden scratched his message in the coffin lid.

He was the hostage, so that Jurek could force Cornelia to do what he wanted – not the other way round.

He needed her, not the churchwarden.

The last entry in Cornelia's journal concerns trials of a YK prosthesis, with a functioning grip in the hand controlled by wires.

Perhaps that was when she realised he was planning to kill more people, and that she had saved the life of a sadistic serial killer.

49

Seven hours later the dog handler drops Saga off on Timmermansgatan. She runs the last block to her building on Tavastgatan, rushes up the stairs, gets in her flat, locks the door behind her, checks it, then pulls the curtains in all the windows.

The sky is black above the rooftops.

She goes into the kitchen and starts calling colleagues involved in the search for her dad. No one has anything to report yet, but one tells her he's going to be getting the results from eight base stations tomorrow.

Saga swallows an impulse to shout and swear at him.

Instead she explains very calmly that her dad has been buried alive, and that he might not survive the night.

'Please, try to put more pressure on them,' she pleads. 'I need the results this evening, it could make all the difference.'

She hangs up, wipes the tears from her cheeks, takes off her dirty clothes and tosses them in the laundry basket, then has a quick shower to clean the wounds on her legs and arms before they get infected.

She cut herself badly in the undergrowth behind Cornelia's house.

It was already dark by the time the dog handler arrived.

Saga was watching from the veranda when she drove up in an old estate car. She stopped behind the Jeep in the carport, got out, put a rucksack down on the ground, then opened the back of the car.

A tall woman in her thirties, Amanda was wearing a black cap over her strawberry-blonde hair, black hunting clothing, and heavy hiking boots with ankle supports and ski-boot fastenings.

She gave the two police dogs some water after the drive, and Saga went up to her.

'You found us,' she said, holding out her hand.

Amanda seemed shy, she averted her gaze a little too quickly, then introduced her dogs.

Billie, a Belgian sheepdog, specialised in finding dead bodies, picking up the smell of cadavers and dried blood. Her head was black, but her thick mane was almost reddish-blonde.

Ella, a black retriever, was trained to find people alive. She had been flown down to Italy after the most recent earthquake.

Saga crouched down and talked to Ella, hugging her and patting her behind the ears, and telling her she had to find her dad alive.

Ella stood still, listening, and wagging her tail.

Though she wasn't wearing suitable clothing, Saga decided to go into the forest with Amanda and the dogs. She needed to be sure they didn't miss anything when they got tired, that they didn't miss any trace of a scent. They used their torches to light their way, letting the dogs decide which direction they should take.

It took them almost six hours to search the dense forest. Saga tore her jeans and kept catching her hair on jagged branches.

Amanda had superimposed a grid on a satellite map so that she could mark off the sections as they searched them.

They reached Björknäs without having found any trace of Valeria or Saga's father.

By the time they got back to their vehicles, Saga had begun to feel the cold and the dogs were showing signs of fatigue; Ella had white froth at the corners of her mouth, though she still wagged her tail when Saga petted her, while Billie had seemed nervous, whimpering, and twitching her pointed ears as if eager to be away.

Now Saga turns the shower off and dries herself, puts plasters on the deepest cuts, puts on clean underwear, a pair of loose velour trousers and a washed-out T-shirt, then puts her shoulder holster and pistol back on.

She gets her protective vest and stuffs it into a canvas bag, along with a knife and several boxes of ammunition.

On the hall floor in front of the door she lays out her motor-bike helmet, overalls and boots.

She needs to be ready if they find her dad. She needs to be ready to leap into action if they get any sort of tip-off, if anyone sees the Beaver or Jurek.

She opens her gun-cabinet, takes out a small Sig Sauer P290, checks that it's loaded, feeds a bullet into the chamber, releases the safety catch and fastens it under the kitchen table with a piece of duct tape.

She puts the roll of tape down, then stops and forces herself to stand completely still.

She's starting to act like Joona.

If anyone could see her now they'd think she was paranoid.

She needs to pull herself together and think clearly.

Pellerina is safe.

She repeats that several times to herself.

Pellerina is safe. And Saga is not going to give up until she's found her dad.

It's a terrible situation, but she can cope.

One day all this will be nothing but memories, she tells herself. Painful memories, but they'll fade a bit more with each passing year.

She takes a wine-box out of the larder, pours herself a glass of red, looks at the trembling surface and takes a sip.

Saga sits down at the kitchen table, drinks some more, takes out the second-hand pay-as-you-go mobile and calls Pellerina, even though they've already spoken on the phone twice today. She hasn't told her sister that the reason she hasn't been to see her is because it's too dangerous. She doesn't want to scare Pellerina, but she knows that a single visit could give away her secret address.

She misses her sister badly, wishes she could cuddle and joke with her, but she can't let herself give in.

'Sabrina's really nice,' Pellerina says in her slightly breathless voice.

'Do you think you'll be able to sleep OK if she's with you?'

'Why can't you be with me?'

'I have to work.'

'At night.'

'Is that OK?'

'I'm twelve now.'

'I know, you're a big girl.'

'We can say goodnight if you've got to work,' her sister says.

'I've got time to talk a bit longer.'

'It's OK.'

'Goodnight, Pellerina, I love you,' she says.

'Saga?'

'Yes?'

'I was thinking,' she says quietly, then falls silent.

'What are you thinking?'

'Have I got to stay here so the clown girls don't get me?'

50

Saga checks that her front door is locked, then puts her holster and pistol under the other pillow on her double bed.

It took her almost an hour to calm Pellerina down enough for them to be able to say goodnight.

First they talked about how the clown girls were only make-believe, then Saga steered the conversation onto the film *Frozen*, but just as she was about to end the call Pellerina started begging her to go and get her.

She could hear that her sister was still crying when they eventually ended the call.

Saga turns the light out, rolls over onto her side, and lays her head on the pillow.

She feels tiredness sweep through her body and closes her eyes, but then she starts thinking about her dad and her increased heart rate pulses in her ears.

This is his second night in a grave.

The temperature will fall below freezing, the ground will harden, the grass start to sparkle with frost.

She has to find her dad.

And then she has to find and kill Jurek. He's hiding out there somewhere. She needs to lure him into the light and finish what she once started.

Saga has just entered deep sleep when she dreams that a rough hand is stroking her cheek.

It belongs to her mum, who's grown old. When Saga realises that she's still alive, she feels full of an intense gratitude.

She tries to explain how happy she is.

Her mum stares at her, shakes her head, walks backwards through the room, hits her back against the window, and manages to get tangled up in the cord of the blind.

Saga jerks awake and opens her eyes. It's dark in the bedroom. She's only been asleep for an hour.

She blinks and tries to figure out what woke her up. Her phone is charging, and its screen is dark.

She's just telling herself that she needs to get back to sleep when she sees the thin figure sitting on the chair next to the window.

She starts to wonder if it's her dad, then fear takes over, and adrenalin surges through her nervous system.

She realises who it is.

Her heart is pounding as she slips her hand under the other pillow, but her pistol is no longer there.

'Little siren, always lethal,' the man on the chair says.

It's a voice she'll never be able to forget, a voice she's heard so many times in her nightmares.

The chair creaks as he leans over to one side, turns the standard lamp on, and looks at her.

'And still just as beautiful,' he goes on.

Jurek Walter's pale eyes and wrinkled face are turned towards her.

He's sitting up straight with her pistol and holster in his lap. He has a deep scar running across one cheek, and part of his ear is missing. He's wearing a check shirt and the shiny plastic of his prosthetic hand looks like that of a small doll compared to his rough right hand.

Keeping her movements unhurried, Saga sits up in bed. Her heart is beating so fast that her breathing is ragged. She knows she has to calm down, knows she has to play along until she can get to the pistol in the kitchen.

'I thought I'd killed you that time,' he says. 'But I was in a hurry, I was sloppy.'

'I thought I'd killed you,' she replies, and swallows hard.

'You very nearly did.'

'Yes, I've read what Cornelia did,' Saga says, breathing through her nose. 'But I don't understand why you're putting yourself through all this, you could have gone to hospital, got proper care, avoided the pain.'

'Pain doesn't frighten me, it's part of life,' he says calmly.

'But when will you be finished, when will all this be over?' she asks, a shiver running down her spine as his pale eyes focus on her again.

'Over?' he repeats. 'I live to restore order . . . and I'm inexhaustible, I was robbed, and that created a hole that needs to be filled.'

'I understand,' she replies, almost silently.

'I had to survive . . . Joona took my brother from me, and I assume you realise that I'm going to take everything away from him.'

At the thought of that he seems almost to smile for a few seconds. The pattern of wrinkles deepens like a mesh spreading across his face.

She considers his remark, about thinking he'd killed her. It's true, he hit her extremely hard, so hard that she passed out, but she's sure he didn't think he'd killed her.

For some reason he let her live.

And for some reason, he wants her to believe that that was a mistake.

She has to remind herself that Jurek lies all the time. Whether you believe the lies or see through them, you fall into the trap regardless.

Her only hope is to focus on finding some way of getting to the kitchen with enough of a head start to reach the pistol.

'You still run your finger along your left eyebrow when you think,' he says.

'Good memory,' Saga says, lowering her hand.

'Do you know, I noticed that you were looking at me through your eyelids when I came into the bedroom . . . If you'd woken up then, you'd have had your Glock in your hand—'

Jurek breaks off, stands up and walks calmly over to the gun-cabinet, where he locks the pistol away.

'It's fascinating, isn't it, the little evolutionary detail of our eyelids?' he goes on, turning to face her once more. 'We can see changes in the light when we've got our eyes closed, movement, silhouettes . . . and the brain registers sensory perceptions in our sleep.'

Saga turns her face away so as not to reveal how agitated she feels. She tells herself not to lose control now, she needs to stay calm, but she can't understand how he knows her secrets.

When she was small, she often had trouble getting to sleep; of a night she would lie awake, listening and registering the slightest movement through her eyelids.

Whenever she thought she saw something, she would open her eyes and check her bedroom.

She's never told anyone about this compulsive behaviour, not even a boyfriend, and she's never written about it in any diary.

Almost all children have compulsive thoughts, but what makes the memory of this one so painful is that she later realised it was connected to genuine survival. When her mum had her manic episodes, she used to imagine all sorts of things, seeing enemies everywhere and getting aggressive.

Saga needed to wake up if her mum crept into her room in the night, so she could calm her down.

Saga knows Jurek's trying to provoke her. She needs to focus, keep the conversation going, not let him trick her.

He wants her to believe that he can see right through her.

But of course he can't.

She needs to think.

Maybe she told him that bit about eyelids when she was in the high-security unit, when she was drugged.

She was given Trilafon and Cipramil, as well as intravenous injections of Stesolid, and Haldol Depot directly into her muscles.

The strong medication must have affected her judgement and caused lapses in her memory.

That's the only logical explanation, she thinks, and meets his gaze again. His pale eyes are observing her as if he's trying to determine what effect his words have had on her.

'Your sister was hiding behind the curtain,' he said. 'I realised that afterwards . . . very good, you've trained her well.'

'What are you doing here?' she asks.

'Do you really want to know?'

51

Saga pushes the covers back, lowers her feet to the floor and stands up. She doesn't have to play by his rules.

'Sit still,' he says.

All she can think about is getting to the kitchen, snatching the pistol from under the table, and shooting him in both thighs.

And once he's lying on the floor, she'll shoot him in his good arm.

Which would render him all but harmless.

She'll put him in the bath and let him bleed until he tells her what she wants to know. He'll talk, and as soon as she finds out where her dad is, she'll kill him.

'I just want some water,' she mutters, and turns towards the door.

She knows what Joona said: don't wait, kill Jurek instantly, as soon as you get the chance. He'd have said that the likelihood of finding her dad alive would only shrink if she listened to Jurek, even if she did have the advantage.

Jurek gets up from the chair as she walks across the bedroom. She can feel his eyes following her, lingering on her face, neck, the plasters on her arms.

'Stay here,' he says.

She turns towards him, scratches her stomach and looks him in the eye.

'I'm not going to try to escape,' she smiles, then carries on into the hall with no urgency.

She hears him follow her, but can't figure out how big her head start is. The light from the standard lamp shows her shadow sliding across the wall, closely followed by his.

Without stopping, she nudges the bedroom door and carries on towards the kitchen.

As she emerges into the hall she realises that Jurek is right behind her. He's not going to let her go to the kitchen on her own.

She glances at the closed front door, and the clothes and helmet on the floor.

Perhaps she could run away from him and grab the gun.

She hesitates, because the kitchen door is closed, and the moment is gone. When she passes the dresser with her keys and some scented candles on top of it, she can hear his breathing behind her.

Without any hurry, she opens the door to the kitchen, turns the light on and walks over to the sink without looking at the table.

Jurek watches her as she waits for the water to run cold. She fills a glass, then turns to face him and drinks.

His check flannel shirt is hanging down over the narrow prosthetic hand, whereas the right sleeve is pushed up to the elbow. His time as a soldier and his work as a mechanic made him tough, she thinks, looking at the oddly coarse hand, the muscles and thick veins beneath the wrinkled skin of his lower arm.

When she casts a quick glance at the table, she sees that one of the chairs is in an unfortunate position. She'll have to shove it out of the way to reach the gun.

Saga drinks some more, then gestures towards the table with the damp glass in her hand.

'Shall we sit down instead?'

'No.'

The pistol weighs so little that it only took one strip of tape to fasten it. That will save her vital seconds. Because even if she tears the tape off with the pistol, it won't get in the way when she shoots.

Jurek goes over to the counter and takes a glass from the wall cupboard. She moves a little further away, a few steps closer to the table.

The moment she hears the tap run she walks quickly and silently towards the hidden weapon. She puts the glass down, shoves the chair aside with one hand and reaches under the table with the other. Just as she's about to grasp the gun he shoves her, pushing her forward with great force.

She tumbles over two chairs and hits the wall with her shoulder blade, sinks to one knee, tries to get to her feet and fumbles across the table for support.

The glass container full of cornflakes falls to the floor and shatters.

He yanks her hard by the hair, brings the prosthetic down on her ear so hard that she collapses sideways, sending one chair flying as she tries to stay on her feet.

Her whole head is ringing from the blow.

He lashes out again, and Saga jerks her head out of the way and hits him in the face with a right hook.

His hand grabs her neck and starts to squeeze her throat. He pulls her towards him and hits her across the cheek and neck with the hard prosthesis, making her vision flare.

He's acting without any sign of fury, just cold efficiency.

Blood is running down her cheek from a cut in one eyebrow.

He jerks her sideways by the neck and hits her again, she tries to protect herself with her hand but can feel her legs starting to buckle.

He strikes her head again, and she falls, hitting her temple on the wooden floor.

A rush of emptiness sweeps through her.

Her toes are tingling.

She blinks but can't see anything.

On some level she realises that he's dragging her by the hair back to the bedroom.

Jurek sits her in the chair by the window, pulls off his belt, wraps it round her neck and ties it to the back of the chair.

She can't breathe.

She can make out Jurek standing in front of her, not moving, just watching her. The prosthesis has come loose in the struggle and is hanging from its straps and the shirt.

Saga tries to insert her fingers under the belt to stretch it. She's struggling to get air into her lungs, kicking out with her legs, trying to topple the chair but all she can do is bang it against the wall.

Her field of vision contracts and she sees flickering images of Pellerina against a white sky before he suddenly loosens the belt around her neck.

She coughs and gasps for breath, leaning forward over her knees as she spits bloody saliva onto the floor.

'Sit up,' he says calmly.

She straightens up, coughs again. Her face and neck are throbbing with pain. Jurek is standing by her bookcase, pulling the duct tape from the little pistol with his mouth.

Her vision is still shaky.

With three short steps he's in front of her, squeezing her cheeks together and pushing the short barrel into her mouth. Then he pulls the trigger.

The gun clicks, but it isn't loaded, he's removed the bullet.

She gasps and feels sweat trickling between her breasts.

'I don't know where Joona Linna is,' she manages to say.

'I know,' Jurek says. 'You don't even know which continent he's on right now, I know him, he doesn't tell anyone anything, it's the only way . . . If I thought there was the slightest possibility that you knew something about Joona, I wouldn't hesitate to cut your face off, piece by piece.'

'So why have you taken my dad, then?'

'I don't mean any harm,' he says. 'I'm almost done with you, you helped me get out of the secure unit, that was your only function.'

She wipes the blood from her mouth with the back of her hand. Her whole body is shaking with shock.

'So what are you doing here?' she asks.

'My brother has no grave, nothing,' he says. 'I want to know where he is.'

'They might have scattered his ashes in the garden of remembrance somewhere?' Saga suggests in a hoarse voice.

'I've tried to find out.'

'I have absolutely no idea. In certain special cases they keep the location secret to avoid it becoming a place of pilgrimage, but that—'

'That's as may be, but I want to know where he is,' Jurek says. 'There must be documentation . . . Naturally, I don't believe in God, but I'd have liked to bury my brother for my parents' sake . . . Igor had a difficult life, those years in the children's home in Kusminki broke him . . . And the Serbski Institute made him who he was . . .'

'I'm sorry,' Saga whispers.

'You have almost full access within both the Security Police and the National Operational Unit,' he says slowly. 'I'll give you your father in exchange for my brother.'

'I want my father alive.'

The wrinkles in Jurek's face deepen into what might be a smile.

'I want my brother alive . . . But it will be sufficient if you can provide documentation showing where he's buried.'

Saga nods and thinks that the only reason Jurek could have reacted so quickly in the kitchen was that he wasn't looking at the tap at all when he was pouring a drink, it was just a ruse to find out where the gun was hidden.

'You're going to do this for me,' Jurek goes on. 'Even if it means surrendering classified material, even if you have to break the rules.'

'Yes,' she whispers.

'Tomorrow – we'll meet around the same time, somewhere else.'

'How will I know where?'

'I'll send you a text.'

52

As soon as Jurek has gone, Saga locks the door, limps to the gun-cabinet, checks that her Glock is loaded and puts her holster on. She checks the door and windows once more, looks in the wardrobe and under the bed, then goes into the bathroom to inspect her injuries.

She washes her face, rinses her mouth and dries herself, then tosses the bloody towel in the bath and goes and sits on her bed with all the lights on, and starts to search through the Security Police database.

She gives up after three hours.

It's morning by the time she stops.

She can't find any information about where Jurek Walter's dead twin brother is.

Saga feels how sore her body is when she gets up from the bed and pulls on a pair of jeans and a soft sweater.

Before she leaves the flat, she makes another attempt to conceal the bruises on her face and neck with make-up.

The large investigation room at the National Operational Unit is deserted. Saga walks past the map of Europe that covers almost the whole of one wall and stops in front of the blurred pictures of the Beaver from the Belarusian security-camera footage.

Every detail they've noted so far takes on a completely new meaning now that they know Jurek is behind everything.

They had thought they were looking for a murderer who was trying to cleanse society, who saw himself as some sort of superhero. In reality, the Beaver was no more than a slave, a domesticated butcher.

Saga can hear voices in the corridor. Nathan is exchanging a few words with a colleague over by the coffee machine as he waits for his espresso.

The preliminary investigation has suddenly become the largest in the country and they'll shortly be meeting the leadership team. They have almost unlimited resources, but Saga knows that isn't going to save her dad.

She has to find Jurek's twin brother's remains.

Nathan comes in and drops his heavy bag on the floor before he looks at her.

'What happened to you?' he asks, putting his cup down on the desk.

'Oh, you know, I went through the forest with Amanda and the dogs . . . wrong clothes entirely.'

'You look like you've been in a boxing match.'

'Feels a bit like it too,' she says, then turns her face away.

Nathan drinks some coffee, then sits down.

'I stopped off at the lab and picked up two reports.'

'Have you had time to read them?' Saga says in a hoarse voice.

'I've only leafed through them, but they're fairly confident they've identified Cornelia's cause of death.'

'She hanged herself?'

He pulls out a thick folder from his bag, opens it and takes out the two preliminary pathology reports. He puts his reading glasses on, leafs through one of them and traces the lines with his forefinger.

'Let's see,' he murmurs. 'Yes, here it is . . . "The cause was total blockage of arterial flow to the brain."'

'Can I look?'

Saga sits on the edge of the desk and starts to go through the material. She stops when she reads that Cornelia's brother had been lying in his grave behind the churchwarden's cottage on

Högmarsö for at least three months, but died of dehydration one week after Cornelia committed suicide.

'They each helped Jurek, and now they're both dead,' she says, slipping down from the table.

She thinks about all the deals Cornelia and Erland must have made with Jurek. Their attempts to be helpful in order to save themselves and each other could well have been the cause of their deaths.

They had no idea how dangerous he was.

Joona used to say that every deal you make with Jurek only leads you deeper into the mire.

Saga imagines an old-fashioned fishing net in shallow water, where wooden rings form a tunnel you can't escape from. Each section is designed to make it easy for the fish to swim into easily, but impossible to get out of.

Saga's mobile buzzes. A text saying that the police have issued a national alert, and that Interpol have been brought in.

'A national alert,' she says in a subdued voice.

'Yes, I heard.'

'They still haven't identified the Beaver?'

'No.'

Saga goes over to the map of Lill-Jans Forest and the Albano industrial estate. She looks at the railway line and distribution of burial sites. Once upon a time Jurek kept a large number of victims buried alive there.

She stares at the markers on the map, trying to understand how Jurek could keep track of all the graves, spread out across something like three million square metres.

And this was just one of his cemeteries.

He must have had maps somewhere, or lists of coordinates.

But in all their years of searching, they've never found anything like that.

They haven't even found where he actually lived.

The flat where he was registered was evidently no more than a façade.

And there was no trace of Jurek in the old workers' barracks where Jurek's brother was hiding out. Forensic experts and teams of dogs searched the whole quarry, the surrounding buildings and bomb shelters, but it was as if Jurek had never even been there.

'Nathan, what actually happened to Jurek Walter's twin brother?' she asks. 'To his body, I mean, where is it now?'

'No idea,' he replies, laying out photographs on the table.

'If the body still exists, I'd like to take a look at it,' Saga says, when she's confident she can keep her voice steady. 'At the injuries, you know, the old scars on his back.'

Nathan shrugs his shoulders.

'There's a comprehensive report from the Karolinska, and at least a thousand pictures in the archive.'

'I know, but I'd like to take a look with my own eyes. It's not important, though . . . Do you know who was in charge of the post-mortem?'

'I don't actually remember, but probably Nils.'

'OK.'

Nathan rolls his chair over to the computer and logs in, sits in silence for a while, types something, then clicks the mouse.

'Nils Åhlén,' he confirms.

'Can I see?' she asks, going over to stand behind him.

He gestures towards the computer and moves out of the way. She pulls up a chair and starts looking for information about whether the body was retained for some reason, but finds nothing. Just tables documenting all the injuries, the weight and condition of every organ.

She tells herself she's going to have to call Nils when she gets a moment to herself. Maybe she should go into the bathroom and call him now?

From the corner of her eye she sees Nathan pinning the pictures from Jurek Walter's file on the wall.

His official police photographs show him from the front and in profile.

He's got older, has more scars and is missing his left arm. But the calmness in his wrinkled face and pale eyes is unchanged.

'The meeting's about to start,' Nathan says.

Her phone rings as she's switching the computer off.

'Bauer,' she says as she takes the call.

'We've found your dad's car,' a female officer tells her, panting as if she'd run to give her the news.

Barkarby Flying Club, the road and the area around Lars-Erik's car have been cordoned off. The police haven't found any visible signs of a struggle, but they discovered his smashed mobile in the frozen mud ten metres from the vehicle.

The crime scene investigators have been through the mechanics' sheds, the green hangars housing the small sports planes, the club building and overgrown landing strip.

The search party looking for Lars-Erik sets off from the gravel road beyond the fluttering cordon-tape.

The winter grass is stiff with cold. Red- and yellow-brick buildings rise up above the treetops, like sombre witnesses to the search.

Saga hasn't been able to get hold of Nils Åhlén. He's on a plane, flying back from a conference in Melbourne, and won't be home until eight o'clock that evening. The thought that Nils might know something about Jurek's brother is the only thing stopping her from panicking right now.

Police officers with dogs and volunteers from the Missing Persons organisation form long chains. They've all been told to look out for pipes sticking up from the ground, or soil that seems to have been disturbed recently.

Ninety people in yellow vests start to move across the grass, through patches of woodland, poking at dense patches of under-growth with sticks, searching alongside roads and along paths.

When they come to a halt after searching the sandy slopes of the nearby motocross course, Saga walks off to one side and calls Randy. He doesn't answer, and a heavy feeling of loneliness fills her chest.

'They've found Dad's car, I'm going to stay out here as long as the search is going on . . . please, call me when you get this,' she says in her message, then goes back to her place in the chain and carries on across Järvafältet with the others.

*

It's eight o'clock in the evening, and Saga is waiting in the Falafel Bar. She slips down from her high stool and takes the bag of food from the counter.

The search was called off at half past six, when they still hadn't found any trace of her dad.

Saga knows she needs to find out where Jurek's brother's remains are to stand any chance of getting her father back.

She goes back to her flat, locks the door, puts the bag of food down on the kitchen table, checks all the windows and cupboards, looks under the bed, pulls the curtains, switches all the lights off and then calls Nils Åhlén.

'I've literally just switched my phone back on,' Nils says in his nasal voice. 'The plane's not finished taxiing.'

'I need to ask you something.'

'We'll be done with the post-mortems tomorrow or—'

'Listen,' Saga interrupts. 'I'm calling because you did the post-mortem on Jurek Walter's twin brother.'

'Igor.'

'What happened to his remains?'

'I don't remember,' Nils mutters. 'But I assume we followed the usual procedure.'

'Can you find out?'

'Someone stole the body from the cold store,' he says in a subdued voice.

'Stole?'

'Right after we'd finished the post-mortem.'

'Why would someone want to steal his body?' she whispers.

'I don't know.'

Saga takes a few pointless steps forward, then turns and lean against the window, feeling the cool of the glass against her sweaty back.

'Could it be a coincidence?' she asks. 'Medical students messing about? Someone who just wanted a dead body?'

'Why not?' he replies.

'Nils, please tell me what you know, this is really fucking important.'

'I don't know anything,' he says slowly. 'And that's the truth . . . but I only mentioned the theft to one person, the only person I thought needed to know about it . . . I thought he'd be upset, but he took it very calmly.'

She stares into space, aware that he's talking about Joona, and that he's the one who for some reason took the body.

'Do you have any idea where the body might be now?'

'I haven't made any attempt to find out, because there was no practical need to,' Nils replies bluntly.

They end the call, and Saga stands in silence for a while.

The body is gone.

She had been sure Nils would be able to help her, that there was a reasonable explanation for where the body had ended up.

Her dad has been buried alive, and she has nothing to offer in exchange for his release.

She takes the plastic carton of falafel out of the bag, gets out some cutlery and sits down at the kitchen table.

Saga looks at her mobile. She hasn't called Pellerina today, because she doesn't feel up to lying to her again. She needs to rescue their dad first.

53

Darkness will soon fall on the fields and meadows; the colours of the landscape are already diluted and watery.

As usual the wind is blowing from the southwest, and the bare branches of the weeping willow are swaying gently.

Joona and Lumi are on their last shifts of the day while Rinus rests in his room.

They're in the surveillance room, the largest in the building. They've put their empty coffee mugs down on a box of ammunition.

The regimented timetable and monotonous tasks mean that days in the safe house tend to blur together.

'Zone 2,' Lumi says, closing the shutter over the opening.

She puts her binoculars down on the plain wooden table with its fixed felt covering, rubs her eyes and looks at the time.

Zone 2 covers the fields towards Eindhoven and a distant greenhouse.

All the zones overlap, and take account of the idiosyncrasies of the landscape.

It's impossible to keep an eye on the whole of their surroundings at all times, but as long as they stick to the plan, the risk of anyone approaching the workshop without being spotted is kept to a minimum.

'Zone 3,' Joona says, looking at his daughter.

She's sitting on her chair, staring at the floor.

'Ninety minutes to go before we wake Rinus,' Joona says.

'I'm not tired,' she mumbles.

'You should still try to get some sleep.'

Lumi doesn't answer, just stands up and walks past the table where Joona's phone is charging.

She stops in front of the large monitor screen. It's divided into sections, showing the workshop and the inside of the garage from various angles.

The smooth reinforced walls blur together in the gloom.

Rinus has repainted the pillar that had been worn smooth by the hydraulic shutter.

The old, crooked door is swaying in the wind.

Lumi walks back, past the row of hatches covering the firing holes looking down on the garage, and sits on her chair again without looking at her dad.

'How long are you planning to keep us in hiding?' she asks after a pause.

Joona looks out through one of the openings with his binoculars, lingering on a dense patch of bushes in front of a water-filled dyke.

'This is starting to feel like Nattavaara,' Lumi goes on. 'I mean, if Saga hadn't found us we'd still be there – wouldn't we?'

Joona lowers the binoculars and turns towards her.

'What am I supposed to say to that?' he asks.

'I'd never have gone to Paris.'

Joona raises the binoculars and scans the next part of the sector, a furrowed field and the clump of trees where the underground passageway emerges.

'What if the high-ups in the police didn't listen to Nathan?' Lumi goes on, talking to his back. 'What if they don't believe you? I mean, then Valeria wouldn't have any protection . . . would she be OK if that's the case?'

'No,' Joona says.

'And you don't care – I can't get my head around that.'

'I couldn't stay, I had to leave in order to . . .'

'To save me – I know,' she says.

'You're on zone 4.'

'Dad,' Lumi says as she gets to her feet. 'I'm doing all this

273

because I promised I would, because it matters to you, but this isn't going to work forever . . . I'm already falling behind at college, I've got a social life, this is so fucking useless, on every level.'

'I can take your zones,' he says.

'Why would you do that?'

'If you want to draw, read, eat—'

'Is that what you think I'm talking about?' she snaps. 'That I want to sit and draw instead of doing my duty?'

'It doesn't bother me,' he says.

'Well, it bothers me!' Lumi says, snatching her binoculars from the table.

She walks past Joona, stops at the window next to the filing cabinet and opens the shutter.

Beside the partially collapsed outbuilding behind the workshop the drainpipe sticks up like a huge straw.

An old tractor tyre is lying on the edge of the field. The lights of cars on a minor road in the distance flicker between the tree trunks.

Everything is peaceful.

Lumi closes her shutter and puts the binoculars down. She can't bring herself to say the name of the zone she's just checked. Instead she crosses the room, pulls the curtain aside, and walks out.

Joona moves on to zone 5, looks through the binoculars, lingering on the neighbouring farm in the distance, where an old bus is parked up in the yard.

In his notes to Nathan Pollock he asked him to leak information to the evening tabloids as soon as Jurek Walter was dead and Nils Åhlén had categorically confirmed the death.

At least once a day Joona checks every page of the papers' online editions, but there's been nothing so far, which means that Jurek is still alive.

And Joona knows what Jurek is capable of.

He keeps hearing him whisper that he's going to take his wife and daughter, that he's going to trample him into the dirt.

But Joona can understand his daughter. For the past two years she's been living her own life, a life she could only have dreamed about before.

And to her, Jurek Walter isn't a real threat.

He wasn't dead, as they had believed when they left their hiding place in Nattavaara, and nothing had happened to her.

She's been living the sort of life any young, independent woman might.

Joona checks the farmyard and bus in the distance again before closing the shutter and putting the binoculars down.

He goes to the kitchen to get coffee, past the curtain and stairs down to the ground floor, opens the door and blinks in the bright light.

Lumi is standing by the worktop with her phone clutched to her ear. Her cheeks are red as she defiantly meets his gaze. He marches over to her, snatches the phone, and ends the call.

'I need to speak to my boyfriend – and you can't—'

Joona throws the phone on the floor and stamps on it, smashing it to pieces.

'You're mad!' she yells. 'What's wrong with you? You're so fucking cool the whole time, but you're really just scared, like some old guy hiding in a bunker with loads of guns and tinned food, so you can survive some fucking war that isn't even real.'

'I'm sorry I dragged you into this, but I had no choice,' Joona says with sombre calm, pouring the last of the coffee from the jug.

Lumi hides her face in her hands and shakes her head.

'You think everything I do is dangerous,' she mutters.

'I'm worried about you.'

She takes a deep, shaky breath.

'I didn't mean to shout, but it makes me so angry, because this isn't working, in fact it's totally fucking claustrophobic,' she says quietly, sitting down at the kitchen table.

'We don't have a choice,' Joona replies, drinking some of the bitter coffee.

'I haven't told you about Laurent,' she goes on in a calmer voice. 'I'm in a relationship with him, he's important to me.'

'Is he an artist too?'

'He's involved in video art.'

'Like Bill Viola.'

'Well done, Dad,' she says in a subdued voice. 'Like Viola, only more modern.'

Joona walks over to the sink and rinses his mug.

'You can't do that again,' he says.

'I can't bear the thought of him panicking – I mean, what's he supposed to think when I suddenly vanish?'

Lumi's hair has come loose from her ponytail, and the tip of her nose is red.

'If you call Laurent, Jurek will kill him, and before he dies he'll reveal the number you called him on.'

'You're mad,' she says, and swallows hard.

Joona doesn't respond, just goes back to the surveillance room. He picks up the binoculars, opens the shutter for zone 1 and starts again.

54

It's almost dark enough to have to swap the binoculars for the night-vision rifle-sights in order to keep watch over the flat landscape around the workshop.

Joona is checking the boarded-up main house and abandoned garden furniture.

He hears Lumi enter the room and glances over at her. She's stopped just inside the curtain, with her hand on a stack of chairs.

He goes back to watching, checking the barrier and narrow track that leads off to the main road.

'Are you OK? Are you sure you're really OK, Dad?' Lumi asks, wiping tears from her cheeks. 'It's not that long since you got out after spending all that time in prison . . . all you said was that you had to help an old friend, but I'm guessing it was really about Jurek.'

'No,' he replies, and moves on to zone 2.

He checks the immediate vicinity through the binoculars, first the dark bushes along the dyke, then he raises the binoculars towards the distant greenhouse.

'It's always him, whenever you lose your judgement,' Lumi goes on. 'I know what happened to Samuel Mendel, and how badly that affected you, that you felt you had to sacrifice us to—'

'Quiet,' Joona interrupts sharply.

A light is flickering at the top of the binoculars' lenses, like a blue rainbow. Only for an instant. He looks through the window past the binoculars and just catches sight of a mobile phone going dark in a large hand.

'Wake, Rinus, we've got visitors,' he says in a low voice as he identifies two figures in the darkness.

Lumi hurries out of the room, simultaneously drawing her pistol.

Joona can make out the curve of the taller man's head against the slightly lighter background. The figure is moving towards the workshop before disappearing behind something.

He hears Lumi come back with Rinus.

'I can't see them any more, but they're close,' Joona says.

'How many?' Rinus asks.

'Two.'

Lumi quickly takes a semi-automatic rifle from a wooden crate, inserts a full cartridge and puts the gun on the table, then takes out another one, inserts a cartridge and lays it next to the first.

'I don't think it's Jurek,' Joona says, looking Rinus in the eye.

Lumi moves over to the monitor as she checks the emergency bag containing her passport, cash, water, emergency flares, and a pistol.

Joona raises the binoculars again and quickly scans the whole sector before moving on to the next.

The weak light of the monitor is lighting up Lumi's anxious face. She's concentrating on the external cameras that show what's happening in the immediate vicinity of the workshop and garage.

The low light makes the images grey and grainy.

Suddenly two figures emerge from the darkness.

Their pale outlines move along the side of the workshop and step over something lying on the ground.

'I can see them,' she says.

Rinus goes and stands next to her as he fastens his protective vest.

The diodes that piece together the image from the infrared heat-sensitive cameras make it look like the two figures are moving through a snowstorm.

They seem to be emitting a kind of pale dust.

They stop in front of the large garage doors.

Lumi catches a glimpse of them on the cameras inside the building as the loose door sways in the wind.

Joona is moving round the zones so they're not taken by surprise by any more intruders.

Rinus picks up one of the semiautomatics from the table.

It isn't possible to see what the two men are doing outside the garage.

On the monitor Lumi sees one of them hold the door open for the other.

'They're coming in,' she says under her breath.

Joona and Rinus are standing beside her watching the screen.

The two intruders turn round and the monitor flares white when one of them raises a camera and takes a picture.

Joona releases the reinforced shutter.

It slams shut instantly behind the intruders, the clang echoing off the walls.

The two men cry out and stumble backwards against the solid wall, scrabbling around it in panic.

Rinus switches the floodlights on and Lumi and Joona see that they've caught two youths. One is hammering against the door with his hands, and his hat has fallen off. He has a full red beard and torn jeans. The other is gasping for breath. He's shorter, with dark hair, and is wearing a denim jacket with a fleece lining.

They turn round in the enclosed space with a look of abject fear on their faces, trying to understand what's going on.

Rinus opens one of the firing holes and the young men's agitated voices suddenly sound louder.

He calls out something in Dutch and the two men stop at once and put their hands in the air.

'Don't frighten them,' Joona says.

The men follow a series of short commands from Rinus. They turn to face one wall, kneel down, put their hands behind their backs, and then lean forward to rest their chests and one cheek against the wall.

That's one of the best ways to control an enemy – when they're in that position, it takes them much longer to launch any sort of counter-attack.

Joona realises that the two youngsters are nothing to do with

Jurek, but seeing as they could still be dangerous he keeps them covered with one of the semiautomatics while Rinus goes down to them.

One of them gets so frightened when the door opens that he almost loses his balance.

Rinus walks in, lowers his pistol, puts it back in its holster, then goes over and pats them down.

'What are you doing here?'

'We're looking for a good place to hold a party,' the bearded man says in a subdued voice.

'Stand up.'

They both get cautiously to their feet, and their breathing speeds up when they see Rinus's scarred face.

'A party?' he asks.

'Factory Dive – one night, one stage, three acts,' the younger one in the denim jacket says.

'Sorry,' the bearded man blurts out. 'We thought the place was abandoned. We live in Eindhoven, we've driven past it loads of times.'

'It says private property on the signs.'

'They always say private property and no trespassing,' the shorter man says.

55

Saga puts her phone and pistol down on her kitchen table. It's late evening. The wind is blowing so hard against the window that it's rattling. A strip of dark glass is visible between the curtains.

She's felt oddly vacant since her conversation with Nils Åhlén.

She has nothing to negotiate with now, and needs to change her strategy.

It isn't easy to understand why Joona took the body.

Joona has always responded to Jurek with unexpected harshness, and has been prepared to do things no other police officer would do.

Jurek has a very orderly mind, and his only mistakes have happened when he lost control for a moment.

Joona probably took the body to prompt another of those moments.

He'll have buried it somewhere, unless maybe he froze it.

Joona could never have predicted that she would need it.

If only he would get in touch, Saga thinks, trying to eat some of her cold food.

She's just wondering about phoning Nils again to ask about the cold store at the Karolinska Institute when her mobile starts to buzz on the table.

She starts, then smiles with relief when she sees that it's Randy. She nudges the tub of cold food aside and picks up the phone. 'Randy?' she says.

'I've only just heard your message, I've been in the dark-room – how are you doing?'

'Fairly good, under the circumstances,' she murmurs.

'Shall I come over?'

'No, I—'

'I'd be happy to.'

'I have to work,' she says.

'It's past eleven o'clock,' Randy says quietly.

'I know.'

'Can I ask what's going on?'

After talking to Randy, Saga drags the armchair from the living room into the hall, turns the volume of her ringtone up as far as it will go, puts it on the dresser, makes a quadruple espresso, puts her shoes and coat on, then sits down on the armchair and stares at the front door with her pistol in her hand.

Randy told Saga to call him whenever she wanted, if she wanted to talk, or – if she felt like having company – he could come and sleep on the sofa.

But Saga is starting to realise that she needs to deal with this on her own.

Otherwise she won't get her dad back.

They've finished searching the woodland around Cornelia's house with dogs, and have been across Järvafältet with lines of officers and volunteers.

It's almost unbearable.

He could be lying in a coffin like the churchwarden, struggling to get enough air through a narrow tube.

The strong coffee has gone cold by the time Saga drinks it. She puts the cup down, glances quickly over her shoulder, then settles down to watch the door again.

She knows she ought to be exhausted after the exertions of the past twenty-four hours, but it's as if her brain can't relax.

If Jurek does get in touch tonight, she's going to say she's expecting information about his brother's remains tomorrow.

She can't tell him that Joona took the body.

She's not going to negotiate with Jurek, but at the same time she needs to let him know that he'll never find out where his brother is if her dad dies.

By two o'clock in the morning she's almost fallen asleep when her phone suddenly buzzes to say she's got a text message.

Her hands start to shake as she takes the phone off the dresser and tries to see what it says. The bright light of the screen makes her pupils contract. The letters slide sideways as she reads: *Hasselgården, entrance C1, ward 4, 2.30.*

With a feeling that everything is happening too slowly, she goes and gets a sheet of paper from the printer, writes down the address and time and leaves the sheet on the kitchen table.

If she doesn't come home or get in touch, someone will find the note.

She snatches up her pistol and two cartons of ammunition.

As she runs down the stairs she looks up Hasselgården and discovers that it's a care home for people with dementia, run by a private company whose website proclaims care of the elderly to be a growth market.

Saga pulls the tarpaulin off, starts her motorbike, and rides away from Södermalm into the cold winter's night.

She changes up to fifth gear on the straight part of Bergslagsvägen, and her head jerks back as the bike accelerates.

The lights on the tall posts in the middle of the road flash past.

The name Hasselgården, with its suggestion of hazel trees, makes her think of a red wooden building from the last century with creaking floorboards and traditional fireplaces, but as Saga approaches the home she finds a dirty high-rise block with salmon-pink plaster and brown window frames.

She stops and turns her bike round fifteen metres from entrance C1, puts her pistol in her pannier, and leaves her helmet on the handlebars.

The door of the main entrance is unlocked.

She glances at the plan of the building and fire escapes, then takes the lift up to the fourth floor.

The machinery whirrs into action with a hiss.

Saga thinks that she misjudged Jurek, he was stronger and faster than she could ever have imagined.

The only reason she's still alive is that he wants something.

Maybe it is just to reclaim his brother's remains, but she has to be prepared for the possibility that he wants something more.

She'll listen to him, talk to him – she needs him to believe that he's messing with her head, finding his way into the darkness inside her.

But as soon as she finds out where her dad is, she'll dispatch a rescue team, and then she'll do everything she can to stop Jurek.

She knows she can't afford any more mistakes, the next time she reaches for a gun she needs to be certain that she's going to kill him.

He's extremely dangerous, but not to her, not at the moment.

She can exploit the fact that he's interested in her.

This isn't a fairy tale about Beauty and the Beast.

He isn't in love with her, but she can tell that he sees something special in her.

That was what Joona meant, that Jurek is interested in what's going on inside her, her inner catacombs.

She needs to exploit that.

Saga repeats to herself that she mustn't let herself be drawn out, mustn't let herself be provoked, but that she's going to have to let him inside, just a little, to prompt him to reveal anything.

It might well be dangerous, but she has no choice.

She succeeded last time, and she's planning to succeed again.

She's going to stick to the truth.

Exchange darkness for darkness.

She looks at herself in the lift mirror. Her eyes are dark and impassive. Her face is bruised, it looks like someone else's.

56

The lift doors slide open and Saga steps out onto the fourth floor. Three metres in front of her is a glass door with a sign saying Ward 4. She can see the illuminated lift and her own reflection in the door, but it's hard to make out the corridor beyond.

A woman's screams cut through the walls.

The lift doors close behind Saga. The light shrinks to a narrow strip, then vanishes altogether.

Suddenly the darkened ward is visible through the door.

An old man is standing looking at her with his nose pressed against the glass. When she meets his gaze, he turns and hurries away.

She cautiously opens the door, and makes sure that it shuts behind her.

The old man is dragging a tube along the floor behind him.

The subdued lighting reflects off the grey linoleum. A black handrail runs along one wall.

One of the doors on the left is open.

Saga moves forward slowly, trying to see if there's anyone hiding behind the door.

The row of sprinklers in the ceiling cast shadows that look like spiked flowers.

She's getting closer to the open door, but just before she gets there it slams shut with a bang.

A man is talking with a put-on voice, and it sounds like he's rearranging the furniture.

The next door is also open.

She approaches it warily, each step revealing more of the small lobby, bathroom door, and part of the flowery wallpaper.

A thin woman is sitting asleep in a wheelchair in the middle of the room. She has a blue-black mark on the back of one hand from a cannula.

Someone's giggling further along the corridor.

Saga moves on slowly, glancing at the emergency exit, and noting that the door opens outwards.

She knows that Jurek is much stronger than her.

She's spent countless hours in the gym and on shooting ranges.

Jurek's fitness comes solely from combat situations, where he was forced to kill to survive.

She steps over a crutch lying on the floor and carries on along the corridor.

There are splashes of red-brown liquid on the scratched skirting board and textured wallpaper.

The lift whirrs into motion behind her.

With silent steps she reaches the unlit staff room. She can hear a bleeping sound, some sort of alarm.

'Hello?' Saga says tentatively, and walks through the doorway.

Faint light is coming from one side, illuminating a dining table with a Christmas cloth and a bowl of oranges.

She feels a chill rush of adrenalin when she catches sight of the blood that has been trodden across the floor in the L-shaped kitchen.

The fridge is open, that's where the alarm is coming from.

A pool of blood leads off to the side.

Saga looks at her own reflection in the dark window, and the empty doorway out into the corridor.

She turns the corner and sees a middle-aged woman lying on the floor behind an overturned chair.

The glow from the fridge doesn't reach the woman's face, but Saga can see her dark blue trousers and T-shirt.

Her laminated name-badge glints on her chest.

Saga moves closer and sees that one of the woman's trouser

legs has ridden up. Her shin has been snapped in two, the jagged bone is sticking through the blood-stained nylon of her socks.

Her head is in darkness, but as Saga moves closer she discovers that her nose and the entire middle of her face have been smashed in.

The linoleum floor beneath her is covered in blood.

The woman's upper jaw and nose cavity have been pushed back into her skull, leaving her lower teeth bare.

Saga turns and feels her legs shaking as she walks back out into the corridor.

She opens the cabinet on the wall and takes out the heavy fire-extinguisher so that she has some sort of weapon.

From behind one door comes a sound like a child crying, but it must be one of the patients, a senile woman with a high voice.

Saga reaches the dayroom, with an electric Advent candelabra in the window. A large man is sitting on the sofa with his face turned towards the switched-off television.

'You can stop right there and put your hands up towards the ceiling,' he says in a low voice.

She puts the fire-extinguisher down on the floor as he stands up and turns towards her. There's no doubt that he's the man known as the Beaver.

He's big, bigger than she'd expected. He's holding a saw in one hand, an ordinary handsaw with a rusty blade.

The Beaver is wearing a crumpled black raincoat, and the pearl earrings are swaying from his earlobes.

'Saga Bauer?' the Beaver says.

He blows his cheeks out, drops the saw on the floor and starts to walk towards her. The look in his narrow eyes is sad and serious.

'I'm going to check you for weapons, and I want you to stand completely still,' he says in a dark voice.

'I assumed I should come unarmed,' Saga says.

He stops behind her and starts to run his big hands over her neck, under her arms, down her chest, stomach and back.

'This is an intimate situation, and I'm not particularly comfortable with it either,' he explains as he starts to feel between her legs and buttocks.

'Perhaps that'll do now,' she says.

Without answering he carries on down her thighs and shins, then stands up and checks her hair, before finally asking her to open her mouth and checking inside with the light on his phone.

'Jurek told me not to bother with the other bodily orifices,' he says.

'I'm not armed,' she repeats.

'And you won't be needing this,' he says, picking the fire-extinguisher up with one hand.

He starts to walk and she follows him along the corridor. When he leans forwards to put the fire-extinguisher down Saga sees that he has a fat wallet in his back pocket.

Further down the corridor an old woman is walking along with a rollator. She stops at every door, tugs at the handle, crying that she's going to beat all the children.

The Beaver shows Saga into a dark room that smells of pipe tobacco and disinfectant hand-gel.

'Jurek will be here shortly,' he says, switching the light on.

'Is he your boss?' Saga asks.

'He's more like a strict older brother, I do whatever he tells me to.'

Saga walks past the small kitchen area and discovers that there's an old man lying in the bed crying. He has grey hair, thin arms, and a washed-out nightshirt. A large plaster is hanging loosely from his cheek.

'Where is everyone?' he sobs. 'I've been waiting and waiting, but where are Louise and the boys, I'm so alone . . .'

'Stop whining, Einar,' the Beaver says.

'Yes, yes, yes,' the old man says, and presses his lips together.

The Beaver takes his black raincoat off, crumples it up and pushes it behind the radiator.

She thinks about the recording of him shooting a man in Belarus, and the trail of frenzied destruction in the bar on Regeringsgatan.

'I know how I look, but I'm more intelligent than most – 170 on the Wechsler scale.'

'Everyone's different,' Saga says warily.

The Beaver squints at her, then smiles, revealing his crooked front teeth.

'But I'm unique,' he says.

'Would you care to elaborate?'

'If you think you'd understand.'

'Try me.'

'I have an allele, a variant gene that means I can incorporate specific mutations, like IVF, only naturally . . . I was born with a sort of sixth sense.'

'How do you mean?'

'The simple version is that it's on the precognition spectrum . . . Most people don't believe me when I mention it – not that that matters. The truth is that I have an ability, I know who's going to die first almost every time I enter a room.'

'You know who's going to die first?'

'Yes,' he replies seriously.

57

The Beaver purses his lips and closes his eyes, as if he's trying to see into the future to see which person in the room is going to die first. A few seconds later he opens his eyes and nods sadly.

'Einar,' he replies, then leans his head back in a silent laugh.

When the old man hears his name his upper body starts to rock catatonically as he begins to whimper again.

'Where are you? Louise? I'm waiting and waiting . . .'

The Beaver sighs, walks over and presses the old man's mouth so hard that blood starts to run down his chin, then he punches him, making his head bounce against the wall.

'He's just senile,' Saga says.

The Beaver wipes his hand on his trousers and walks back to Saga. Einar is sobbing quietly in his bed, asking in a bewildered voice after Louise and the boys.

'Can you guess why I wear my pearls?' he asks.

'As a tribute to an important person in your life,' she replies.

'Who?'

'Will you tell me where my dad is if I guess right?'

The door opens and Jurek Walter walks in, wearing the usual check shirt, labourer's trousers and heavy shoes.

Without so much as looking at them he goes over to the kitchen area and pours a glass of water. His prosthetic hits the counter with a dull clang as he turns the tap off.

'Isn't this place unnecessarily risky?' Saga asks. 'Why don't you live in your own place?'

Jurek drinks the water, then rinses the glass.

'I haven't got a home,' he says.

'I think you've got a house,' Saga goes on. 'It's probably not completely isolated, seeing as you seem to think it would be a risk taking the Beaver there.'

'A house?' Jurek repeats in a low voice, turning his pale eyes on her.

'Your early childhood was spent in Leninsk,' she says. 'Near the cosmodrome. Your name was Roman, and you lived in a house with your brother Igor and your father.'

'Yes, well done,' Jurek says drily. 'I guessed it was by tracking my father's movements that Joona Linna found the gravel pit.'

He looks down at the floor and tries to adjust the straps of the prosthesis.

'But here in Sweden . . . why didn't your brother live with you?' Saga goes on.

'He wanted to live at the quarry. He needed to be near Father's things, the furniture he recognised – I suppose some places have a sort of magnetic attraction that keeps you there.'

The Beaver goes over behind Jurek and tries to adjust the straps under his shirt. The prosthesis seems have twisted slightly and he's trying to loosen it.

'Just take it off,' Jurek says curtly

With a calm smile the Beaver starts to undo the straps across Jurek's back.

'A prosthesis never obeys the way you want it to,' the Beaver explains to Saga. 'It's almost as if the power relationship is reversed when you start to adapt to the limitations of the prosthesis.'

He rolls Jurek's flannel shirt up, gently releases the arm's fixture, and pulls it out from the sleeve along with the straps.

Saga catches a glimpse of the end of the stump before the shirt falls back into place. It's very high up the arm, not far below the shoulder. Cornelia has stretched the skin over the stump and made sure the stitches and sutures were on the inside of the arm.

The Beaver puts the prosthesis in the sink and ties a knot in the loose sleeve of Jurek's shirt.

'You know there are more modern prostheses?' Saga says.

'I don't really miss the arm anyway,' Jurek replies. 'It's just a cosmetic issue, an attempt not to attract attention.'

Saga looks at the blood-stained plastic hand sticking out of the sink, and the sand trickling from the cup.

'Why did you put Cornelia's brother in a grave?' she asks.

'Cornelia was threatening to commit suicide, so I took her to the island and made her watch while I buried him.'

'But it didn't work,' Saga says.

Jurek makes a resigned gesture with his hand, then takes hold of the knot in the other sleeve.

'I'd like to have kept her,' he says. 'But when she realised I'd tracked her daughter down in Fort Lauderdale she hanged herself . . . she thought that would save her daughter, but obviously it hasn't.'

'You're really not interested in the killings though,' she says hoarsely.

Those pale eyes focus on her once more, and she holds his gaze without blinking.

'That's a good observation,' Jurek says.

The Beaver takes out a frying pan and puts it on the hotplate, then gets eggs, cheese, and bacon from Einar's fridge.

'I don't even think you wanted to kill me before, like you mentioned the last time we met,' Saga says, with a feeling of taking a leap in the dark.

'Perhaps not,' he replies. 'Perhaps that's the way it is with sirens. You don't want them to die – and that's what makes them so dangerous. You know they're going to ruin everything, but the thought that they might disappear is simultaneously unbearable.'

The Beaver turns on the extractor fan above the stove, then starts to melt some butter in the pan.

'Let's go to the dayroom,' Jurek says.

They leave the Beaver cooking and go out into the corridor. Jurek pushes a wheelchair out of the way with no trace of urgency.

'I remember what you said about the first times you killed anyone,' Saga says as they walk.

'Is that so?'

'You said it was strange . . . like eating something you didn't think was edible.'

'Yes.'

'So how is it now?'

'Like physical labour.'

'And it never felt good?' Saga says tentatively.

'Oh, yes.'

A woman is screaming so hard behind one of the doors that her voice breaks.

'That's hard to imagine,' Saga says.

'"Good" might not be the right word, but the first time I killed anyone after Father's suicide . . . it felt calming, like when you've solved a complicated riddle . . . I hung him up on a spike and told him why it was happening.'

'So that was when you explained the way you saw things to him . . . about how you were going to restore order or however you want to put it,' Saga says as they pass the fire-extinguisher on the floor.

Jurek doesn't answer.

They reach the dayroom where the Beaver was waiting for her when she first arrived.

An old woman is standing on the other side of the sofa, poking her stick at the floor in front of her, muttering something, then starting the process all over again.

Jurek gestures to a table where there's a small portable laptop. They walk round the dark aquarium and sit down opposite each other. Jurek's empty shirtsleeve ends up on the table and he brushes it off with his right hand.

Saga looks over at the old woman behind the sofa and swallows hard. From this angle she can see that she's poking at a severed head with her stick. The woman doesn't seem to understand what's on the floor in front of her but is still anxious, as if she can't quite put her finger on what's wrong, and somehow imagines she can put it right with her stick.

The slowly rolling head belongs to a man in his thirties with a neat black beard. His glasses have fallen off and are lying in the pool of blood.

58

Saga looks away from the senile old woman and can hear the sound of her own breathing. She looks at the dark aquarium and thinks that she can handle this meeting, provided she remains calm.

'Hasn't it ever felt good for you?' Jurek asks.

'Only once – when I shot you,' she replies, looking him straight in the eye.

'I like that,' Jurek says.

'Because you tricked me into thinking I'd killed my own mother,' she goes on, but regrets it immediately.

She doesn't want to talk about her mother.

She never wants to talk about her, it doesn't do her any good.

The old woman catches hold of the glasses with her stick and backs away, leaving a trail of blood after them. She stops and looks over towards the door, mutters something to herself, seems to forget about the glasses and starts to walk towards the corridor.

'I assumed you did that intentionally,' Jurek says, leaning back in his chair. 'It would have been perfectly natural, but I was wrong.'

'Yes.'

'I know you were only eight years old,' he goes on. 'And, in purely legal terms, you had no responsibility for her, but obviously you could have saved her, that's always an option.'

'You don't know what you're talking about,' Saga says, feeling the weight of each breath.

'I don't know anything about you, I'm not claiming that, but I assume you went to school like all Swedish children.'

'Yes.'

'Are you saying that no one noticed anything? That no one noticed that you sometimes hadn't slept for days, that you came to school with bruises on your face and—'

'Mum never hit me,' she interrupts, then purses her lips.

'She was fairly heavy-handed, though? You said you never wanted to take your jacket off because you were ashamed of all the bruises.'

Saga tries to smile wearily, in an attempt to hide how agitated she feels. Jurek takes nourishment from other people's darkness.

He thinks he can shock her, get her off balance with his cruelty, but she's already thought all these things, that's why she keeps that door firmly closed.

'Mum never hit me,' she says in a calmer voice.

'I didn't say she did. You survived, it was OK, but that gave you a chance to save her,' he goes on, wiping his hand on the front of his check shirt.

'I understand what you're doing,' Saga says.

'All you had to do to save her was tell someone about your situation,' Jurek says slowly. 'But for some reason you thought that would be disloyal. And that was what killed your mother.'

'You don't know anything,' Saga says.

Her lips are dry, and when she moistens them she can feel her mouth trembling.

He can't know anything, but she remembers the morning when she had been awake for three days and her mum felt better and made pancakes for breakfast. Before Saga went to school, her mum made her promise not to say anything about what had happened that night.

It was a long time ago, and Saga no longer remembers what had happened, all she remembers is that her mum said Saga would end up in a children's home if she said anything.

She slowly gets up from the chair and turns away.

Maybe it was just a throwaway remark, but why would she say she'd lose custody if Saga said anything.

'I'm not saying you wanted to kill her,' Jurek goes on, talking to her back. 'But you neglected to save her, and that's perfectly understandable, given what she'd done to you.'

Saga realises she's let Jurek inside her head.

She looks up, stares at the simple floral pattern of the wallpaper and tries to compose herself.

It doesn't matter, she tells herself. This is part of the plan, she can handle it.

She knows that his technique of mixing the truth with lies has an ability to open up the doors that lead to the catacombs. There's no danger if she puts a stop to it there, he won't get any deeper now.

She realises that he's right when he says that someone at school must have understood things weren't right. She remembers having bruises on her neck and upper arms, and she knows she used to be incredibly tired. They tried to talk to her, of course, took her to see the school nurse and the counsellor.

She turns back towards Jurek, clears her throat quietly, then looks him in the eye.

'My mum was bipolar, and I loved her, even if it was hard sometimes,' she explains calmly.

Jurek runs his large hand over the top of the computer.

'It isn't inherited,' he says.

'No.'

'But there are genetic vulnerabilities that increase the risk of a child having the same condition by a factor of ten.'

'Genetic vulnerabilities?' she says with a sceptical smile.

'Abnormalities in the configuration in the genes that control perception of time are passed down, they're supposed to work on a frequency of twenty-four hours, of course, but if they don't, then the risk of bipolar disorder increases.'

'I sleep well.'

'But I know you have periods of hypomania . . . when you get incredibly focused, think fast and are easily irritated.'

'Are you trying to tell me I'm mad?'

Jurek's eyes remain firmly focused on her.

'You have a darkness inside you that's almost a match for mine.'

'What does your darkness look like?'

'It's dark,' he says with a trace of a smile.

'But are you healthy or are you mad?'

'That depends who you ask.'

Jurek stands up and walks over to one of the doors. He listens, glances out into the corridor, then returns to Saga. The empty sleeve swings as he walks.

'Isn't your brother's illness inherited, then?' Saga says when he's sitting down again.

'Igor was just downtrodden.'

'Why didn't you look after him?'

'I did . . .'

'I was there in the gravel pit with the forensics team, I looked inside those barracks, went down into the old shelter, I saw everything.'

'Nothing escapes forensics,' Jurek sighs and leans back.

'Your brother lived in utter misery,' Saga says. 'Did you ever go there, make sure he had a hot meal, sleep under the same roof?'

'Yes.'

'You treated him like a dog.'

'He was the best dog I've ever had.'

'And now you want to bury him like a human being?'

He smiles joylessly at her.

'I've requested all the files about your brother,' she goes on. 'The request needs to be authorised, it'll take a few days.'

'I'm not the one in a hurry, am I?'

'You only get the information if I get my dad back,' she says, and feels her chin start to tremble. 'I know how it sounds, but the best thing would be for you to let him go at once.'

'You think so?'

'I promise, you'll get all the information relating to your brother's body, but if my dad dies you won't get anything.'

'So don't let him die, then,' Jurek says simply.

He opens the laptop and turns the silvery computer towards her.

A web-chat program is already running. Using peer-to-peer technology, this computer is connected to another computer in another location. The two screens show what's happening in front of the other computer in real time.

Saga can see that the other computer is trained on a cramped space with rough cement walls, lit by a bare bulb in the ceiling.

'What's that supposed to be?' Saga asks, even though she knows the answer.

Black shadows are moving across the cement wall – as if they were reacting to her voice – then, a moment later, a figure appears off to one side of the screen.

It's her dad.

He's started to get a white beard, his glasses are gone, and he's squinting in the harsh glare of the bulb. His brown corduroy jacket is dirty and sandy. Something scares him and he flinches as if he's expecting to be hit.

'Dad,' Saga cries. 'It's me, Saga.'

When he hears her voice he starts to cry. She can see his mouth moving, but there's no sound. He doesn't seem to have been seriously injured, but there's some dried blood on his face and white shirt.

'Please, don't get upset,' she says to the screen.

Her dad approaches the computer, she sees the light of the screen reflect off his face. Trembling, he reaches out with his dirty hand. He tries to say something again, but she can't hear anything.

'Dad, listen,' she cries. 'I'm going to find you, I promise . . .'

Jurek breaks the connection and closes the laptop, then sits and studies her as if she were part of an experiment. With patient curiosity those pale eyes of his linger on her face.

'Now the darkness will close around him again,' he eventually says, very calmly.

59

Saga pulls the key out of the door and hangs it round her neck, covers the keyhole with duct tape, then tapes over the letterbox and turns round.

The light from the bathroom is falling across her face at an angle. She has a deep wrinkle between her eyebrows and lack of sleep has left her skin looking almost transparent.

The T-shirt under her jacket is wet with sweat around the neck.

She's already searched her flat. That was the first thing she did when she got home.

She pushes past the armchair, goes into the kitchen and opens one of the drawers. The sheet of paper with the address of Hasselgården on it flutters as she walks past.

She takes out two sturdy kitchen knives, goes into the bedroom and tapes one to the back of the open door.

She and Jurek have met twice now. Maybe she could have killed him on the first occasion if she'd hidden her pistol better, if she'd been aware of him entering the flat.

It's possible that she actually registered his presence in her sleep, through her eyelids, but dismissed the warning. She's been sleeping with Randy too much, she's no longer as alert as she used to be.

Saga tapes the other knife to the side of the toilet bowl, steps back to check that it can't be seen, then turns out the bathroom light.

Her phone is lying dormant on the dresser in the hall. She hasn't had any more messages.

Saga's eyes are burning with tiredness as she goes into the living room to fetch the standard lamp. The wooden floor is covered with her dirty footprints. She puts the lamp in the hall, switches it on and points it directly at the door so it will dazzle any intruders.

Thoughts are swirling through her head, images tumbling towards her in a torrent.

The dead bodies at the care home, her dad's frightened face.

His left eye was wounded, drooping slightly.

He was moving like someone who was dying.

Saga swallows hard and forces herself not to start crying, that would be completely pointless. If she can't sleep, then she needs to make use of the time, concentrate, think.

She sits down on the armchair with her pistol in her hand, the bag of ammunition by her feet.

Saga looks at her phone again, but the screen is dark. She puts the pistol on the arm of the chair and wipes her sweaty hand on her trousers.

She really should try to get some sleep, maybe dig out the morphine pills she's saved.

That would calm her down.

Jurek isn't likely to contact her again tonight. He thinks she isn't going to be getting any more information about his brother's remains until tomorrow.

She picks up her pistol again and stares at the front door.

There are air-bubbles trapped beneath the silvery tape.

She slowly closes her eyes, leans her head back and sees the light from the standard lamp through her eyelids.

She detects a slight change and immediately opens her eyes again.

It was nothing.

Saga can't help thinking that they didn't have to kill the night staff, they could have tied them up, locked them in somewhere. It must have been the Beaver. Jurek doesn't enjoy killing, it's of no significance to him.

If it was Jurek, then he did it because he wanted to frighten her, remind her how dangerous he is, that he's serious about her not getting her dad back unless she comes up with information about his brother's body.

She realises her hands are shaking when she checks again that her phone is charged and the volume turned up.

It's half past five.

Joona wouldn't have been happy with the way she's handling this. He would have told her to kill Jurek the first chance she got, even if it cost her dad's life.

That's impossible for her.

It's not a choice she can make.

Joona would have said that the cost keeps on rising with every second Jurek remains alive. It doesn't stop until you've lost everything.

Perhaps she's wrong, but it feels as if she and Jurek were sitting at a chessboard once more.

She was trying to lure him out through an opening in her defence.

That was the plan, anyway.

But what was she getting in return?

It must be something, seeing as you can't move a piece without leaving a gap.

It feels like she's missed an important detail, something she brushed past, something that could be pieced together with something else.

Her tiredness is suddenly gone.

Jurek managed to steer the conversation on to her mother even though she had drawn a sharp line there.

It was odd how easily that had happened.

She had felt she had control over the situation, that she had merely been denying false claims about her mum, but still managed to reveal that her mum had been bipolar.

It probably doesn't matter, but it was unnecessary.

Sometimes she feels like a butterfly he's trying to catch, but sometimes it's as if he's already got her in a glass jar.

Jurek Walter is smart.

He fed her a series of false suppositions before claiming that her mum had harmed her.

He was just guessing – but now he knows.

Every conversation with Jurek is a precarious balancing act.

She rubs her face hard with one hand.

She has to think.

Her memories of the conversation are growing weaker by the minute.

Jurek sounded cold when he said his twin brother was a dog; that was part of his strategy, he wanted to see how she reacted to his harshness, she's sure of that. But when he talked about different homes, that was probably genuine. He said that some places have a sort of magnetic attraction that draws you back time after time.

'Damn,' she mutters, and gets up from the armchair.

There was something she'd meant to remember.

But it was as if the sight of the dead bodies had erased her ability to think strategically.

Saga glances at the door, then goes into the kitchen, puts her pistol on the counter and opens the fridge.

When she asked about his brother, she had allowed Jurek to steer the conversation to her mum's bipolar disorder.

What had she got in return?

He was almost obliged to give her something.

Saga pulls a cherry tomato from the vine, pops it in her mouth, bites down and tastes the sharp explosion.

She tried to provoke him by saying he hadn't looked after his sick brother, said she had seen the misery he lived in when they searched the old workers' barracks at the gravel pit.

That was when it happened.

Jurek's voice took on an unexpectedly derisive tone when she spoke about the police forensics team going through every corner of the gravel pit.

Nothing escapes forensics, he said, seeming to imply that they had actually missed the most important thing.

Saga pulls the clingfilm off a plate of leftovers and starts eating with her fingers as she tries to think through the entire conversation again.

Jurek claimed that Joona managed to find his brother after their escape from the cosmodrome in Leninsk because of their father's work at the gravel pit.

She chews the cold pasta, swallows, then pops some of the chicken in her mouth, tasting the lemon and garlic on it.

The Beaver was standing behind Jurek, helping undo the straps. He spoke about prosthetics, and the fact that you start to adapt to their limitations.

A pointless contempt for weakness, Saga thinks. In her mind's eye she sees the Beaver putting the prosthetic in the sink, then some sand had trickled out of the end of it.

She saw it, but didn't understand at the time.

Jurek is living out at the gravel pit, that's the only plausible answer.

He's been there the whole time, she realises.

With trembling fingers she puts the empty plate in the sink and pulls the carton of yesterday's falafel out of the fridge. She chews quickly, then bites the end off a green pepper.

The gravel pit is the magnetic place, she thinks. That's where everything began and ended, that was where their father died, and that was where Jurek's twin brother died.

When he said 'nothing escapes forensics', he meant the exact opposite.

There must be another bunker, one that they didn't manage to find. Perhaps it's even further underground, beneath the ones forensics have already searched.

Saga can't help grinning to herself.

It could all fit

She goes through the conversation again as she eats dried-up hummus and carrot sticks, drinks juice straight from the carton and wipes her sticky fingers on her jeans. She goes to the table, turns the sheet of paper over and starts to write down the key points, starting with the sand trickling out of the prosthetic.

Jurek hasn't revealed anything obvious, but, taken as a whole, it's possible that he let something slip.

He claimed he had lived with his brother, but there was no trace of him either in the buildings or down in the bunker.

The perfect hiding place. Jurek knew that the police wouldn't find the hidden room, seeing as they'd already tried looking with all the resources at their disposal.

The cement wall that had been visible behind her dad could very well belong to a bomb shelter from the Cold War.

And once the connection with her dad had been broken, Jurek had said: *Now the darkness will close around him again.*

He didn't say anything about a grave, nothing about digging.

Saga is almost certain her dad is in the gravel pit in Rotebro. She hurries out into the hall and grabs her phone from the dresser.

60

After finishing her call to her boss, Verner Sandén, Saga sits down in the armchair with her phone in her hand, feeling a frightening rush inside her. He had listened carefully to what she had said, only patronised her once, and agreed with her analysis on almost every point.

When she explained the plan she had worked out, he was silent for a few seconds, then gave her the go-ahead to put together a small team. She would have access to rapid response officers from the National Response Unit, as well as an experienced sniper.

'I'm shaken up and pretty tired . . . but maybe we can finally put an end to this, maybe we can save my dad, maybe Valeria too,' Saga had said.

She stands up and goes into the kitchen.

The sky is getting lighter through the closed curtains.

When the police arrived at the care home, Jurek and the Beaver had long since left the building.

It isn't certain that the operation this evening will succeed, she could be completely wrong, she has to bear that in mind, but right now she feels a huge sense of relief at just having a plan.

She's going to prepare a trap that can be called off and evaporate like mist if circumstances change.

But with a bit of luck she'll be one step ahead of Jurek for a few seconds, and if that's true, they'll be the last seconds of his life.

The plan entails her being in position at the gravel pit with the sniper and rapid response team when Jurek contacts her with the location and time of their next meeting.

She'll tell him she'll see him there, and if he shows himself he can be taken out.

Saga opens her laptop again and examines the satellite and drone pictures. It's a fairly large area, with extreme drops in level.

She looks at the long grey block of the workers' barracks, which form a narrow strip between the forest and the pit where sand was extracted.

Beneath them are the bunkers.

She calls her boss again and says she needs another two snipers.

Verner replies that she'll have the whole team at her disposal in good time.

Saga puts her laptop and a scatter cushion with gold embroidery on it from the sofa in a blue nylon bag from IKEA, fetches her Game of Thrones mug from the kitchen, and unplugs the standard lamp.

It's already night by the time Saga and Nathan Pollock approach the meeting point on the narrow road west of Rotebro.

Nathan's phone buzzes, a text message from Veronica. She's sent him a red heart.

'I signed all the papers,' he says.

'Good.'

'I have no idea why I was being such a pain.'

The twelfth-century church at Ed shimmers like a white jewel in the darkness, beside the slumbering fields and black lake.

The team is already there.

Their black vehicles glint like splashes of ink in the distance.

Nathan turns onto a bumpy track, drives past the wall of the church and the signs warning of military manoeuvres.

It's just past midnight, and if Jurek follows the same pattern as previous nights they still have plenty of time to take up their positions.

Scattered lampposts light up the deserted car park.

Nathan stays in the car while Saga goes to see the team. She shakes hands with each of the six men from the National Response Unit, their commanding officer, and the forensics officers from the Security Police. Then she goes over to the three snipers who are standing slightly apart from the others.

Two of them are from the Special Operations Group in Karlsborg, plain-clothed men in their thirties. Linus is tall and blond and holds Saga's gaze slightly too long when they say hello, whereas Raul has deep scars across his cheeks and hides his mouth with his left hand when he smiles.

Behind them stands Jennifer Larsen from the Stockholm Police. She's dressed in black, has her brown hair in a thick plait, and has tied sports tape round her right hand.

'Do you feel like coming along for a while, then?' Saga says.

'Anywhere you say,' Linus smiles.

'Good,' Saga says, without smiling back.

'Just tell me who we're going to shoot,' Raul says.

'I'm going to need some time to set up my equipment and sort out the ballistics,' Jennifer says.

'How long?'

'Twenty minutes should do it.'

'You'll have more than half an hour after my briefing.'

'Perfect.'

The three snipers follow Saga back to the rest of the group. The entire area around the medieval church is quiet.

A half-moon trembles on the thin ice covering the lake.

So far Jurek has suggested a new meeting place each time, to avoid potential traps. If Saga is right, and Jurek is hiding out in the gravel pit, her plan might well succeed.

When Jurek contacts her, she's going to claim that she knows where his brother's remains are, but say she needs proof that her dad's still alive before she'll agree to an exchange.

Perfectly reasonable.

What Jurek doesn't know is that they've already got snipers outside his hiding place. The moment he shows himself, one of the snipers will have time to incapacitate him.

The only thing that happens if she's wrong about his hiding place is that the operation gets called off.

The most dangerous scenario is if the snipers miss or merely injure Jurek and he manages to get away.

If that happens, the rapid response team will storm the building.

But if Jurek gets away and her dad isn't there, she'll probably never find out where he is.

And all trust between her and Jurek will be gone.

The same thing applies if Jurek realises they're there, if he's got some sort of alarm system or hidden-camera surveillance.

But this is her only chance.

She would never have gone through with this operation if the odds weren't as good as they are.

Saga gathers her team in a circle, hands out maps of the gravel pit, and meticulously goes through the positioning of each sniper. Jurek Walter won't be able to leave the old workers' barracks without finding himself in a perfect line of fire. She shows the rapid response team which way to go in, where to gather, entry routes for ambulances, and somewhere a helicopter would be able to land.

While she delivers the operational tactics briefing, she thinks about what Joona said about disregarding all caution, all regulations when it comes to Jurek Walter. The only thing that counts is killing him. That's worth all the losses, all the potential consequences you could possibly imagine.

'So you don't want us to shoot the other one, the tall guy?' Linus asks.

'Not until the prime target has been incapacitated.'

'Incapacitated?'

'This should be regarded as a hostage situation,' Saga explains, and hears the tension in her voice. 'You're not to hesitate, you're not to miss, and you'll only get one chance.'

'OK,' Linus says, holding his hands up.

'Listen, everyone . . . to remove any trace of doubt when the situation becomes critical, I want to stress that the word incapacitate means that the shot needs to be fatal.'

The circle around her falls completely silent. A cold wind is blowing from the churchyard, lifting the frozen leaves from the ground.

'This isn't a complex operation when it comes down to it,' Saga goes on in a slightly milder voice. 'The various stages are clear, you've all been briefed, and we break off if anything goes wrong . . . I'll be with sniper number one, that's you, Jennifer, and we maintain strict radio silence until the order to proceed is given.'

61

The snipers return to their cars and start to get their rifles, helmets and camouflage nets out.

They change into warm, waterproof clothing in the dim light from the boots of the two vehicles.

Saga sees Raul do a little roll of his hips with his hands behind his neck once he's pulled his trousers on.

She goes over to the group from the National Response Unit to confirm their tactics when they force open the reinforced doors.

The men are specially trained for hostage situations, where storming the location is the only alternative.

'It's possible that the hostage is in a bad way, and a pressure wave could do serious harm,' she says.

'We'll start with welding arcs on the hinges and bolts,' the group leader says.

Saga is about to discuss the use of explosives as a last resort, but stops when she hears the snipers arguing.

'What the hell are you doing?' Jennifer asks angrily.

Linus looks at his friend with a grin and shakes his head.

'What did you just do?' she asks.

'Nothing,' he replies.

Saga sees him calmly fasten his camouflage trousers. He has broad shoulders, and is at least a head taller than Jennifer.

'I'm thirty-six years old and I've got two children,' Jennifer says.

'I've worked in the police for eight years, and no one just happens to pinch another person's nipple. That's a tactic used to humiliate and exclude women from certain professions.'

'All that matters to us is how good a shot you are,' Linus says coldly.

'Listen,' Saga says, stopping in front of them. 'That was fucking uncalled for and fucking unprofessional . . . No, shut up. Jennifer's right, every woman's had that happen to them, no one likes it, so lay the fuck off in future.'

Linus's cheeks are flushed.

'So call my boss and get me fired. I'm one of your best, but now that you ladies have teamed up . . .'

'We'll deal with this afterwards,' Saga says.

The men check their equipment with sullen looks on their faces. Saga goes over to Jennifer's car and sees that she's mounted a night-sight on her rifle, and has wrapped four magazines in camouflage tape, all lined up in the boot.

'I need three snipers,' Saga says. 'There's no time to find a replacement for him.'

'Don't worry,' Jennifer says, pulling some stray strands of hair from her mouth.

She fastens a knife in her belt, above her left hip, then puts her protective vest on and fastens the straps at the side.

'You're going to be lying over four hundred metres from the target area,' Saga says.

'I'll make the necessary adjustments,' Jennifer says.

'You handled those idiots well,' Saga says in a quieter voice.

'I used to let things like that go,' she replies wearily. 'And, oh, you know . . . felt ashamed of it. But now I've got way too much going on in my life to tolerate any more shit. My mum's got Alzheimer's and the rest of the family are already fighting over the inheritance.'

'I'm sorry to hear that,' Saga says.

'But the worst thing right now is that my husband's determined to run the Stockholm Marathon.'

'They all have their little projects,' Saga replies. 'I mean, my guy's got it into his head that he's a photographer.'

'Not naked pictures?' Jennifer asks with a wry smile.

'Yes, but *very* artistic,' she smiles.

'My husband went through that phase too . . . the marathon is much worse. I hope you manage to avoid that one.'

Saga is about to reply when her phone buzzes in her hand. She reads the short text message from Jurek: *Lidingö golf club 2 a.m.*

She takes a couple of steps away from Jennifer, composes herself, thinks through how to reply, then taps with trembling fingers: *I know where your brother's body is now. Before any exchange I need to see that my dad's OK.*

She reads her message twice, takes a deep breath, then clicks send. There's no way back now, she thinks. She's just lied to Jurek, and it's going to be very hard to maintain that lie if anything goes wrong.

While she's waiting for him to reply she looks out across the fields.

The forest is dark behind the church. The amber-coloured lighting on the façade makes the little building shimmer like molten glass.

There's a chance she might be able to put everything right.

Her phone buzzes again. Saga looks at the screen and shivers when she reads: *Make sure you've got a laptop handy.*

She walks across the car park with her heart pounding and raises her voice so everyone can hear her.

'Listen, we've had word from the hostage-taker, the situation is now live, you know what to do, take up your positions, make sure none of you is spotted, and await further orders.'

62

Saga is in the lead minibus, parked on a forest track on the top of the Stockholm Ridge, approximately one kilometre from the edge of the large gravel pit where she thinks Jurek is hiding out.

She's been sitting there for forty minutes now.

To be on the safe side, the forensics officers and team leader have left her alone in there.

They've cleared the inner panel inside the van and have set up a white backdrop. Saga is leaning against it, sitting on her cushion with her laptop on her knees and the Game of Thrones mug beside her. The only light comes from the screen and the standard lamp she's brought from her flat.

If she doesn't move the laptop, it will look like she's sitting at home in her flat when their computers connect and the cameras are activated.

She thinks through what she's going to say if Jurek asks her to take the laptop into a particular room in her flat. Hopefully it will be enough if she tells him the battery's charging and that they might lose their connection if she moves.

The cars passing by on the main road are almost inaudible, but the siren of an ambulance down on the motorway reaches into the minibus.

The snipers ought to be in position around the old workers' barracks now, and the rapid response team will have split into three pairs in the forest up above.

Saga thinks through the coming conversation once more. She's going to suggest an immediate exchange, but without seeming to be in too much of a hurry. Jurek takes nourishment from their conversations, the feeling that he's dissecting her soul.

She controls her breathing, feels the gentle movements of her stomach, and breathes out more slowly.

When the burbling sound indicating an incoming skype call starts up, Saga feels oddly calm.

It's almost as if she's got opiates in her system.

She moves her cold fingers over the pad, moves the cursor to the green symbol, and clicks to accept the call.

Jurek's face appears on her screen. He's disconcertingly close. She can see the network of wrinkles and countless scars on his forehead, chin, and one cheek.

Jurek's eyes inspect her calmly.

He's wearing an unbuttoned black hooded anorak on top of the same check shirt he was wearing last time. He's not wearing the prosthetic. The sleeve of the anorak is hanging empty. She can make out the shape of the stump beneath the fabric.

'You should have found your dad's car by now,' he says.

'I knew it wouldn't lead us anywhere, but I joined in with the search because it was expected of me,' she replies honestly.

Somewhere behind Jurek comes the sound of tired coughing. He doesn't react to the sound, his pale stare doesn't deviate from her face for a moment.

'I've been thinking about what happened when you found my brother,' he says.

'You'd been given a high dose of Cisordinol and happened to mention Leninsk,' Saga says.

'No, that . . . you couldn't have understood what I said.'

It's impossible to tell if he's feigning surprise, or if he genuinely didn't know that.

'That was how we found you.'

He breathes in and leans closer to the screen. Saga forces herself not to look away.

'You know that Joona executed my brother?'

'How do you mean?' she asks quietly.

'According to the post-mortem report, he shot Igor in the heart from such close range that the powder from the barrel penetrated his skin.'

Saga has also read the post-mortem report, and knows that Jurek is right, in purely technical terms. There were no witnesses when Igor died, and Joona refused to answer any questions at the obligatory debriefing that gets triggered automatically when firearms are discharged.

'I know Joona intended to arrest your brother,' she says in a steady voice. 'Something must have happened, or he wouldn't have fired.'

'Why not? People flatter themselves by claiming there are accepted norms for human behaviour . . . but everyone is basically jealous, cowardly, full of hate . . . bound by their environment and ready to defend their territory with unpalatable aggression . . . destroy other people . . . because in the end, when you're still alive and sitting down to dinner with your family, other people's suffering means nothing.'

'I want to see that my dad's OK,' Saga whispers.

'I want to see that my brother's OK,' he says, turning his computer.

Bare cement walls flicker past the camera in the top edge of the laptop before it stops on Saga's dad.

He's lying curled up on his side on the cement floor, next to a blue plastic drum. His bare feet are sandy, and his corduroy jacket is filthy.

'Lars-Erik, sit up,' Jurek says.

Saga sees her dad curl up, but he makes no move to sit up.

'Sit up now,' Jurek says, kicking him gently in the shoulder.

'Sorry, sorry,' her dad whimpers, and sits up against the wall, trembling.

He squints into the light, and almost topples over, but puts his hand on the floor to steady himself. He has traces of blood under his nostrils, on his cracked lips and in his white stubble.

Her dad is looking in surprise at Jurek, who turns his back on him and returns to the computer.

'Are you giving him water?' Saga asks.

Jurek sits down in front of the screen again. His pale eyes study her face.

'Why do you care so much about your dad all of a sudden?' he wonders. 'A few years ago you didn't even know if he was alive or dead.'

'I've always cared about my dad,' she says, swallowing hard. 'And I need to be certain you're going to let him go if I give you what you want.'

'The Beaver will drive Lars-Erik to a petrol station, where he'll be given a mobile to call you.'

'OK,' Saga whispers.

Jurek leans closer to the screen and studies her intently.

'How did you find out where my brother's remains are?' he asks after a pause.

'I can't tell you that,' she says, and notices that the laptop has started to tremble on her lap.

The silence between them grows. Jurek very slowly tilts his head to one side without taking his eyes off her.

'How do I know you're not trying to trick me?' he asks calmly.

'Because you wouldn't be asking that question if you thought I was.'

Jurek's lips form a thin smile, and Saga thinks that if she's wrong, if Jurek and her dad aren't here in the gravel pit, then she'll go through with the exchange anyway. She'll lie about knowing where his brother's body is, say it's being stored in a secret cold store at the Karolinska Institute.

Jurek stands up and takes the laptop with him as he leaves the room where her dad's lying. Saga catches a glimpse of a small room with cement walls before he closes and locks a thick steel door and sets off along a dark tunnel.

'We'll soon be finished with each other,' he says into the computer. 'But I need to see you one last time to find out why someone took Igor's body.'

'I promise you'll get your answers,' she says. 'Should I set off to Lidingö golf club right away?'

'You'll get a new address,' he replies, and ends the call.

63

Saga quickly pulls on her camouflage gear and protective vest, fastens the holster round her hips and pulls on her rucksack. She takes out a compass, then starts to run through the forest.

The muted light of her torch picks out a grey path across the black ground. She veers round a tree and jumps over some huge roots.

In four hundred metres she'll have to switch the torch off, and then it will be extremely dark.

She counts her steps and turns round, keeping her head down, and pushes through a dense thicket backwards, then turns and runs again.

She slows down when she's a hundred metres or so from Jennifer's position, breathing through her nose. She checks the compass, switches the torch off, and bends to duck under a low pine branch.

She moves cautiously forward, holding one hand out, dodges a tree, and slips on a rock.

To her left she can make out a floodlight in the gravel pit, but it's too far away to be of any use to them.

Her phone buzzes and she stops, breathes cold air into her lungs, opens her pocket, takes it out and reads:

Järfalla ice hall, 3 a.m.

She keeps moving, thinking that she can be at the ice hall in fifteen minutes by car. If she's wrong, or if for some reason they miss Jurek, she'll set off there on her own and carry on as if nothing had happened.

When the ground starts to slope downwards she slows her pace even more, treading carefully so as not to make any noise, not to snap any twigs, or send any cascades of stones rolling.

Even though Saga knows where Jennifer is, she still has trouble spotting her. She's cut some branches to give herself some cover, she's wearing camouflage gear and a net over her helmet, and is lying on her stomach with her legs wide apart, with the barrel of her rifle sticking through a clump of heather.

Saga approaches at a crouch, and sees that Jennifer has heard her, but she doesn't take her eye off the night-sight for a second.

It isn't possible to make out the workers' barracks in the darkened gravel pit four hundred metres away.

Not even the outline.

Everything is black.

Saga knows there's a fence in front of the sheer drop to the bottom of the pit, almost fifty metres below the original ground level.

There's a floodlight on a post maybe two kilometres away, but it's little more than a white dot against the black sky.

They maintain radio silence until the final order to go ahead or break off.

Saga lies down on her stomach a short distance from Jennifer. She can smell the pine needles and damp earth. She brushes a branch away from her face and takes her image-enhancing binoculars from her rucksack.

They look like any other modern binoculars but pick up ultraviolet light where the human eye would only see darkness.

A micro-channel plate multiplies the electrons that are released by the incoming photons, and recreates a visible image.

Saga looks into the darkness and sees a radiant, emerald-green world. Most of the light captured by the enhancer seems to be coming from the floodlight on the pillar in the distance. But, in the glow of that, the barracks and broken tarmac are now visible.

That was where they started to extract sand on an industrial scale many years ago, and that was where Jurek's father ended up when he fled to Sweden.

The old workers' barracks have been abandoned for years. Some are almost intact, but others are in ruins, barely more than foundations now. Almost all the windows are broken, the roofs have collapsed and there are piles of overgrown bricks.

A crow calls in the distance.

Saga scans the target area, following the line of the buildings and scrutinising the weeds and piles of scrap and rubble.

Everything is a luminous green, and looks oddly plastic.

The shadows make the ground look like the surface of water in a pool.

In the forest on the other side she can just make out the other snipers. The lighter circle close to the ground must be the lens of the night-sight, which would fit with Linus's position.

Jurek hasn't had time to get out yet, but it won't be long now.

There are no cars parked nearby, perhaps he's left it in the industrial estate by the motorway, or possibly in Rotebro. Either way, he'll have to set off soon if he's going to get to the ice hall in time.

Saga checks that her pistol is still in its holster, and glances quickly at Jennifer. In the tiny amount of light given off by the night-sight, all she can make out is part of her cheek and one eyebrow.

Saga scans the barracks once again through the night-vision binoculars. She checks it piece by piece: the doors, collapsed walls, piles of bricks. The green world is peculiarly lifeless.

She stops.

There's a candle burning in one of the windows.

She's on the point of breaking her silence when she realises what she's actually looking at. The light from the floodlight is being reflected in a splinter of glass left in an otherwise shattered window.

She needs to pull herself together.

There's no room for any mistakes.

She checks the last building in the row – the one that's been almost razed to the ground – before starting again.

It's so quiet that she can hear when Jennifer swallows.

Saga doesn't know how the snipers' night-sights will react to

Jurek's black anorak, if he's going to be swallowed by the shadows because of the sharp contrast.

That would make it much harder to get a clean hit.

He's thin, and can move with remarkable speed.

They won't get many seconds to line up the crosshairs on his chest and squeeze the trigger.

There's a noise in the forest, like a branch breaking.

Saga looks back into the darkness, suddenly worried about tunnels and other entrances, that Jurek could get out of the quarry through a hidden exit.

Perhaps she's made a huge mistake. What if she's ruined the chances of an exchange by being greedy and wanting too much?

Her dad has been broken down by pain and dehydration.

Valeria is probably in an even worse condition – if she's still alive.

They've got ambulances waiting by the Bredden traffic interchange.

There are two helicopters in the air above Kallhäll. They can't be heard here, but they're only a minute and a half from the gravel pit.

The moss crunches quietly beneath her as she moves one elbow.

Saga looks at the barracks again, going from door to door, then suddenly pans to one side to look at the entrance from Älvsundavägen. Someone's dumped rubbish down the slope. The half-overgrown gravel track leads to a wire-mesh fence that's supposed to stop people entering the more dangerous area. A sign with the name of the security company is lying in the grass. Further away are the rusting remains of a car, with weeds growing through the chassis.

Saga looks back at the barracks again. Everything is frozen in shades of pistachio and seaweed.

Down in the pit are the sifting machines and huge crushers with their conveyor belts, and even further away is the entrance from Norrvikenleden, which is where the office and weighbridge are.

Jurek must be here, she thinks. He locked a huge steel door behind him when he left her dad. It looked like an old bunker, with a sandy cement floor.

Then again, there are more than sixty-five thousand bunkers in Sweden.

He could be anywhere.

What if she's read too much into her observations? She can't have done, surely? She's been through the list hundreds of times, and both Verner and Nathan agreed that the operation was justified.

For some reason Saga finds herself thinking back to last summer, when she and Pellerina found a dead swallow in the garden in Enskede. Pellerina filled the shallow grave with flowers and wild strawberries before gently laying the bird in it.

A torn sheet of plastic is swaying in one of the doorways.

The wind seems to be getting stronger, whistling through the forest behind them.

Suddenly bright light makes the entire landscape seem over-exposed, like the glare from a soundless explosion.

64

Saga lowers the binoculars and sees a car that's turned in from the main road and is now rolling towards the fence. The light from the headlamps sweeps across the old paint tins, empty bottles, pieces of old tyres, a white oven with its door hanging open.

The woman in the passenger seat undoes her seat belt.

The young man says something.

Saga doesn't understand what they're doing, it looks like the woman is trying to climb over the driver's legs. Greasy blonde hair hangs over her face. Holding onto the steering wheel with one hand, she turns round, pulls her dress up over her white backside, and sits astride the man.

This can't be happening, Saga thinks.

They could ruin the entire operation.

Saga checks the barracks again, sees a darting light from the corner of her eye, turns quickly back to the car and realises that the guy is filming them having sex on his phone.

The door of the third barrack has swung open, possibly because of the wind.

Jennifer is breathing slowly.

The operation will have to be called off soon.

Light fills the landscape again, turning it radiant white. The car reverses out, they're already finished, the windscreen is misted up.

Not exactly a feature-length film, Saga thinks to herself as she looks at the window of the building where Jurek's father hanged himself.

Time is running out. They should have seen Jurek by now.

Saga hears Jennifer's breathing speed up, and quickly scans the target area again, but everything looks quiet.

An old bedstead and some wet cardboard.

There's a slab of concrete lying on the tarmac. It's cracked in the middle, and the rusty reinforcement rods are visible in the gap.

The wind has grown stronger, so Jennifer has to adjust the range on her rifle to compensate.

Saga looks at the time.

She can stay for another four minutes before she has to set off for the ice hall.

The likelihood that Jurek is here has shrunk dramatically.

A large bird moves through the treetops above them.

She tries to see anything in the dense green darkness behind the barracks, the image shimmers around the outline of the buildings.

It's time for her to leave if she's going to make it to the meeting, she's aware of that, but she still scans the area again, just as rigorously as before.

Piece by piece, she checks Jurek's father's old home. The ragged curtain is swaying in the wind. She's about to move on to the next building when something catches her attention at the end of the row. She pans across to the building that's collapsed completely.

Dark green light spreads out across the foundations, the remains of one wall, collapsed tiles, and a fallen roof beam.

Saga holds her breath.

The image flickers, and as it stabilises again she sees movement, close to ground level.

'The far building,' Saga says, and hears Jennifer move the barrel of the rifle through the heather.

A thin figure is emerging from underground, step by step by step.

There must be some stairs there.

'I see him,' Jennifer says quietly.

The man straightens up and becomes a thin silhouette against the pale green glow from the distant floodlight.

Only when he takes a few steps forward is Saga sure it's him. The moss-green shimmer surrounds his outline, but she recognises the black anorak and the empty sleeve fluttering in the wind.

'Fire,' Saga says over the radio, staring at the flickering image.

He's heading towards the edge of the forest, and will soon be hidden behind the next building.

They've got less than three seconds.

The hood is pulled up, but the anorak remains undone. The check shirt is visible when the wind grabs the loose sleeve.

'Fire,' she repeats, as Jennifer fires her rifle.

Saga sees the shot hit, fairly high up his torso, she's almost certain that the jacketed bullet passed right through his body.

Jurek takes a small step to one side, then carries on.

The echo of the shot bounces off the buildings.

Saga can't breathe, she almost drops her binoculars. She looks over towards the barracks again with her bare eyes, but everything is dark, there's nothing in sight.

With shaking hands she raises the binoculars again. Linus fires from the other direction.

Blood flies out behind Jurek.

He stops.

She can see that clearly.

Jennifer fires again, and hits him right in the middle of his chest. He falls sideways like a slaughtered animal, and lies there absolutely still.

'Target one down, target one down,' Saga reports to the team leader, and gets to her feet.

She drops the binoculars on the ground and rushes through the edge of the forest and down the slope.

She triggers little avalanches of stones as she goes.

She doesn't care about the risks, about the Beaver.

As she runs she draws her pistol.

She can't see him now, but keeps telling herself that he must be dead, he must be dead.

Crouching, she runs along the side of the building, pulls her torch from her belt and switches it on, climbs over an old pallet, then sees the body in the wavering beam.

It's still there.

Crouching to get under a fallen beam, she stumbles and reaches out for the wall for support, and steps over a sodden mattress.

The rapid response team come running up behind her. Saga can hear the rustle of their equipment, the thud of boots, but doesn't take her eyes off the body for a moment.

He's lying by the remains of the foundations, twisted on one side, with blood spattering the heap of bricks.

She suddenly imagines that he lifts his head, that his neck strains and the back of his head lifts off the ground, just for a moment.

Her heart is beating far too fast.

The butt of the pistol is slippery in her sweaty hand.

Joona's words about Jurek being a child soldier flash through her mind. He doesn't care about pain, and will do whatever it takes to survive.

A sheet of plastic billows out, blocking her view.

She stops, holds the torch alongside her pistol, tries to find a line of fire, sees the light caught by the plastic, catches sight of him on the ground and fires three shots.

She sees the body jerk with the impact, and feels the recoil linger in her right shoulder.

She moves forward, holding the plastic back with one hand, and tries to blink away the flare of the shots.

Numbness from the shots is fizzing like bubble-bath in her ears.

A pane of glass cracks beneath her right boot.

She reaches the body and keeps the pistol trained on it as she kicks the lifeless body onto its back, and finds herself looking at her dad's face.

She doesn't understand.

It isn't Jurek, it's her dad lying there, it's her dad that they've shot.

He's dead, she's killed him.

The ground lurches and she falls to one knee.

Everything collapses around her.

Saga reaches out her hand, and her fingertips touch his bearded cheek as everything turns black.

65

Saga is sitting motionless on a chair in a treatment room at the Emergency Ward of the Karolinska Institute. She has the blanket from the ambulance round her shoulders.

Nathan Pollock is standing beside her, trying to get her to drink some water from a plastic cup.

Her protective vest and rucksack are back at the gravel pit, but she's still wearing her camouflage clothing.

Her pistol and holster are hidden by the blanket.

She's pale and in a cold sweat. Her forehead is dirty and her cheeks streaked with tears. Her lips are as pale as aluminium, her pupils oddly enlarged.

She doesn't answer any of the doctor's questions, and doesn't even seem to notice when he disentangles her arm from the blanket to take her pulse.

Her hand is limp, and there are traces of brown blood under her fingernails.

The hospital works closely with the National Centre for Disaster Psychiatry and the Crisis and Trauma Centre.

The doctor straightens up, takes out his phone, and calls one of the duty psychiatrists.

Saga hears what he says about dissociation and amnesia, but can't be bothered to protest, there's no point.

She just needs to think for a bit before she carries on.

The doctor leaves them alone, shutting the door behind him.

Nathan crouches down in front of her and tries to smile at Saga's frozen features.

'You heard what he said, you're a victim, and it's perfectly natural to experience feelings of guilt about surviving . . .'

'What?' she mutters.

'It isn't your fault, you're a victim, there was nothing you could have done.'

Saga looks at the floor, and the scratches and marks left by small rubber wheels, and vaguely remembers yelling that it was her fault when they forced her into the ambulance. She was crying and repeating that Jurek was right, that she hadn't cared if her dad was dead or alive.

'It was a trap,' Nathan says gently, trying to catch her unseeing gaze.

Jurek hadn't made a mistake when he led her to think about the gravel pit. The whole thing had been planned in minute detail. He made sure she saw the sand trickling out of the prosthetic arm.

He probably made up his mind when she tried to reach the pistol hidden in her kitchen. That was when he knew for certain that she wanted to kill him.

And the game changed tone and direction.

Jurek understood precisely how she thought.

He knew what the trap should look like, and how he should lure her into participating in his terrible plan.

It was basically a conjuring trick, an illusion – a check shirt and an anorak.

Her dad's collarbone and shoulder were broken, and his arm strapped tightly to his back so that the sleeve would hang loose.

Jurek led her dad up the stairs and let him go while he himself left the bunker via a passageway to the pump-house in the edge of the forest. He had dug the tunnel beneath the rubble and ruined buildings.

With the help of tracker dogs, the police were able to reconstruct Jurek's passage through the forest and along the edge of the gravel pit to the allotments in Smedby.

Saga had slumped to her knees beside her dead father. Time had stretched out into a huge, gaping hole. She was no longer aware of the rapid response team who were searching and securing the barracks. They made their way down the steps, checked the corridors and forced open the steel door inside the shelter.

There was no one there.

No Jurek, no Beaver, no Valeria.

There were no more bunkers, forensics hadn't missed anything.

The rapid response team had even drilled into the reinforced cement floor of the bunker, but there was nothing but sand beneath it.

In order to deceive Saga, Jurek had been keeping her dad in the same bunker where his brother kept the previous victims.

The location of Jurek's real hiding place remains unknown.

The glare of the fluorescent light in the ceiling is falling across Saga's face almost directly from above. There are dry pine-needles in her hair. Beads of sweat merge and trickle down her cheek.

A nurse comes in and introduces herself, asks Nathan to leave them alone, then tells Saga that she's going to give her a sedative to help her sleep.

Nathan gets to his feet and gently squeezes her shoulder before he leaves.

While the nurse prepares the Stesolid Novum injection, Saga starts to think about eyelids again, and the fact that they're transparent, that you never quite stop being aware.

'I have to . . .'

She stops and slowly stands up from the chair, holding the nurse off with one hand as she makes her way out of the room.

With the blanket round her shoulders she leaves the Emergency Ward. She walks out into the chill morning air, through the huge buildings, and leaves the hospital precinct.

Saga knows what she has to do, what she ought to have done a long time ago.

She needs to fetch Pellerina, leave the country, and go into hiding somewhere.

Karlberg Palace shimmers bright white in the morning mist as she crosses the bridge over the railway line. The blanket falls off in front of the broad flight of steps leading to the palace but she doesn't notice.

Her grey camouflage clothing is dark with blood on the arms and chest.

She sat with her dad in her arms, pressing his head to her chest until the paramedics arrived.

She crosses the narrow Ekelund Bridge to reach Stadshagen, then walks along Kungsholms strand until she gets to P O Hallmans gata.

She rings the doorbell but gets no answer. Just as she's about to ring again, she changes her mind.

She no longer knows what she's doing there.

Pellerina is safer inside the flat than outside.

She isn't in danger.

Really Saga just wants to hug her, hear her wise words, feel her love.

Holding back tears, she takes out her pistol, checks the magazine and makes sure it's working.

Then she starts to walk towards Police Headquarters.

She has one more task to complete, and it can't wait. She needs to locate a new hardness inside herself, track Jurek down, and kill him.

66

Joona puts the night-sight down on the table and gazes out across the landscape. There are no lights on in the neighbouring farm in the distance, but the sky is starting to brighten slightly on the horizon. The haze in the air catches the light of the town.

It looks like the whole of Weert is in flames.

On the other side of the dimly lit room Rinus switches surveillance zones, pulls a chair over to the window and opens the hatch.

Lumi is standing in front of the monitor.

She hasn't spoken to Joona properly for two days, isn't looking at him, and only responds very curtly to direct questions.

Joona scans the grass in front of the old bus, the front wheels, headlights, windscreen and along the flat roof.

The starry sky looks like it's covered in gauze.

Joona thinks back to their life in Nattavaara, the last time they were in hiding from Jurek. He trained his daughter so she'd be as prepared as possible if the worst happened.

They grew closer to each other.

He remembers the crystal-clear black sky, and how he taught her to navigate by the stars.

In the Northern Hemisphere you can always get your bearings from the North Star.

It's always directly to the north, and doesn't move in relation to the rotation of the Earth like other stars.

'Can you still find the North Star?' he asks.

She doesn't answer.

'Lumi?'

'Yes.'

'It's at the end of the Plough, you just have to—'

'I don't care,' she says, cutting him off.

'No,' Joona says.

He raises the rifle's night-sight again and checks his zone, piece by piece. They mustn't let themselves get complacent, tell themselves that nothing's going to happen.

Yesterday he read about a major police operation outside Stockholm in one of the papers, but there was no indication of what it had been about.

He's lost track of the number of times he's looked for a message from Nathan, with one of the evening papers reporting an unconfirmed rumour that a hitherto unknown serial killer has been killed during the course of a police operation.

But seeing as no one printed anything like that, Joona has to assume that Jurek Walter is still alive.

He has to protect Lumi, but if the Swedish police don't manage to stop Jurek soon, they'll cut back on Valeria's protection.

The current situation isn't sustainable for much longer.

Joona thinks about all the information about Jurek he's looked through over the years. He even had all his father's letters from Leninsk to his family in Novosibirsk translated.

Vadim Levanov was a rocket engineer, extremely interested in space exploration. Joona recalls one letter about George O. Abell, the American who discovered the Medusa Nebula.

It forms part of the constellation of Gemini.

Back then it was thought to be the remnants of a supernova, but it was actually a planetary nebula – gas that's been expelled from a red giant right at the end of its existence.

Joona thinks about the fascination expressed in Vadim Levanov's letter as he explained that the constellation of Gemini would soon change, seeing as a nebula of this type has such a short life – only a million years.

Joona moves to zone 3, opens the hatch and looks out at the telephone mast and clump of trees.

'Dad, you probably did the right thing last time,' Lumi says, and takes a deep breath. 'Jurek had an accomplice . . . that's why Samuel Mendel's family went missing even though Jurek was being held in isolation. We know that now. And I understand that . . . that you probably saved my life, and Mum's, by cutting all ties with us.'

Joona lets her speak as he watches the clump of woodland where the hatch from the hidden tunnel is concealed. A plastic bag has blown in and caught on some brambles.

'But it was still a high price to pay,' Lumi goes on. 'Mum got used to it, to grieving . . . her life was put on pause . . . I was just a child, I adapted, forgot about you.'

Joona checks the edge of the patch of trees. The front scoop of a large digger is lying on the ground. He always spends a long time looking at it, because it would be a good position for a sniper.

'Are you listening?' she asks.

'Yes,' he replies, lowering the night-sight.

He closes the hatch, turns and meets her blank gaze in the gloomy room. When her brown hair is hanging over her forehead, she's the spitting image of Summa.

'Sometimes I got teased for not having a dad,' she says. 'It sounds so old-fashioned, but single mums really weren't that common back then . . . and we didn't have a single picture of you. How was I supposed to explain that?'

'It had to be done,' Joona replies.

'According to you,' she points out.

'Yes.'

'Can't you try to understand how this feels for me? You call me and tell me to drop everything and . . . oh, forget it, there's no point going on about it,' she says. 'But all this, because you've got it into your head that Jurek isn't dead. Maybe you're right this time too – we don't know – but the situation is very different now, because I'm an adult, and I make my own decisions.'

'That's right,' he says in a low voice.

She leaves the monitor and walks over to him. She stands there with her arms wrapped around her, takes a deep breath, then carries on.

'I mean, life isn't all about surviving, it's about living,' she says. 'Even if I've said lots of things because I've been angry, I know you're worried about me, that you're doing this for my sake, and I'm not ungrateful, I'm really not, even if I'm not as convinced as you are that Jurek has come back from the dead.'

'He has,' Joona says.

'OK, but apart from that . . . at some point you have to make a decision – how am I going to respond to fear?'

'What if you die? What if he takes you?'

'Then that's just the way it is,' she says, meeting his gaze.

'I can't accept that.'

She sighs and goes back to the monitor.

Rinus is sitting perfectly still, looking out at his zone through his binoculars. Even if he doesn't understand Swedish, he knows enough to stay out of this.

Joona opens the hatch for zone 2 and looks out across the fields towards Eindhoven. The greenhouse is so far away it looks like a pin-prick of light. He picks up the night-sight and looks at it. A luminous golden mirage. He's got the focus adjusted as far as it will go, but even so, he can't tell if the dark outlines behind the glass are plants or if there's someone standing there.

He knows he can't force Lumi to stay here. He can try to persuade her, but when it comes down to it, it's her choice.

She'll end up going back to Paris soon, no matter what he says. And before that, someone has to stop Jurek Walter.

Once, when he was child, Joona was on the island of Oxkangar in the Finnish archipelago, and the water in the inlet was perfectly smooth.

He was walking along the shore as usual, looking for bottles with messages in them.

A duck was floating maybe twenty metres out, a mallard, a brown female with five little ducklings in a nervous little row.

He doesn't know why he's never forgotten that.

One of the ducklings fell behind and was attacked by a seagull. The mother returned to the lone chick and chased the larger bird away. But then another gull attacked the rest of the ducklings.

Joona yelled and tried to scare the gulls away.

The mother flapped back to the four ducklings, but then the first gull attacked the lone duckling and snatched it up in its beak.

The duck rushed back and the gull dropped the duckling. Its neck was bleeding, and it was squeaking in its high voice.

Joona grabbed some stones and tried to throw them at the gulls, but couldn't reach.

The mother was getting desperate. The second gull was attacking the four ducklings again, pecking at them and trying to catch one. The mother had to give up. She left the lone duckling to save the other four. The first gull turned sharply in the air, dived at the injured duckling, pecked at it, caught it by one tiny wing and flew away with it.

That's precisely the tactic that Jurek uses.

Joona moves on, opens the hatch of zone 1 and looks out at the old house and narrow track. Before he has time to raise the night-sight he spots lights, bouncing up and down.

'A vehicle,' he says.

Rinus starts systematically checking the other zones while, without a word, Lumi feeds five cartridges into the sniper rifle and passes it to Joona.

He quickly mounts the sight on it, rests it on the window and watches the car as it comes closer along the narrow track. The headlamps bounce in time with the potholes in the tarmac. He can see at least two people through the windscreen.

'Two people,' he says. They stop in front of the barrier.

The beam of the headlamps lights up most of the track leading to the main house. One door opens and a woman gets out of the car. She looks around, climbs over the ditch and takes a few steps into the meadow. She unbuttons her jeans, pushes them and her underwear down around her ankles, then crouches with her legs apart.

'Just stopped to pee,' Joona says, lowering his rifle and removing the sight again, without taking his eyes off the two people.

The second person is still in the car. The glow from the dashboard lights up the end of a nose and a pair of eyebrows.

The woman gets up and fastens her jeans, then goes back to the car, leaving a piece of tissue on the ground.

Lumi mutters something and goes off to the kitchen as Joona watches the car reverse out of sight.

When the lights have disappeared he takes the cartridges out of the rifle and puts the gun back.

Joona walks across the room, pushes the curtain aside, opens the door and goes into the kitchen. Lumi is standing in front of the whirring microwave. There's a ping, then it falls silent. She opens the door, takes out a plastic mug full of steaming hot noodles and puts it on the table.

'You're right,' Joona says. 'I'm scared of Jurek, I'm scared of losing you, and that's exactly what he's exploiting . . . I've been so certain that the only way to protect you was to disappear, hide . . . you know, all this.'

'Dad, I'm only saying that this won't work long-term,' she says, sitting down at the table.

'I know, and I understand that, of course I do, but if you agree to stay here for a bit longer, I'll go back to Sweden and meet Jurek.'

'Why are you saying that?' she asks, trying to swallow her tears.

'This has turned out wrong, I have to admit that, I thought Saga and Nathan would be able to track Jurek down fairly quickly . . . I mean, he's in one of his active phases, and they've got all the material, plenty of resources, but . . . I have no idea why things haven't gone the way I hoped.'

'What are you going to do?'

'I don't know, but I've realised I can't run away from this, it's down to me to stop Jurek.'

'No.'

He looks at her face for a while, her lowered gaze, the sad set of her mouth.

'It'll be OK,' he says almost silently, then goes back through the curtain to the surveillance room.

Rinus has moved his chair to zone 3. He lowers his binoculars and listens as Joona explains his new plan.

'I trained you, so you'll do a good job,' Rinus says in his terse way.

'If I'm still welcome after all this, I'd love to come and visit you and Patrick in the spring.'

'As long as you can put up with him calling you Tom of

Finland,' Rinus says, and for the first time in several days a trace of a smile crosses his scarred face.

It's dawn by the time Lumi walks to the car with Joona. The barrier has been opened and the narrow tarmac track lies like a thread of silver through the damp meadow.

They look over towards the main road.

Thin veils of mist are hanging over the fields.

Joona's plan is to drive back to the South of France, then catch the first available flight to Stockholm, as quickly as he can, without giving away their hiding place.

They're both aware that it's high time he got going. Lumi's cheeks are pale and the tip of her nose is red.

'Dad, I'm sorry I've been so awful,' she says.

'You haven't been,' he smiled.

'Yes, I have.'

'You were right, it's good that you didn't back down,' he says.

'I didn't mean you should set off at once, though. We could stay here a bit longer, that wouldn't be a problem, would it?' she says, and swallows hard.

He wipes the tears from her cheeks.

'Don't be upset, it's going to be OK.'

'No, it isn't.'

'Lumi.'

'Let's stay, please, Dad. We . . .'

Her voice breaks and the words turn into hacking sobs. Joona hugs her and she holds him tightly.

'I can't bear it,' she says.

'Lumi,' he whispers to her head. 'I love you more than anything, I'm so proud of who you are, and there's nothing I want more than to be part of your life, but I have to do this.'

He holds her until she runs out of tears and starts to breathe more calmly.

'I love you, Dad,' she says between sniffs.

When they finally let go of each other, remorseless reality kicks in again: the narrow track, the waiting car.

Lumi blows her nose and tucks her handkerchief in her pocket.

She smiles and does her best to pull herself together. Their breath clouds in the cold air.

'Remember, none of this is your fault, not in any way whatsoever. If it goes wrong,' Joona says, 'it isn't your responsibility. This is my choice, and I'm doing this because I believe it's the right thing to do.'

She nods and he walks round the car and opens the door.

'Come back to me,' she says in a low voice.

He looks her in the eye, then gets in the car.

The engine starts and the rear lights colour the track beneath her feet red.

Lumi stands with her hand over her mouth and watches him leave.

The car disappears from sight.

When she can no longer see him she closes the barrier, pegging it with the rusty bolt, then walks back to the workshop.

67

Sabrina Sjöwall knows her job, and is aware of the situation, but she hasn't been told why the Personal Protection Unit has decided that the threat against Pellerina Bauer is so serious that only the highest level of security measures would be sufficient.

Unquestionably, the most important aspect of witness protection is keeping the address secret.

The girl's location isn't mentioned in any lists or reports. Only those directly involved within the police are aware of the address.

The flat is on the ninth floor, and consists of five rooms and a kitchen. Unnecessarily large for a single child, of course, but sometimes whole families are protected here.

The front door looks the same as all the others in the stairwell, but this one should in theory be able to withstand an attack from a rocket launcher.

Life is supposed to feel as normal as possible. The furnishings are simple but pleasant, with brown leather sofas, throws, wooden floors and soft rugs.

It all seems normal, even if the world takes on an oddly soft shimmer thanks to the thermoplastic windows.

Sabrina is dressed in civilian clothing, but she's got her Sig Sauer P226 Legion by her hip, and has her portable radio unit slung over the left shoulder of her jacket.

She has blue eyes and dark brown hair, worn in a plait

down her back. Her knees hurt, though she runs every morning, goes to the gym and attends tactical shooting training.

She's 1.8 metres tall, has sturdy hips and large breasts. She's always struggled with her weight, and has lost four kilos since she stopped eating sweets last summer. She tries to keep an eye on the calories, but she can't stand being hungry all the time, it makes her weak and messes with her concentration.

For the past six years Sabrina has worked in the Personal Protection Unit in Stockholm, and has had more than twenty previous assignments like this, but this is the first time she's been in this particular flat.

Being a bodyguard for anyone who has been put on the witness protection programme is extremely demanding. The social aspects are as important as the purely technical side of things. You have an ultimate responsibility to maintain your charge's mental health.

Sabrina calls to Pellerina that tea is ready.

She's piled their plates with rice and fish-fingers, peas and crème fraiche flavoured with saffron and tomato.

Pellerina comes running in wearing her fluffy slippers, and treads intentionally on the sill of the kitchen door to make it squeak. It could be the tiny brass nails, or perhaps the wood is splitting, but for some reason it makes a high-pitched squeak whenever you step on it.

Sabrina has never spent any time with someone with Down Syndrome before, she's actually always been a bit scared of them, unsure of what to say.

But Pellerina is wonderful.

It's very obvious that the girl is trying to hide how worried she is about her dad and older sister, Saga, but every so often she declares that her dad's a cardiologist, and sometimes has to work nights.

She used to go to a nursery that was open at night, but now Saga stays with her instead.

Pellerina spends a lot of time thinking about her missing dad, she worries that he's fallen off his bicycle and broken his leg, and wonders if that's why he hasn't come to fetch her.

Pellerina eats four fish-fingers, but doesn't touch the peas, just arranges them in a circle round the edge of her plate.

'My dad's a hen, I used to have to feed him peas and sweet corn,' she says.

Once Sabrina's finished clearing up in the kitchen it's time for *Swedish Idol* in the living room. Pellerina takes her glasses off and pulls the footstool over to Sabrina. She's the judge, and has to sit on the stool while Pellerina mimes and dances to Ariana Grande songs.

An hour later it's time for Pellerina to go to bed, after brushing her teeth and going to the toilet.

Sabrina pulls the curtains in the bedroom. They sway gently, and the rings tinkle on the pole.

'You can still be scared of the dark even though you're twelve,' Pellerina says quietly.

'Of course,' Sabrina replies, and sits down on Pellerina's bed. 'I'm thirty-two, and sometimes I get scared of the dark.'

'Me too,' Pellerina whispers, fiddling with Sabrina's silver cross.

Pellerina tells her about the chain email that frightened her. That if you don't send it to more people, the clown girls will come and hurt you at night. Sabrina reassures her, and eventually manages to make her laugh. They say goodnight and agree to keep the door open slightly and leave the bathroom light on.

Sabrina walks across the soft carpet in the living room, goes out into the hall and checks that the front door is locked, even though she knows it is.

She doesn't know why she feels so uneasy, but she's got an anxious feeling in the pit of her stomach.

She goes and gets a glass and the large bottle of sugar-free Coca-Cola from the kitchen, returns to the living room, settles down on the sofa and starts to watch a dating show on television.

It's so ridiculous that her face feels hot and she has to take her jacket off.

She fans herself with her hand, then leans back again.

The pale light of the television plays across her slightly sullen-looking features. The shadows of her head and shoulders rise and fall in strength on the wall behind her.

She goes through to the kitchen again, makes herself a sandwich at the pine table, does what she needs to on Facebook and Instagram, then goes and brushes her teeth.

Maybe it's because of the nagging feeling in her stomach, but she's always struck by her own loneliness when she's on an assignment like this.

She's a fairly shy person really.

Her sister's been trying to get her to try internet dating.

No one wants to be alone, but at the same time Sabrina feels she has some sort of need for that.

She can't explain it.

She often finds socialising exhausting.

Like the time her neighbour invited her out to dinner.

She managed to get out of the situation without coming across as too weird, saying she had to help her mum with her Christmas decorations.

That conversation with her neighbour has been bothering her for weeks, to the point where she hardly dares go out into the stairwell now.

Perhaps her shyness is something to do with her job, perhaps she just needs to be alone when she's not working, sleep in her own bed without having to worry about anyone else.

Her mum also takes a lot of time, even though she's moved into an assisted flat. She has her own apartment with access to centrally prepared meals, and a shared space for activities.

Her mum has always been a bit New Age. It makes her happy, breathes fresh life into her. But since she moved into the new flat she's hooked up with a group of spiritualists.

Sabrina isn't sure what she thinks about that. Her mum has told her she's been in contact with her dead father, and that he's very angry.

He keeps shouting at everyone, and calling her a trollop and a whore.

Sabrina inherited the large silver cross from her grandfather. She isn't really even a Christian but she always wears it, possibly as some sort of protective talisman.

Sabrina has tried to ask her mum who the spiritualists' medium is, but all she's been told is that it's one of the residents.

342

Mediums usually offer support and comfort.

This sounds more like manipulation, some sort of personal attack.

Sabrina feels sorry for her mum, for being tricked into believing that her father's angry with her.

It's very sad.

Apparently, three weeks ago her grandfather told her mother to hang herself.

It was then that Sabrina decided she'd had enough. She threatened to report the medium and the managers of the home, and told her mother that she wouldn't visit her again unless she stopped seeing the spiritualists.

She went back last Sunday anyway.

Her mum had got a new wig, with tight, light brown curls down to her shoulders. It didn't look anything like the hair she used to have.

Her mum offered her 'afternoon tea' and got out a three-tiered cake stand.

They looked in the old photograph album from when Sabrina was little, then worked their way back in time, to her parents' wedding, then her mum's school graduation.

When they came to a black-and-white photograph of her grandfather, her mum didn't want to look any further.

She clung to the album without saying anything.

Sabrina had never seen that photograph before.

Her grandfather was standing under a ladder that was leaning against a building, with an angry frown on his face. He was wearing a strange, tight-shouldered jacket with the silver cross outside it, and was holding his hat in one hand.

Sabrina tried to get her mum to turn the page, but she didn't want to, just sat there in her ugly wig, staring at the picture.

Before Sabrina goes to bed she does another circuit of the flat, checks on Pellerina and makes sure all the windows are shut and locked, then goes into the hall and switches the monitor on so she can see the door to the street and the landing outside the reinforced door.

There's a pushchair parked on the other side of the lift.

Last night the doorbell rang, someone down in the street, but there was no one there. Probably someone pressing the wrong button.

Sabrina turns the monitor off, goes into her bedroom, puts her phone on to charge, lies down on the bed fully clothed, with her pistol still in its holster, and switches the light out.

The screen on her phone glows for a while before going dark. Sabrina stares up at the ceiling, closes her eyes, and thinks about that fact that someone's coming to relieve her tomorrow.

68

Sabrina Sjöwall starts and opens her eyes in the darkness. Adrenalin courses through her body.

Someone's banging hard on the door of the flat.

She gets up from the bed, wobbles and reaches out to the wall with one hand.

'What the hell is the time, anyway?'

She adjusts the cross round her neck as she walks past Pellerina's room. She crosses the darkened living room, bumping into the footstool with a dull thud.

Her jacket is still lying on the sofa.

There's another knock on the door.

Sabrina scratches her stomach and puts her hand on her holstered pistol as she walks out into the hall.

She turns the light on so she can see the buttons, then switches on the monitor on the wall beside the entry-phone.

The black-and-white image flickers, then becomes sharper.

It's her mum.

Her mum is standing in the stairwell banging on the door.

She's wearing that curly wig and staring into the camera.

Her face is visible in the light of the entry-phone's buttons, but the stairwell behind her is completely dark.

How on earth has her mum found her way here?

Somehow she's managed to get through the door down in

the street, got the lift up, and is now standing outside the door of the flat.

Sabrina swallows hard and presses the button for the microphone.

'Mum, what are you doing here?'

Her mum looks round, she doesn't understand where her daughter's voice is coming from, then bangs on the door again.

'How did you find your way here?'

Her mum holds up a scrap of paper on which she'd written the address, then puts it back in her handbag.

Sabrina tries to understand how this has happened. She was visiting her mum when she got this assignment. She must have repeated the address out loud while she was on the phone, and her mum must have thought she was saying it to her.

When her mum takes a step back she's almost swallowed up by the darkness in the stairwell. Her face becomes a grey shadow.

'Mum, you need to go home,' Sabrina says.

'I hurt myself, I . . .'

She leans into the light again, feels beneath the wig and shows her bloody fingers.

'Oh God, what's happened?' Sabrina says, unlocking the door.

She presses the handle down, looks at her mum on the monitor, and sees a thin man stepping quickly out from the darkness.

She only opened the door a crack, and starts to pull it shut again when she feels someone grab hold of the handle on the other side.

'No one dies,' her mum cries. 'He promised me that—'

Sabrina braces one hand against the doorframe and pulls with all her strength. She can't understand what's happening. The other person is too strong, the gap is slowly getting wider.

She isn't going to be able to hold them back, she lets out a whimper, the handle is already starting to slip out of her sweaty hand.

Sabrina tries to pull the door shut one last time.

Impossible.

She lets go and rushes back into the flat, stumbling over Pellerina's fluffy slippers and hitting her shoulder against the wall, knocking a framed poster to the floor.

Sabrina runs straight through the dark living room and into Pellerina's bedroom, lifts the warm body out of bed, hushes her, then hurries along the passageway, past her own room and into the bathroom.

She closes the door silently, locks it and turns the light out.

'Pellerina, you need to be completely silent, can you do that?'

She can feel the girl shaking.

'Yes,' she whispers.

'You need to lie in the bath the whole time and not look up – we can pretend it's a special bed for you to sleep in,' Sabrina says.

She places some large towels in the bathtub, then lifts the girl over the edge so she can lie down.

'Is it the girls?' Pellerina asks in the darkness.

'Don't worry, I'm going to take care of it, just try to stay really quiet.'

Pellerina had told her before that a friend's cousin had ended up blind, the nails were still in her eyes, it had been in the newspaper, but the police hadn't found the clown girls because they were hiding in the forest.

Sabrina had calmed her down and explained that that was only a made-up story – people tell you it's real, but it isn't. The same thing used to happen when she was little.

She picked a funny example and managed to make Pellerina laugh before she said goodnight to her.

Sabrina moves away from the door, unfastens her holster and draws her pistol, feeds a bullet into the chamber and releases the safety catch.

'Are you OK, Pellerina? Are you lying down?'

'Yes,' the girl whispers.

Sabrina is aware that her portable radio is in the jacket she left lying on the sofa last night. She's supposed to keep it with her at all times, so she can always contact the command centre at once.

This wasn't supposed to happen.

She's been careless.

Her phone is lying on the bedside table, in full view. If the man has been in there, he's probably taken it.

She can't believe that she let herself be tricked into opening the door.

She thought her mum had had a fall and needed help.

But someone must have given away the location of the safe house, seen her go in, then traced her mother and fetched her from her assisted housing.

There's a dull clang from the bath when Pellerina moves.

'You have to lie still,' Sabrina whispers.

Sabrina thinks about the thin man who appeared out of the darkness, and the door handle slipping from her grasp.

Slowly her eyes are getting used to the darkness. Very faint light from the lamp in the hall is actually reaching the bathroom.

The faint glow is like a watery strip under the bathroom door. Just enough to reveal that there's someone standing right outside.

69

Sabrina stands absolutely still in the dark bathroom, staring at the light under the door.

She's breathing as quietly as she can, and can feel sweat running down her back.

She hears a metallic sound somewhere in the flat.

The man must be in Pellerina's room. She can hear the rings moving along the rail as he opens the curtains.

Sabrina puts her ear to the bathroom door.

He's searching Pellerina's room. The magnetic lock on the wardrobe clicks as he opens the door, and the empty plastic hangers clatter against each other.

Then footsteps again, it's impossible to tell in which direction.

Sabrina aims the pistol at the door and moves back. She stares at the unbroken strip of light beneath the door.

Her heart is beating fast.

The man is systematically searching through the flat, it's only a matter of minutes before he finds them. She needs to fetch the radio from her jacket on the sofa, get back to the bathroom and sound the alarm.

If he's not armed with a gun she can probably hold him off long enough until backup arrives.

She can tell he's walking through the living room again. His footsteps vanish as he crosses the rug, then reappear.

He's heading towards the hall, the other bedrooms and possibly the kitchen.

'Wait here,' she whispers to Pellerina.

Sabrina hesitates for a moment, turns the lock silently, pushes the handle down and gently inches the door open.

She keeps the barrel of the pistol aimed at the crack in the door, her finger resting on the trigger as her other hand nudges the door open.

Sabrina steps out, sweeps the passageway with the pistol, making sure it's secure.

The heavy silver cross sways between her breasts.

She closes the bathroom door and looks along the dimly lit passageway towards the two bedroom doors and the opening to the living room.

Everything is quiet.

Sabrina passes the first door and sees that her mobile has gone. She keeps going, constantly looking between the living room and the other bedroom door.

She stares at the doorway to Pellerina's room and shivers as she passes it.

Slowly she approaches the living room.

The wooden floor creaks behind her.

Every door represents a point of danger.

She sticks close to one wall of the passageway and keeps the pistol aimed in front of her, and now she can see the soft living room rug and the end of the sofa where her jacket should be.

Sabrina looks back and gets the impression that the handle of the bathroom door has moved slightly.

She keeps going. There's no other option. She needs to get into the living room even though the man might be waiting for her just inside.

Everything is silent.

Sabrina bends her arms, holds the pistol in front of her face and tries to control her breathing.

The sill of the kitchen door creaks. The man must have stood on it.

She reacts instantly, quickly takes the last few steps along the corridor and hurries into the dark living room.

She checks around the walls, then sinks to one knee and sweeps the pistol from right to left around the room.

The glow from the light in the hall reaches across the floor, all the way to the half-closed kitchen door.

Bloody footprints lead in both directions across the parquet floor.

Sabrina stands up, walks round the large sofa and sees that the radio is still hanging over the left shoulder of her jacket.

Just as she's about to reach out for it she hears a kitchen chair slam into the table.

The kitchen door opens and Sabrina sinks down behind the sofa.

His footsteps come closer.

She glances at the pistol in her right hand. The barrel is resting on the soft rug.

She's breathing far too fast.

He's in the living room now, his steps are slower on the wooden floor, and fall silent completely when he crosses the rug.

He's only three metres away.

Sabrina tries to shuffle sideways so he won't see her if he carries on through the room towards the bathroom where Pellerina's hiding.

Her pulse is thudding in her ears, making it hard to hear what he's doing.

It sounds like he's walked into the footstool.

Now he's approaching the sofa, heading straight for her.

She realises she's about to be discovered. If he takes just another few steps he'll see her lying on the floor.

So it has to happen now.

She leaps to her feet, holding the pistol with both hands.

But there's no one there. She sweeps the room with the gun.

He's gone.

She must have heard wrong.

With trembling hands, she frees the radio from her jacket and starts to walk back to Pellerina.

It takes only a couple of seconds, nevertheless it's too late when she realises he was crouching down at the other end of the sofa.

He has stood up and is right behind her now.

She spins round with the pistol but her hand is blocked abruptly and the blade of a knife is thrust up into her armpit.

The pistol falls onto the rug, bounces, then slides across the wooden floor.

The pain in her armpit is so intense that Sabrina can't resist when the man drags her sideways and kicks her legs out from under her.

She falls heavily and lands across the coffee table. The edge hits her like a blow from a baseball bat.

The fruit bowl shatters.

She tumbles onto the floor and tries to cushion her fall with her hand, but can't avoid hitting the back of her head on the floor.

The oranges from the fruit bowl are rolling across the rug.

She lets out a gasp and tries to get up.

Warm blood is pulsing from her armpit.

It sounds like she's standing on a beach looking at the sea, but she realises it's just her own breathing, that she's heading into circulatory shock.

The man stamps hard on her shoulder and looks at her. His wrinkled face is perfectly calm.

He bends over and moves the heavy silver cross aside so it won't damage the blade, holds her still, then brings the blade down hard between her breasts, through her breastbone and straight into her heart.

A large wave rolls in and breaks with a hissing sound.

The man stands up.

Sabrina can only see a hazy figure, a thin outline.

He got the knife from the kitchen, didn't even bother to make sure he was armed when he arrived.

She thinks about the photograph of her grandfather standing under the ladder, then the wave washes over her and everything turns black and cold.

70

As the plane begins its descent over Stockholm, Joona sees that the country is covered with snow, apart from the bigger lakes which are open and black. Fields and patches of forest drift past in leaden colours.

After going through passport control he heads to the left-luggage lockers, taps in the code to one of them and takes out the bag containing his identity papers and the keys to the flat on Rörstrandsgatan. He switches back to his true identity and takes a taxi to the long-stay car park in Lunda industrial estate.

He pays the fee, then gets in the car and unlocks the glove compartment.

His pistol's still there.

Dusk has already started to fall by the time Joona arrives at the Department of Forensic Medicine. A suspended streetlamp is swaying in the wind, its light swinging back and forth across the almost empty car park.

Joona gets out of the car and buttons his jacket over his shoulder holster as he strides through the main entrance.

Nils Åhlén is pulling off a pair of disposable gloves when Joona walks into the main pathology lab.

'Are you coming?' Joona asks.

'Are you aware of what's happened, Joona?' Nils replies, dropping the gloves in the bin.

'All I know is that Jurek is still alive, you can tell me the rest in the car.'

'Sit down,' Nils says in his hoarse voice, and points to a metal chair.

'I want to get going at once,' Joona says impatiently, but stops when he sees the look on the professor's face.

Nils looks at him sadly, then takes a deep breath and starts to tell him about everything that's happened since Joona went away.

Joona stands and listens as Nils tells him that no one believed Jurek Walter was behind the murders because of the recording from Belarus, showing the man known as the Beaver killing a security guard.

When Nils takes his glasses off and tells him that Valeria was never given any protection at all, Joona slumps heavily onto the chair and covers his face with both hands.

Nils tries to explain how Joona's theory was dismissed, because all the evidence seemed to disprove it: the footage, the method, and all the witness statements which seemed to point to the Beaver as the sole perpetrator.

It wasn't until the churchwarden was found buried that Jurek's name cropped up again. Now they know that it was the church-warden's sister who took care of Jurek's injuries and amputated his arm.

Joona's face is impassive and his pale grey eyes look glassy as he lowers his hands and meets Nils's weary gaze.

'I have to go,' he says quietly, but doesn't move.

Nils carries on, telling him about what happened in the green-house, then at the school. Joona nods slowly as he hears about the circumstances surrounding Saga's father's death.

When Nils tells him that Pellerina is missing and her body-guard murdered, Joona gets to his feet, leaves the room and hurries for the exit.

Nils catches up with him in the car park and gets in the passenger seat as Joona starts the engine.

The winter evening is dismal and alien, as if someone had ripped reality apart and replaced it with a lonely, abandoned world.

They drive along dark, wet streets, past parks with climbing-frames left empty in the cold.

During the short drive to Police Headquarters Nils Åhlén tells Joona what little Saga has said about her encounters with Jurek Walter.

'She doesn't want to talk, doesn't want to write any reports,' Nils explains heavily. 'It seems like she's blaming herself for everything that's happened.'

A couple of years ago Jurek exploited her to escape from a secure psychiatric unit. Saga, however, had managed to secure information from him that led to the death of his twin brother.

Wet snow starts to fall on the water as they drive along Klarastrandsleden. The headlights stretch out into oily smears.

Now Jurek has returned from the dead and, following his usual practice, has taken the people closest to Saga. But at the same time he's deviated from his normal pattern, Joona thinks as he listens to Nils.

He tricked her into killing her own father.

That's indescribably cruel.

But Jurek Walter isn't a sadist.

At first Joona wonders if Jurek is behaving differently because he's fascinated by Saga's beauty and darkness.

Maybe it hurt more than usual when she started to deceive him? Was that why he was taking such brutal revenge?

'No,' Joona whispers.

This goes much further than that. Jurek has set this entire drama in motion to unbalance her.

No one can defend themselves against Jurek, not him, and no one else either.

They cross Sankt Eriksbron and approach Kronoberg Park, and the old Jewish cemetery where Samuel Mendel and his family are buried.

Snow is blowing towards them along the road. He eases his foot off the accelerator, but it feels as if they're still moving forward at speed.

Joona parks outside Police Headquarters and he and Nils walk in through the large glass-covered entrance.

They take the lift up and walk past Joona's old room, knock on the door of the conference room and walk in.

Saga Bauer barely reacts when she sees him. She looks up briefly, then carries on writing a list of names on a whiteboard.

'Saga, I'm so sorry, I've just heard—'

'I don't want to talk about it,' she says, cutting him off.

Nathan gets up from his computer and shakes hands with Nils and Joona. His face looks ravaged, and he almost seems on the brink of tears. He tries to say something, but stops and covers his mouth with his hand.

Joona turns back towards Saga and sees that she's written the names of everyone who has been found buried, in the order they were reported missing.

'Where do you think that's going to lead?' he asks.

'Nowhere,' she whispers.

'There are plenty of us working on this now,' Nathan says. 'The chiefs are with us, along with the National Murder Unit, Forensics, plenty of detectives, things are heating up . . .'

'While we're rummaging through the bins,' Saga says without looking at them.

'I hear what you're saying,' Joona says. 'But we're all here now, the four individuals who know more about Jurek Walter than anyone else in the world.'

Saga pus her pen down and looks at him with bloodshot eyes. Her lips are cracked, and one cheek and her throat are covered with yellow bruises.

'It's too late,' she says hollowly. 'You came back too late.'

'Not if we can save your sister and Valeria,' he replies.

71

Nathan's ordered food, and they eat while they work. Nils Åhlén is talking on the phone to a colleague in Odense as he spears pieces of lettuce with a plastic fork.

Joona has dragged the desk lamp over, and it's shining down on the contents of his boxes: water-damaged notes, fuzzy pictures, printouts from the population registry, smudged pencil-written letters in Cyrillic script.

Slushy rain falls against the windows and runs down onto the dirty sills.

Saga doesn't touch the food, but drinks a little mineral water as she sends a formal request to the police in St Petersburg for access to their reports.

Joona clears the table, puts Saga's salad in the fridge, then carries on looking through every detail of the new investigation.

He makes his way along the wall of photographs from the new crime scenes and stops in front of the pictures from the nature reserve in Belarus.

'Jurek leaves nothing to chance, even though it can sometimes look that way,' Joona says. 'But he's still human, and he makes mistakes . . . Some of those mistakes are traps, but others are doors . . . I know he's here in the details, he thinks in set ways.'

Nathan busies himself adding new details to the database. After a while he wonders out loud if it's time to make a noise in the media, pleading with Jurek not to harm Pellerina.

They all know it would be pointless, but no one can be bothered to argue with him.

Saga goes over to one of the windows and looks out.

'We haven't got time to be sad, that can wait,' Joona says.

'OK,' she sighs.

'I understand that this is terrible, but we need you,' he goes on.

'What could I possibly do?'

'You've spoken to him three times, maybe—'

'It won't lead anywhere,' she exclaims. 'We won't find a damn thing, I thought I had a chance, but I didn't, he was way ahead of me.'

'It can sometimes feel like that.'

'He makes you believe lies, he makes you lose your footing,' she goes on, rubbing one eyebrow hard. 'I like to think I'm reasonably smart, but I made every mistake I could possibly have made.'

'He makes mistakes too,' Joona says. 'It's possible to read him—'

'No, it isn't.'

Nathan gets up from his chair, loosens his tie, and undoes the top button of his shirt.

'Joona wants us to try to work out how Jurek thinks,' he says. 'Everyone has their own rules, their own system . . . he had loads of people buried in the same place, Lill-Jans Forest. I mean, why there, of all places? How was he able to remember where all the coffins and barrels were?'

Saga sweeps a heap of reports off one of the tables.

'This is stupid,' she says in a trembling voice. 'We aren't the ones making the rules here, why are we even pretending that we are? We've lost, and we're going to have to do whatever he says.'

'So what's he saying?' Joona asks. 'You haven't told us what he—'

'Stop!' she interrupts. 'All I need to know is what you've done with Igor's body, that's what he wants . . . I don't give a damn about anything else, I just want to get Pellerina back, she's terrified of the dark, she's—'

'Saga,' Joona says. 'This isn't about Igor's body, that's all part of the lies, the manipulation.'

'No, it's important to him,' she sobs.

'It isn't important, he isn't sentimental or religious, he doesn't care about someone's remains.'

Joona is thinking that Jurek exaggerated his interest in his brother's body because he already knew that Joona had taken it.

That was the only reason he said he was prepared to swap Saga's father for his brother.

The idea was that if Saga started to look for the body, she would realise that it was Joona who had taken it. She'd have to contact him to get her dad back, and thereby reveal where he was hiding.

It was a smart and cruel ploy.

It was a brutal plan, and it would probably have succeeded if Saga had had any idea where he was.

She was merely a means to an end, again.

Joona looks at Saga's anguished face and thinks: I'm the one Jurek's obsessed with, and he needed an accomplice who he could share that obsession with. That's why my number was in the German paedophile's phone, that's why the grave-robber took Summa's skull. But Jurek chose the Beaver – and there are no limits to what he's prepared to do.

'I've talked to Jurek,' Saga goes on in a tense voice. 'He wants Igor to have a proper grave, and I need to be able to tell him where the body is if he calls again.'

'He won't call – he was lying to you if he said that.'

'Great, then all we have to go on are lies,' she says quietly, brushing away her tears and sitting down again.

'They won't all be lies – that's why you have to tell us every detail of your conversations.'

'There's no point. I've got a bloody good memory, but Jurek is in a completely different league. He has total recall of everything I've ever said to him, from the moment we first met in the secure unit. It's crazy – every gesture, every intonation . . . We don't stand a chance, we're still no nearer to catching him.'

'The first time you met him he mentioned Leninsk, and that was enough, we stopped him,' Joona points out.

'That was sheer luck.'

'No, *you* did that, you got him to talk, he wanted to get inside you, and he happened to give you something he hadn't planned to.'

'That's what I thought at the time,' she says quietly. 'But he tricked me, the whole thing turned out to be one trap after another.'

'Have you written down your conversations?'

'I didn't want to,' she whispers.

'But you can remember them?'

'Stop it,' she mutters, and bites her trembling lip.

'I know you can remember everything if you try.'

'That's enough,' she says, louder, and little red dots start to appear on her forehead.

'Tell us where he lives,' Joona says in a sharp voice.

'Who?'

'Jurek.'

'If I knew that, I'd—'

'But what do you think?' he interrupts. 'You've talked to him, you should be—'

'I don't know!' Saga yells.

'Maybe you do,' Joona persists.

'Stop it!'

'Tell us what you think when—'

'I don't want to! I don't want to . . .' she sobs.

'Saga, I'm going to ask you some questions, and you need to try to answer them.'

'I can't deal with any more of this shit right now.'

'Of course you can.'

'Be gentle with her,' Nathan says.

'Shut up,' Joona says, and goes and stands in front of Saga. 'You talked to Jurek, and I want to know where he's hiding.'

'The rest of us will leave,' Nils Åhlén says.

'You're staying,' Joona snaps.

Saga is staring at him wide-eyed. Her breathing is laboured, as if she's been for a long run and is exhausted.

'I can't bear to think about him, don't you get it?' she says. 'He humiliated me, I can't stand myself—'

'Try to think about him anyway,' Joona insists.

Saga takes a deep breath and looks down at the floor.

'OK, it doesn't matter,' she says. 'I got the impression he was living in a house, because he reacted when I said that, but that was probably just another trap.'

'What exactly did you say?'

She raises her head and looks at him with her tired blue eyes.

'I said I thought he had a house, and that it probably wasn't all that isolated, seeing as he thought it was too risky to let the Beaver live there.'

'What did he say to that?'

'He used what I'd said, turned it back on me and got me to believe he was hiding in the gravel pit. It seemed logical. Because there's something about him and the places he's lived.'

'Yes, there is,' Joona says.

Joona goes over to look at the various maps, then bends down and picks up a folder containing registry printouts, rental contracts, and tax demands from one of the boxes.

'Maybe because he fled from Leninsk, was thrown out of Sweden, ended up in the wrong country and had to make his way back here?' Nathan says quietly.

'Jurek never lived in that flat in Södertälje,' Joona says as he leafs through the folder. 'There were no personal belongings there, no trace of him . . . he probably only ever went there to collect the post.'

'And he didn't live in the gravel pit either, that was all a lie,' Nathan goes on. 'We've been in with diggers . . . the barracks have been demolished, the whole area excavated. There are no more bunkers.'

'But he did live there as a child, we know that much,' Joona says thoughtfully.

'Yes,' Saga whispers.

'And while he was recovering, he lived with the churchwarden's sister,' Nathan reminds them.

'Jurek was close to death when Cornelia found him . . . it's all in her journals, every detail of the operations,' Nils points out.

'Under the name of Andersson . . . the most common surname in Sweden, just to mess with us,' Nathan sighs.

'He's not messing with us,' Joona says.

'But we can't ask everyone called Andersson for an alibi,' Nils says.

72

The hours pass, and the work of pulling the vast amount of material into some sort of manageable shape continues in silence.

Joona blows on his coffee and looks at the map of Europe with the locations of where the rejected accomplices were found or murdered.

The lights flicker from a disruption in the electricity supply.

He turns to the map of Norra Djurgården and looks at the pins which mark each individual grave in Lill-Jans Forest and the industrial estate.

'How was Jurek able to find the graves in the dark?' Joona asks.

Nathan searches for his reading glasses among the papers on the table, but as usual they're perched on his forehead.

'We've tried with coordinates and prime numbers, we've run it through the best programs we've got – geometry, trigonometry, all that sort of thing.'

'He isn't a mathematician,' Joona says, studying the pattern of the graves.

'There is no fucking system,' Saga sighs.

'Hold on,' Joona says quickly, still staring at the map.

'Can't we just admit that?' she whispers.

'No.'

'Being stubborn isn't enough,' Saga says. 'It's time to rethink this, we need to ask the public for help.'

Joona moves along the wall, looks at the pictures from the gravel pit, Cornelia's house and the flat in Södertälje.

'Sometimes I understand his way of thinking,' he says in a low voice, thinking that it feels like he's on his way to interpreting the undercurrents, nudging towards the answers.

He goes back to the map of Lill-Jans Forest, follows the old railway line with his finger, looking at the pins that mark each individual grave.

'Are they randomly placed?' Nils asks.

'It's the twins,' Joona says, and starts to pull the pins out.

'What? What do you mean?'

'Gemini, the constellation,' Joona says, pulling out more pins. 'That's how he can remember where the graves are.'

Joona pulls out the last pin, takes the map down off the wall and holds it up to the light, so that it shines through the small holes in the paper.

'Do you remember Jurek's father's letter about the Medusa Nebula?' Joona asks.

'Yes,' Nathan says.

'That's part of the same constellation.'

Joona puts the map down on the table and draws lines between the tiny holes: the image resembles a cave-painting of two people holding hands.

'The constellation of the Twins,' Nathan says slowly.

Saga goes and stands behind Nathan as he looks up a photograph of the constellation on his phone and enlarges it. He puts the map over his phone and enlarges the image a bit more. The holes in the map match the stars almost exactly.

'This is mad,' Nathan smiles, looking at the others.

'We took his bishop,' Saga mutters.

She sinks onto a chair and runs her hand gently across the table.

'Saga . . . we're still deep in the catacombs together,' Joona says. 'And it's your move again. Your move.'

'Now we know it's possible to see through him,' Nathan says hoarsely. 'He was following a pattern . . .'

'An order,' Saga says quietly.

'What?' Nathan asks.

She swallows and closes her eyes to help find the right words.

'Morals have no meaning to him, we know that, not that it matters,' she says, looking Joona in the eye. 'But he does subscribe to a certain sort of order.'

'What are you thinking?' Joona asks.

She rubs her forehead hard.

'I don't know why I said that,' she sighs.

'Back up, go back,' he says quickly. 'What were you thinking when you used the word order? That sounds significant. What sort of order did you mean?'

She shakes her head, wraps her arm around her, looks down at the floor and sits in silence for a long while before she finally speaks.

'When we were in the secure psychiatric unit, Jurek and I used to talk . . . about what it was like the first time he killed someone,' she begins, and looks up.

'He said it was like eating something he didn't think was edible,' Joona says.

'Yes, but the other day, when I met him in the care home, he compared killing with physical labour . . . He doesn't kill for fun, we know that, but I asked him if it had ever felt good, killing someone.'

She falls silent again.

'And it hadn't,' Joona says.

Saga meets his gaze.

'No, but the first time, the very first person he killed in Sweden after his father's suicide . . . he said it made him calmer, as if he'd solved a riddle . . . A riddle about how to restore order, I thought . . . because that was when he realised that instead of killing the guilty, he was going to take everything away from them.'

'Do we know who his first victim in Sweden was?' Nathan asks.

'No,' Nils replies. 'We haven't found enough bodies.'

'Could . . . could the first victim's name have been Andersson?' Saga asks, wiping her mouth with her hand.

'You're thinking that might be why Jurek told Cornelia that

was his name?' Joona says. 'That he took his new name from his first victim.'

'The same way he'd assumed the name Jurek Walter before he returned to Sweden.'

'Good thinking, Saga,' Joona says. 'Very good.'

She nods, with a feverish look in her eyes, and looks on as Nathan starts to search for the name in Jurek's files.

'No Andersson, nothing,' Nathan whispers in front of the computer.

'Then it's a victim we don't know about,' Joona says.

'Come on, we need to think,' Saga says, and pauses to draw a ragged breath. 'When Jurek returns to Sweden after all those years and finds his dad dead, when he thinks of the loneliness that has almost driven him to suicide . . . who's the first person he thinks of then, who does he want to destroy?'

'The people who took the decision to separate Jurek and his brother from their father, the officials in the old Alien Persons Department,' Nils Åhlén suggests.

'It's none of them, they committed suicide several years later, they're on the list,' Joona says.

'So who does he kill first?' Nils asks.

'Maybe the foreman at the pit? That's what I'd have done. Check him out . . . the man who took Jurek and his brother,' Saga says, wiping her mouth with the back of her hand again. 'I mean, he was the one who started it all. He could just have told their dad to keep his kids under control – that's what a lot of people would have done, and that would have been the end of it.'

'Can we find out his name?' Nathan asks, clicking at the computer.

'It must be possible,' Saga says.

Nils starts searching old reports on his own laptop.

'I know I've got the notes somewhere,' Joona says, pulling a bundle of notebooks out of a box.

'Jan Andersson,' Nils says, and looks up from his computer.

'That was the foreman's name?' Saga asks breathlessly.

'Yes, but it doesn't fit,' Nils says. 'He wasn't the first victim . . .'

'What?'

'He's alive,' Nils says, and reads on. 'Jan Andersson and his family are still alive, that's why the investigation never picked him up.'

'Would Jurek have ignored the man who reported his family to the police?' Nathan wonders sceptically.

'Well, Jan Andersson is retired now, and his daughter lives in Trelleborg,' Nils goes on. 'His wife's dead, but his brother's still alive. He's got a large family in Lerum.'

'I think Jan Andersson has been dead for many years,' Joona says slowly.

'What do you mean?' Nils asks.

'Jurek hasn't just taken his name, but his whole identity,' Joona says. 'That's why it looks like he's still alive.'

'You mean Jurek is drawing his pension, paying his bills . . .'

'Yes.'

'In that case, he's probably living in Andersson's house in Stigtorp,' Nils says, turning his laptop towards them.

73

Valeria is freezing all the time now, and she's lost the feeling in her feet. The pressure sores on her back keep waking her up. It's so dark and silent here beneath the floorboards that she's lost all track of time.

To eke out the supply of water, she waits until her thirst is almost unbearable before drinking any. That will extend the chances of her being found, but it's also making her weaker.

She tells herself that by now someone must have realised what happened in her greenhouse, must have seen the blood and the body in the car. Her sons are bound to have contacted the police, and everyone will be looking for her.

Valeria lies still and listens out for any sign of life, but dozes off and is dreaming about a rowing boat full of water when she suddenly wakes up to the sound of a girl's voice, very close to her.

'Daddy? Daddy?'

Valeria drinks some water to get her voice back.

'Daddy? Saga?'

'Hello?' Valeria says, and clears her throat cautiously. 'Can you hear me?'

The girl falls silent abruptly.

'My name is Valeria, I'm locked up too . . . right next to you.'

'I'm freezing,' the girl says.

'Me too, I'm freezing as well, but we're going to get out of here . . . What's your name?'

'Pellerina Bauer.'

'You were calling for Saga – do you know Saga Bauer?'

'Saga's my sister,' the girl says. 'She's going to rescue me, because she's a police officer.'

'Who was it who took you, Pellerina – do you know?'

'No.'

'Did you see him?'

'He's old, but really, really quick . . . Sabrina was looking after me when he arrived, I was hiding in the bath and I kept as quiet as a mouse, but he still found me.'

'What happened?'

'I don't know, I woke up and it was completely dark . . . I'm twelve years old, but I'm still a bit scared of the dark.'

'I was scared of the dark when I was twelve, but you don't have to be scared now, because I'm here the whole time, and you can talk to me as much as you like.'

Valeria has worked out that the man and woman who gave her the water are dangerous. Jurek must have lied to them, frightened them. They think they're safe as long as they do what he tells them, as long as they hold her captive and keep her in a coffin. But Pellerina is only a child. It's hard to imagine what Jurek might have said to them to make them treat her like this.

Time passes in the darkness beneath the house. The long hours merge together. Valeria is feverish and her head aches. Pellerina is freezing, and very thirsty.

All they can do is try to hold on until they're rescued.

At first Valeria talked about her greenhouses to help calm Pellerina down, she described the different plants, the fruit trees and raspberry canes. Now she's making up a long story about a girl called Daisy and her puppy.

The puppy has fallen in a hole and Daisy is looking everywhere for it. Pellerina keeps talking to the dog, trying to comfort it and tell it that the little girl is going to find him soon.

Valeria has figured out that Pellerina was in some sort of secure accommodation when Jurek came for her. That means that her own disappearance hasn't gone unnoticed. The police know what's happened, and presumably are conducting an intensive search for the girl. Time's starting to run out. Valeria can feel her general condition deteriorating fairly rapidly now, and a child won't last long without water.

She describes how Daisy keeps looking in different places, and keeps finding different clues: the dog's favourite toy, a bone, his collar.

Valeria falls asleep in the middle of the story, but wakes up when someone walks across the floor of the room above them.

There's a scraping sound as the floorboards are lifted off.

'Be ready, I'm about to open it,' the woman says sharply.

'I'm ready,' the man says.

'Shoot if she tries to get out.'

Valeria's mind is racing as she hears them loosen the straps around the other coffin. They're afraid of Pellerina too. What on earth has Jurek told them?

'OK, open up,' the man says.

They nudge the lid open.

'Hold her down,' the woman yells.

'I'm trying, I'm trying!' the daughter replies.

'Let me out!' Pellerina sobs.

'Hit her!' the mother cries. 'Hit her in the face!'

There's a loud slap and Pellerina starts to whimper in pain.

'Lie still!' the man roars.

'Hello?' Valeria calls out. 'What are you doing?'

'Give her the bottle of water.'

More thuds, and Pellerina starts crying even louder.

'Calm down, Anna-Lena,' the man says.

'For Christ's sake, she was the one who burned him, she was the one who—'

'I don't want to be here,' Pellerina sobs.

'Just drink,' the woman snarls.

'I don't want to! I don't want to!' Pellerina cries. 'I want to go home to—'

Pellerina gasps as someone slaps her again, then starts to cough.

'She's bleeding,' the daughter whispers.

'Can you hear me?' Valeria calls. 'Why are you hurting a child?'

'And you can shut up!' the woman yells.

'Can you tell me why you're keeping a little girl down here?' Valeria asks. 'Her name is Pellerina, and—'

'Don't listen to her,' the woman interrupts.

Valeria weighs up the possible consequences before she speaks, but there's no time to think things through and she decides to risk it anyway.

'Pellerina has nothing to do with this, her dad took an overdose and she's only staying with me until he gets out of rehab.'

'We know everything,' the man says.

'Good, because I'm not going to make any excuses,' Valeria says. 'I'm a junkie . . . and I was so fucking desperate when it happened.'

'What's she saying?' the daughter asks.

'I'm so sorry for what I did, I swear—'

'Shut up!' the woman shouts.

They close the lid of Pellerina's coffin again and Valeria hears them tighten the straps.

'The man you've met, his name is Jurek . . . he just wants his money, I don't know what he's going to do with me, but that's my own fault, I borrowed loads of money for smack and then took off . . . I get that you want to punish me, but if you let Pellerina die, you're no fucking better than I am.'

'He said we weren't to listen to them,' the teenage girl whispers.

'When the withdrawal kicks in you start to panic, it's like something takes you over, you'll do anything for half a gram . . . I burned him to get money, and his phone . . . Pellerina doesn't know anything about this.'

'He said it was her, the abortion who burned those letters into Axel's face,' the teenage girl says.

'No, it was me, she can't even write . . . I branded him with those letters so he'd get money from the cashpoint.'

'Shoot her, shoot her through the lid,' the woman sobs.

'Calm down,' the man says. 'We can't, you know what we have to do.'

'Give me the rifle,' the woman says. 'I'm going to shoot her.'

'That's enough!' the man roars.

The woman goes on crying, and walks away across the floor.

'It's cold down here and we're freezing,' Valeria says. 'I don't think Jurek wants me to die, because then I won't be able to pay back the money I owe him.'

'What the hell are we supposed to do?' the man asks in a more subdued voice.

She hears them start to put the floorboards back over the hole again.

'Pellerina's only a child, her parents are addicts,' Valeria goes on in a stronger voice. 'I don't know why you're being unkind to her . . . if you won't let her out, then at least give her some warm clothes and food.'

She starts to cry as the footsteps fade away across the floor and everything goes quiet again.

'Drink some water even if they were horrid to you,' she says into the darkness.

Pellerina doesn't answer.

'Did they hit you with the stick? Pellerina? Were they mean to you? Can you hear me? You know I was lying to them when I said I burned that boy? They thought you'd done it, but I knew that wasn't true. It isn't good to tell lies, you're not supposed to, but I did it so they'd let you out. Sometimes you have to say silly things. But I promise you, I've never hurt anyone like that . . . have you?'

'No,' the girl whispers.

'But they think we have, that's why they're not letting us go.'

74

After a quick briefing the National Response Unit teams set out from their base in Solna.

Two black vans and a white command vehicle are now driving at speed past Rinkeby and Tensta, following a black Volvo.

Nils Åhlén has gone home, but Nathan Pollock is in the white minibus with the team's commanding officers.

Joona Linna is driving the first car in the convoy, with Saga Bauer sitting beside him with her eyes closed. They've both been given direct orders to stay in the background and not take an active part in the operation.

'Saga, how are you doing really?' Joona says.

'Fine,' she snaps.

'You know you can leave all this to me?'

'All I know is that I have to find my sister,' she replies in a subdued voice.

Both Saga and Joona are having trouble believing that they're going to find Jurek in the house, but they still have a tingling sense of having some sort of advantage, that it isn't absolutely impossible that they're going to beat Jurek.

Joona has uncovered a vital part of Jurek's system.

What looked like either a chaotic or fiendishly complex method was actually following a simple pattern: the stars' alignment to each other in a constellation that Jurek and his twin brother felt an affinity towards.

It's perfect on every level.

The stars that make up the twins' heads are called Castor and Pollux. According to Greek mythology, Castor and Pollux were twin brothers who were raised by the gods.

Only one thing separated them.

Pollux was immortal, but Castor was mortal.

When Castor was killed in battle, Pollux went to Zeus and asked to be allowed to share in death with his brother, and that his brother might in turn be allowed to share his own immortality.

The twins therefore take turns, spending every other day in Hades.

The dusty weeds by a crash barrier sway as they drive past, and an empty crisp packet flies into the air.

The convoy crosses the bridge at Stäket, passes a sports ground and takes the exit for Kungsängen.

Saga is holding a map on her lap on which two houses are circled in red.

Even though she lost the game of chess against Jurek, she still managed to identify the truths his lies were based upon.

She understood that Jurek's first murder was the clue to his psyche. It had given him the notion that there was a way for him to restore justice.

Saga managed to connect that first murder with the name Andersson.

Joona concluded he had adopted his first victim's entire identity.

Nathan managed to track down Jan Andersson's daughter, Karin, at her place of work: the Bjurfors estate agency in Trelleborg. When he contacted her, she said she hadn't spoken to her father in twenty years. He had always been an alcoholic loner, but he would send her a Christmas card every year. He still does, but that's the only indication that he's alive. She tried to call him at first, but he never answered and never phoned her back. She sent letters and invited him to christenings and crayfish parties, but he never answered and eventually she gave up.

Three of the vehicles turn off in the small village of Brunna, while the fourth carries on to the military base at Granhammar Castle.

The retired foreman, Jan Andersson, owns two small houses in Stigtorp, on the outskirts of Kungsängen. They're slightly apart from other houses, but not completely isolated.

Many years ago, Jurek murdered Andersson and stole his identity. He draws his pension and pays his bills. This is the identity he uses whenever he has to show ID or travel abroad.

The frozen ground slopes down towards the water. In the steepest parts, bare rocks stick out, but otherwise the pine forest is dark and dense.

The vehicle stops on a forest track to the north of Stigtorp. Saga stays in the car while Joona goes to talk to the rapid response team who will storm the house.

Twenty metres into the forest is a cliff from which you can see the whole of the little community: eleven houses in four clusters.

A white van is parked on the gravel in front of the three buildings belonging to Hultström's Tractors.

The two houses owned by Jan Andersson are nestled against the edge of the forest.

The rapid response unit can be down in Stigtorp in less than five minutes.

The officers from the other van have already split up. One group is waiting in a RIB boat out in Garnsviken, and the other is approaching the two houses on foot through the forest.

When Joona reaches the team, the officers are sitting on the ground in their heavy protective vests, chatting among themselves. Their breath clouds in the icy air. They're all clutching semiautomatic rifles in their laps, the most compact version of Heckler & Koch's G36 series.

One of them is lying on his back with his eyes closed, as if he were trying to sleep; another is eating dried fruit, and offers some to the man sitting beside him.

The men need to be able to switch quickly between extremely demanding situations and rest, moments of high adrenalin and relaxation.

The group leader, known as Thor because of his big beard, has an oddly gentle manner. Joona listens as he gives out orders in a surprisingly soft voice.

'Was I the only one watching the match when the alarm went off?' one of them says.

'It's always the same,' another one smiles. 'The minute you light the barbeque or take a beer out of the fridge.'

'This counts as a party for me,' one red-haired officer says.

'Definitely, as long as the bastard's actually hiding in that cottage,' the first one says.

'Don't think this is going to be an easy job,' Joona says.

'Maybe you don't know it, but this is exactly the kind of thing we've spent years training for: going in and incapacitating someone who's taken hostages,' the man with red hair replies, and looks over at Thor.

'I hope that's what's going to happen, but I don't think it will be,' Joona says bluntly.

'Come over here,' Thor says to him.

They walk behind the black van. The sound of the motorway carries on the wind.

'What are you doing?' Thor asks gently.

'Jurek Walter is dangerous,' Joona replies.

'So we've been told.'

'Good,' Joona says.

He sees his own reflection in the black paint of the van, dressed in a grey suit beside the heavily equipped police officer.

'Anything else?' Thor asks.

'I respect your team. From everything I've seen, you're good . . . but Jurek is far more dangerous than you imagine.'

'I'll raise that with the team.'

'If you like, I'd be happy to come with you.'

'Thanks, but we'll be OK,' Thor says, and pats Joona on the shoulder with a smile. 'I mean, we're talking about one, maximum two perpetrators, aren't we?'

Joona looks at one of the officers, who's kneeling down and playing with a police dog.

'Jurek is an elderly man now,' Joona says slowly. 'But he has more experience of combat than any of you comes anywhere close to . . . He's been a soldier for years, he's killed hundreds . . . and before that he was a child soldier. It's all he knows.'

'OK,' Thor whispers.

'If he is in that house, most of you are going to die,' Joona says, looking him in the eye.

'I certainly hope not,' Thor says, without looking away. 'But we've already said goodbye to our families.'

'I know.'

All the officers in the rapid response unit have recorded videos to be given to their families in the event they're killed in service. They're stored on USB sticks and kept in sealed envelopes inside a safe back at headquarters.

Thor opens the rear door of the van and takes out a box of distraction grenades, then responds to a call on the radio from the operational commander.

The other team is in position.

The officers get silently to their feet and put on their balaclavas and helmets. Their semiautomatics swing soundlessly on their leather straps.

75

Thor and his team follow the steep path down towards the water. They maintain a distance of approximately four metres between them.

The path is covered with pine-needles and cones. The water in the inlet has frozen, the temperature must have dropped at least ten degrees since yesterday.

Thor can't stop thinking about the tall superintendent with the Finnish accent and deadly serious manner.

Most people tend to be impressed when they meet the rapid response team, but Joona Linna had only seen their weaknesses, and seemed genuinely concerned for their safety.

That annoyed Thor.

And he doesn't usually let himself get annoyed.

In a childish attempt to seem brave or adult, he'd told him that they'd already said goodbye to their families.

He knows perfectly well that neither he nor anyone else in his team is prepared to die.

They all fend off the thought of death, and tell themselves that they take these risks to help make the world a safer place.

Thor thinks about those brief farewell messages. They were given templates to help them, so they could prepare in advance of the recording. The whole situation was far from natural, and he probably sounded oddly detached as he said goodbye to his mother and his wife Liza.

He knows he looked into the camera when he addressed Liza. He spoke slowly, the way you were supposed to, and repeated that he loved her several times, and apologised for letting her down.

It was only when he started talking to his daughter that the tears appeared. A chasm opened up, quite unexpectedly. All he could do was try to explain to her who he is, so that she'd have something left of him when she grows up.

At the point where the terrain flattens out, the team reaches a junction and turns right. Three hundred metres further on the forest opens onto the broad clearing containing the scattered group of buildings.

Areas of gravel and yellowed grass slope down towards the choppy water.

Thor rests his finger on the grip of his semiautomatic.

He gestures to his team to spread out along the side, passing close to a rusty diesel tank perched on some breezeblocks.

A dog is barking inside one the buildings occupied by Hultström's Tractors, but the police dog doesn't react at all, doesn't even prick its ears, just sticks close to Thor.

The tall, corrugated metal garage blocks their view as they walk past one end of it. Thor swings his rifle quickly round the corner and finds himself looking at the yellow metal trailer of a dumper-truck. A few hundred metres away there's a house right by the water, with waves lapping across its jetty.

The team moves on. The gravel crunches beneath their heavy boots, and their equipment rattles quietly as they move.

The two houses that Jurek Walter has taken over lie at the far end of the clearing. The front one blocks the second one from sight almost completely. So far Thor can only make out the tiled roof and satellite dish.

The window of the first house is dark, and reflects the cloudy sky.

Thor's group make no attempt to conceal their approach.

It doesn't matter if they get seen, because all possible escape routes are covered. The terrain is rough on almost all sides, with bare rocks and steep drops. The forest along the shore is the only real escape route, and that's where the other team is posted.

Thor's orders are to storm the house, rescue the hostages and incapacitate the perpetrator.

He has his rifle raised as he marches towards the first building, not taking his eyes off it.

The plaster has crumbled from the end of the building, revealing the brickwork underneath. There's a grubby lace curtain hanging in the single window.

The dog starts to pant and raises its nose.

'What's wrong?' Thor whispers, moving cautiously sideways across the yard so he can see the other house.

He looks back at the lace curtain.

Did he just spot movement behind it?

His heart starts to beat faster.

He stops and points his rifle at the window.

It was nothing.

He's about to move on when he sees a shadow behind the curtain, quick movement in the little room.

He gestures to the team that they have a potential hostile ahead.

Thor moves forward slowly, and from the corner of his eye he sees one officer move off to the left, and another sink down on one knee.

Thor's crosshairs are trained on the window with its peeling wooden frame.

A shadow appears behind the curtain, then a head.

He's about to pull the trigger when he realises there's a deer inside the room.

Through the lace curtain he can see the animal's ears twitch nervously. Its breath billows around its black nose.

He stretches his arm out sideways with his hand clenched and the team spreads out, divides and passes the house on both sides.

Suddenly there's a clatter of hooves as the deer turns in an instant and rushes out into the forest.

Thor walks round the house and discovers that one wall is missing. There are piles of leaves in the corners, and weeds and scrappy saplings growing from the open floor.

He trains his rifle on the next house.

A red cottage with a glazed veranda, half-hidden by trees, as if it's being swallowed by the forest.

The house is neglected, but seems to be intact.

All the windows are covered by dark-blue roll-blinds.

Beside the house is a bare patch of cement protected from the wind. Rainwater has frozen to ice in a dome-shaped barbeque that's standing next to the front door, along with a plastic chair that's blown over.

They all know what's expected of them.

Once the door is forced open, Thor will go in with two of his men.

He presses up against the wall beside the door.

Two of his men are aiming their semiautomatics at the house as he pulls on a protective mask and fixes the torch to his rifle.

When the team leader gives the final order to storm the building, the windows are shattered by tear-gas grenades.

They detonate almost simultaneously with a deep sucking sound.

Splinters of glass fall to the ground.

The pale smoke filters out past the roll-blinds and veranda.

Thor is already sweating.

One of the officers saws the front door open with a huge angle-grinder.

Distraction grenades explode in a storm of noise and blinding light

The door is lifted out and Thor enters the house.

The torch on his rifle picks out a smoke-filled tunnel through the hall and into the kitchen.

Two officers follow him, covering the sides of the house.

He can already feel the tear-gas burning the bare skin not covered by his mask.

He can hear the dog barking again in the distance.

Thor thinks about the beautiful police officer who was waiting in the car. He couldn't help glancing in her direction.

The windscreen reflected the treetops and white sky. Behind the reflection he could see her sorrowful face, as if in a dream.

After securing the kitchen and bathroom, Thor approaches the closed door to the bedroom. The floorboards creak under his weight. He gestures to one of the officers, who steps up and stands beside the door.

The torch on his rifle trembles on the door handle and brass lock.

Thor is breathing faster now, feeling that he can't quite get enough oxygen.

He counts down from three, puts his finger on the trigger, then walks up and kicks the door open. A grey cloud billows out towards him and for several seconds he can't see a thing.

76

The operation is over by the time Joona and Saga come down to Jan Andersson's house. The National Response Unit are still searching the rest of the area with the dog.

Everyone knew that the odds of taking Jurek by surprise and incapacitating him weren't great, but seeing as their main goal is the rescue of Pellerina and Valeria, they had no choice but to go ahead with the operation.

Joona looks inside the first house as he passes. There are sacks of grass seed and compost on the floor, barbeque tools hanging on a hook on the wall, and a rusty animal feeder is swaying from the lamp-hook.

Thor is standing in the doorway of the larger house with his gas-mask in one hand. His neck is red and his eyes are streaming.

'We're all still alive,' he says in a hoarse voice when he catches sight of Joona.

'I'm pleased about that.'

'You'll have to put surveillance on this place and call us in if he comes back.'

'He won't come back here,' Joona replies.

'You haven't been inside yet. Are you sure that this was his place? We didn't find any weapons, nothing.'

Joona goes over and topples the domed barbeque. The ice breaks and black water runs out. Among the clumps of wet ashes on the grass is a vacuum-packed pistol.

Thor's pale blue eyes stare at the gun.

'How did you know that?'

'Jurek isn't a barbeque kind of guy,' Joona says, drawing his Colt Combat and releasing the safety catch.

It's a good hiding place for a reserve weapon, easy to grab if you have to leave quickly. Jurek had moved the barbeque from the dilapidated house, but left the cooking implements behind.

The wind comes straight off the water here, and no one would have a barbeque right in front of their door when the paved area was more sheltered.

Saga pulls her pistol from her shoulder holster and follows Joona into the house.

The floor in the gloomy hallway creaks. A single military jacket is hanging on a hook, and there's a pair of muddy boots standing on a rack.

They carry on into the kitchen. The blind has been torn down and a tear-gas canister is lying amidst the broken glass on the linoleum floor.

On top of the dirty cooker there's a frying pan with a thick layer of grease the colour of wax. A coffee-cup, fork, and clean plate have been left on the table out on the veranda.

There are dead flies and wasps along the bottom of all the windows.

Joona opens the fridge and finds butter and fresh eggs. Saga finds a bag of bread in the larder and holds it up to the window to check the date.

'Baked yesterday,' she says quickly.

Joona goes back out into the hall. He gently nudges the bathroom door open with the barrel of his pistol. There are several bright yellow disposable razors on the basin. Next to the tap there's a toothbrush perched in a streaked glass.

Saga goes into the bedroom.

There's a row of photographs on top of a dark, wooden chest of drawers.

Jan Andersson's family, his daughter, and wife.

Joona comes in behind her and holsters his pistol as he spots the tear-gas canister in the middle of the unmade bed.

'He's been living here all these years, but he hasn't changed a thing, not one detail,' Saga says, opening the wardrobe. 'This bed's where he's been sleeping, isn't it? He's kept the fridge stocked and hung his clothes in the wardrobe next to Jan Andersson's.'

They search the room, even though deep down they know they're not going to find anything useful.

There's a Bible in the drawer of the bedside cabinet, as well as a pair of reading glasses and a jar of indigestion pills. Joona feels under the drawer and leafs through the Bible.

They spend two hours looking for maps, addresses, anything at all that could lead them to Valeria and Pellerina.

The tingling sense that they're finally closing in on Jurek slowly fades away.

When Joona and Saga walk outside again the rapid response unit is gone. Everything they found inside the smaller house is neatly lined up on the paved area. Nathan has moved the plastic chair and is sitting in the middle of the sacks and buckets, sheltered from the cold wind.

'They checked in all the other buildings, spoke to any neighbours who were home,' he says. 'Jurek seems to have kept to himself, they've only seen him at a distance a few times in all these years.'

Saga walks slowly along the row of lawnmowers, pots of paint, boxes full of old electronics.

'If there's anything that could help us, it should be here,' Saga says. 'This is his place, the house, we've obviously found where he's been living.'

'And that's why there are no graves nearby . . . just as there weren't any in the gravel pit,' Joona says.

'Home and burial sites are kept separate,' Nathan nods.

'Yes,' Saga sighs.

'We've got experts examining Jan Andersson's bank account to see if it's possible to link purchases with locations,' Nathan says.

'It won't be,' Joona says, looking towards the dark forest behind them.

'Come on, Pellerina and Valeria have to be somewhere – it must be possible to find them,' Saga says.

'We know he used a constellation to keep track of the coffins in Lill-Jans Forest,' Nathan says, thinking out loud. 'That means he uses systems, and that we can decode them.'

'We know him, we're getting closer,' Joona goes on. 'He assumed the foreman's identity, called himself Andersson . . .'

'Because this is where everything changed for him,' Saga says.

'But where the hell are the rest of the graves?' Nathan asks.

Saga pulls out her map and unfolds it. The large sheet of paper rustles in the cold wind. They look at the houses in the clearing, the road through the forest, the small community closer to Kungsängen.

Joona looks at the red circles around the two houses, the narrow inlet, the bridge, and road leading towards Jakobsberg and Rotebro.

'He's done it again,' he says in a low voice.

'What?' Saga asks.

'The Twins, only on a different scale. This time the constellation is much, much bigger,' Joona replies, pointing at the red circles on the map. 'This is us, at the place where Jurek lived for years, this is where he kept coming back to, this is Pollux, the head of one of the twins . . .'

'Slow down,' Nathan says.

'Look,' Joona says, pointing to the workers' barracks at the gravel pit in Rotebro. 'This is Castor, the head of the other twin. And of course that was where Jurek's brother lived. It's the same thing again, he keeps using the same constellation the whole time, the same mental picture.'

'Like a mind palace,' Nathan says.

Joona adds the other stars that make up the constellation, then draws lines between them so the image becomes clearer: twin boys with their heads almost touching, holding hands.

'This star, the gravel pit, that's Igor's head,' Joona repeats. 'And, at this scale, his left hand is in Lill-Jans Forest in Stockholm.'

'Because he was watching over the graves there,' Saga whispers.

'These are the coordinates we're looking for,' Joona says, pointing at the map. 'We have seventeen precise points, and we've already searched three of them. I promise you, Pellerina and Valeria are somewhere among the ones that are left.'

77

Emilia is wearing a black kimono and has her red hair loosely tied back after her shower. In one hand she's holding a dog-eared textbook, *Mathematics* 3, that she found on the kitchen table.

Her stepson, Darian, is in his last year of high school, and is doing his homework in his room with a friend.

The Do Not Disturb sign he stole from a hotel has fallen off the door handle.

Emilia opens the door and enters the narrow passageway with a pair of boxing gloves on the wall, steps over the jackets on the floor, then turns the corner to enter the main part of the room.

She can hear the sound of waves, and a lot of sighing.

Dorian and his friend are sitting on the floor with their backs to her, they haven't noticed her coming in.

She stops when she realises they're watching porn on a laptop: the screen shows a blonde having sex with two men at the same time.

Emilia can't help spying on the boys for a moment. She stands still and looks at their serious faces from behind and off to one side. Their eyes are open wide, their trousers tight across their crotches.

The woman in the film is being taken from behind by one man, while the other is thrusting into her mouth.

Emilia stares at the young men as they concentrate on the screen, then slowly moves backwards, and accidentally kicks a skateboard with her foot.

Dorian quickly shuts the laptop.

She turns back towards them, pretending not to have noticed anything, and tells them they left the textbook in the kitchen as she walks over to them.

They're clearly both embarrassed, and lean forward to hide their crotches, thank her for the book and say they're going to carry on studying.

'Dorian? What are you two up to?'

'Nothing,' he replies quickly.

'I know you're hiding something.'

'I'm not.'

'Move your hands,' she says, in a slightly sterner voice.

Dorian blushes but does as she asks. His jeans are so tight that the zip in his crotch is clearly visible. Emilia crouches down with an expression of feigned concern on her face, before the seriousness of the moment hits her.

'What's this?' she asks, and swallows hard.

She runs her hand gently across her stepson's crotch and tries to hide the fact that she's breathing faster as she squeezes his stiffness. His blond friend is staring at them, unable to understand what's going on.

'Can I see?' she asks, running two fingers across the taut denim.

Dorian looks away, undoes the button of his jeans and starts to pull the zip down when the picture freezes.

The director stops the rough-cut of the introduction to the scene and closes down the program on his computer. He's putting together a first cut because the producer is going to be calling in today to see how far they've got.

Emilia comes back into the studio from the dressing room in a thick towelling dressing-gown. Her heavy mascara has left a line of black dots below one eyebrow.

She watches as the director puts his reading glasses down next to the computer and says something to Ralf, who's in charge of the cameras.

They've fallen behind schedule, but Ralf doesn't seem bothered. Emilia has met him many times before. He's over sixty, and has been married to the same woman for more than twenty years. His face is tanned and slightly puffy. His Smiths T-shirt is pulled tight across his stomach, and he's wearing washed-out jeans with a brown leather belt, kneepads and a pair of black Crocs.

Emilia hasn't worked with this director before. He looks stressed, and is evidently more accustomed to directing adverts. He has a big black beard and a shaved head, and is wearing Adidas trousers and a blue shirt with dark sweat patches under the arms.

Swedeep Pictures is a recently established production company that's still looking for premises of its own.

This isn't a real studio, just an old industrial building with a polished cement floor. It might have been used as a warehouse by some wholesaler. Beside the front door is a tatty advert featuring a picture of a doctor smoking.

It isn't an ideal location for recording, but the hired cameras are decent quality and the scenery looks real enough. It probably came from a genuine television studio, borrowed or stolen from a store somewhere.

They record thirty and sixty seconds of the sex scenes at a time, then have a ten-minute break.

It would be impossible otherwise.

Emilia has got rid of her nicotine chewing-gum and drunk some mineral water.

The long oral scenes are done now.

According to the script, first she sucks her stepson, then his friend, while the stepson licks her.

Now they're going to do vaginal penetration, followed by anal and more sucking, then double penetration, and finally cumshots to the face.

Very original, as she muttered to herself during the read-through.

The director and Ralf spent the morning setting up, and by the time she arrived at eleven they were ready to run through that day's scenes with her. They don't exactly have high standards for the acting, but she still gets directed.

Look at the door, look at him, stretch your wrists.

Smile when you say his dad's at work.

Just like in fairy tales, it's always the stepmother who's the dangerous one.

They usually film using three cameras, except when they're doing the extreme close-ups. Then Ralf uses one camera and the steadycam.

The new guy calls himself Dorian. He's only twenty, has short dark hair, green eyes, and tattooed arms.

She's checked his medical certificate, it was issued on Monday by the same doctor she goes to.

Dorian was brought in after the original guy was fired on the first day. The producer got angry and dragged him out by the hair because he was snooping through the things in the store-rooms next to the dressing room.

The producer attended the first day of shooting, and said they'd been given permission to use the premises by a friend, and repeated that they needed to respect that.

Presumably the friend has left some belongings in the store-room next to the women's dressing room. There's no lock on the door, but no one's allowed to go in there, that was one of the conditions.

Emilia couldn't help thinking that the friend probably didn't know what his premises were being used for.

The producer walked up to each of them in turn, looked them in the eye, and said that the storeroom was absolutely out of bounds.

Emilia prefers professional partners, ones who just do their job.

The biggest problem with beginners is that they sometimes think it's about sex, and make a real effort to get her excited.

She's worked with guys who thought she could actually have an orgasm while they were recording.

The odds of that happening really aren't that high.

Back at the start, she actually came close a couple of times, when she was performing with her ex. He was the one who got her started in the business. Before she met him she had no self-confidence at all, and had even tried to commit suicide. They'd had to pump her stomach.

Obviously she feels what's going on, her nerves get stimulated during vaginal intercourse, but there's no excitement at all, she doesn't get wet.

It's all about the money.

At least, unlike the guys, she gets paid well. She's never understood why they do it. Being in a porn film isn't exactly the sort of thing you can boast about.

She does her best to avoid seeing the films; it makes her feel weird, seeing herself on screen. She remembers the first time she watched while they were editing, and saw a huge, shiny penis slipping inside her.

The same thing, every time.

Emilia has thought a lot about an article she read recently, about two female directors who make feminist porn films. She got curious and considered contacting them, but couldn't pluck up the courage. She was too worried that they would look down on her.

Emilia hangs up the dressing-gown and lies down on the bed again. The football poster on the wall has fallen off, but it doesn't matter, seeing as they're about to do the close-ups.

She grabs the plastic tube and squirts more lubricant into her vagina. The make-up artist comes over and wipes away any that's in the wrong place, then applies powder to take the shine off her skin.

Dorian is standing beside the bed, masturbating to get his erection back. His face shows no emotion as he stands there with his back hunched.

The heat from the lamps makes her shiver until she warms up.

While she waits for Dorian to be ready she looks around at the set, the lights, the reflective screens, the soft-boxes.

She looks at the row of small windows up by the ceiling, and sees a bit of Christmas tinsel hanging from a grille in the wall.

The director and Ralf are waiting in silence. There's nothing to say, everyone knows what they have to do.

Dorian breaks into a sweat as he masturbates and the make-up artist goes over and pats his cheeks and chest and applies some more powder.

No fluffers any more, Emilia thinks. She feels a bit sorry for the men, having to take care of themselves, eating loads of Viagra and wanking.

It's easy enough to fake ejaculation, but they have to manage to get an erection for themselves.

Emilia is careful not to take any responsibility for the guys who have trouble. She tries to stay out of it and does her best to hide her irritation and impatience when they take too long.

Dorian is sweet, and is so keen to impress.

Earlier that day he'd had a bit of trouble, his hands were cold, and he kept shaking and muttering to himself.

'Come on,' she says gently.

'It's not going to work,' he replies, giving her a pleading look.

'Idiot,' the director mutters.

Ralf sighs and adjusts one kneepad.

'Come on, it's OK,' she says. 'Let's pretend it's just you and me . . .'

Dorian walks round the bed and lies on top of her, she helps him in and keeps hold of his semi-hard penis.

'You know, you really have got a great cock,' she whispers.

'This isn't working,' Ralf says, starting to remove the camera from the steadycam.

Dorian lies down heavily on top of her, his stubble against her cheek, and slowly starts to move his hips.

'It's just you and me here now,' Emilia whispers.

She can feel his heartbeat start to speed up, and puts her arms round him even though that's against her rules. She usually tries to relax as much as she can, to stop herself getting tired, and to avoid injuries.

'Don't stop now.'

Emilia groans in his ear and feels him growing and getting hard.

'God, this is great,' she lies, and catches Ralf's eye.

'OK, camera rolling,' the director says.

'Lie on your side,' Ralf says, kneeling down with the camera in front of the bed.

'Keep going, keep going, I'm going to come soon,' she whispers.

'On your side,' the director repeats.

Dorian lets out a groan and she feels him ejaculate, three hard pulses, and his back feels sweaty under her hand. His body relaxes and he gets heavier, then rolls onto his side and whispers sorry.

'Jesus, this can't be happening,' the director sighs wearily.

Emilia lies back and can't help laughing, but stops at once when she sees that the thickset producer has come into the studio.

He's standing just inside the door in a black raincoat. His broad shoulders are dusted with a thin layer of snow.

She goes completely cold when she remembers what she did yesterday. Without looking at the producer, she gets off the bed and puts her dressing-gown on. Dorian's semen is trickling down the inside of one of her thighs.

Emilia doesn't know why the order not to look in the forbidden storeroom had the opposite effect on her. Maybe it's because she doesn't like being treated like a child.

When Ralf needed a long break to copy the recordings from the memory card, she went into the corridor, past her dressing room, and stopped in front of the metal door.

There was a hole in the door where the lock should have been. She was only planning to bend over and look through it, but found herself reaching for the handle and opening the door instead.

She couldn't help it, despite what had happened to her first leading man.

The storeroom was dark, but she'd been able to make out something to her left.

There had been a dusty smell of freshly sawn wood in the air.

She had lit the torch on her phone, letting its chalk-white glow tremble across the bare concrete walls.

In the far corner was a dark blue tarpaulin covering what looked like furniture or boxes.

Emilia remembers hearing the director talking to the two guys in their dressing room. She'd hesitated for a moment, then crept further into the storeroom.

She'd taken hold of one corner of the tarpaulin, but it had been far too heavy for her to lift with one hand.

So she had put her phone down on the floor, letting its cold light shine straight up at the ceiling.

Using both hands, she'd managed to fold back one corner of the tarpaulin.

Then she had quickly picked up her phone and aimed the torch at it.

She saw a coffin made of unpainted plywood resting on two sawhorses.

On the floor beneath had been a circular saw and some grey boxes full of nails and brackets, straps and blocks of veneer.

She'd crouched down and shone the torch further under the tarpaulin. Next to a row of large blue plastic barrels was a half-finished coffin, the right size for a child.

78

The temperature has fallen to sixteen degrees below freezing. The heat inside makes Joona's face flush as he hurries along the corridor. His pistol is knocking against his ribs under his jacket. A notice about this year's Christmas collection comes loose from the wall and drifts to the floor as he passes.

Carlos is standing beside his aquarium, and has just finished feeding his fat goldfish when Joona opens the door.

'No, you have to share,' Carlos is saying, tapping the glass.

Joona has already called him from the car to tell him they've cracked Jurek's code, meaning that there's a chance they can rescue Pellerina and Valeria.

He requested an immediate operation involving the collective efforts of the Stockholm Police, National Response Unit, and Special Operations to check out the coordinates of the fourteen remaining stars.

Carlos listened and said he understood, but because this would entail the largest police operation in Swedish history, he would have to go via the National Police Committee and ask for a green light from the Ministry of Justice.

'Have you spoken to them yet?' Joona asks.

Carlos looks away from the fish, sits back down on his chair, and sighs.

'I explained that you'd identified fourteen addresses where

Jurek Walter might be . . . I didn't mention the constellation, I don't think that would have helped.'

'Probably not.'

'Look, you have to understand that I tried,' Carlos says awkwardly. 'I stressed how urgent this was and so on, but the Justice Minister was very clear. He isn't going to authorise any more operations . . . Hold on, Joona, I know what you think . . . but try to see it from his point of view, this is about kidnap, not terrorism.'

'But we—'

'There's no obvious threat, the general public aren't in danger,' Carlos interrupts.

'Call and say we'll accept a smaller operation focused on eight locations.'

Carlos shakes his head.

'There aren't going to be any more operations at all, not until we have definite proof of where Jurek or his victims are.'

Joona gazes out through the window behind Carlos, at the dark treetops in the park, the frosted grass hillocks.

'This isn't good,' Joona says in a low voice.

'We've already used the Rapid Response Unit twice this week,' Carlos reminds him. 'With nothing to show for it.'

'I know.'

'You have to understand.'

'No,' Joona replies, looking him in the eye.

Carlos lowers his gaze, runs one hand across the top of his desk, then looks up again.

'I can reinstate you, if you like?' he says.

'Good,' Joona replies, then leaves his boss's office.

He takes the lift to the tenth floor, walks quickly along the corridor and opens the door to the investigation room.

With the help of their technical experts, Nathan and Saga have put together a precise map matching the constellation, using the house in Stigtorp and the workers' barracks in the gravel pit as their starting points. There were only 200 metres between the twins' heads in Lill-Jans Forest, but this time there are 8,000 metres between the heads, and 86,000 metres from head to foot.

'This version of the constellation is four times the length of Manhattan,' Nathan points out.

They've pinned the map to the wall next to the photographs of the gravel pit, the Beaver and the various crime scenes.

Jurek's brother Igor represents Castor, whose hand is on the smaller version of the constellation of Gemini in Lill-Jans Forest. The stomach is located on Ekerö, and the feet down in Tumba and Södertälje.

Saga takes her jacket from the hook on the wall and pulls out the hat she'd stuffed into one sleeve.

'Print out the exact addresses and coordinates,' Joona says.

'We're going to have a meeting of all the teams as soon as we can organise it,' Nathan says, standing up from his place at the large table. 'I'm going to need at least three command vehicles.'

'I forgot to mention, we're going to have to handle this on our own,' Joona says.

'OK,' Saga sighs.

'So it's over before we've even started,' Nathan says, sinking back down onto his seat again.

'Nothing's over, we carry on,' Joona says. 'The only difference is that we're going to have to search the locations one at a time, just us.'

'Fourteen stars,' Nathan says.

Saga puts her jacket and hat on the table, grabs the list from the printer and hands it to Joona.

'You're both in agreement . . . that Pollux in the constellation of Gemini represents Jurek, because the star for Pollux's head is located at his house?'

'And the other twin . . .' Nathan frowns.

'Castor,' Joona fills in.

'His head matches Igor's home in the gravel pit,' she concludes.

'And the interesting thing is that Castor's hand in the large version of the constellation is where the graves Igor was responsible for were located,' Joona says.

'Yes.'

'That makes me think that there's a symbolic logic, that these stars represent more than coordinates to Jurek.'

'I agree,' Saga says.

'And because we need to take a quick decision . . . I think we have to follow the same logic, that Jurek has abandoned the stars that make up Castor now that Igor's dead.'

'Which leaves us with eight locations,' Nathan says.

'Take another look at Pollux,' Joona says. 'Where are Valeria and Pellerina?'

'I'd start with the hands,' Saga says.

'One hand is indicating an industrial estate in Järfalla, the other a summerhouse south of Bro,' Nathan says, showing them on the map.

'Joona?' Saga says.

'We go to the industrial estate,' he says. 'That's where the twins are holding hands, as if the dead brother is handing responsibility to watch over the graves to Jurek.'

Saga and Nathan don't say anything else, and the three of them run out of the room, pulling their jackets on as they hurry along the corridor.

Saga and Joona are in one car, Nathan in another. On the E18 both cars get up to 160 kilometres an hour, but by the time they turn off Viksjöleden they're down to half that.

They're now following the satnav's instructions as they head along Järfallavägen beside the railway tracks, into a rundown industrial estate.

Rubbish has blown into the weeds along the tall fence.

They pass low buildings made of concrete and metal sheeting, tarmacked areas full of shipping containers, stacks of pallets and a row of abandoned caravans.

They slow down and turn right by a sign advertising car servicing.

Slowly they drive past vacant buildings surrounded by trucks, old trailers, poles with tatty company flags hanging from them. They pull up in the empty car park in front of JC's Car Service.

An advertising hoarding has blown over.

The three of them get out of their cars.

It's very cold, a snowstorm is approaching from Russia, the Swedish Met Office has issued a level 2 warning.

They pull on their protective vests and check their weapons. Nathan lifts a Benelli M4 Super 90 from the boot of his car, a semiautomatic shotgun used by rapid response units around the world.

Joona grabs the bag containing the bolt-cutters, crowbar, lock-pick gun, and angle-grinder.

Saga checks her Glock, then slips it back in her holster.

Nathan wraps his shotgun in a waterproof jacket.

They set off.

The industrial building at Åkervägen 14 is owned by an export company registered in Poland, but whose ownership is rather unclear.

It's located precisely where the two twins' hands meet when the constellation is superimposed on the map.

There's no one in sight anywhere.

The tarmac has been left pitted and damaged by heavy trucks.

The shabby building is tucked behind a tall fence with three rows of barbed wire above it. Immediately below the zinc roof there's a row of narrow windows that runs the whole length of the building. At one end there's a loading bay and a large retractable metal door to allow goods in and out.

Crows are crying loudly around a skip at the end of the turning circle.

The entrance to number 14 is blocked by a heavy gate bearing the logo of a security company.

Joona puts the canvas bag down, takes out the bolt-cutters, and cuts through the lock.

It clatters to the ground and Joona kicks the pieces into the ditch, opens the gate and walks in.

A commuter train passes behind the building, making the bushes by the fence sway.

There's a dented metal advert for Camel cigarettes on the wall next to the door. The rust from the screws has run down over the face of a smoking doctor.

They stop and listen, but there's no sound from within.

Saga uses the lock-pick gun to unlock the door.

Nathan unwraps his shotgun.

Joona puts the canvas bag full of tools on the ground, draws his pistol, looks his colleagues in the eye, then opens the door and goes in.

He checks the cramped lobby.

There's nothing there apart from an empty coatrack and a junction box with ceramic fuses.

The main circuit breaker is switched off.

Saga and Nathan stay close behind him as he goes over to the next door. He can hear Nathan's breathing behind him.

Holding his pistol at face-height, he gets ready to cover the right-hand side of the room, while Saga takes the left and Nathan the area in front of the door.

Joona cautiously presses the handle down, then shoves the door open, and points his pistol into the large space.

They count down from three.

Sounds from outside reach into the room through the row of narrow windows up by the roof. There's a strip of lighter patches across the bare cement floor.

Saga follows Joona in and they systematically check the dark corners in unison.

Nathan walks towards the middle of the room and sweeps round with the barrel of the shotgun.

The large space is empty.

Their footsteps echo off the bare walls.

Joona turns round.

One end of the room consists almost entirely of a single huge door, made up of horizontal metal strips, that can be raised up into the roof.

There's nothing here, the floor has been scrubbed clean.

There's a bit of tinsel hanging from an air-vent, swaying jerkily in the draught.

Without a word they cross the floor towards a dark corridor. Using the same system as before, they search two more empty rooms and the bathroom.

Judging by the marks on the linoleum floor, there were once shower cubicles next to the drains.

The last room is an empty storeroom, with a bit of sawdust on the floor.

They return to the large room. Joona walks to the middle of

the floor and turns round, looking at the narrow windows, the blank walls.

'I'll check out the back,' Saga says, and sets off.

'Has this place ever had anything to do with Jurek Walter?' Nathan wonders.

'Yes,' Joona says in a low voice.

'I mean, the whole idea with the constellation could be wrong,' Nathan says.

Joona doesn't answer, just walks over to the retractable door leading to the loading bay. The floor is scratched, the metal sill buckled.

He follows the black-rubber seal with his eyes, then turns to look at the room again.

Dust particles are floating in the weak sunlight.

The floor is perfectly clean. It hasn't just been swept, it's been scrubbed. Recently, too.

Joona walks over to the drain in the floor, kneels down and detects a strong smell of bleach.

He removes the grille, pulls out the filter and sees that it too has been cleaned.

Nathan mutters something about going outside, and walks out.

Joona gets to his feet and glances over at the loading bay again, then walks slowly after Nathan.

He stops at the open door to the lobby. This part of the building is darker.

Joona looks at the hinges and door. He closes, then opens the door again.

There's a long strand of hair stuck to one of the screws holding the sill in place.

Joona moves to one side, stands right by the wall and inspects the edge of the door.

There are three small ovals, not far from the floor.

At first he thinks they're knots in the wood that are visible through the paint, but the angles of the ovals prompt him to bend over and photograph them, using the flash on his phone.

The corner lights up, then goes dark again.

He hears a loud, scraping sound outside. Like a digger dragging a scoop across the ground.

Joona enlarges the image on his mobile and sees that the ovals are actually bloody fingerprints.

Someone's been dragged through this door and tried to hold on.

He can't see any blood in the lobby, but it looks like a fitted carpet has recently been removed – fragments of glue are still visible on the cement.

Joona goes out into the cold air and sees around thirty crows circling a white industrial unit some distance away. They're focused on a skip that's in the process of being lifted onto a truck. That's where the noise is coming from.

Saga comes round the corner of the empty building. She shakes her head, and seems to be holding back tears.

Several of the crows land and start pecking at the ground where the skip was standing.

The truck rolls out through the gates of VVS Enterprises and turns slowly onto Åkervägen.

Joona runs out into the road, stops right in the middle of it and gestures to the driver to stop.

The heavy vehicle slows down, rolls towards Joona and comes to a stop with a hiss.

The driver winds his window down and looks out.

'What the hell's your problem?' he calls.

'I'm a police superintendent with the National Operational Unit, and—'

'Have I broken any laws?'

'Take the key out of the ignition and throw it on the ground.'

'I pay your wages, and—'

'Otherwise I'll shoot your tyres out,' Joona says, pulling his pistol from its holster.

The keys rattle as they hit the tarmac.

'Thanks,' Joona says, and climbs up onto the truck.

He heaves the heavy metal bar aside to open the skip, pulls the hatch open and is met by a terrible stench.

Beneath a pile of old drainpipes, insulation and packaging, damp cardboard and a broken toilet seat are six black bin-bags.

The bottom of the skip is covered with blood.

A naked arm is sticking out from a tear in one of the bags, broken at the elbow, dark with internal bleeding.

The hand is small, but not a child's.

The six bin-bags are large enough to contain a body each.

Six people killed at the place where the twins hold hands.

The building was scrubbed clean, and the bodies dumped in a skip.

Joona pulls out his mobile and calls Nils Åhlén. While the call goes through he looks down into the skip again, staring at the broken elbow and the odd angle of the lower arm. He thinks about the bloody fingerprints on the doorframe, looks at the pale hand resting on the black plastic, then sees that two of the fingers are moving.

79

Valeria wakes up in the darkness with a splitting headache. They've put some thick socks on her feet, and laid a blanket over her. Even so, she's so cold that she's shaking.

'Pellerina? Are you cold?'

Valeria fumbles for the water bottle, unscrews the lid and drinks the last drops.

'Pellerina?' she says, louder this time. 'Are you there?'

When the girl doesn't answer, Valeria smiles so broadly that her dry lips crack. They've taken her up into the house. That must be what's happened. Seeing as she herself has been given a blanket, at least some form of communication has been established. She was taking a risk when she pretended to be a drug addict, it could have gone badly wrong.

She still doesn't know what they think she's done, but if she'd told them the truth and denied everything they'd never have listened to her.

Valeria doesn't know where she got it all from, but she did her best to use her time as an addict to sound plausible.

She's sure they'd already noticed the ugly scars on her arms.

Valeria has never tried to hide them, never enquired about plastic surgery, because she thinks she deserves the contempt they sometimes prompt in other people.

Her own sense of shame is so much worse.

The family had probably already been having trouble believing that Pellerina was involved. When Valeria confessed that they were both being punished for her drug debts, things became more comprehensible to them – and at the same time, more morally confused.

The last time they removed the floorboards and opened the coffin she had sat up, even though they were yelling at her to stay down, calling her a junkie whore and saying they were going to shoot her in the head.

'Do it, then,' she had replied. 'Then you'll be responsible for my debts to Jurek.'

'Shut up!' the woman had said.

'I need you to know that I'm sorry for everything I—'

'You want us to forgive you?' the man interrupted. 'Is that it? You're scum, you're not even human.'

'Stop talking to her,' the woman whispered.

'I don't want to do bad things,' Valeria said. 'It was only that I couldn't borrow any more, and the withdrawal kicked in and I was just so desperate . . . You never worry about AIDS or over-dosing, or getting beaten up or raped . . . but withdrawal terrifies you, it's like being in hell.'

'I hope you're there now,' the man says.

'It's really cold, I can't feel my legs any more . . . I don't think I can survive another night . . .'

'That's not our problem,' the woman said, weighing the axe in her hands.

'Did Jurek tell you to kill us?'

'We're just guarding you,' the man replied.

'We're not supposed to talk to her,' the teenage girl blurted.

'I don't want to frighten Pellerina,' Valeria went on. 'But she's small, she'll soon freeze to death – you understand that, don't you?'

'Lie back down,' the man said, taking a step towards her and raising the rifle.

He was so close she could see the blond hairs on his arms.

'I mean, you could take us up into the house, I'm so weak I probably can't even stand up now . . . you could tie me up, you're armed, after all—'

They threw a bag of food scraps into the coffin, forced the lid down again, and tightened the straps.

Valeria's fingers were too weak to untie the knot, so she had to rip the bag open with her teeth.

She ate a little of the boiled potatoes and sausage and almost threw up, but concentrated on keeping the food down.

Her stomach warmed up and her thoughts drifted off in a very odd way, and she realised that the food was drugged, and that they were either sedating or killing her.

For a few moments she dreamed about a pink hummingbird and a beautiful Chinese tapestry moving in the wind before she jerked and opened her eyes in the darkness.

The seal around the lid of the coffin started to glow white and blue. She thought she could hear loose straps fall onto the dry earth beneath the house, the clatter of a winch.

In her drugged state, she thought that they were opening Pellerina's coffin. She thought she could hear her crying as they lifted her up into the house.

Valeria has no idea how long she's been unconscious.

It feels like at least a day.

Her head aches and her mouth is dry.

She realises that they drugged her so they could put more clothes on her. They must have believed her story about being an addict, and that Pellerina hadn't burned anyone's face.

Pellerina isn't down here with her any more, maybe they've even let her go. Now Valeria has to try to save herself, try to turn her story against Jurek, get them to understand that he was using her.

80

Saga washes her face in the basin of one of the toilets of the Intensive Care Unit on the fourth floor of the Karolinska Hospital.

She tells herself once more that she needs to pull herself together. But the tears bubble up again and she sits down on the toilet seat and tries to breathe slowly.

'I can do this,' she whispers.

She had been round at the back of the industrial unit, kicking a pile of frozen autumn leaves and walking along the fence by the railway line when she heard Joona call out that he'd found something in a skip.

A train rattled past.

It was as if she'd fallen through the ice on a lake and was sinking through freezing water.

The weeds were swaying in the wind as dust and rubbish were swirled into the air.

The sudden fear was like an immense, all-encompassing tiredness.

A chance to give in, to lie down on the ground, and stop time.

Instead she'd clung to the low fence backing onto the railway embankment.

And when she heard Joona call out that one of them was still alive, she began to walk, as if through deep sand.

She didn't notice her bag falling to the ground. It must have slid off her shoulder.

All she could think was that she should have let Jurek kill her. It was all her fault.

Black crows were perched on the ground outside the premises of VVS Enterprises.

Saga turned the corner and stepped out into the road, saw the truck carrying the skip, and caught a glimpse of the driver through the windscreen.

Joona was shouting something, and Nathan turned towards her. She had seen her own terror reflected in his face. He'd walked towards her, holding his hands up to calm her, and stopped her from going any closer.

'My sister,' she mumbled, trying to get past him.

'Please, wait, you have to—'

'Who is it who's still alive?'

'I don't know, the ambulance is on its way, and—'

'Pellerina!' she cried.

She thinks back to how Nathan held onto her, telling her she had to wait, then she ended up sitting in Joona's car a few hundred metres away, shivering.

Three police cars and six ambulances arrived.

Their blue lights flew across the buildings and fences, casting quick shadows across the tarmac and bushes.

Through the car's windscreen she watched the paramedics work.

At first the activity around the truck was frenetic and intense.

But everyone apart from the naked woman was dead. Saga could tell from the way they were handling the bodies.

There were three people standing in the skip, cutting the bin-bags open and lifting out body after body.

Saga tried to see if any of the bodies looked like a child's, but she was too far away and her view was obscured. One ambulance reversed out, and uniformed officers cordoned off the area.

She only managed to catch a glimpse of one of the shattered bodies as they were lifted out of the skip and lined up on the ground. She saw a narrow leg hit the rusty edge of the skip, and a black bin-bag stuck to a thickset man's back.

The first ambulance left the area, taking the woman away. She heard the sirens start to blare as it pulled out onto Järfallavägen.

Saga couldn't tell if Valeria was among the dead, or if Pellerina's naked body was lying at the far end of the row.

She opened the car door and got out. She didn't want to go, but she had to.

It felt like she was wading through water, thick, blue, sluggish. She wasn't sure she'd be able to make it.

Joona had been standing to one side of the paramedics. He didn't see her coming. She tried to read his face.

He looked sad, focused.

Saga walked up to the cordon. One of the uniformed officers recognised her and let her through.

She heard herself thank him, and carried on, stopping a few steps away from the bodies, bloody and horribly pale.

Neither Pellerina nor Valeria were among the dead.

She'd had to check several times.

The body at the far end was a young man in his twenties, with green eyes and dark hair. His throat had been cut, and his face and one side of his head had been badly beaten.

Saga had staggered and reached out to the fence for support, then walked off through the weeds, back to the road, where she stood for a while with her hands resting on the bonnet of one of the police cars. She remembers seeing her face hazily reflected in the white paint, and thinking that she really ought to go back and help. When she turned round, the paramedics were lifting the naked man onto a stretcher.

She sank into a crouch with her back against the front wheel of the police car, covered her face and wept with relief and gratitude that Pellerina wasn't among the dead.

Eventually Joona came over and sat on the ground beside her. He had brought a blanket from the ambulance which he wrapped round her.

'I thought she was one of the bodies,' she said, wiping her tears away with both hands.

'It's OK to feel relieved, even if other people have suffered.'

'I know, it's just that . . . This isn't like me, but I just can't . . . I can't bear the thought of anyone hurting her,' she said, and tried to swallow the lump in her throat. 'Pellerina is the wisest, most wonderful—'

'We're going to find her.'

'What's the plan now?' Saga asked, trying to pull herself together.

'If they can save the woman's life, I need to talk to her,' Joona had told her. 'And after that I'm going to the summerhouse where Pollux's other hand is located.'

'I'll come with you,' she said, but didn't move when he stood up.

'You don't have to, you know.'

Saga rinses her face in the basin again, then dries herself off with paper towels and walks out of the hospital toilet. As she makes her way down the corridor she thinks about all the other people – parents, children, wives, boyfriends, and siblings of the dead people in the skip – who would be getting terrible news that day. This time she has been given a reprieve, she can still hope for a happy ending.

The unconscious woman has been identified as Emilia Torn. She was driven to the Intensive Care Unit at the Karolinska Hospital, where the decision was taken to sedate her. Both her arms and one leg are broken, she has severe trauma to the back of her skull, she's been bitten in the neck, cut across the stomach, and has lost a lot of blood.

Joona comes running over with a set of protective clothing in his hands just as the doctor is about to go into the operating theatre.

'Wait,' he says. 'I need to know if there's any chance of talking to the patient. I'm a police officer, and—'

'Then you know how this works,' the doctor interrupts.

'There are more lives at stake.'

'She's already been sedated, and is about to be anaesthetised properly so—'

'I was the one who found her, I only need a couple of minutes,' Joona interrupts, pulling on the protective tunic.

'I can't let you impede our work,' the doctor says. 'But you can have a try before we intubate.'

They go into the operating theatre where the staff are busy

preparing. An anaesthesiologist is disinfecting the woman's groin at the top of the leg that isn't broken, then inserts a catheter into the vein.

The woman's face is pale and yellowish, her skin already sweaty from the morphine. Some of her red hair is stuck to her cheek with congealed blood. Her broken arms are mottled with internal bleeding.

'Emilia? Can you hear me?'

'What?' she replies, almost inaudibly.

'Was there a child in the building, a little girl?' he asks.

'No,' she whispers.

'Think, was there a little girl with Down Syndrome?'

'I don't understand, he killed Ralf . . . he stamped on his face, then cut the guys' throats, then attacked me and—'

'Who did? Who did this?'

'The producer, he just went crazy, he—'

'Do you know his name?'

'Auscultate heart and lungs,' the doctor says, looking at the carbon-dioxide monitor.

'Do you know how I can get hold of the producer?'

'Who the fuck are you, anyway?' she murmurs.

'My name is Joona Linna, I'm a superintendent at—'

'It's all about you,' she says in an uneven voice.

'What do you mean?'

'He kept shouting, saying you'd be trodden into the dirt, that you'd—'

Her body starts to shake and she coughs up blood over her chin and chest. Joona steps back to get out of the way of the team of doctors and nurses. He leaves the room, pulls off the protective clothing, then hurries along the corridor to the waiting room.

Saga and Nathan are sitting next to each other on one of the sofas, staring at their phones. Saga's face is tense, her eyes bloodshot.

'It doesn't look like Pellerina was there,' Joona says.

Saga nods to herself, then puts her phone away, and meets his gaze. Nathan moves the pile of brochures from the low table and spreads out the map with the constellation of Gemini drawn on it.

'Seven locations left,' he says. 'Presumably we start with the other hand, the summerhouse?'

'Maybe we've been thinking about this wrong,' Joona says.

'How do you mean?'

'I'm convinced we're going to find something there, but this is personal for Jurek, he said he wants to trample me into the dirt.'

'The feet, you mean?' Nathan says, looking up at Joona.

They bend over the map again and scrutinise it. The star marking Pollux's left foot is in the middle of a road in Södertälje. But his right foot is located on a detached house north of Nykvarn.

81

While they were at the hospital the storm swept in across Stockholm, bringing huge amounts of snow and lowering the temperature still further.

Joona is driving fast through the heavy snow along the E20, heading towards Nykvarn. The snow has already settled between the lanes and along the verge.

Saga checks her pistol, then inserts the magazine.

Joona changes lane and overtakes a lorry on the wrong side.

A cloud of dirty snow flies up onto the bonnet and windscreen.

According to the property registry, the house that Pollux is standing on is owned by a middle-aged couple with two children. Tommy and Anna-Lena Nordin run their own business, recruiting staff for other companies. Their daughter Miriam is fifteen, and goes to the high school in Tälje, and their son Axel is eight, and attends Björkesta School in Nykvarn.

Joona accelerates and the noise inside the car gets louder.

As they're approaching the Almnäs junction, Joona sees a flashing blue light in the rear-view mirror. He slows down and pulls over to the side of the road.

In the back seat Nathan smiles, cradling his semiautomatic rifle on his lap.

The police car stops behind them, the front doors open and two uniformed officers get out. The female officer rolls towards them, breasts thrust out, while the man unfastens his holster.

They've stopped a dirty BMW that was doing 180 kilometres an hour. They already know that the car is registered to a man who has been given an unconditional discharge from prison, and they're about to discover that the three people sitting in the car are heavily armed.

Considering the circumstances, it really didn't take Ingrid and Jim of the Södertälje Police long to re-evaluate the situation.

At first Joona was reluctant to accept their offer of help, because they had no idea how dangerous the operation could turn out to be.

'They're experienced officers,' Nathan said. 'And we've been promised backup as soon as we've got proof of where Jurek is . . . We need their help to get inside the house.'

So now Saga is sitting in the back seat of the police car, going through the details of the operation with the two officers.

They're following Joona's BMW along the old Strängnäs road. Snow flies up behind the two cars.

Ingrid and Jim have a thermos of coffee and a bag of saffron Lucia buns on the console between them.

They're driving past the broad expanse of Vidbynäs Golf Club with its snow-covered bunkers and greens as Saga goes on sketching out possible scenarios.

'The most dangerous possibility is that Jurek and the Beaver have taken over the house and are waiting inside, heavily armed, for us to show up,' she says.

The police car almost slides as it turns right at Turinge Church and follows Joona's BMW along a narrow road.

'As long as we don't have to do the triathlon,' Jim says in a thick rural accent.

'Nothing's worse than the triathlon,' Ingrid replies, in the same accent.

They laugh, then apologise and explain that they sometimes pretend to be Sture and Sten, two old men from Skaraborg.

'They can't stand physical exercise,' Ingrid says with a smile.

'We invented them when we started training for the triathlon together,' Jim explains. 'We've been at it for four years now, coaching each other . . .'

'And now Sture and Sten are terrified, because we've signed up to do a full-length triathlon in the French Alps.'

'Nothing's worse than the triathlon,' he says.

'Sorry, we're very silly,' Ingrid laughs.

'Well, we're not *that* silly,' Jim says, in his exaggerated accent.

They have to drive round the whole golf course to get to the house in Mindal. Beyond the manor house there are no further tyre-tracks in the snow. Bright orange poles mark the edges of the road to stop anyone driving into the ditches or fields.

Joona and Nathan pull over to the side of the road. The snow crunches as the tyres compact it before finally coming to a halt.

As soon as the police car and Saga have gone past, they get out of the car, step over the ditch and head up into the forest to make their way round to the back of the house without being seen.

It's almost twenty degrees below freezing and the cold is stinging their faces and making their eyes water.

The snow is nowhere near as deep among the trees, and is littered with fallen pine-needles and cones.

As they walk, Joona scans the ground for any air-pipes, disturbed soil and bare ground.

A few snowflakes drift down through the trees.

After fifteen minutes they catch sight of the back of the house between the trees. They carry on cautiously before stopping at the edge of the forest.

The thick snow has blanketed the landscape in a deafening silence.

The house is modern, fairly large, two storeys with a black-panelled roof and grey façade.

Nothing about it suggests violence and death.

The snow on the lawn at the back of the house is untouched, gently undulating over flowerbeds and garden furniture.

Joona takes out his binoculars and starts to check the windows, one after the other. The curtains upstairs are all drawn.

He takes his time, but can't see any sign of movement, no shadows.

Everything is quiet, but there's something unsettling that he can't put his finger on.

He moves down with the binoculars and sees that drifts of snow have built up against the veranda doors on the ground floor. Through the frosty glass he can make out a conservatory containing a sofa, two armchairs and a polished cement fireplace.

There are blankets folded neatly over the arms of the chairs, and the glass table is clean and bare.

Joona lowers the binoculars and looks at Nathan. His face looks sombre, his nose red with cold.

'Nothing?' Nathan says with a shiver.

'No,' Joona says, then realises what it was that was unsettling him.

It wasn't anything he saw, but something that was missing from the picture. An ordinary middle-class family with two children, and there wasn't a single Christmas decoration in sight on 12 December. No Advent candelabra or stars in the windows, no strings of lights, no decorations in the garden.

The police car has driven right up to the house in Mindal and parked in the snow-covered drive.

Saga and the two officers are sitting in the car, looking at the house.

The snow is falling more heavily now.

Through one window they can see a girl wearing headphones, doing her homework.

The snow on the drive is untouched. No vehicles have come or gone since the snow started falling.

One door of the double garage is open. Saga can make out a golf-buggy, a few sun-bleached cushions for garden furniture, a huge barbeque, a lawnmower and a spade with a rusty handle.

The radio crackles and Joona's voice breaks the silence.

He and Nathan are in position at the back of the house. They can't see anyone, and there's nothing remarkable except the absence of any Christmas decorations. They're staying hidden in the forest, but are ready to go in through the back door if necessary.

Saga gets out of the car with the two uniformed officers. Ingrid starts to cough as she breathes the cold air into her lungs.

'OK?' Jim asks quietly.

She nods and the three of them walk towards the house. Through the window they see a man removing shiny cutlery from a dishwasher.

He's wearing a pastel-blue shirt with the sleeves rolled up.

They stop in front of the door, stamp the snow from their shoes, then ring the doorbell.

Saga moves aside, puts her hand in her pocket, and takes hold of her pistol.

The breath is like smoke around their mouths.

Her face is stinging with cold.

They hear footsteps inside as someone approaches the door.

Saga reminds herself that Jurek or the Beaver could be inside the house, and that Pellerina and Valeria could be buried in the garden or in the forest behind the house.

The lock clicks and the door is opened by the man from the kitchen. He looks tanned, has a blond moustache, and tired rings under his eyes.

He's standing on the white marble floor in his socks. Behind him a broad staircase leads up to the second storey and down to the basement.

'Tommy Nordin?' Saga asks.

'Yes,' he replies, looking at her quizzically.

'We've had a report about a disturbance.'

'A disturbance?'

'We need to come in and talk to you and your wife.'

'But there haven't been any disturbances here,' the man says slowly.

'All the same, we need to talk to you, seeing as we received a report,' Saga says.

The girl who had been sitting at the kitchen table comes out into the hall. Her movements are strangely drowsy. She's taken her headphones off. Her straight blonde hair is hanging beside her cheeks, and she's drawn in her eyebrows and applied make-up to cover the spots on her chin. Her lips are thin and she's dressed in jeans, white socks, and a Hollister polo-shirt with a dirty collar.

'Ask Mimmi,' the man says, nodding towards the girl. 'Ask

her . . . Anna-Lena and I have split up, I haven't seen her in the past two months, she's moved to Solna with our son.'

'So it's just the two of you living here?'

'Yes,' the father replies.

'Then you won't mind us coming and taking a look around,' Jim says.

'Don't you need a warrant from a prosecutor to do that?'

'No,' Saga replies curtly.

'We can question and arrest someone without a permit,' Ingrid explains.

'That sounds like a threat,' the man says, stepping aside so they can go in.

82

In the hall Saga unbuttons her jacket so she can quickly reach the pistol in her shoulder holster.

She blows on her cold fingers as she looks over at the staircase.

There are no lights on upstairs or down in the basement.

Ingrid is leaning against the wall with one hand as she wipes her shoes on the doormat.

There's a sudden clatter as Jim accidentally knocks into a long-handled broom.

There are dust and hairs caught in its head.

They follow the father into a large, open-plan kitchen. The dining room is separated from the kitchen by a full-length white screen.

'We do have a home-cinema system that can be quite loud,' the father says, running his tongue over his front teeth.

The girl says nothing, just walks slowly back to the island unit and sits down on the barstool in front of her schoolbooks again.

Saga can't help thinking that Joona's right. Even though the parents have separated, it's odd that they haven't put up any Christmas decorations in the kitchen or dining room.

It feels as if time has stood still in here.

There are white orchids in the window.

The snow-covered golf course is visible through the trees.

A frosted-glass door leads through to the living room, and there's a half-open wooden door leading to a corridor.

'Would you like coffee?' the man asks.

'No, thanks,' Saga replies.

The thin screen between the kitchen and dining room is semi-transparent, and sways gently in the slightest draught.

The man carries on emptying the dishwasher, lining up the clean glasses on the worktop.

'Could you leave that for the time being?' Saga says.

He turns and looks at her with a deep wrinkle between his eyebrows.

'Have you had any visitors recently?' she asks.

'What do you mean by visitors?'

'What do you think?'

He scratches the top of one arm, then goes on emptying the dishwasher.

Saga watches him, changes position and sees that he's broken out in a sweat.

'No visitors?'

She moves the screen aside with her hand and walks into the dining room, past a large table with a stone top, then turns back towards Tommy Nordin again.

'If it wasn't a domestic row, what was it?' Saga says, addressing her words to the screen.

'Like I said, we were probably watching a film,' the father says.

Through the screen, the kitchen looks like it's covered in thick fog. Saga sees the girl glance unhappily at her father.

'Every day?' Saga asks.

'It varies.'

'Which days this week?'

Ingrid straightens up and sticks her chest out beneath her uniform, and Jim is standing with one hand on his holster watching the man.

Saga goes over to one of the windows overlooking the snow-covered garden. Flakes are still falling, only to be swallowed up by the existing whiteness. The branches of the fir trees are weighed down. She leans closer to the pane and feels the cold through the glass. A trail of dark footprints leads from the entrance, round the garage and over to a snow-covered playhouse.

Her heart starts to beat faster.

What have they been doing in the playhouse?

The number of footprints indicates that they've been there several times.

She goes back into the kitchen, round the island unit, and feels her hand trembling as she puts it down on the marble top.

Very cautiously, she slips her other hand inside her jacket and takes hold of her pistol.

From this position she can cover both father and daughter, as well as the entrances to the living room, corridor and hall.

'When did you stop using the playhouse?' Saga asks the girl.

'Don't know,' she replies quietly, and goes on staring at her books.

'After the first summer?' Saga suggests.

'Yes,' the girl nods, without looking at Saga.

'So what do you keep in there?' Saga asks the girl.

'Nothing,' she says quietly.

'Look outside,' Saga says. 'There are deep footprints in the snow.'

The girl doesn't look, just keeps her eyes trained on her books.

'The neighbours have two little girls, they sometimes use it,' she whispers.

'In the winter?' Saga says, letting go of the pistol.

'Yes,' the girl says, still not looking at Saga.

'Hasn't this gone on long enough, now?' the man says, rubbing the back of his neck hard.

'Soon,' Jim says amiably.

'You can start by showing my colleague your bedroom,' Saga says.

'Look, I'm really not happy with this . . . this is an invasion of privacy, I haven't done anything.'

The girl lowers her head slightly and covers her ears, but seems to realise what she's doing and puts her hands back down on the worktop.

'Soon as we've taken a look around, we'll leave you in peace,' Jim says.

Saga thinks she can hear knocking through the walls. She holds her breath and listens, but it's all quiet again. Maybe it was just snow falling from the roof.

The father dries his hands on a check-patterned tea-towel, then tosses it on the counter and walks towards the hall.

His dark blue socks are so worn that his white heels are visible through them.

Jim glances at Ingrid, then follows the man out of the kitchen. The two men's footsteps echo into the kitchen as they go upstairs.

The girl hasn't turned the page of her book once. She's still staring at the opening page about Sweden's years as a great power.

'Your name's Miriam?' Saga says.

'Yes,' she says, and swallows hard. 'Everyone calls me Mimmi.'

'And you're at high school?'

'First year.'

Ingrid has walked over to the frosted door leading to the living room.

'What subjects?' Saga asks.

'Soc . . . social sciences.'

'Did you hear those thuds?'

The girl shakes her head and Saga notices that she's got grubby plasters on her thumbs.

'What year do they say Sweden first became a great power?' Saga asks.

'What?'

'Which century?'

'I don't remember,' the girl mumbles and closes the book.

'Do you remember if you've had any visitors in the past week?' Saga goes on.

'I don't think so,' she says in a monotone.

'Mimmi,' Saga says, taking a step closer to her. 'I'm a super-intendent in the police, and I can tell that something's happened here.'

The girl's been biting her pen, the end is chewed and squashed. She carries on staring at the table.

'What's happened here?' Saga persists.

'Nothing,' Mimmi whispers to herself.

'Why haven't you got any Christmas decorations up?' Ingrid asks amiably.

'What?'

'Why haven't you got any Advent stars, or gingerbread biscuits?'

The girl shakes her head as if the question was annoying and irrelevant.

Saga wonders if they're a perfectly ordinary family that hasn't yet been drawn into Jurek's world, a family who are blissfully unaware that one of the constellation's stars is located right where their house is.

But at the same time it's obvious that they're hiding something. Both father and daughter have a look of raging panic in their eyes.

'Can you show me your room?' she says.

'It's in there,' the girl says, pointing at the door leading to the corridor.

'Show me.'

The girl gets to her feet without a word.

'Who is it who plays golf?' Ingrid asks as they set off.

'The whole family, but I do a bit of extra work coaching kids.'

Saga and Ingrid follow the girl through the door to the corridor. The passageway is fairly long and ends at a bathroom. A thin line of LED-lights runs along the bottom of the left-hand wall.

Two doors lead to the children's rooms. According to the signs, the first is Axel's, the second Mimmi's.

The floor outside the boy's room is ice-cold. A sign saying 'No entry' has been taped to the door beneath the sign.

Saga gestures to Ingrid to stay in the corridor while she goes into Mimmi's room with her.

They pass the small door of a closet under the stairs leading to the upper floor. The girl automatically closes the door as she passes it.

On the wall above the unmade bed is a poster of a very thin David Bowie holding up a thick book with a black star on it, like some evangelical priest.

There's a box of sleeping pills on the bedside table.

In the corner, on the back of a chair, hangs a Halloween mask, some sort of zombie: a bloody skull jutting out from a man's torn mouth.

'So you've passed the princess stage,' Saga says.

'Yes,' the girl replies.

It sounds as if someone's banging on a door a long way away.

'Did you hear that?' Saga says, looking at her.

'No,' the girl says slowly.

Saga looks towards the window. Large snowflakes are falling through the light radiating from the room.

'And just you and your dad live here?'

The girl doesn't answer, merely prods the repulsive mask absentmindedly.

The ceiling creaks and Saga assumes that Jim and the girl's father are on their way back downstairs.

'Sit down on the bed,' she says.

The mattress springs protest as the girl obeys. The bottoms of her white socks are filthy.

'Mimmi . . . you know you're going to have to tell me what's happened,' Saga says seriously.

'It would probably be better if I died,' the girl whispers.

83

Ingrid is standing in the corridor, listening as Saga talks calmly to the girl in her bedroom. It seems to her that this family has been badly damaged by the divorce, all their happiness has gone.

Ingrid looks hesitantly at the door to Axel's room. She isn't sure if the superintendent meant for her to go in there, or just wait.

Dust is drifting along the floor of the corridor, lit up by the white glow of the LEDs.

She presses the handle down and goes into the boy's room.

It's dark and cold.

She can hear a faint scraping, rasping sound.

There are large model aeroplanes hanging from the ceiling on nylon threads.

Through the wall Ingrid can hear Saga Bauer talking to the daughter.

There's a strong smell of rotting flowers in the air.

She steps further in. Her uniform creaks with her body's movements.

The window is wide open, letting the ice-cold wind in. The catch is rattling with the gusts and the curtains are billowing.

Several sheets of paper have blown off the desk.

Something's terribly wrong.

The aeroplanes swing in a fresh gust, and the door to the corridor slams shut. The wardrobe creaks.

Ingrid looks at a poster of the superhero, Wonder Woman, with her shield on her back, as she walks further into the room.

A boy is lying on the bed, staring up at her with reddish-brown eyes.

He's almost entirely covered with flowers.

His face is covered with black burn marks, and his greenish torso is swollen with gas.

He must have been dead for a week, maybe longer.

'Bauer, you need to see this,' Ingrid calls out loudly.

The curtain billows again, then sinks back.

From the corner of her eye Ingrid sees the wardrobe door open. A chill runs down her spine, she turns and just has time to see the hard expression on the woman's face before the axe hits her in the head. The back of Ingrid's head thuds into the wall with the superhero poster. The thick blade has penetrated so deeply into her brain that everything goes dark and silent. She doesn't even notice as her legs buckle beneath her and she ends up lying on her back with her neck against the wall at an unnaturally sharp angle as blood gushes onto the floor.

After saying it might be better if she was dead, the girl clams up entirely. She stops answering questions and sits there tight-lipped with her head bowed. When Saga hears her colleague call her, she tells Mimmi to stay where she is and wait until she comes back.

'Promise not to move,' Saga says.

She hears a loud thud against the wall, and the pin-board above Mimmi's desk shakes.

Mimmi stares at Saga with a look of horror in her eyes, then clamps both hands over her ears.

Saga goes out into the corridor, but Ingrid isn't there. She looks towards the kitchen, then notices that the door to the boy's bedroom is open slightly.

'Ingrid,' she says quietly.

Saga moves closer and feels the cold wind from the dark room, hesitates, then steps into it. The curtains are fluttering in front of the open window, snow is swirling in, and petals are drifting across the floor.

Behind the heavy scent of hyacinths is the stench of death. It isn't a conscious perception, but it makes her more wary.

A pale reflection slips across one wall.

Saga takes another step into the room and simultaneously notices the axe swinging towards her from one side.

All her years of boxing have taught her to judge the direction of the blow correctly. She instinctively lowers her head and slips backwards and off to one side. The blade of the axe misses her face and slices into the plasterboard, before coming to rest on an internal beam.

Saga stumbles out into the corridor before the woman has time to pull the axe loose. She reaches out to the wall to keep her balance and backs away as she draws her Glock from its holster.

Aiming the pistol at the door, she retreats a bit further and glances quickly over her shoulder.

There's no one behind her.

The bathroom door is closed, but the light is on inside.

'Ingrid?' she asks in a loud voice.

There's no answer, and Saga turns back quickly towards the boy's room.

Without making a sound the woman has managed to get out into the corridor. She's standing motionless, the axe over one shoulder, looking at Saga. Her face is taut, focused. Tiny specks of blood are spattered across the woman's glasses, neck and both arms.

Saga backs away slowly, raises her pistol and puts her finger on the trigger.

'Police!' she declares, squeezing the trigger past the first notch. 'Stay where you are and put the axe down on the floor!'

Instead of doing as she says, the woman sets off towards her. Breathing hard through her nose, she's approaching with long strides.

Saga supports her pistol with her left hand, quickly lowers the barrel and shoots her in the thigh. The bullet passes straight through the muscle and blood sprays out behind her. The woman lets out a groan, but keeps moving.

The leg of her trousers turns dark with blood.

Saga backs into the bathroom door.

The woman's lips narrow as she keeps walking. She raises the axe, bringing down the ceiling lamp.

It goes out and crashes to the floor.

Saga shoots the woman twice in the chest. The recoil slams her right shoulder blade into the door.

The cloud of powder dissipates.

The woman stops, reaches out for the wall with one hand, drops the axe and slumps down heavily onto the floor. Her blood-spattered glasses drop into her lap, her head falls forward, then jerks sideways several times.

The moment the first shot goes off Joona kicks in the narrow glass door to the conservatory. The lock comes apart with a crash. The door flies open and the glass shatters, spreading splinters across the parquet floor.

Joona runs in with his pistol drawn. Nathan rips the plastic bag from his semiautomatic and runs after him.

Joona points the pistol at the sofa until he's past it, then aims at the door to the kitchen.

Nathan is covering their backs as they hurry past the fireplace.

Their reflections fly across the windows looking out onto the dark forest.

Joona stops in front of the door and catches Nathan's eye.

'We go in together,' he says quietly. 'You take the left side, ninety-five degrees.'

He counts down with his fingers, then opens the kitchen door. They run in and secure the most dangerous angles systematically.

Empty.

Joona signals to Nathan to guard the door to the hall as he walks round an island unit with some schoolbooks and a mobile phone on it.

He points his pistol towards the screen leading to the dining room.

Their movements have made the fabric sway.

Darkness has fallen in the garden outside, and it's hard to see anything through the screen. Joona can barely make out the table, chairs and sideboard.

He hears two more pistol shots from the corridor.

'What the hell's going on?' Nathan whispers, looking round.

Joona slips behind the screen, simultaneously training his pistol on the door to the corridor. He looks over at Nathan, and sees him turn his back on the door to the hall just as it starts to open behind his back.

'The hall!' Joona calls out.

Nathan only has time to start turning round before the father comes into the kitchen and fires his shotgun at him.

The hail of bullets rips the back of Nathan's skull off.

Blood and brains spray across the island unit and across the screen.

Joona rushes forward as Nathan falls to the floor.

His pistol is aimed at the father's chest, the line of fire through the thin fabric perfect, but Joona doesn't shoot.

Nathan's dead body falls heavily to the ground and ends up on its side.

Without letting go of the shotgun, the father wipes away the blood that landed on his face with his shoulder.

He doesn't spot Joona until he's emerged from behind the screen.

Before the father has time to aim the gun at him, Joona shoves it aside with one hand and hits him across the face with the pistol.

The shotgun goes off and hits the ceiling.

The man staggers sideways and tries to grab the gun.

The blast rings in their ears as fragments of plaster and dust rain down on the pair of them.

Joona slams his right elbow into the man's cheek.

It's a solid blow.

The man's head thuds against the wall and he sinks to one knee. He isn't even aware that Joona has snatched the shotgun away from him.

Blood is running into his moustache from both nostrils, and his eyes look dazed. He reaches out to the wall and tries to stand up. Joona takes a step forward and kicks him hard in the chest, and he jerks backwards and slides across the floor.

'Stay there,' Joona says, then stamps on the shotgun, shattering it.

Coughing hard, the man gets his breath back as heavy footsteps echo on the stairs. Jim walks in, looking very pale, with blood running down one cheek.

'Shit, he knocked me out,' he mutters, then stops in the doorway when he sees Nathan's body.

84

Saga is stepping over the dead woman's body when she hears a shotgun-blast from the kitchen. She aims her pistol at the door and moves silently along the corridor. The barrel quivers slightly as the shotgun goes off a second time.

Saga waits a few seconds, then goes into Axel's room, sees the boy's body on the bed, and confirms that her colleague is dead before she returns to Mimmi's room.

Silence.

The girl has opened the window and climbed out. She's only got socks on her feet. Her footprints through the snow lead in a wide arc around the house.

Saga takes out her radio and calls Joona. When he tells her that Nathan's dead she feels like curling up in a ball and sobbing.

But at the same time she realises that the insane rage of the family means that Jurek has been here.

And if Jurek has been here, they may know something about Pellerina and Valeria.

Saga quickly tells Joona what's happened, that the young boy, Ingrid, and the mother are dead, and that she's about to go after the daughter.

'Get going, find her,' he says.

It's snowing more heavily now, and her footprints will soon be covered.

Holding the window open with one hand, Saga climbs up and

sits on the sill. The black tin creaks as she shuffles further out, braces herself with her hands, then jumps.

She lands softly on the snow and takes a step forward to stop herself falling.

The girl has a five-minute head start, at most, and her tracks are still visible.

Saga runs round the house, and can feel the wetness of the snow that's got into her shoes and trousers.

The snow has blown into large drifts behind the garage. She keeps moving, pistol in hand. It's darker there, as if the forest was casting a dark light across the garden.

The playhouse is rust-red, with white detailing and a black roof, and white windows with net curtains.

The original footprints are scarcely visible through the freshly fallen snow, like a shallow stream, but the new prints are perfectly clear.

It's dark inside the playhouse, but all the footprints lead straight to the small door with its stained-glass window.

Saga walks through the snow, looks over her shoulder, stands beside the door and knocks.

'Mimmi? Come out now.'

She knocks again, then waits a few seconds before reaching over and pushing the handle.

She tries pushing and pulling, but the door's locked.

'Mimmi, can you open the door? I only want to talk to you, I think you can help me.'

Saga thinks she can hear a noise, the sound of something being dragged across the floor, something heavy.

'I need to come in,' she says.

She breaks the little window in the door with her pistol, hears the glass hit the floor inside, then sweeps the barrel of the pistol around the edges to get rid of the worst of the splinters.

The inside of the playhouse is completely dark.

A rancid smell hits her as she tries to reach in with her arm. Her sleeve rides up a bit before coming to a stop.

The opening is too small.

Saga takes her jacket and top off, dropping them on the ground. She's only wearing a white vest now. Her sports bra is visible through the thin cotton. Her thin arms with their sharply defined muscles are covered in bruises and scratches.

The cold feels oddly sharp against her bare skin, and every snowflake that lands on her burns like a stray spark from a sparkler.

She tries to look through the hole in the door.

There's no movement inside.

Holding her pistol in her right hand, she moves closer to the hole.

As soon as she puts her arm through, the girl starts to scream, so loudly that her voice breaks. Saga tries to reach the lock, but she needs to push her hand even lower.

The girl stops abruptly.

Saga leans against the door, cutting her armpit, reaches the handle on the inside and finds the key, which is still in the lock.

She tries to turn it with stiff, frozen fingers. She hears the shuffling sound again, but forces herself to go on.

She loses her grip, then finds the key with her fingertips and tries again. The lock clicks and Saga withdraws her arm.

She pushes the handle down, opens the door, and moves out of the way.

Nothing but silence.

It's too dark for her to be able to make out anyone inside the playhouse.

'Mimmi, I'm coming in now,' Saga says.

She crouches down, and has to put one hand on the floor to get through the low door.

The room smells of damp and wet clothes.

Saga bumps into a piece of furniture in the darkness, bends over and sees a toy stove with some pine cones in a small saucepan.

'We need to talk,' she says quietly.

A bulky figure moves slightly over in one corner. The girl is sitting on the floor wrapped in blankets and covering her ears.

When Saga gets used to the darkness she can make out the girl's pale face, the look of abject terror in her eyes, and her pursed lips.

*

Joona drags the father into the dining room and secures him to one leg of the heavy table with his handcuffs. Then he tears down part of the screen and lays it over Nathan's body.

Nathan's been his friend and colleague since Joona started work at the National Crime Unit. He can't count the number of times he's visited over the years, just to sit down and collect his thoughts in Nathan's company.

Joona notices that a thin arc of blood has already seeped through the fabric around Nathan's head.

Jim is sitting on one of the high-backed chairs at the dining table. He's pale and his face is shiny with sweat, and he's unbuttoned the collar of his uniform.

'Ambulances and more police are on their way,' Joona says to Jim. 'But it would be great if you could help Saga look for the girl, we can't let her get away.'

'What?'

'If you can manage that?'

'I just need . . . I think I heard what Bauer said,' he says. 'Is Ingrid dead? Did they kill her? Is that true?'

'I'm sorry,' Joona says. 'I'm so sorry.'

'No . . . we were warned, you tried to stop us,' he says, rubbing his face hard with one hand. 'What the hell is wrong with these people? We were only trying to help them, and they—'

'I know,' Joona interrupts calmly.

'I just don't get it,' Jim mutters, and looks at Joona as if he can't remember who he is. 'I'll go after the girl,' he says, and sways slightly as he gets up from the chair.

'Remember, she's only a child,' Joona says.

Jim doesn't answer, and walks out into the hall, pulling his torch from his belt as he goes. The front door opens and closes again, a little too hard.

The remains of the fabric screen sway in the air.

Joona is certain that Valeria and Pellerina are buried here somewhere. A dog handler is on the way. Assuming they're still alive, there's no time to lose. The temperature has fallen from zero to minus nineteen in the past twenty-four hours.

Joona walks round the table, looks out at the snow-covered landscape, then turns back towards the man. He's lying with his cheek against the floor. His blond moustache is dark with blood and one of his eyes is badly swollen.

'You'll be taken into custody and formally arrested soon,' Joona says. 'But if you help me now it's possible that your situation could be improved.'

'You don't understand anything,' the man slurs.

'I know that Valeria de Castro and Pellerina Bauer are here somewhere.'

'It was self-defence, survival . . .'

'Tommy,' Joona says, crouching down to look the man in the eye. 'I could have shot you but I didn't – because I need answers . . . I know you've met Jurek Walter. You have to tell me what he made you do.'

85

Saga has pulled her jacket back on inside the playhouse. She offered her jumper to Mimmi, but got no answer.

It's obvious that the girl has hidden here many times before, she's got blankets and a sleeping-bag, there's a bucket in the corner that smells of stale urine, and the floor is littered with empty biscuit packets, drink cans, and sweet wrappers.

'So, why do you hide in here?'

'Don't know,' the girl says blankly.

'Because you can't handle what's been happening in the house?'

Mimmi shrugs her shoulder almost imperceptibly.

'We're actually here because we're looking for a woman and a girl, Valeria and Pellerina.'

'Oh.'

Saga takes out her mobile and shows her a few pictures of them. Mimmi looks at them very briefly, then lowers her eyes. Her face looks like it's sculpted out of ice in the cold glare of the screen.

'Do you recognise them?' she asks.

'No,' the girl replies, and turns her face away.

'Take another look.'

'I don't want to.'

The playhouse goes dark again when Saga turns the screen off and puts her phone back in her pocket.

'Whatever you've all been doing here, it's over now, and things aren't going to be very pleasant for a while, lots of police and officials, but how that all turns out for you is going to depend on the answers you give me.'

'Oh.'

'Shall we go back to the house?'

'I can't,' she says in a shaky voice.

'I understand. I saw your little brother,' Saga says.

Mimmi starts to cry just as a beam of light reaches into the darkness inside the playhouse. Saga crawls over to the window, and hears the spiders' webs tear as she opens the curtain.

It's Jim, approaching the playhouse with a torch in his hand.

The beam forms a swirling tunnel that bounces down towards the snow with each step he takes.

He's following their footprints.

'Bauer? Are you there?'

'We're in here,' she calls back.

There are heavy footsteps outside, then the door opens and Jim crawls into the playhouse. He's breathing heavily as he puts the torch down on the doll's cot. The beam shines through the bars, filling the small space. The furnishings are old and have been damaged by damp, the pink wallpaper is coming away from the walls, there are spiders' webs hanging from the broken lamp hanging from the ceiling, and the windowsill is covered with dead flies.

'I was told to come and look for you,' he mumbles, knocking the stove over as he sits down on the floor.

The playhouse creaks as he turns and makes his way over to the girl. His breathing is shaky and he has transparent snot dripping from his nose.

'It was you, wasn't it? You killed my partner,' he says in an anguished voice, and suddenly he's holding his pistol to the girl's head.

'Jim, take your finger off the trigger,' Saga says quickly.

'Did you really have to kill Ingrid?' he asks, with a sob in his voice.

'Calm down, Jim,' Saga says firmly. 'Take your finger off the trigger and put the gun down.'

The pistol wavers in front of the girl's face. Jim's forehead is shiny with sweat and his eyes are wide open.

'How does it feel now?' he asks in an agitated voice, jabbing the barrel and making her head rock.

'Please, don't do it,' Saga says. 'I know you're upset, but it wasn't—'

'How does it feel?' he yells.

'Good,' the girl replies, looking him in the eye.

The pistol trembles in his hand again.

'Listen, Jim, it wasn't Mimmi who killed Ingrid,' Saga says. 'But—'

'It was her mum,' Saga says. 'We didn't know she was there, she was hiding.'

'Her mum?'

'She was hiding in the boy's room.'

'What the hell is wrong with you people?' he says weakly, lowering his pistol.

Saga takes the pistol out of his hand, puts the safety catch on, pulls out the magazine, and removes the bullet from the chamber.

'Go out and make sure the ambulances find us,' she says.

He wipes his nose with the back of his hand and crawls out, hitting his head on the doorframe, and closes the door behind him.

'I'm sorry he threatened you. He'll be reported and will have to leave the force, but people sometimes do terrible things when someone close to them dies.'

Mimmi nods weakly and looks at her.

'I know you can help me,' Saga says.

'You don't understand, I can't.'

'Look at these pictures again,' Saga says, bringing up the images of Valeria and Pellerina on her phone.

'I know who they are,' she snarls, batting the mobile away. 'It was them who did it, don't you get that? They burned him, they killed him . . . Are they going to get away with that? It isn't right, they've ruined everything . . .'

Saga sits down on the floor beside her and puts one arm round her shoulders. In a low voice Mimmi tells her about the man from the Russian security service. She doesn't remember his name, but he had tracked the woman and child all the way through Ukraine and Poland to Sweden. They're both seriously mentally ill. They met at the Serbski Institute, and managed to escape from there. They have a secret pact, they travel around, focusing on a particular family and killing them all, one after the other.

'They always start with the youngest child,' she whispers.

'Where are they now? Do you know?'

She takes a deep, shaky breath and explains that the man from the Russian security service is going to get them out of Sweden and make sure they face justice in Russia.

'I know you're not supposed to do that sort of thing, but here in Sweden all they'd get is medical treatment and then they'd be released, and then they'd come here and kill us . . . in Russia they'll be sent to Penal Colony 56 for the rest of their lives.'

Saga brings up a picture of Jurek on her phone.

'Is this the man?'

Mimmi lowers her gaze and nods.

'Do you know where Valeria and Pellerina are now?'

'No,' she says faintly.

'I have to find them, because they haven't killed anyone—'

'My little brother, they killed him, they burned his face, then broke his arms and—'

She starts to sob loudly with her mouth open.

'Mimmi, did you see that happen? With your own eyes?'

The girl just goes on crying.

'You never saw who killed your brother, did you?'

Mimmi calms down slightly, but her breathing is still ragged.

'He told us all about it,' she sniffs. 'Every detail, he was so sorry he hadn't got here in time to save Axel.'

'This man doesn't work for the Russian security service. It was him who killed your brother, and somewhere Valeria and Pellerina are lying buried in coffins . . . because that's what he does.'

The girl gets to her knees and is sick in the bucket. She pauses for breath, then throws up again. She sits down heavily, leans back against the wall and wipes her mouth on her sleeve.

'Show me,' Saga says.

*

Joona is standing by the dining room window again, looking at the playhouse. The light from Jim's torch is shining through the open door and three windows, spreading out like a cross of light over the snow.

The footprints have disappeared completely now.

He can see the large dining table and the man on the floor reflected in the glass. He's lying on his side with his hands over his head. Joona has told him that they'll soon have tracker-dogs at the house but the man maintains his silence, although Joona suspects that he's starting to realise his mistake.

The light inside the playhouse suddenly changes, and Saga crawls out with the torch. She turns and helps the girl out.

They walk back towards the house through the deep snow.

In spite of the poor light and clouds of breath around their mouths, Joona can see the change in their sombre faces.

He meets them in the hall, then follows them downstairs to a den with brown leather furniture and a billiard table.

The ceiling is low and there's a faint basement smell.

The girl tries to push the billiard table aside and Joona goes over and helps her.

The small metal castors under the legs of the heavy table leave deep marks in the Persian rug.

None of them says anything.

Slowly they roll the table aside until it hits the wall. A picture frame rattles and one of the balls bounces off the side-cushion.

Joona and Mimmi pull the large rug in the opposite direction.

A jagged rectangle, approximately one metre by two in size, has been cut into the floorboards. Joona takes out his knife, nudges one edge up, takes hold of it with his fingers and lifts the panel.

The beams and insulation under the house rise up with the boards.

He takes a firmer grip and catches his lower arm as he drags the panel out of the way.

The girl has sunk down onto the floor by the billiard table and covered her ears with her hands.

Joona goes over to the opening and feels ice-cold air flowing up through it.

'Oh, God,' he whispers.

'Hurry up,' Saga whimpers.

On the ground beneath the house are two unpainted coffins with straps around their lids. They're surrounded by splinters and sawdust. The only sound is Saga's rapid breathing.

86

Joona is pacing restlessly up and down the corridor outside the Emergency Room of the Karolinska Hospital in Huddinge, waiting for news.

He's lost count of the number of times he's passed the two badly worn chairs outside the treatment room and the table covered with information leaflets.

His hair is a mess, his face tired and worried, his eyes an intense silver-grey, and his shirt and trousers crumpled. He's washed the worst of the blood and dirt off his face and hands.

Unfiltered images from the confusion in that basement room keep overwhelming him. Fragments of the scene, suddenly lit up by the beam of the torch are rushing through his mind.

The images are horrific.

Nathan's brutal death, the two coffins under the house, the stench of the bodies, the fear in the paramedics' eyes, and the screams of the teenage girl as she was led away by a female police officer.

For something like the fortieth time, Joona stops at the windows in the black doors at the end of the hospital corridor, sees the backs of the two uniformed police officers standing guard outside, then turns and starts to walk back again.

Security in the hospital is tight: sixteen officers are guarding the Emergency Room, but Joona knows that nothing is over until they've caught Jurek Walter.

The doors at the far end of the corridor swing open automatically and an elderly woman is wheeled in on a trolley.

Joona thinks back to Saga's panic-stricken reaction.

She was holding the torch with both hands, but couldn't stand still. The shadows kept shaking and lurching aggressively up the walls.

Her angst was like a caged animal's, there was no way for her to vent it.

Joona keeps pacing the corridor. Four wooden rails run horizontally along the walls to stop trolleys and beds from damaging the walls. The lights in the ceiling glint like misty clouds off the grey linoleum floor.

He can't stop thinking about it.

The clasps made a loud snapping sound when they came loose, and he tore at the straps, scratching his back on the rough edge of the sawn floorboards.

The harsh light of the torch cut through the dust his shoes had churned up from the dry ground.

He grabbed hold of the lid of the first coffin with both hands and wrenched it aside.

Valeria was lying there, covered with a grey blanket, like a corpse wrapped in a winding sheet after an earthquake.

Her grey, dirty face was still, her lips were cracked and her eyes closed.

She didn't react until the harsh light hit her face, and she started fumbling for the lid with her hands.

'No more,' she sobbed, trying to get up.

'Valeria, it's me, Joona,' he said. 'We've found you, we're here now.'

Her whole body was shaking, she couldn't believe it was him, she kept flailing her arms, and managed to hit him in the mouth.

He helped her out, and the blanket slid off as she struggled over the edge of the coffin. She was blinking in the light, dazed and confused, and almost fell, then started to crawl towards the other coffin.

'Pellerina,' she whimpered as she tried to force the lid open.

She was too weak, and couldn't use her swollen hands; her nails were broken and her fingertips caked with blood.

'Open the coffin!' Saga cried. 'You've got to get it open!'

Joona stops in the corridor and leans against the wall with both hands. Two nurses hurry past in pale blue uniforms.

He looks down at the strips of tape on the floor that indicate where trolleys and beds should be parked, but all he can see is the basement room in the house: yellow jackets with wide reflective strips, wet boots, and him pulling Valeria away from the second coffin and passing her up to the first paramedics to reach the scene.

One of the paramedics started to cry.

The stretcher hit the side of the staircase, knocking flakes of paint to the floor.

Saga dropped the torch, it hit the edge of the floorboards and landed on the dry soil next to Valeria's coffin and rolled under the house.

Joona cut the straps on the other coffin, dropped his knife and heaved the lid off.

Saga screamed until her voice broke and someone tried to hold her back, but she pulled free and fell on her knees at the edge of the roughly sawn hole, whispering her sister's name.

Pellerina was lying in the coffin in a pair of baggy trousers and a padded blue jacket. Her pale face was completely motionless, and she didn't react to the light of the paramedics' torches.

Her little round mouth was sunken, her cheekbones very pronounced.

Joona gently lifted Pellerina's body out of the coffin, holding her to his chest like a sleeping child, with one hand behind her neck and her head against his cheek. He couldn't hear a heartbeat, couldn't feel a pulse.

'No, no, no,' Saga sobbed.

Another stretcher arrived just as Joona detected faint breath from Pellerina's mouth.

'I think she's alive. Hurry up, she's alive!' he cried. 'Take her, she must have hypothermia . . .'

Trampling on the empty plastic bottles and bags in the other coffin, he lurched forward and held the girl up to the two paramedics. They laid her down gently on the stretcher. Saga stroked her cheek and kept telling her that everything was going to be all right now.

Joona walks to the end of the corridor again, looks at the two police officers, then turns and walks back to the door of the treatment room.

He runs his hand through his hair, then sits down on one of the chairs. It creaks as he leans back, resting his head against the wall.

Just as he's getting up again the door opens and a doctor in a short-sleeved white tunic and trousers comes out.

'Joona Linna?' she says.

'Is she conscious?'

'I tried to tell her she should rest before seeing anyone, but she was adamant that she wanted to see you.'

'How is she?'

'It's too early to say, she's extremely weak.'

The doctor explains that they're still waiting for test results, but that in her opinion Valeria's condition is no longer life-threatening. When she was brought in she was suffering from sepsis, acute dehydration, malnourishment and, above all, hypothermia. Her body temperature registered 32 degrees in the ambulance, but they've managed to bring that back up to normal levels in the past five hours using hot air and internal warming. Her hands and toes were frostbitten, but it now looks unlikely that they'll have to be amputated, as first feared.

Joona thanks the doctor, taps gently at the door and goes in.

Valeria is lying in a hospital bed with the rails on both sides raised. Her face is pale and thin. She's connected to a pulsoximeter, ECG and blood-pressure monitor, is being fed oxygen through her nose, and has cannulas on the insides of both elbows.

'Valeria,' he says softly.

He walks over and touches her hand. She opens her eyes and looks at him tiredly.

'Thanks for finding me . . . bastard cop,' she smiles.

'They say you're going to be fine.'

'I'm already fine.'

She purses her lips and he bends over and kisses her. They look at each other for a moment, then become serious again.

'They won't tell me anything about Pellerina,' she says quietly.

'Me neither . . . she barely had a pulse when we found her.'

Valeria's eyelids are heavy and she lets them close. Her dark curls are spread across the pillow, almost reaching the thin pine headboard set into to chrome frame of the bed.

'What happened in that house?' she asks, opening her eyes again. 'I mean, why were they doing that to us?'

'It's too soon to talk. You need to rest. I'll sit here with you.'

Valeria moistens her dry lips.

'But I need to know,' she says. 'I figured out that they were angry with us, they thought it was our fault their son died.'

'It sounds like Jurek told them some story, but I don't know the details, Saga was the one who questioned the daughter,' Joona says, pulling a chair over to her bed.

He only has time to tell her that Nathan and a colleague from the Södertälje Police were killed in the operation before Saga comes into the room. She's obviously been crying a lot, her eyes are red and swollen.

'Pellerina's been sedated,' she tells them in a subdued voice. 'Her condition's critical, they've raised her body temperature, but they're having trouble with her heart, it's beating far too fast . . .'

Saga's voice cracks and she swallows hard.

'They had to use a defibrillator to slow it down . . . What if she never wakes up?' she whispers after a pause. 'Then that coffin will be the last thing she ever experienced . . . darkness, loneliness.'

'We talked the whole time,' Valeria says, then has to cough.

'Did you?' Saga asks, staring at her with a despairing look in her eyes.

'She wasn't scared, I swear, she wasn't,' Valeria goes on. 'She was cold and thirsty . . . but we were lying next to each other and she only had to say my name and I'd talk to her . . . she was sure you were going to rescue her, and you did.'

'She doesn't know I was there,' Saga whispers.

'I think she knows,' Valeria says.

'I should get back to her,' Saga says quietly, and blows her nose.

'Of course,' Joona says.

'Did you hear that the prosecutor in Södertörn has remanded the father in custody?' Saga asks, tossing the tissue in the bin next to the basin.

446

'Yes,' Joona says.

'So why were they doing that to us?' Valeria asks.

'It was Jurek, he destroyed that family,' Saga says. 'They hadn't done him any harm, but he needed that location, and he needed their loyalty for a few weeks . . . So he murdered the youngest child and blamed you and Pellerina, got them to hate you.'

'That's appalling,' Valeria whispers, and coughs weakly again. 'Can't someone stop him?'

'Yes,' Joona replies.

'Not you, you've done more than enough already,' she says quickly.

'Valeria, I'm staying here until you're feeling better,' Joona says. 'But this isn't over yet. Jurek Walter isn't finished, he'll be coming back for you . . . there's no need to be afraid now, though, there are sixteen police officers here in the hospital, and that will keep him away . . . But sooner or later the level of protection will be reduced.'

'What are you planning?' Saga asks.

'I'm going to carry on with the constellation . . . it's a gamble, but the star that represents Pollux's heart . . . it's located on a small island in Lake Mälaren.'

'You know you can't do this on your own,' Saga says heavily. 'I'd be happy to go with you, you know that, but I have to stay with Pellerina, I have to be here when she wakes up.'

'I can handle it.'

'Listen to her,' Valeria says, her voice agitated.

'Joona, you can't do this alone,' Saga repeats. 'It's too dangerous, you know that, you have to talk to Carlos.'

'There's no point.'

'A small team from the National Response Unit,' Saga pleads.

'No,' Joona says.

'How about Rinus Advocaat – can't you call him? He could be here in a few hours,' Saga says.

Joona's face stiffens and he puts one hand on the chrome bedframe.

'I didn't think you knew about Rinus,' he says quietly.

'You talked about him after Disa's death,' Saga says. 'You were almost dead yourself, but I understood that you trusted him. Can't you ask him to help?'

'No,' Joona replies, looking at her with eyes that have never been darker than now.

'Oh, no . . .' Saga says with fear in her voice. 'Joona? Tell me it isn't true.'

'How bad is it?' he asks gruffly.

'When Jurek took Pellerina, I panicked and tried to get hold of you, I had no other choice.'

'Saga . . .' Joona says, getting up heavily.

'I was panicking,' she says, almost inaudibly. 'I thought you could tell me where Jurek's brother's remains were.'

'What did you do?' Joona asks.

She rubs her eyes hard to get rid of the tears.

'It's probably nothing, but I thought that if you were going to hide, then you'd need help . . . Nils would do anything for you, but he isn't tough, not in that way . . . which is why I thought of Rinus, so I called him at home in Amsterdam, and spoke to a guy called Patrick . . . he said Rinus was at work, and I gave him my number . . . no one ever got back to me.'

'Is there any way Jurek could have had access to your phone?'

'Sorry,' Saga whispers.

'Then he's going to take my daughter,' Joona says, and starts to walk towards the door.

'Run!' Valeria says.

Joona hears Saga apologising once more in the treatment room just before the door closes behind him.

87

Lumi systematically moves the night-sight across the middle of zone 1, lingering on the bushes and garden furniture, before moving on to the abandoned main house.

Everything is peculiarly quiet tonight.

She looks at the boarded-up door and the warped sheets of plywood over the windows.

She lowers the sight to get a broader overview and looks out. She mustn't let her concentration slip.

The temperature has stayed below freezing over the past few days, and the sky is unusually clear for this part of Europe.

Without the night-sight the old house is invisible in the darkness. From time to time the headlamps of trucks on the motorway shine through the bushes and trees.

Grey light is lying like a dome over the nearest village, Maarheeze, and in the distance the lights of Weert are caught by particles in the air, forming a colourless aurora in the night sky.

Lumi raises the night-sight again and moves closer to the workshop, scanning the overgrown piece of machinery in the ditch. She's always thought it looked like a huge hair curler.

It's actually the rotating cylinder from the front of a combine harvester.

Slowly she follows the pitted gravel track leading to the workshop, all the way round the meadow to the barrier where she said goodbye to her dad.

It had been dawn then, with mist hanging over the fields.

She thinks of how her self-confidence evaporated and she started to cry.

As she studies the narrow road leading to Rijksweg, she allows herself to think the horrible thought that she sent her dad off on a mission from which he might never return, straight to the person he had wanted to hide from.

That first day when she was alone in the workshop with Rinus had been tense and quiet.

They got on with their tasks, followed the routines, but even after completing a shift, grabbing a meal and a shower and a few hours' sleep, there was still a lot of time left over.

They started to keep each other company, getting coffee for one another, sitting and making small-talk, and eventually started talking properly.

Rinus understood that she was sad after the row with her dad, and told her about the time, many years ago, when he first heard about Jurek Walter.

'Joona called me on a secure line and I told him about this place. I know he wanted to come here, and hide away with you and your mum, but in the end he decided on a different option . . . You must have been, what, four years old when you left Sweden?'

'Three,' she replied.

'But you're alive, and you've got a life.'

She nodded in the darkness, then stared at the distant green-house through the binoculars.

'I've got a life now . . . I grew up with my mum in Helsinki, I used to be very shy,' she said. 'And now I live in Paris and have got loads of friends, it's ridiculous . . . I've got a really handsome boyfriend, I never thought that would happen, I mean, I always thought, you know, who's going to want me?'

'The young are very careless with their youth,' Rinus muttered.

'Maybe.'

'Does Joona know you've got a boyfriend?'

'I have mentioned it.'

'Good,' he nodded.

Lumi thinks about that first conversation with Rinus as she

moves her chair and the night-sight to zone 3. Without any urgency she goes and gets her bottle of water, the blanket, and the sniper rifle, which she lays down on the floor in front of her by the wall.

She sits and looks out into the darkness. All she can see through the hatch is the red lights on the telecoms mast, and the distant glow of Eindhoven about twenty kilometres away.

Near the central station there's a youth hostel where Joona has rented a room for her, in case she ever has to flee from the workshop.

She's about to raise the night-sight again when Rinus comes in with two cans of cola and a bag of warm popcorn. His shift doesn't start yet, but he usually shows up an hour or so early, so they have time to chat.

'Were you able to get any sleep?'

'One eye at a time,' he jokes, handing her one of the cans.

'Thanks.'

She puts it down on the floor next to the rifle, then starts to check the closest part of the zone, the patch of gravel and the tumbledown barbed-wire fence in front of the meadow.

Rinus eats his popcorn in front of the monitor showing the inside of the garage and the immediate vicinity of the workshop.

She follows her usual routine, scanning the sector in sections, moving from the meadow to the clump of trees where the secret tunnel emerges.

'I was thinking about what you said this morning, about never having any really long conversations with your dad yet,' Rinus says. 'I never did with mine . . . His name was Sjra, have I told you that? You only find that name down here . . . he never even went north of the Waal. We were very Catholic and . . . I don't know, Dad meant well, but the church was like a prison to me.'

'What about your mum?'

'She's been to see me and Patrik in Amsterdam a couple of times, but I don't think she's really understood that he's the love of my life, even though I've told her we're getting married.'

Saga moves the night-sight to the large scoop lying at the edge of the trees.

'Before I met Laurent, I was seeing an older man. He was married, ran a gallery,' she tells him.

'I tried that as well,' Rinus says, putting the popcorn down on the floor. 'Well, he didn't run a gallery, but he was older . . .'

'Father complex,' she smiles.

'I was really flattered at first, impressed by everything he said . . . but it didn't work, he kept belittling me for my opinions the whole time.'

Lumi lets out a sympathetic sigh.

'I broke up with gallery-owner because he wanted to set me up in a flat he rented . . . so I'd be available as his lover when-ever it suited him.'

'Laurent sounds much better,' Rinus says.

'Yes, he is . . . He's got a few things he needs to work on, but he's pretty OK.'

At two o'clock precisely Rinus takes over, and moves the chair to zone 5. She passes him the night-sight and rifle, then stands behind him with the can of Coke in her hand.

'What's happening with your college work while you're away?' he asks.

'I don't know. I'm supposed to be working on a graphics project on the theme of "dysfunctional integration",' she replies.

'What's that?' Rinus asks.

'No idea,' she smiles. 'That's probably what I'm supposed to be finding out.'

'It makes me think of families, and the way they . . . I don't know, but they never seem very well matched.'

'Maybe that's a bit too easy.'

'Love . . . or sex,' he suggests.

'Good, Rinus,' Lumi smiles.

'A flash of creative genius,' he laughs, and fans himself with his hand.

She laughs, looks at the time, and says she'll bring him his meal once she's done her exercise. She walks off towards the firing holes looking down on the garage. She brushes the curtain aside, walks round the stairs leading to the ground floor, opens the door and goes past the kitchen.

Her own room is warm and she turns the thermostat on the radiator down slightly. She finds a pair of clean underpants, then grabs the bag containing her gym clothes from the floor.

When she walks back she hears the floor in the corridor creak behind her. Thinking that she's dropped something, she stops and turns round.

All she can see is the closed door to the last bedroom and the blocked emergency exit with the words Stairway to Heaven.

She walks past the kitchen again, through the door at the top of the stairs, and goes down to the ground floor.

When she passes the storeroom where they keep the food and weapons, she hears the electricity box ticking quietly beside the wardrobe.

On one of their first days there she tried pushing through the hanging clothes to check the escape route. She heaved the heavy steel beam aside, opened the door and felt the cool air from the tunnel rush up and hit her face.

She puts her bag down on the wooden bench in the changing room and slips her gym clothes on, hanging her cargo trousers, sweater, and vest on one of the hooks.

She lifts one foot onto the bench and ties her lace, sees a loose wooden bar lift up a few centimetres at the other end, and thinks out of sheer habit that she could pull it off and use it as a weapon if need be.

Lumi goes into the exercise room and cycles for an hour at a relatively fast pace, then does press-ups and sit-ups on the cold floor before returning to the changing room, pulling off her sweaty clothes and going into the bathroom.

She locks and checks the door. The wet-room is cold underfoot and her skin comes out in goosebumps all over her body.

Every time she showers she checks the bathroom cupboard, taking out the plastic bag containing the pistol and checking that it's loaded. The sights on it are a little too close together for her liking: ideally the gap between them shouldn't be that small when speed is more important than absolute accuracy.

She puts the gun back, closes the mirrored door, and looks at her tired face.

The light in the ceiling flickers.

There's a thin layer of dust on top of its white glass dome. Its light spreads across the ceiling like a hazy circle.

Holding the white shower curtain back with one hand, Lumi turns the water on, then moves out of the way as it starts to fall from the showerhead in the ceiling.

Only a man would choose not to have an adjustable shower when they were installing a bathroom, she thinks.

The first drops form grey rings on the white polyester. The roaring sound fills the bathroom. She waits until the warmth of the water steams out towards her and the mirror starts to mist up.

88

Lumi steps into the shower, pulls the curtain behind her and shivers as the hot water washes over her.

She's thinking about Laurent, the way he would sit on her bed naked, strumming his guitar with a cigarette between his lips.

The water cascades over her head, the walls of the shower and the curtain.

She starts to warm up, her muscles relax after being tense for so many hours.

Lumi hears a scraping sound through the walls and pushes the curtain aside to look at the lock on the door.

Cooler air hits her.

There are small pearls of condensation on the basin and toilet.

After the shower she's going to cook some spaghetti, open a jar of pesto, and maybe have half a glass of wine before she goes to bed.

She soaps her armpits, breasts and thighs.

The lather runs down her stomach and legs and vanishes into the drain in the floor. The white shower curtain becomes slightly translucent when it's wet.

The wooden unit beneath the basin looks like a dark shadow.

Like someone crouching down.

Lumi looks down at the floor and can't help thinking about her dad. She's worried that he hasn't been in touch yet.

She tilts her head back, closes her eyes and lets the water wash over her face and run into her ears.

Through the gentle rumble of the water she imagines she can hear voices, men screaming in pain.

She wipes the water from her eyes, spits and looks at the trembling shower curtain again, at the shadow beneath the basin.

It's the bathroom cabinet, that's all.

As she's reaching for the shampoo, the lamp suddenly flickers.

The light becomes weaker, before everything suddenly goes completely dark.

Her heart starts to pound.

She turns the shower off, pushes the curtain aside and listens.

All she can hear is the drops of water still hitting the floor.

She quickly dries herself in the darkness, gets the pistol out of the cupboard, releases the safety catch, manages to find the door, unlocks and cautiously opens it.

The hinges creak softly as the door swings open.

It's pitch-dark out there.

She reaches for her bag, hurriedly gets dressed, then snatches up the pistol again.

She crosses the floor without a sound, crouches down, opens the door and looks out.

The entire ground floor is in darkness.

She listens, and thinks she can hear footsteps upstairs.

She puts one hand on the wall and follows it to the junction box, opens the metal hatch and feels for the switches and circuit-breakers.

They're all set correctly.

In theory, it's impossible to cut off the electricity unless you have a digger and manage to hit the cable by chance.

She turns round. Grey light is bouncing off the walls.

It's coming from the upper floor.

She hears footsteps on the stairs.

A flickering light reaches the ground floor.

She quickly moves back, presses up against the wall and raises the pistol, seeing as there's no way she can get into the clothes closet without being seen.

Her sweater is damp and cold against her back from her wet hair.

It's Rinus, with a torch in one hand and his pistol in the other.

'I'm here,' she says in the darkness, lowering the barrel of the pistol towards the floor.

'Lumi?'

His voice is wary, but he doesn't sound alarmed.

'I checked the fuse-box,' she says. 'None of the fuses have blown, nothing.'

They go back upstairs, past the curtain, and into the surveillance room. The monitor showing pictures from the security cameras has died.

As Rinus moves between the various zones, Lumi opens a wooden crate and swaps her pistol for a G36 Kurz, a good, short-barrelled assault rifle that's easy to handle in confined spaces. She quickly inserts a magazine, then tucks two more in the pockets of her trousers.

'OK, there's a total power cut south of here,' Rinus says, lowering the binoculars. 'Maarheeze and Weert are both dark.'

'I actually got a bit scared,' Lumi confesses, going over to him. 'I was in the shower when everything went out.'

'I want us to remain on high alert until further notice,' he says.

'OK,' she says, and goes over to zone 5.

Through the night-sight she looks at the neighbouring farm and the old bus. There are no lights in any of the windows, everything is dark.

She checks the zone's meadows, ditches, and fences faster than usual before she moves on.

Angling the night-sight lower, she slowly follows the gravel track from the workshop, round the meadow and up to the closed barrier.

Suddenly she stops, almost instinctively.

She's seen a movement.

Her eyes registered it and she reacted before her brain had processed the information. She scans back along the empty track and starts again.

A couple of hundred metres from the barrier she slows down.

There's something in the ditch.

The weeds are moving.

She breathes out when a black cat jumps up and runs across the track.

'The power should be back on soon,' Rinus says behind her.

'Let's hope so,' she replies.

The alarm system has switched automatically to back-up batteries that will last about forty-eight hours, but the security cameras have been knocked out, and the hydraulic door can't function without mains electricity.

Lumi raises the night-sight again and looks at the abandoned house, the bushes and old garden furniture, the door and boarded-up windows, the collapsed drainpipe and the barrel of rainwater.

Dry leaves are blowing across the yard.

She's about to check the main road when she notices that the barrier has been opened.

'Rinus,' she says, and a shiver runs down her spine.

'A car,' she goes on. 'A car's come through the barrier with its lights off.'

She can't make out the driver's face. Rinus rushes over and takes the night-sight from her.

'Jurek Walter,' he says curtly.

'We can't be sure of that.'

'Lumi, it's happening. Make sure you've got your bag,' he says, quickly pulling on a protective vest.

89

They both hear the sound of the car approaching the workshop with its lights switched off. Somehow Jurek Walter has found their hiding place and sabotaged the substation on the outskirts of Weert to cut off their electricity.

Lumi blackens her face and wipes her hands on a cloth, pulls on her watertight camouflage jackets and changes into a pair of sturdy fluoro-plastic trainers.

Rinus is busy over by the ammunition boxes, lit up by the masked beam of the torch. Its weak light plays across an open box of 5.56 x 45mm Nato bullets. Their pointed copper tips glint in the light.

They've rehearsed tactics for a wide variety of scenarios countless times. Lumi knows she can just grab her rucksack and escape through the tunnel, but for some reason Jurek wants them to see him coming. It isn't certain that he's in the car. Maybe he's out there somewhere, keeping watch with a thermal camera, waiting for her to run from her hiding place like a frightened rabbit.

Rinus picks up a plastic container full of magazines containing different combinations of tracer, armour-piercing, and live ammunition, and carries them over to one of the windows.

The magazines are transparent, so you can see what sort of ammunition they contain, but Rinus has his own system so he can identify them with his fingertips in total darkness.

The car is slowly approaching across the yard, at an angle that requires Lumi or Rinus to open the hatch completely and lean out to be able to fire at it.

'How many people do you think are inside?' Lumi asks.

'I'm guessing two,' he says.

'But we can deal with eight, that's what we've said.'

Rinus folds a sheet of plastic back and drags a wooden crate across the floor.

'The only thing that would be hard to handle is if he tries to burn the building,' he says, opening the crate. 'But your dad didn't think that was likely, seeing as Jurek wants to take you alive.'

Rinus takes out three packs of explosive putty, puts two in his green canvas bag, then cuts the third in two, through the wrapper, and wipes the knife on his trousers.

The explosive gives off a faint smell of ammonia.

He pulls four Russian fuses with sturdy detonators from a smaller box and drops the box on the floor.

'I don't think he'll try to force the door downstairs, it would take him too long to get hold of explosives or antitank rifles in the Netherlands.'

'You think he's brought a ladder?'

'I don't know, but he's got something planned,' Rinus says, turning the torch off again. 'Because if I was going to break in here, I'd choose the emergency exit . . . and I'd assume it was guarded and mined.'

'Yes.'

As a result, Rinus isn't planning to mine the door itself, but rather the corridor a little way along. Moving quickly, he feels his way through the darkness, brushes the curtain aside and folds it back, hurries past the stairs and the creaking door. He switches the torch on again, runs over to Lumi's room, and puts the bag down on the floor.

He looks over at the sealed emergency exit at the end of the corridor, estimates the average stride and pattern of movement.

Immediately behind the doorframe to Lumi's room he fastens an entire pack of explosives with duct tape approximately one metre off the floor.

The charge is completely invisible from the corridor, and powerful enough to blow up half of the upper floor.

He presses the fuse into the grey mass, then takes down the religious picture from the opposite wall, ties a length of thin nylon thread to the screw, rehangs the picture, stretches the thread diagonally across the passageway to the explosive, and ties it to the pin in the detonator. He removes the safety catch, then slowly backs away from it.

If you stand still and move your torch around, you can just make out the glint of the nylon thread, but otherwise it's impossible to detect.

You'd have to move very slowly, inching your way forward.

The moment you feel the thread against you, it's already too late.

Three centimetres is enough to pull the pin out and trigger the detonator.

Rinus sets up a similar trap immediately after the door to Joona's room, putting the charge behind the fire-extinguisher on the wall and fastening the thread across the corridor to a screw in the skirting board.

He retreats to the kitchen and quickly constructs a fake trap by stretching a thread an inch or two above the floor and fastening it to a bag of empty bottles next to the door.

It will take time to disarm that as well.

He moves back, closes the creaking door to the corridor, glances at the staircase leading down to ground level, then tapes half a pack of explosive at head-height, inserts the fuse, and runs the thread from the detonator to the door handle, then removes the safety catch.

He turns the torch off and goes back to the surveillance room. He knows that Jurek is very experienced, but it would take an entire bomb squad hours to disarm that corridor.

'He's driving right round the workshop,' Lumi says quietly as she hears the loose gravel clattering against the chassis of the car.

She moves sideways to be able to see the car. It slows down and stops in front of the main doors, maintaining an angle that makes it impossible to hit from any of the hatches.

'It's stopped,' she says.

From where they are, only part of the rear bumper and boot are visible.

'What's he doing?'

'I can't see. The car's stopped, but I don't know if he's still inside.'

Rinus switches to a magazine that he's marked with a cross of red tape, to indicate that every tenth bullet includes phosphorous that will leave a trail of light in the darkness.

The car is running in neutral, its engine rumbling softly.

The loose garage door is creaking in the wind.

Lumi scans the scene outside again. An empty bottle of washer fluid is rolling across the yard. The bare branches over by the barbed-wire fence are trembling.

The car engine starts to rev louder.

A bird takes off and flies away.

The cloud of exhaust fumes grows, and drifts off on the wind towards the meadows.

The car reverses one metre, stops, and goes on revving.

He wants us to see this, she thinks.

Suddenly he puts the car in gear and accelerates so hard that gravel flies up behind the car. There's a loud crash as the car drives straight through the double doors, followed by a clanging thud and the sound of breaking glass when it hits the reinforced wall and stops.

The engine falls silent.

One of the garage doors breaks free of its hinges and falls to the ground with a crash.

Lumi hurries across the floor and looks through one of the internal hatches. The garage is dark and silent. A smell of metal and petrol hits her nostrils.

'Stay back,' Rinus says, going over to the next hatch.

Without a sound he pushes the barrel of his assault rifle through the hole, angles it downward, then waits several seconds before leaning forward to look through the sights.

The image is blurred and grainy.

As if he's looking through murky water, he sees a car with its front smashed in. The bodywork is crumpled and the windscreen smashed. Tiny, sparkling cubes of glass are scattered across the bonnet.

Inside the car he can make out the rounded shape of a head in the driver's seat.

He automatically puts his finger on the trigger, but he can't fire from this angle.

'What's happening?' Lumi says beside him.

'I don't know.'

He moves to the furthest hatch, pushes the barrel through, waits, then looks through the sights. The front right wing of the car has broken off and is lying on the garage floor. One windscreen-wiper is moving sluggishly back and forth even though the glass has gone.

Rinus puts his finger on the trigger again and accidentally knocks the barrel against the side of the hatch, and a metallic sound rings out.

Slowly he moves the barrel towards the driver's seat, and sees a hand resting on the steering wheel.

He follows the row of white buttons on a blood-stained shirt towards the collar and a gold necklace.

And then he sees the face.

It's Patrik.

He's injured, but still alive. Blood is running from his nose, down over his mouth. His glasses have fallen off, and he's blinking slowly.

Rinus is absolutely certain he didn't tell Patrik where he was going. He just said he had to go away for work, and never mentioned that he was going into hiding with Joona and Lumi.

But he's aware that Patrik has known about the workshop for years. As a Jewish homosexual, he got a bit paranoid when the far-right populists were gaining ground in the Netherlands. When things were at their worst, Rinus took him to the workshop in an effort to make him feel safer, to show him that there was a plan if everything went wrong.

90

Rinus's anguished heart is pounding hard, and the sights tremble. The seconds tick past. Patrik's mouth is slightly open, the way it usually is when he's asleep.

With his finger on the trigger, Rinus starts to look for Jurek, scanning the inside of the car through the sights, then around the sides.

The darkness beneath the car looks oddly fluid.

The floor looks wet.

The front tyre is muddy, and curved fragments of the head-lamps lie like shells on a beach.

Suddenly the image flares white, and Rinus instinctively jerks his face back.

The glare lingers on his retinas in the darkness.

Lumi is moving between the zones to check their surroundings.

Rinus looks down into the garage again, not through the sights this time, and sees a dancing glow beside the car.

It flits up against the wall, anxious as a caged bird.

Something's burning.

Rinus quickly switches to another hatch and looks down. A strip of burning cloth is hanging out of the car's petrol tank.

'Patrik!' he yells through the hatch. 'You have to get out of the car!'

He runs back to the first hatch. In the dancing light he sees Patrik tiredly open his eyes.

'Patrik!' he cries. 'The car's going to explode! Get out of the garage, you have to get out of—'

The explosion comes in two hard bursts. The garage fills with fire. Metal and glass are blown up at the ceiling and out into the yard.

Rinus staggers backwards.

Flames shoot out through all the hatches.

There's a loud clattering sound from the garage as car parts rain down across the floor. The fire roars loudly.

'Was Patrik still in the car?' Lumi asks, her voice numb.

Rinus nods, and looks at her with strangely lifeless eyes before he shuts the hatches, one by one.

Lumi hurries to the last zone and opens the hatch. In two places outside the workshop she can see vivid yellow flames, and pitch-black columns of smoke.

'He's burning old tyres,' Lumi says.

She pulls on her lightweight rucksack, thinking that Jurek is trying to divert their attention or distract any thermal cameras.

He's going to try to break in anytime now, she thinks, and moves to the next zone.

What's he waiting for?

In the flames of a burning tyre she sees that the large combine-harvester drum is no longer lying in the ditch. The dead grass has been torn away and there are deep tracks running across the yard and round the building.

They hear heavy thuds from the bedroom corridor, and the sound echoes through the building.

Rinus hangs a number of hand-grenades from his belt.

There's a creak, then several seconds of silence before more thuds, and the alarm linked to the emergency exit goes off.

'He's inside, isn't he?' Lumi asks, even though she knows the answer.

Adrenalin kicks in at once and her mind becomes icily clear. Jurek has leaned the combine-harvester drum against the wall like a ladder, broken the door open and got in.

'Come with me,' she says.

Rinus just turns away and switches the alarm off. A frightening silence descends, then there's a tinkling sound from the kitchen.

Jurek has dismantled the first two traps and made it past the fake one in a matter of seconds.

'Thanks for everything,' she whispers.

He has his back to her, and nods to himself, then turns and meets her gaze, unable to bring himself to smile.

Lumi brushes the curtain aside, spots the explosive that's been fixed to the door to the corridor and hurries down the stairs.

As soon as she's gone, Rinus sets up one last trap behind the curtain, pulling the thread one metre above the floor and removing the safety catch, then retreating and taking up position.

He hears a scraping sound, then the door to the corridor opens with a soft creak.

There's no explosion.

Jurek must have nudged the door open very slightly, stuck a thin knife blade through the gap, pulled it up and cut the thread.

Rinus can't understand how he's able to identify and disarm the traps so quickly.

It's as if he had a map and knew exactly where the explosives had been positioned and how they were constructed.

Through the night-sight of the assault rifle Rinus sees slight movement in the curtain, then the glint of a knife blade. It slips up the gap between fabric and wall and cuts the thread to his last trap.

Rinus fires through the curtain in a downward diagonal pattern.

The noise of the shots fills the room, the barrel flares and he feels the familiar recoil of the weapon in his shoulder.

The empty cases clatter to the floor.

Rinus counts the bullets, stops at the ninth, then takes aim at the explosive and fires the tenth shot.

The blazing phosphorous charge leaves a dark trail through the darkness.

The explosive detonates instantly.

He tries to take cover, but the speed of the detonation is incredibly quick.

The pressure-wave hits Rinus's chest and the back of his head slams into the wall.

The entire section of wall surrounding the curtain disintegrates, the floorboards are ripped up, debris flies through the room. The railing on the stairs and the door to the corridor are gone.

Rinus manages to get up on one knee as splinters and plaster rain down on him and empties the rest of the magazine in three seconds.

He fires through the remains of the wall and the jagged opening to the kitchen.

He quickly rolls sideways, releases the magazine, and inserts a fresh one, but it's too late.

A thin man is running at him along one wall.

Rinus draws his knife and stands up in the same movement, then swipes in an unexpected direction, from below and off to one side.

But the man deflects his arm and sticks a narrow blade into his side, just below the strap of his protective vest.

Beneath his ribs, up towards his liver.

Rinus ignores the pain and changes the direction of his knife, aiming at Jurek's neck as he takes a step back and pulls out the pin.

Almost without a sound, the detonator explodes inside Rinus.

His legs buckle and he hits the floor hard, and his eyelids flutter as blood gushes out of the small hole in his side.

Only now does he realise what's happened.

It wasn't any ordinary knife.

When Jurek disarmed one of the traps, he took the Russian detonator with him and attached it to some sort of blade or spike.

Rinus raises his head slightly and sees Jurek standing in the window with the night-sight from his assault rifle.

The pain in his side is like a terrible attack of cramp.

The floor is already wet with blood.

He lowers his head again, panting from the exertion, and loosens a hand-grenade from his belt to blow them both up.

But it's already too late.

Jurek is heading towards the stairs. If he knows about the escape route, he'll be able to see Lumi running across the fields.

91

Lumi folds in the shoulder-support of her assault rifle, closes the door to the closet, steps over the paper bags full of shoes, forces her way between the hanging clothes and removes the bar across the steel door.

Just as she is about to go into the small hallway she hears stuttering automatic fire, then a loud explosion.

She carefully closes and locks the door behind her.

More automatic fire licks like a metronome in the walls, followed by silence.

Lumi's hand is shaking as she switches her torch on. She hurries down the narrow concrete steps to a smaller room and another steel door.

She has to shove her shoulder against the door to get it to move. It swings open with a creak, and she shines her torch into a cramped passageway with earth walls. The wooden planks in the roof are held up by thick posts. Small drifts of soil and stones are lying here and there on the loose planks of the floor of the tunnel.

The light of the torch sways as she shines it towards the entrance to a large concrete pipe.

Even though Rinus described the escape route as 'a tubular section' two hundred and fifty metres long, she didn't realise he was literally talking about a buried pipe.

An underground passageway designed to work on one single occasion.

It's a very simple solution.

Presumably the most difficult bit was the connection between the building and the pipe.

It feels as dangerous as an old mine-shaft.

Lumi lets the steel door swing shut, then hurries across the uneven planks, crouches down and goes into the tunnel.

She runs along it, bent almost double.

Her rucksack scrapes against the roof.

She counts her steps as she moves as quickly as she can.

The light of the torch catches on the joins between the sections of pipe, like a sequence of thin rings ahead of her.

The barrel of the rifle knocks against the side of the pipe.

She stumbles over an uneven join, falls forward and braces herself with her hands, and breaks the glass of the torch. When she gets up again she feels a sharp pain in one knee, but limps on.

Warm blood is trickling down her shin inside her trousers.

The torch is working, but the beam is no longer as focused.

She thinks about the explosion and gunfire, and knows she has to keep going. She forces herself to run again.

Jurek could well be dead.

Rinus is very experienced. She's seen his hands assemble weapons in a matter of seconds as he tells her about Patrik's many sisters.

He taught her how to make an invisible holster for a pistol using a metal coat-hanger, and a silencer out of a plastic bottle, some aluminium mesh and a bit of wire-wool.

She's watched him practising knife-fighting in the darkness, seen the precision and speed of his movements.

It doesn't seem possible anyone would be able to beat him in close combat, but she has to assume the opposite, assume that she's fleeing for her life.

The light of the torch is bouncing along in front of her, glinting off the water that's gathered along the bottom of the pipe.

Suddenly she imagines she can hear steps behind her, and terror seizes her heart. It's probably just the echo of her own movements, but she stops and switches the torch off with trembling hands, points the assault rifle behind her, unfolds the shoulder-support and looks through the night-sight.

There's nothing in sight and everything is black, seeing as there's no ambient light down here for the sight to enhance.

She waits and tries to blink away the sweat running into her eyes.

The only sound is her own breathing.

She folds the shoulder-support away again, turns round and switches the torch back on.

It clicks, but doesn't come on.

She tries again, and shakes it gently, but nothing happens.

She stands there, eyes wide open, staring into total darkness.

Careful not to cut herself, she removes the last of the broken glass and feels the small bulb, presses it in slightly, and tries switching it on again.

It works, shining up towards the low roof in a blurry, elliptical ring.

Crouching down again, she carries on running through the pipe.

The air feels thin, and she's breathing too shallowly.

As she runs, she multiplies the number of steps and the length of her stride, and when she figures out that she shouldn't have more than forty metres left, she stops and shines the torch ahead of her.

The beam is blurred, but she can see that the end of the tunnel is full of earth, right up to the top. This end of the tunnel seems to have collapsed, sealing the pipe.

She tries to keep her breathing calm, keeps going, then puts the torch and assault rifle down, crawls up the pile of earth and starts digging with her hands. She heaves the soil behind her with a growing feeling of panic.

Her back is wet with sweat, her heart pounding in her chest.

She tries to tell herself that it's a good sign that the soil isn't densely packed. If all the ground above her had collapsed, it would be impossible to dig through with her bare hands.

Going back isn't an option, and she can't stay where she is.

She cuts her fingertips on a sharp stone but doesn't stop digging.

Gasping for breath, she moves backwards and heaves the soil and stones further into the pipe, then keeps digging until she eventually reaches the top of the heap.

Snatching up the torch, she shines it along the passageway and sees that one of the supports has given way, letting an avalanche of earth in.

The plank in the roof is bowed, but still resisting the weight above it.

Lumi enlarges the opening, then shoves the assault rifle and rucksack through before squeezing after them.

Dry soil trickles down over her neck and back.

As carefully as she can, she crawls along the bare connecting section, into a small room with cement walls.

The collapsed soil has reached halfway across the floor.

She wipes her filthy hands on her trousers, then starts to climb a ladder that's fixed to the wall to reach the steel hatch in the roof. With her bruised and bleeding fingers, she loosens the rusty fastenings, pulls the cross-strut out and pushes up with one hand.

The hatch is stuck.

She undoes the waist-strap of the rucksack and uses it to strap herself to the ladder so she can use both hands.

She makes sure that she's not going to fall, then lets go of the ladder, puts her hands flat against the hatch and uses both her arms and legs to push.

It makes a frosty, crunching sound.

She takes a deep breath, concentrates and pushes hard again. The ladder creaks alarmingly and her muscles tremble. Slowly the hatch starts to move. Soil falls onto her face as the grass and moss give way.

Lumi switches the torch off and crawls out into the cold air, closes the hatch, brushes grass and leaves over it with her hand, then shuffles backwards down the far side of the clump of trees.

She looks up at the night sky and locates the Pole Star to make sure she's got her bearings right.

She runs across the dark field at a crouch. After five hundred metres she takes cover in a ditch and looks back for the first time.

The car tyres are still burning in the yard, casting an uneasy glow over the metal walls, but apart from that everything looks peaceful and there are no signs of movement. She adjusts the assault rifle to its triple-shot setting, then scans the field and clump of trees through the night-sight before she starts to run again.

Some birds take off close to her and she instantly throws herself to the ground and crawls sideways into a deeper furrow.

After a few seconds she points the rifle back towards the workshop, looks through the sights and sees the combine-harvester drum leaning against the wall.

The ground seems to be swaying in the glow of the burning tyres.

She lowers the gun and looks at the building with just her eyes. The two plumes of flame are leaning in the wind, and when they straighten up again she thinks she can make out a thin figure.

She quickly raises the rifle and looks through the sights, but all she can see now are the white fires and the pulsating façade of the building.

Without looking back, she runs over the hard field along a dyke, climbs over an electric fence, and crosses a meadow.

She passes the dark greenhouse at a distance, the one she looked at so many times from the workshop.

There are leaves pressed up against the dark glass.

An oil drum is standing next to the door.

Lumi follows the track to the main road, the E25, and starts to walk parallel to it.

She keeps the assault rifle hidden from passing cars.

The dirty weeds shake as they drive past, and an old milk carton slides along the road.

Without stopping, she pulls some dry grass from the side of the road and wipes her face. The sharp pain in her knee has faded to a dull ache.

Her dad was right.

Jurek Walter did manage to find them.

She knows that's what's happened, but even so her brain is having trouble accepting that all this is happening, that it's real.

It's starting to get light by the time she reaches Eindhoven.

Rubbish and leaves are lying in drifts beside a noise-barrier.

The ground shakes as a truck drives past.

She limps past a huge roundabout, walks through a small

patch of woodland and finds herself in a part of the city full of fairly old buildings, houses with brown-brick walls and white woodwork.

The streets are still deserted, but the city is slowly waking up.

An almost empty bus pulls away from a stop.

Lumi wipes the blood from her hand on her trousers, then starts to dismantle the rifle as she walks.

She drops the magazine down one drain, the bolt down another, and the rest of the gun in a skip full of builders' rubble.

She crosses the ring-road and enters the centre of Eindhoven, steps into a doorway, turns her back on the streets and shrugs off the rucksack. She looks quickly through the plastic folder containing her passport, hotel key and cash, then takes out the pistol and checks that it's fully loaded.

She tucks the pistol inside her jacket before carrying on.

A young refuse collector jumps down from his van and stops beside the rumbling vehicle, staring at her.

She turns away before he has time to say anything, then runs two blocks.

She strides past a row of closed shops, crosses a murky-looking canal, and carries on through the city centre towards the station. She walks past the cycle-park in front of the station to the entrance of the hostel.

Lumi goes in and walks through the garish yellow lobby with its pale blue sofas and pink garlands.

She's filthy and smeared with blood.

Her hair is hanging in dirty clumps, her mouth tightly closed, and her eyes strangely intense in her dirt-streaked face.

A group of youngsters standing in the lobby clutching heart-shaped balloons falls silent abruptly when they catch sight of her. Lumi walks straight through the group towards the lifts, as if she hasn't even seen them.

92

After he left the hospital, Joona flew straight to Antwerp, hired a black Mercedes-Benz, and drove due east along the E34. It was early morning, and still very dark. The motorway was almost empty, and he had no trouble sticking to a speed of 180 kilometres an hour.

Jurek broke Saga and tricked her into contacting me, Joona thinks as he drives.

By claiming this was all about his brother's body, he made her feel she had the advantage.

But the only thing he wanted was to find out where Lumi was hiding.

And there's a long way to go before dawn.

The flat landscape is black.

He catches up with a gleaming silver tanker, overtakes it, and watches it disappear in the rear-view mirror.

Joona crossed a boundary when he shot Jurek's traumatised brother. He had no choice, but it left a stain on his soul.

According to the post-mortem report, the brother's remains were transferred to the Karolinska Institute's surgical department for use in research.

Joona is aware that he stole the body for emotional reasons, then had it cremated, and scattered the ashes in the same garden of remembrance where the twins' father's ashes had been scattered.

Presumably Jurek has visited the garden and seen his brother's plaque next to his father's, and realised that it was Joona who had done that.

Jurek knew that Saga's enquiries would lead back to Joona.

That was why he said he'd exchange her father for information about his brother, Joona thinks, as he crosses the border into the Netherlands halfway across a viaduct.

He drives past a petrol station with a large car park. Rows of trucks and caravans glint between the trees.

The road is straight, and the sky above the expansive landscape dark. Scattered settlements sparkle like amber jewels.

Because he ran from the hospital and drove straight to the airport, he hasn't had a chance to get hold of a gun. All he can hope is that he gets to Lumi before Jurek, and can take her to another colleague in Berlin.

The motorway is lined by tall pylons with four separate layers of cables. Farms and industrial units flash past through the trees.

Immediately after a large sports-ground with rows of football pitches lit up by floodlights, he pulls into the right-hand lane and turns off onto the E25.

It didn't take long for Saga to realise she was going to have to ask me what happened to Igor's body, Joona thinks.

But it wasn't until her dad was dead and Jurek had snatched her sister that Saga cracked and tried to get hold of me.

Everyone has their own breaking point.

Joona's heart starts to beat harder when he sees that the whole of Maarheeze is in darkness, the result of an extensive power-cut.

It seems to stretch all the way to Weert.

And is probably also affecting Rinus's hideaway.

He leaves the motorway and has to lower his speed as he drives along the narrow road that runs parallel to the motorway.

The house and fields lie in darkness.

Long before he reaches the turning he sees blue lights flashing across the tarmac and black tree trunks.

A white police-van is parked beside the turning.

The yellow and blue stripes on the front doors and sides flash between the bare branches of the bushes.

Joona turns and drives straight through the cordon tape, thundering along the narrow track towards the main buildings.

He can see five police cars parked on the far side of the meadow, and there are two ambulances and a fire-engine next to the workshop.

To make sure he doesn't block the way for the ambulances he pulls in sharply in front of the abandoned house and stops beside the old garden furniture. He gets out of the car without bothering to shut the door and runs across the meadow.

One of the garage doors is lying on the ground, and the debris from an explosion is visible in the yard and tall grass.

The blue lights chase each other across the metal walls, vehicles and uniformed police officers.

Joona realises that he's too late, that the battle is over.

There are police everywhere, he can hear them talking on their radios, realises that they're trying to figure out the severity of the incident and establish an investigative team. Someone somewhere is worrying that there could be more explosives and wants to wait for the bomb squad.

An Alsatian is tugging anxiously at its leash, barking loudly.

Joona passes the melted remains of a burned tyre and walks up to one of the uniformed officers, shows his ID and tells him that Interpol have been called in. He pretends not to hear the officer telling him to wait, just lifts the cordon tape walks into the garage.

The reinforced walls are smeared with soot, and the fire has left a strong acrid smell.

The remains of a burned-out car are resting against the internal wall.

Its petrol tank has exploded, tearing large parts of the chassis away with it.

There's a charred body sitting in the driver's seat, weirdly contorted.

Joona walks through the sawn-open armoured door.

He opens the fire cabinet and snatches up the axe that's hanging beside the extinguisher, then hurries towards the staircase.

If Jurek is still here, he needs to make sure that he's dead.

The door to the closet and the emergency escape route is closed.

He can hear voices from up above.

The stairs are littered with plaster and splintered wood from an explosion. The debris crunches beneath his feet.

The internal walls upstairs are almost non-existent now, and the remaining fragments are perforated with bullet-holes.

Two paramedics are lifting someone onto a stretcher. One leg is hanging limply over the edge, and Joona can see blood-stained trousers and a military boot.

The axe swings in Joona's hand as he approaches the man on the stretcher.

The beam from one of the paramedic's head-torches is aimed downwards, and Joona catches a fleeting glimpse of Rinus's blood-smeared face.

Joona climbs over a blackened beam and puts the axe down against the wall, staggering slightly at a sudden flash of pain from a headache.

There's a loud ringing in his ears.

Rinus has an oxygen mask over his mouth and nose. His eyes are staring up at the ceiling. He seems to be trying to figure out what's going on.

'Lieutenant,' Joona says, stopping beside the stretcher.

With a weak hand, Rinus pulls the mask aside and moistens his mouth. One of the paramedics lifts his foot onto the stretcher and straps the belt across his thighs.

'He's gone after her,' he says almost inaudibly, then closes his eyes.

Joona rushes down the stairs, out through the garage, past the police officers who are waving the first ambulance through. With panic roaring in his head, he runs across the frost-covered meadow towards the car.

*

93

Joona reverses out, brakes and slides backwards on the gravel, changes gear and puts his foot down. A cloud of dust flies up from the ground.

There's a police car in the way.

Joona swerves and drives straight through the rose bushes and across the ditch. There's a bang and the glove compartment flies open, scattering documents across the floor and passenger seat.

He swings up onto the rutted track again and increases his speed. The yellow grass whips the sides of the car.

A police officer is busy putting up fresh cordon tape as Joona drives straight through it.

He turns left when he reaches the police van, skidding across the narrow road and up onto the bank, shattering a small wooden warning sign and scraping the side of the car against the barrier separating the smaller road from the motorway.

Soil sprays up behind the car as the tyres thunder across the uneven ground.

The car lurches back onto the tarmac and races along the road, in the opposite direction to the traffic on the motorway on the other side of the barrier.

It will soon be light.

A group of people is waiting at a bus stop.

Joona puts his foot down and overtakes a tractor, then reaches Maarheeze and heads down a hill. He wrenches the wheel to the right and passes beneath the motorway. He's going so fast that the car slides across the carriageway and hits the concrete wall side on.

The driver's window shatters and small cubes of glass fly into the car.

He accelerates again and turns left at the roundabout, straight across the entrance to a petrol station, sending an advertising hoarding flying.

Jurek is used to operations behind enemy lines, and Lumi won't realise he's following her, she'll show him the way to the student hostel.

Joona overtakes a horsebox on the slip-road, pulls out onto the motorway, passes a truck on the wrong sides and puts his foot down as hard as he can.

The wind roars through the broken window.

He drives through a patch of forest and soon reaches Eindhoven.

The sky is slightly lighter over to the east now, and the city is glowing in the last of the darkness.

Brown brick buildings flash past.

He's rapidly approaching a junction, the lights are red and one car has already stopped, and there's a bus approaching from the right.

Joona blows his horn and passes the waiting car, drives straight out into the junction, accelerates hard in front of the bus, and hears it brake and thunder past just behind him.

He crosses three lanes and swerves into Vestdijk, across the canal, and steers into the bus lane.

Large modern buildings rush past.

A delivery truck and two smaller cars are blocking the two lanes in front of him.

They're going far too slowly.

Joona's migraine suddenly explodes behind one eye. It's still only a precursor to the real thing, but the car lurches and almost drives into the oncoming traffic before he regains control.

He blows his horn, but there's nowhere for the other vehicles to go.

Joona pulls into the red cycle-lane and passes them on the inside, tearing a rubbish bin from a post. In the rear-view mirror he sees it fly across the pavement and shatter a shop-window.

The car swerves out onto the road again, the wheels thundering over the kerb.

He turns sharp right on shrieking tyres, into 18 Septemberplein. Maybe he's already too late.

Joona races over a pedestrian crossing, brakes and turns sharp left, across the path of oncoming traffic, and into the square in front of the station.

Pigeons fly up from the ground.

The flat, glass-fronted bulk of Eindhoven station is tucked next to the student hostel.

It's too early for most of the morning commuters. There aren't many people moving about behind the glass doors.

A beggar is kneeling on a piece of cardboard next to a stack of free newspapers.

Joona pulls in beyond the row of waiting taxis and stops.

Glass cascades from his clothes as he gets out of the car and starts to run towards the hostel.

He automatically starts looking around for some sort of weapon.

There's a uniformed police officer standing in the empty arcade by the yellow ticket-machines. He's hunched over, eating a sandwich from a bag.

Joona changes direction and walks towards him. The policeman is middle-aged, with blond sideburns, and almost white eyelashes.

Pieces of lettuce keep dropping from the sandwich.

Joona darts behind two pillars and approaches the officer from behind. He reaches forward, unfastens the man's holster, and snatches his pistol.

The police officer turns, his mouth full of food. He has a pair of sunglasses sticking out of his breast pocket.

'Interpol, this is an emergency,' Joona says, glancing over at the hostel.

He starts to walk away, but the police officer grabs his jacket. Joona pushes him hard. The man's head hits the wall and he drops his sandwich.

'Listen, lives are at stake here,' Joona says.

The policeman pulls out his baton and raises it to strike, Joona manages to parry the blow but still gets hit in the cheek.

He wraps his arm around the officer's shoulder and jerks him backwards, sending him sprawling to the floor. Leaning on one hand, he tries to get up, but Joona stamps on one of his knees.

The police officer lets out a cry of pain.

Joona grabs his radio and runs over to the hotel, tossing the radio onto the roof of a currency-exchange bureau on the way and swerving round the overflowing bicycle-park.

He checks the magazine as he runs towards the door of the hostel.

It looks like it contains eight or nine bullets.

Joona can still hear the policeman screaming as he strides into the hostel.

It's early morning, but already there are around twenty young-sters hanging about in the lobby and lounge.

Joona keeps the pistol aimed at the floor.

Two of the lifts are broken and the third is stuck on the eighth floor, where Lumi's room is.

Joona's headache is making his vision flare. He yanks open the door to the stairs and starts to run up them.

His footsteps echo through the stairwell.

His pulse is thudding in his ears by the time he reaches the eighth floor. His thighs are tight from the exertion, his shirt wet against his back.

He walks quickly along the corridor, turns a corner and sends a display of brochures about activities offered by the hostel flying.

'Wacht even.'

A young man is standing in Joona's way, pointing and appar-ently meaning that he should pick the brochures up.

Joona keeps going, shoving him out of the way and pushing past. Another man standing in one of the doorways has been looking on. He starts to protest, but abruptly falls silent when Joona points the pistol at his face.

He can hear a faint ticking sound.

Joona runs along the corridor to Lumi's room.

The lock has been broken and the room is empty.

The bed is untouched, and Lumi's bag is sitting on one of the chairs.

The wastepaper basket has been knocked over.

Joona's heart is pounding so hard he can feel it in his throat.

He hurries out of the room, rushes round the corner and finds himself looking at Jurek's pallid face at the end of the corridor.

He has a rope over his shoulder, and is dragging a large, plastic-wrapped bundle into the waiting lift.

The glare of the wall-lamp glints off his rigid prosthetic hand.

Joona raises the pistol, but Jurek is already gone.

He starts to run, and hears a ringing sound as the doors close. Joona rushes over and presses the button, but the lift is already on its way upwards.

It stops at the top, on the twenty-eighth floor.

Joona runs back to the stairwell and starts to climb.

He knows that Jurek could break Lumi's neck at any moment. But that wouldn't be enough for him, his way of working isn't that simple.

Ever since Joona first caught Jurek many years ago there's been a special darkness between them.

Jurek has spent a large part of his life locked up and isolated.

And every day he thought about how to grind Joona into the ground.

He's going to take everyone Joona loves and bury them alive.

Joona will have to spend his life looking for their graves, until he gives up and hangs himself, consumed by loneliness.

That's how Jurek has envisaged his revenge.

He would have been planning to take Lumi with him and bury her somewhere. That's what his instincts are telling him to do, that's how his sense of order manifests itself.

But now that Joona has caught up with him here at the hostel, he has quickly changed his plan.

Just like he did last time, when he took Disa, Joona thinks as he runs up the stairs.

94

Joona reaches the top floor but keeps going, running up the last, narrower flight of steps leading to the roof. He opens the door, checks both sides with the pistol, then walks out into the cold air.

The sun is rising above the wide horizon. The city spreads out in all directions, glass and metal glinting in the light.

Most of the roof of the hostel is hidden by the black construction at its centre, housing the top of the stairwell and the lift machinery.

Joona stands with his back to the wall, trying to catch his breath.

The roof is covered with a layer of polished stones, and a narrow path made of planks has been laid out across it, like on a beach.

Joona looks round and takes a few steps.

There's no one in sight.

Some rusty bolts hold up a mast with a red light at the top of it. White bird excrement has trickled down the side of a ventilation unit.

Joona starts to think that he's been tricked, that he'll have to go back down, when he suddenly sees tracks in the gravel beside the path some distance away.

Something heavy has been dragged across the roof.

Joona starts to run along the side of the machine-room with

the pistol raised. He keeps going across the loose stones, aims the gun round the corner, and catches a momentary glimpse of Jurek before he disappears round the next corner.

Jurek has wrapped Lumi in heavy-duty plastic. Joona has no idea if she can breathe, or if she's even alive. Jurek has tied a thick rope round the bundle, forming a loop that he can hold over his shoulder so he can drag her along behind him.

Joona runs after them.

The stones slide beneath his feet.

He gets back up onto the planks again, runs along the long side of the machine-room, past a row of grey satellite dishes.

The rising sun is behind him, throwing long shadows across the pale stones.

Some distance away, Jurek is dragging Lumi towards the edge of the roof between a ventilation unit and a large array of solar panels.

Joona doesn't know if Jurek is armed.

He can hear sirens down in the street.

Joona moves quickly sideways in an attempt to identify a decent line of fire.

The early morning sun is hitting the solar panels, and the reflection dazzles him.

Jurek vanishes like a shadow behind the glare.

Joona stops, holds his pistol in both hands, and aims at the slender silhouette through the flashes of light.

'Jurek,' he calls out.

The sights tremble as he keeps moving sideways, sees a way through the reflections and fires as soon as he catches sight of Jurek again.

He squeezes the trigger three times and hits Jurek in the back with all three shots. The sharp crack of the shots echoes across the city. Jurek stumbles forward, turns round and draws Lumi's pistol.

Joona fires three more times, right into his chest.

Jurek loses his grip on the gun and it slips through the slats in the path, then he quickly turns away and carries on dragging Lumi towards the edge.

He must have picked up a protective vest from Rinus's workshop.

Joona runs closer.

Jurek is behind the ventilation unit now. Five large fans are whirring behind thick mesh.

Joona catches sight of him again, aims lower and shoots him in the thigh. The bullet tears straight through the muscle. Blood sprays out in front of him, the drops sparkling in the sharp sunlight.

Joona moves closer with the pistol raised and his finger on the trigger. He can only see Jurek intermittently through the chimneys and air-vents.

Lumi is getting far too little air, Joona can see she's suffocating, her lips are blue, her eyes wide open.

Her sweaty hair is stuck to her face inside the plastic.

Joona's migraine flares behind one eye and he almost falls.

Jurek has lifted Lumi up now, and is limping towards the low edge of the roof.

This is his new plan.

Joona will be too late again.

Jurek wants him to plead and threaten, and then watch his daughter fall.

Joona gets past the ventilation unit, quickly takes aim and shoots Jurek in his other leg. The bullet hits the back of his knee and exits through his kneecap.

Lumi lands hard on the round stones on the roof. Jurek staggers sideways, falls onto one hip, rolls onto his stomach and tries to lift his head.

Joona runs forward, still aiming at Jurek. He pulls Lumi away from him and tears through the plastic covering her face.

He hears her gasping for breath and coughing as he turns back to Jurek, presses the pistol against the back of his head and squeezes the trigger.

The gun clicks, then clicks again.

Joona pulls the magazine out.

It's empty.

A helicopter is approaching, and there are more sirens now.

A small crowd has gathered down in the street in front of the hostel. They're all looking up, filming on their phones.

Joona turns back to Lumi, unties the rope around her and tears the plastic away.

She's going to be OK.

Jurek is sitting up against one of the chimneys now. His prosthetic arm has come loose and is hanging from its straps.

He's pulling a long splinter from the path.

Joona feels fire flare up inside him, and is incapable of stopping what has to happen now. Pulling the rope behind him, he stops in front of Jurek and ties a noose.

Jurek looks at him with those pale eyes of his, then lets go of the splinter. His wrinkled face betrays no sign of pain or anger.

Joona widens the noose and sees that Jurek is slipping into circulatory shock from loss of blood.

'I'm already dead,' Jurek says, trying to fend off the rope with his hand.

Joona grabs the hand and twists, breaking the arm at the elbow. Jurek lets out a groan, then looks at him again and moistens his lips.

'If you look into an abyss, the abyss looks back inside you at the same time,' he says, making a pointless attempt to move his head away from the noose.

Joona manages to get it round his neck on the second attempt, tightens the knot at the back of his neck, pulling it so tight that Jurek's breathing becomes a hiss.

'That's enough now, Dad, stop it,' Lumi pants behind him.

Joona walks over to the back of the solar panels and ties the end of the rope to one of the sturdy supports.

The clatter of the helicopter is getting closer.

Joona drags Jurek to the edge of the roof. The prosthesis drags behind him, then falls off altogether. Jurek tenses his neck, coughs and tries to breathe.

'Dad, what are you doing?' Lumi asks in a frightened voice. 'The police are on their way. He'll spend the rest of his life in prison, and—'

Joona drags Jurek to his feet. He's so groggy he can barely stand. Blood is pouring over his shoes from the gunshot wounds.

The tracks of the railway station shimmer like copper wire far below.

They can hear voices from the stairwell.

Jurek's broken arm is twitching.

Joona takes a step back and looks into Jurek's eyes.

There's an odd expression in them.

It's as if Jurek is looking for something in Joona's eyes, or trying to see himself reflected in his pupils.

Lumi has turned away, crying now.

Jurek staggers and whispers something just as Joona shoves him in the chest with both hands, knocking him over the edge.

Lumi screams.

The rope slips quickly across the smooth stones and over the edge of the roof. It makes a ringing sound as it stops and pulls taut. A window below shatters and fragments of glass fall on the crowd gathered on the pavement. The solar panel next to Joona sways and creaks.

Joona runs towards the stairwell, pushing the caretaker aside when he tries to stop him and hurrying down the stairs to the twentieth floor. He hears the screaming before he even reaches the corridor. The door to one of the suites opens and a woman stumbles out dressed in a pair of jeans and a bra.

Joona walks past her into the room, then closes and locks the door behind him.

The window is broken, fragments of glass glinting on the grey carpet and bed.

Jurek is swinging gently in through the window, then out again.

He's dead, his spinal column has snapped.

Blood is running from the deep furrow cut by the noose.

Joona stands in front of Jurek and looks at the thin, wrinkled face and pale eyes.

The body swings back into the room again.

A few pieces of glass come loose from the top of the window and fall onto the sill.

Joona feels an incredible tiredness wash over him, the confused aftermath of a terrible struggle.

Jurek Walter is dead.

He won't be coming back.

The body sways slowly back and forth. The blood from the gunshot wounds drips from his feet, leaving a thin trail across the carpet and window-frame.

Joona isn't sure how long he's been standing staring at Jurek when the lock on the door clicks behind him.

Lumi walks in and tells him very gently that he has to leave the room with her.

Joona looks at Jurek's large hand, his dirty fingernails, lower arm, and blood-stained shirt.

'It's over, Dad,' Lumi whispers.

'Yes,' he replies, looking into Jurek's pale eyes.

Lumi puts her arm round his waist and leads him out of the room, past the caretaker clutching the master key and the waiting police officers.

95

Valeria is dozing in her bed in the Intensive Care Unit, thinking about her brief conversation with Saga just before the nurse came in to administer more morphine.

Pellerina's condition has got worse, her heart has started racing again and defibrillation no longer seems to be working.

Saga was pale, she had dark rings under her eyes and was so agitated that she could barely stand still beside the bed.

She was almost manic, constantly brushing hair away from her face, and wanting Valeria to keep telling her about her conversations with Pellerina.

Valeria described once again how she and Pellerina had spent almost the whole time talking, and reassuring her that her sister hadn't been afraid when she was in the coffin.

'It felt a bit like we were holding hands,' Valeria had said, mainly to calm Saga down.

She nodded, but was clearly having trouble concentrating.

When Valeria woke up in the coffin with a blanket round her and didn't get any response from Pellerina, she thought the family had believed her. She had taken all the blame, saying she would have done anything to get more heroin. Valeria was convinced they had taken Pellerina up into the house, whereas she had actually lost consciousness – that was why she was no longer answering.

A nurse with her hair in plaits and a silver ring through her eyebrow came in to give Valeria more morphine for the pain in her hands and feet.

Saga tried to wait, but got too anxious to stay and hurried back to the surgical department.

Now Valeria's pain is fading, and the room grows darker as her pupils contract.

Everything becomes fuzzy, as if covered in dark grey veils.

The lights all grow ragged circles, like big brass cogs.

The nurse is standing beside her bed, checking her temperature and blood pressure.

Valeria can no longer make out her face, it's just a dark blur now.

Her body feels warm, and pleasantly tingly.

She sees that the buttons on the nurse's tunic have turned slightly yellow when she leans over and explains something to her. Valeria understands everything she says, and is on the point of asking a question when she forgets all about it.

Her eyelids are getting heavier.

The police officers outside the door to her room have finally stopped talking about football.

Valeria wakes up and opens her eyes, but still can't really see.

A different nurse is checking the ECG and blood levels. She has no idea how long she's been asleep.

She tries to focus and looks at the drip-regulator and the glistening drops running into the tube.

Everything slides away again and she shuts her eyes as the nurse makes her comfortable. Valeria is almost asleep when the phone rings.

'My phone,' she mumbles weakly, opening her eyes.

The nurse picks the mobile up from the bedside table and passes it to her. She can't read the screen, but takes the call anyway.

'Valeria,' she says in a tired voice.

'It's me,' Joona says. 'How are you?'

'Joona?' she asks.

'How are you?'

'Fine, a bit groggy from the drugs, but—'

'And Pellerina?'

'Her condition's got worse . . . her heart isn't beating properly, it's too fast . . . It's terrible,' she replies.

'Have you spoken to Saga?'

Valeria feels like a child as the nurse stands by the bed and calmly and methodically wipes the cannula with surgical spirit.

Joona is a long way away, but she can tell that he's different, that something has happened.

'I daren't ask,' she says quietly.

'Lumi's fine,' Joona says.

'Thank God.'

'Yes.'

Neither of them says anything. The distance hisses dreamily down the line. The nurse connects a syringe to the cannula and checks it.

'What happened?' Valeria asks, watching as blood gets sucked into the tube, mixing with the fluid in the syringe.

'Jurek's dead.'

'Jurek Walter's dead?'

'This time he is . . . it's over,' Joona says.

'You finally stopped him.'

'Yes.'

The nurse puts something on the trolley beside the bed, then leaves the room quickly in three long strides.

'You're not hurt, are you?' Valeria asks, closing her eyes again.

'No, but I'm going to be here for a while, I need to answer some questions.'

'Are you going to end up in prison again?' she asks, as she hears the door close softly.

'I'll be OK, I've got the backing of Interpol and the International Liaison Office back home,' he replies.

'You sound sad,' Valeria says.

'I'm just worried about you, and Saga and Pellerina . . . They haven't cut back on the security, have they?'

'This hospital's crawling with cops, I've got two right outside the door, twenty-four hours a day. It feels a bit like being back in prison.'

'Valeria, you need protection.'

'The best thing would be if you came home.'

'Lumi's going back to Paris tomorrow.'

'I'd like to go there too.'

'I'll pick you up as soon as I'm done here.'

'Just need to change into some better clothes.'

'I love you,' he says quietly.

'I've always loved you,' she replies.

They end the call. Valeria smiles to herself. Her eyes are burning with tiredness behind her eyelids. Thinking about the fact that Joona is coming back, she falls asleep with the phone in her hand.

When she wakes up again, the effect of the morphine has faded, leaving behind a faint feeling of nausea.

The police officers outside her door are talking about football and football managers again.

She's lying on her back, staring up at the ceiling.

Her pupils have gone back to their normal size, and her vision is working properly again.

She looks at the square tiles of the suspended ceiling.

One of them has a damp grey patch on it, it looks like a photograph of one of the moon's craters.

She's thirsty, and turns her head to look at the bedside table, but her eye gets caught by the tube leading into her left elbow.

A syringe full of clear liquid is still attached to the cannula.

She remembers the nurse who was with her when she was talking to Joona.

The injection was prepared, but never finished. The nurse just left the room without a word.

There's a small, empty glass bottle on the metal trolley beside the bed. Valeria reaches out for it and turns it round in her hand.

Ketalar 50 mg/ml, she reads on the label.

A drug used to sedate people for operations.

She can't understand why they were going to sedate her. No one's said anything to her about an operation.

While she was talking to Joona she had glanced at the nurse cleaning the cannula in her arm.

She doesn't remember the face, everything was far too blurred.

But she did notice the beautiful pearl hanging from the earlobe above her.

Chalk-white, with a sort of creamy glow around it.

Valeria remembers feeling like a small child while the nurse was fussing about her.

At least two metres tall, she thinks, and shudders.

Saga is sitting waiting for the new cardiologist in a room for relatives in the Heart Clinic's intensive care ward. Her face is tight with anxiety and lack of sleep. There's a crumpled paper cup on the table in front of her.

She brushes a stray lock of hair from her cheek with an agitated gesture, then leans forward so she can see along the corridor.

'This is hopeless,' she whispers to herself.

She stares blankly at the aquarium with its little shoals of neon-tetras, and thinks back to the time Joona came to her dad's house to warn her. As soon as he realised Jurek was still alive, he came to see her and begged her to flee with her family.

She remembers feeling sorry for him, thinking that he'd lost his grip and become paranoid.

When Joona realised she wasn't going to hide, he warned her about meeting Jurek.

Saga gets up from the chair and walks out into the corridor.

She remembers feeling insulted by his warnings, pointing out that she had actually spent more time with Jurek than Joona had.

She was ignoring the fact that Joona had lived with Jurek's presence for years, that he had seen himself reflected in him every day in order to survive the coming confrontation.

Joona's first piece of advice was to kill Jurek immediately, with no consideration for the personal consequences.

The second was that Jurek thinks and behaves like a twin. And that with his new accomplice, he can be in two places at the same time.

The last piece of advice concerned a hypothetical situation in which Jurek had taken a member of her family.

'If that happens,' Joona said, 'you need to remember that you can't make any agreements with him, because they'll never work in your favour . . . He won't let go, and with each agreement you make with him, you'll end up deeper in his trap.'

Saga sinks into a chair and remembers what Joona said, about Jurek planning to take everyone she cares about away from her, not because he wanted them, but because he wanted to get at the darkness inside her.

If only she had heeded any of those three pieces of advice, she'd still have her old life.

Saga knows she betrayed Joona.

Not intentionally, but her contacting Patrik was what led Jurek to Lumi's hiding place.

As if she'd been chosen, like some sort of Judas who needed to exist to bring balance to the world.

Her thoughts are interrupted when a woman in her fifties with shoulder-length blonde hair and no make-up comes over and introduces herself as Magdalena Herbstman. She's the cardiologist responsible for Pellerina's care that morning.

'I can understand that you're worried about your sister,' she says, sitting down.

'The last doctor said that her heart's beating too fast because she was so cold,' Saga says, then clenches her jaw tightly.

Herbstman nods and frowns.

'It's a lot to take in, but, as you say, the cold led to a serious disturbance in the rhythm in one chamber of her heart, so-called ventricular tachycardia, VT . . . And when her heart is racing, that puts your sister's body under a lot of strain. At first the tachycardia worked itself out, that's often what happens, but last night it became even faster and went on for longer, which is why we tried to stop it with defibrillation and stabilising medication.'

'I thought that had helped?' Saga says, starting to bounce one of her legs nervously.

'It did at first . . . but the problem is so severe that she's ended up in what's known as an electrical storm – repeated sequences of tachycardia. We're keeping her sedated and are preparing for ablation.'

'Ablation?' Saga asks, brushing the hair from her face.

'I'm going to insert a catheter into her heart, try to identify the area that's sending out the wrong impulses, and create some scar tissue there instead.'

'What does that do?'

'I want to scorch off the tiny area that's causing the problem. If that works, her heart should start beating normally again.'

'You mean she's going to be all right?'

'I always try to be honest with people . . . your sister's condition is critical, but I promise to do my utmost to help her,' Herbstman says, standing up.

'I have to be with her,' Saga says, getting up so abruptly that her chair slams into the wall. 'I need to see what's happening, I'm going mad sitting here waiting, staring at those damn fish.'

'You can sit with my clinical assistant.'

'Thank you,' Saga whispers, and follows the doctor along the corridor.

Saga thinks that she's going to keep talking to the cardiologist, get her to realise that she and Pellerina are real people, not just patients passing through, not just part of her ordinary working day.

Maybe she should tell her that her dad was a cardiologist, and worked at the Karolinska Institute in Solna.

They may well have known each other.

Saga is shown through a door into what looks like an advanced control room in a recording studio, with a huge array of screens and computers.

She can hear clattering sounds and muffled voices from a loudspeaker.

It all feels like a dream.

There are ECG readings on various screens, the contractions marked by a regular bleep.

She says hello to an older woman but doesn't catch her name. The woman's glasses are hanging round her neck on a gold chain.

Saga mumbles her own name, then walks slowly towards the glass wall.

There are at least five people in the brightly lit theatre. They're all wearing pale blue outfits and masks over their mouths.

A small figure is lying motionless on the operating table.

Saga can't believe it's her little sister.

The older woman says something and pulls out an office chair for Saga. The cardiologist has gone through a door into the operating theatre.

Saga stops in front of the glass wall.

There is a blue sheet covering Pellerina's hips, her upper body is bares, and she has an oxygen mask over her face.

Saga stares at the little protruding stomach and pubescent breasts. Two defibrillator pads are attached to her chest, diagonally, on either side of her heart.

Saga brushes the hair from her face.

She tells herself that if Pellerina gets better it will mean that she didn't get there too late, that she will have managed to save her sister.

If Pellerina survives, then there'll have been a point to everything after all.

The older woman is standing in front of the screens, tapping something on one of the computers. She explains calmly that she's going to be keeping an eye on everything.

'You can sit down,' she says. 'Because I promise that I—'

She breaks off, presses the button on the microphone and tells the team in the theatre that another electrical storm is on its way.

Saga looks at her sister. Pellerina is lying perfectly still, but on the ECG screens her heartbeat starts to race alarmingly.

There's a loud noise from the operating theatre as the defibrillator charges. The team back away just before it goes off.

Pellerina's body jerks violently, then lies motionless.

It looked like someone hit her in the back with a baseball bat.

Her heart starts to race again.

The alarm goes off.

There's another bang, and Pellerina's body jerks up.

Saga stumbles sideways and grabs the desk for support.

The defibrillator whines as it charges again.

Another bang.

Her sister's shoulders fly up and her skin quivers.

The older woman speaks into the microphone, informing her colleagues in the theatre of the various readings.

Pellerina's heart is beating even faster.

The team back away from her and there's another bang.

Her body jerks upwards.

Tears are streaming down Saga's cheeks.

Someone adjusts the blue sheet covering Pellerina's hips, then steps back moments before the next shock.

They defibrillate her sister eleven times to break the recurring VT episodes, and eventually her heart calms down and the readings return to normal.

'God,' Saga whispers, sinking down onto her chair.

She wipes the tears from her face and thinks that everything that's happened, everything that's happening right now, is her fault, her responsibility.

She was the one who revealed Pellerina's hiding place to Jurek. She was confused and numb after their father's death, and just wanted to collect her sister and hide her away somewhere.

Saga had already snatched up the entry-phone when she realised that was way too dangerous, but by then it was too late. She had already shown him the way.

97

Saga is back on her feet, and can feel her legs shaking as she stands in front of the glass wall facing the brightly lit operating theatre, watching the cardiologist work calmly and methodically.

She has inserted a tube into Pellerina's right thigh, working through the veins to her heart in order to find the substrata, the area where the impulses that make her heart race are triggered.

Using fluoroscopy, she can see the exact position of the tube on a large screen.

The cardiologist and her assistant seem to agree on the location that's sending out the wrong signals.

Saga understands that they need to hurry, before the next storm starts.

Everyone in the room is concentrating hard, working in silence.

They all know what they have to do.

The cardiologist is studying a three-dimensional image of Pellerina's heart. She slowly adjusts the catheter, then begins the ablation.

A piercing ringing sound cuts through the room as the doctor burns away the tissue.

The catheter moves a tiny distance.

Saga keeps telling herself that Pellerina wasn't frightened in her coffin, because Valeria was there with her the whole time.

She wasn't scared of the dark then, and she isn't scared of the dark now.

The older woman says something into the microphone in an agitated voice.

Saga glances quickly at the ECG-screens. The waves are getting closer together, like stitches made by a sewing machine.

'Prepare for defibrillation,' the assistant says loudly.

The cardiologist tries, right up to the last moment, to burn away another area, as the ringing tone merges with the whine of the defibrillator as it charges.

The assistant reads out the measurements into the microphone.

The members of the team step back, and the next instant there's a bang.

Pellerina's chest jolts and her head sways sideways.

Another storm has begun.

Saga realises that Pellerina isn't going to be able to cope with this for much longer.

The screens show that her heart is beating far too fast, but her sister is lying on the operating table perfectly still now, as if there was nothing happening inside her.

There's another bang, then another.

Her heart continues to race.

The cardiologist is sweating, talking quickly in an agitated voice, then moves the tube and tries to ablate Pellerina's racing heart.

The anaesthesiologist's hands are shaking as she checks the oxygen supply.

They make another attempt with the defibrillator.

Another bang, but her heart doesn't slow down, then suddenly it stops beating altogether and the line on the ECG-screens goes flat.

For a moment or two there are slight undulations, a faint remnant of the contraction of the atria, then the line goes completely flat.

The system sets off an alarm.

The team starts to massage Pellerina's heart. The cardiologist has stepped back slightly and pulled off her mask. She stares at the screen with an intent look in her eyes, then walks out.

Saga stands behind the glass wall, looking at the man whose hands are on her sister's chest, pressing it in an even rhythm.

The door opens and the cardiologist comes in. She walks over to Saga, says she needs to speak to her, and asks her to go with her.

Saga doesn't answer, just pulls her arm away when the cardiologist puts her hand on it.

'I wanted to tell you in person that we weren't able to find the area causing your sister's ventricular tachycardia,' she says. 'We've tried everything, but we weren't able to stop that last attack.'

'Try again,' Saga says.

'I'm sorry, but it's too late for that now. We're going to have to stop all attempts at resuscitation.'

The cardiologist leaves her by the glass wall and walks out. The man stops massaging Pellerina's heart.

Saga puts both hands on the glass.

They remove the defibrillator paddles from Pellerina's body.

Saga feels like screaming, but stands there in silence.

She turns and walks towards the door, past the assistant, doesn't hear what she says, just walks out into the operating theatre.

The monitors are switched off and the room falls silent as the tube is removed.

Someone pulls the pale blue sheet up over Pellerina's naked chest.

Everything is far too quiet.

The lights above the operating table are turned off.

At first it feels like it's gone completely dark, but the room is still perfectly light.

The members of the team drift off, like ripples in a pool of water.

Leaving Pellerina behind at the centre of the rings.

The plastic covers of the lamps click as they cool.

Saga approaches her dead sister as if in a trance, thinking that they can't stop, they can't give up. She doesn't notice herself walking into a chair that's in the way.

The oxygen mask has left a pink mark on Pellerina's pale face.

You have to try again, Saga thinks.

Her legs threaten to buckle beneath her as she gets closer.

It feels as if she has to cross an entire ocean before she can grasp her sister's limp hand.

'I'm here now,' she whispers.

Her sister looks calm, as if she's sleeping soundly, without nightmares.

Saga hears someone from the team trying to explain to her that Pellerina's heart couldn't cope with the last attack.

His voice tails off and he leaves her alone with her sister.

The nurses clear the equipment away.

Saga has never felt so exhausted in her entire life. She feels like lying down beside her sister, but the operating table is too narrow.

There are drops of blood on the plastic floor next to an instrument trolley covered with haemostats, scissors, and scalpels.

The light reflects off the metal onto the ceiling.

Saga sways as she looks at her sister's little hand in hers, then at her sunken mouth, and pink eyelids.

She knows it's all her fault, she thought she had the situation under control, thought she could deceive Jurek, but instead she killed her own father and led Jurek to Pellerina's hiding place.

It's her fault that her sister is dead.

Saga leans over Pellerina, strokes her cheek, then straightens up and turns away.

She picks up a scalpel from the trolley and stumbles out from the operating theatre.

Two police officers are still on duty outside the door.

She doesn't hear what they say to her, just carries on along the corridor.

The light from the lamps in the ceiling lies like pools of salt on the linoleum floor ahead of her.

The automatic doors at the end of the corridor swing open for a group of nurses.

Saga turns right and goes into the toilet, locks the door behind her and walks over to the basin.

They're all dead – her mother, her father, her sister.

It's all her fault, no one else's.

She presses the sharp blade of the scalpel to her left wrist and makes an incision. The blade sinks almost without resistance through the skin and taut veins, ligaments and muscle, right down to the bone.

When the scalpel cuts through the artery the first jet of blood shoots up across the mirror and tiles.

Tiny red dots spatter the toilet lid and cistern.

She gasps as burning pain from the incision reaches her brain.

The blood is pumping out in strong pulses, hitting the edge of the basin before running down to the plughole.

Her heart starts to beat faster and faster to compensate for the loss in pressure.

She reaches out to the wall to keep her balance.

A sticker from the left-wing youth movement has been half-scraped off the mirror.

Her legs are on the point of giving way.

She sits down on the toilet lid and holds her arm over the basin. Her fingers are ice-cold.

There's a blue plastic shoe-cover on the floor. Daylight reaches in through the crack under the door.

She's breathing faster now, and leans her head back against the wall, closes her eyes and feels nothing but relief.

This is where she's been on her way for so many years.

She hears a distant knock, as if from a different world.

Her pulse is roaring in her ears.

It puts her in mind of a train, the noise as it races over the joins in the track, the lurches as it crosses sets of points.

Her arm falls from the basin.

Saga opens her eyes and stares blankly at the white walls. She's forgotten where she is. She can't find the energy to raise her arm again. The blood runs over her hand and drips onto the floor.

She doesn't hear when the knocks on the door turn into thuds.

The cut is stinging badly.

She gasps for breath and closes her eyes again.

A huge angel is gliding across the floor of a ballroom. Its footsteps make no sound at all as it heads straight towards her, hitting its head on the large chandelier and making it swing.

Its heavy wings are folded behind its back.

The crystal prisms tinkle, then the noise fades.

The angel stops in front of her and looks at her with its sad, welcoming gaze.

Epilogue

It's the middle of May, and the evening is surprisingly mild. The Beaver leaves the Grand Hotel and walks past the little square named after Raoul Wallenberg. The water in Nybroviken is almost as still as the hazy light.

He goes into Riche and pushes his way through a group of youngsters. The music is far too loud, the conversations already stupid.

The Beaver is wearing a crumpled linen suit and a pink shirt that keeps riding up from his trousers, revealing his hairless stomach.

The look in his eyes is calm, but the pearl earrings sway anxiously as he sits down on one of the tall barstools.

'What an evening,' he says to the woman sitting on the stool next to him.

'It's wonderful,' she says politely before carrying on her conversation with her friend.

When the bartender comes over, the Beaver orders five shots of Finlandia vodka.

He looks at the woman's hand resting beside her wine-glass, her neat fingernails and smooth wedding ring.

A glint of light reflects off the bottle. The bartender lines up the five small glasses and fills them to the brim.

'Perfect,' the Beaver says, and knocks back the first.

He looks at the glass in his hand, turning it round in his fingers before putting it back down on the bar.

The Beaver is currently running a locksmith and key-cutting service in Årsta, he's put in a bid on a chemical factory in Amiens in northern France, and is building up a shipping company in Gothenburg.

He feels the warmth of the alcohol reach his stomach and thinks back to the time he paid Valeria de Castro a visit in hospital back in the winter. The plan was to sedate her, then take her to a grave on an island in Lake Mälaren. Because she was tired from the effects of the morphine and didn't recognise him, he was able to prepare the anaesthetic syringe without having to resort to violence. She was talking on the phone, and sounded like she was about to drift off to sleep.

He was about to administer the injection when he heard her say that Jurek Walter was dead.

As he understood it, she had just been told by the person she was talking to.

It sounded like a definite fact, but he remembers thinking that it didn't necessarily have to be true merely because it sounded that way.

'You finally stopped him,' she had said in her tired voice.

When he heard those words he started to hear the mechanical ticking sound inside his head. It was a matter of a few seconds, no more. He saw a large clock-face before him, its Roman numerals picked out in brown and gold.

Tick tock, tick tock.

The ornate minute hand moved forward one notch, and was pointing at the number one as he saw his own face.

He was about to turn back towards Valeria as she lay there on the bed, but his eye was caught by his own reflection in the mirror above the basin instead.

The clock went on ticking, and was pointing at the number two before he saw her face.

He was going to die before Valeria, and he had to leave.

He had already left his signature on the mirror, as a mocking greeting that the police would never understand.

It was only a game, after all.

Two men with beards sit down next to the Beaver and order fancy beer from a Swedish micro-brewery. The slightly older one is evidently the other man's boss. They stand with their backs to the bar and talk about capital investments and try to sound more worldly than they actually are.

The Beaver empties the second glass, then kicks his shoes off onto the floor beside the bar.

'Please, keep your shoes on,' the younger man says.

'I'm sorry,' the Beaver says, looking him in the eye. 'I suffer from water retention, and my feet are swollen.'

'In that case, no problem,' the man grins.

The Beaver nods and raises the third glass to his lips. He downs the burning liquid in one, then puts the glass down.

You can do the whole puzzle for the police, and even hand them the last piece, he thinks. It's like asking a beetle to solve a quadratic equation.

'Nice earrings,' the younger man says.

'Thanks,' he replies. 'I wear them as a tribute to my sister.'

'I'm kidding with you.'

'I know,' the Beaver says seriously. 'Don't worry, it's fine.'

The Beaver walked out of the hospital, throwing away his ID card, keys and nurse's uniform when he emerged onto Katrinebergsvägen.

Seeing as Jurek Walter had saved his life, he had accepted the harsh punishments when he made mistakes.

He would take his shirt off himself, and hand him the belt.

But now Jurek's dead, the Beaver has erased every connection to him. He's destroyed his computers and phones, thrown away the research material and pictures, cleaned and dismantled the guns.

That connection is very nearly at an end, he thinks as he downs the last glass of vodka.

'Nearly,' he whispers, and crushes the glass in his hand.

The only thing left is a small colour photograph that he keeps in his wallet. The fold across the middle looks like a streak of snow, right across Joona Linna's throat.

READ THE
JOONA LINNA SERIES

THE HYPNOTIST

Detective Inspector Joona Linna is faced with a boy who witnessed the gruesome murder of his family. He's suffered more than one hundred knife wounds and is comatose with shock.

THE NIGHTMARE

The lifeless body of a young woman is discovered on an abandoned boat. A man is found hanging alone in his apartment. Should the deaths be treated as suicide or murder? Four people know the answer. But a killer wants them dead.

THE FIRE WITNESS

A young girl has been brutally murdered, her body arranged in bed with her hands covering her eyes. Detective Inspector Joona Linna's investigation descends into more violent territory, leading him to a shocking confrontation with the past.

Follow Lars Kepler:

FROM THE BEGINNING...

THE SANDMAN

Jurek Walter is serving a life sentence. Kept in solitary confinement, he is still considered extremely dangerous by psychiatric staff. When one of his victims is discovered on a railway line, close to death, Detective Inspector Joona Linna must uncover the truth.

STALKER

Several films arrive at Stockholm's National Crime Investigation Department showing women in their own homes, plainly unaware they are being watched. The police don't take them seriously ... until the women are found murdered.

HUNTER

The police offer ex-Detective Joona Linna a chance to clear his name: help Superintendent Saga Bauer track down a vicious killer who hunts in the shadows and is terrorizing Stockholm, before he strikes again.